Barbara CARTLAND

Three Complete Novels of
Royalty and Romance

A Witch's Spell

A Song of Love

Revenge of the Heart

WINGS BOOKS
New York • Avenel, New Jersey

This 1996 edition is published by Wings Books,
a division of Random House Value Publishing, Inc.,
40 Engelhard Avenue, Avenel, New Jersey 07001,
by arrangement with the author.

Wings Books and colophon are trademarks of Random House Value Publishing, Inc.

Random House
New York • Toronto • London • Sydney • Auckland

Printed and bound in the United States of America

Library of Congress Cataloging-in-Publication Data

Cartland, Barbara, 1902–
    [Novels. Selections]
    Three complete novels of royalty and romance / Barbara Cartland.
        p.   cm.
    Contents: A witch's spell—A song of love—Revenge of the heart.
    ISBN 0-517-15045-X
    1. Man-woman relationships—Great Britain—Fiction. 2. Nobility—
Great Britain—Fiction. 3. Love Stories, English. I. Title.
PR6005.A765A6   1996
823'.912—dc20   95-41600
                                                            CIP

8   7   6   5   4   3   2   1

Barbara CARTLAND

Three Complete Novels of
Royalty and Romance

Barbara Cartland: 5 Complete Novels
Moon Over Eden
No Time for Love
The Incredible Honeymoon
Kiss the Moonlight
A Kiss in Rome

Barbara Cartland: 3 Complete Novels
A Night of Gaiety
A Duke in Danger
Secret Harbor

Barbara Cartland: 3 Complete Novels
Lights, Laughter and a Lady
Love in the Moon
Bride to the King

Barbara Cartland: 5 Complete Novels
of Dukes and Their Ladies
A Fugitive From Love
Lucifer and the Angel
The River of Love
The Wings of Ecstasy
A Shaft of Sunlight

Barbara Cartland: 3 Complete Novels
of Earls and Their Ladies
A Gentleman in Love
Gift of the Gods
Music From the Heart

Barbara Cartland: 3 Complete Novels
of Marquises and Their Ladies
Ola and the Sea Wolf
Looking for Love
The Call of the Highlands

Barbara Cartland: 3 Complete Novels
of Dukes and Their Ladies
The Disgraceful Duke
Never Laugh at Love
A Touch of Love

CONTENTS

A WITCH'S SPELL
1

A SONG OF LOVE
163

REVENGE OF THE HEART
313

A Witch's Spell

Author's Note

The belief in Witchcraft is still very strong today and practised in parts of England and Europe. There are two types of witchcraft—Black and White. White witches usually use herbs to cure wounds, sores and diseases.

Ten years ago a White Witch from a coven in the North of England was asked:

"Does a Witch possess what others would regard as 'supernatural' powers?"

The answer was :

"A Witch possesses nothing which is not basic in everyone. People in becoming 'civilized' have lost sight of these powers. A Witch cultivates them, learns how to bring them back into use—how to control them and make the power work."

The terrible cruelty of the witchhunts in England between 1542 and 1684 resulted in a thousand witches being executed. In Scotland the number executed was higher and death was by burning. In Europe from the 15th to the 18th century over two hundred thousand witches died at the stake.

In England in 1736 the statute was repealed and the law no longer punishes witches. By the end of the century the mania for witchhunts in Europe had disappeared. In rural districts however, they are still revered or feared.

CHAPTER ONE

1818

*C*oming from the farm with a basket of eggs on her arm Hermia was humming a little tune at the same time as she was telling herself a story.

Because she was so much alone she invariably enlivened her daily tasks by pretending she was the wife of an Eastern Potentate, or the daughter of an explorer seeking treasures hidden by the Aztecs, or a pearl diver.

Just as she reached the end of the narrow lane which led to Honeysuckle Farm, and was about to join the road which would take her to the village, she heard a man's voice exclaim in a tone of exasperation:

"Damn!"

Hermia started because she had seldom heard a man swear. The country people were God-fearing and soft spoken.

Curious, she hurried down the last few yards of the lane to have her first sight of an extremely well-bred horse.

She appreciated its appearance and saw that its rider was bending down to pick up its off-side hind leg.

She realised that he was looking at the horse's hoof and guessed that it had lost a shoe.

It was something that frequently happened in the

neighbourhood because the roads were so rough, and Hermia suspected that the local Blacksmith was not as skilled as his predecessor.

It flashed through her mind however that she did not recognise the horse or its owner, who at the moment had his back to her.

She, however, walked forward to ask in her soft voice:

"Can I help you?"

The Gentleman bending over the horse's hoof did not turn his head.

"Not unless you have something with which to lever a shoe from a hoof!" he replied.

He spoke in an obviously irritated manner, but with the drawl which her brother had told Hermia was fashionable amongst the Bucks in London, and was affected by the aristocratic visitors who stayed with her Uncle, the Earl of Millbrooke, at the Hall.

She guessed this was where the Gentleman whose face she could not see had come from.

Moving closer she realised that what was upsetting him was that the shoe on his horse's hoof had come loose, but was still attached by one nail which he could not dislodge.

This was an accident which had often happened to the horses her brother Peter rode when he was at home.

Without saying anything she put down her basket and looked at the rough surface of the road. A second later she saw what she sought.

It was a large flat stone and picking it up she moved to the side of the Gentleman who was still struggling to wrench the shoe loose and said:

"Let me try."

He did not glance up at her but merely held his horse's foreleg as he was doing already, and waited while she bent down, slipped the flat stone under the shoe and levered it free from the hoof.

It took a certain amount of strength, but because

she was doing it the right way and with a deft movement of her wrist, the shoe was detached from the
hoof and clattered onto the road, taking the nail
with it.

The Gentleman beside her put the horse's leg down
straightening himself, and said:

"I am extremely grateful to you, and now kindly tell
me where I can find a Blacksmith."

He picked the shoe up from the ground as he
spoke.

Then for the first time he looked to see who had
been skilful enough to help him.

Not realising she was doing so, Hermia as she bent
down to insert the stone under the shoe, had pushed
back her sun-bonnet so that still tied by its ribbons
under her chin, it hung down her back.

Her hair could now be seen curling unfashionably
over her head in a natural and very attractive manner,
and was in the sunshine turned to burning gold.

It was the vivid gold of the daffodils in spring, the
jasmine when it first appears after the cold of the winter, and the corn when it is just beginning to ripen in
the fields.

Anybody who saw Hermia looked at her hair as if
they did not believe it could possibly be natural, but
must owe its vivid colour to the dye-pot.

It complemented the pink-and-white clarity of her
skin and the blue of her eyes, which strangely enough
were the vivid blue of an alpine flower rather than the
soft blue of an English summer sky.

Despite the cynical expression on his face, there was
a look of astonishment in the eyes of the Gentleman.

At the same time if he was surprised by her, Hermia
was certainly surprised by him.

Never had she seen a man who looked so sardonic.

His hair was dark, his features clear-cut, and while
his eye-brows seemed almost to meet across the bridge
of his nose, there was a bored, almost contemptuous

expression in his eyes as if he despised everything and everybody.

They stood looking at each other until the Gentleman said dryly:

"You certainly make me believe that the stories of pretty milk-maids are after all, not exaggerated!"

There was a faint twist to his lips which one could hardly call a smile as he added:

"And of course it is an added bonus that you should be intelligent as well!"

As he spoke he drew something from his waistcoat pocket and put it into Hermia's hand saying:

"Here is something to add to your bottom drawer when you find a hefty young farmer to make you happy."

Then as Hermia would have looked down at what he had given her, he moved a step forward and putting his hand under her chin turned her face up to his.

Before she realised what was happening, before she had time to think, he bent his head and his lips were on hers.

She felt as if he held her prisoner and it was impossible to move or breathe.

Then, as at the back of her mind she knew she must struggle, and at the same time tell him that he insulted her, he released her and with the lithe grace of an athletic man, sprang into the saddle.

While she was still staring at him in bewilderment he said:

"What is more, he will be a very lucky man. Tell him I said so."

He rode off and as Hermia watched the dust from his horse's hoofs rising behind him she thought she must be dreaming.

Only when the stranger was out of sight did she ask herself how she could have been so stupid as to have stood there gaping at him like any half-witted yokel while he kissed her.

It was the first time she had ever been kissed.

Then as she stared down at what she held in her hand, she saw it was a golden guinea, and could hardly believe it was real.

Hermia was used to walking about the countryside by herself and everybody in the village knew her.

It had never struck her for one moment that a stranger might think it odd or as she realised now, mistake her, because of the way she was dressed, for a milk-maid.

Her worn cotton gown was a little too tight from so many washes, her sun-bonnet was faded because she had worn it since she was a child.

Even so she did not look in the least like Molly, the farmer's daughter who helped him to milk his cows.

Nor did she resemble in any way, the middle-aged women who had worked on Honeysuckle Farm, some of them for twenty years.

"A milk-maid!" she whispered to herself, and thought how angry her father would be at what had happened.

Then she could not help thinking it was her own fault.

She had gone to the assistance of the stranger without explaining who she was.

Although he might have guessed from the few words she spoke to him that she was educated, she could hardly blame him for believing her to come from a very different background.

At the same time she thought it was an insult even for a milk-maid to be kissed by a strange man for no reason except that she had helped him.

Because she was not only angry, but in fact humiliated, Hermia's instinct was to throw away the guinea the stranger had given her and hope nobody would ever know what had happened.

Then she told herself that would be a wicked waste of money, for a guinea would buy many of the things which her father paid for himself for the poor and sick in the village.

Times were hard since the war, and it was difficult for the younger men to find employment.

Those who were not fortunate enough to work at the Hall or on the Earl's estate had to feed themselves by growing vegetables and keeping a few chickens.

Hermia looked down again at the guinea and thought that, if she slipped it into the Poor-Box in the Church which usually contained nothing, her father would be delighted.

He would bless the unknown benefactor, which was very far from her own feelings towards him!

As the full realisation that she had been kissed by a man she had never met before and would never meet again swept over her, Hermia said beneath her breath:

"How dare he! How dare he behave to me in such a manner? It is monstrous that no girl should be safe in a country lane from men like him!"

In the violence of her indignation, her fingers tightened on the guinea and she asked herself how she could have been so stupid as not to have returned it to him the moment he gave it to her.

Similarly she should have known when he put his fingers under her chin what he was about to do.

It had however never entered her mind that a man she did not know and who had seen her for the first time would wish to kiss her.

Yet it was just the way, she told herself, that she would expect the Bucks and Beaux whom Peter was always talking about, to behave in London.

She should therefore have been on her guard from the moment she heard the man swearing in the lane, and should have guessed what he would be like, when she saw his horse.

"I hate him!" she said aloud.

Then she found herself thinking that her first kiss was not in the least what she had expected.

She had always thought a kiss between two people would be something very soft and gentle.

Given with love and received with love, it would be something which reminded one of flowers, music and the first of the evening stars coming out in the sky.

Instead the stranger's lips had been hard and possessive and Hermia thought again that he had held her prisoner so that she would not escape.

"If that is a kiss," she exclaimed, "I want no more of them!"

Then she knew that was not true.

Of course she wanted to love and be loved.

It was all part of the stories she told herself in which the wildest adventures carried her to the top of the Himalayas or along crocodile-infested rivers in the centre of Africa.

Then the heroine would find the man of her dreams and they would be married.

Until now the hero had never had a face, but now she was certain of one thing: the man who had just kissed her was the villain in her stories.

As she thought about him and remembered his drooping eye-lids and the cynical twist to his lips, she was sure he not only looked like a villain but even more like the Devil.

'Perhaps that is who he was,' she thought as she picked up her basket of eggs and started to walk slowly homewards.

It was a fascinating thought, and she wondered what her mother would say if when she arrived at the Vicarage she told her she had met the Devil in Chanter's Lane, and he had kissed her.

Moreover if the Devil had done so, that meant she had now become a Witch.

She had so often heard whispered stories from the villagers of how in the dark woods which covered a great part of her uncle's estate Satanic revels took place to which foolish girls had been lured.

Nobody knew exactly what had happened to poor

little Betsy. She had been sane before she went to one, but they said it was Satan himself who had sent her mad.

Her mother replied to such tales by saying that it was a lot of nonsense: Betsy had been born abnormal and her brain was damaged so that there was nothing the doctors could do for her.

But the villagers much preferred to believe that Betsy was Satan's child, and they enjoyed shivering apprehensively when she passed them.

If she was muttering, as she usually did, to herself, they were quite certain she was casting a curse on those she did not like.

There was also a story about another girl who had gone into the woods night after night, and finally had been spirited away so secretly that she was never seen again.

Hermia's father had given the explanation that as a visitor to the village who came from London had disappeared at exactly the same time, it was quite obvious what had happened.

But the villagers were convinced that the girl's fate was the same as Betsy's. She had joined in the Devil's revelries, and he had made her one of his own.

It seemed unlikely, Hermia thought, as she neared the village, that the Devil would ride such an outstanding, well-bred horse or would be dressed by the tailors, patronised by the Prince Regent.

These were, Peter assured her, the only cutters who could make a man's coat fit as if he had been poured into it.

Thinking of Peter made Hermia wish that he was at home. He would certainly think her experience amusing, but not even to her adored brother, to whom she confided almost everything, would she admit that she had been kissed by a stranger. Devil or no Devil.

"Peter would laugh at my being so foolish," she told herself, "while Papa would be furious!"

It was not often her good-natured, happy-go-lucky father was angry about anything.

But she had become aware this last year since she had grown up that he disliked the compliments that the gentlemen who came to the Vicarage, although there were not many, paid her.

She had heard him say to her mother that it was a great impertinence and he was not going to tolerate it.

Although she knew it was very reprehensible Hermia had waited outside the door to overhear her mother's reply.

"Hermia is growing up, darling," she had said, "and as she is very pretty, in fact lovely, you must expect men to notice her, although unfortunately there are not many eligible bachelors around here to do so."

"I will not have any man whoever he may be, messing about with her," the Honourable Stanton Brooke said sharply.

"Nobody is likely to do that," Mrs. Brooke replied soothingly, "but I wish your brother and his wife would be a little kinder in asking her to some of the parties they give at the Hall. After all, she is the same age as Marilyn."

Hermia listening outside the door had given a little sigh and did not wait to hear any more.

She was well aware that her mother resented the fact that the Earl of Millbrooke, her father's brother, and his wife had almost ignored her since she was eighteen.

Not once had she been asked to any of the parties they gave at the Hall for her first cousin.

Hermia knew even better than her mother the reason for it.

Marilyn was jealous.

During the last year when they had done lessons together, as they had ever since they had been small children, she had grown more and more resentful of her cousin's looks and never missed an opportunity to disparage her.

Because she could not find anything unkind to say about her face she concentrated on her clothes.

"That gown you are wearing is almost in rags!" she would say when Hermia arrived at the Hall early in the morning. "I cannot think why you are content to make a scarecrow of yourself!"

"The answer is quite simple," Hermia would reply. "Your father is very rich and mine is very poor!"

She had not spoken resentfully, she had merely said it laughingly, but Marilyn had scowled and tried to think of another weapon with which she could hurt her.

It did seem to Hermia very unfair, even though her mother had explained to her, it was traditional that the oldest son of the family should have everything, and the younger sons practically nothing.

"But why, Mama?"

"I will explain it to you," her mother had replied quietly. "Large estates like your Uncle John's must be passed intact from father to son. If they once started to divide up the land and the money amongst other members of the family there would soon be no great Landlords in England, but only a lot of small-holdings."

She paused to see if her daughter was listening to what she was saying before she went on:

"That is why in all the great aristocratic families the oldest son inherits everything, including the title. The second son generally goes into the Army or the Navy, while the third son becomes a Clergyman because there are always livings of which his father is the Patron."

"So that is why Papa became a Parson!"

Her mother had smiled.

"Exactly! I think in fact, if he had had the choice, he would rather have been a soldier. However, as you know, he is just a poor Parson, but a very, very good one."

That was true, Hermia knew, because her father for all his easy-going nature was extremely compassionate and had a real love of his fellow-men.

He wanted to help everybody who came to him with their problems, and enjoyed doing so.

He would listen for hours, which she knew was something her uncle would never do, to the complaints of some poor old woman about her health, or to a farmer who was having difficulties with his crops.

If a young man found himself in trouble and did not know how to get out of it, her father would advise and help him, often financially.

"I never realised until I took Holy Orders," he had said once, "how many dramas take place in even the smallest village. If I were a writer, I could fill a book with the stories to which I listen every day, and sometimes that is what I think I will do."

"A very good idea, darling," his wife answered, "but as you spend all your free time at the moment riding, I think you will have to wait until you are too old to get on a horse before you start using your pen!"

The great joy of her father, apart from being at home with his wife and family, was to ride his brother's horses and hunt them in the winter.

The Earl was far more generous than his wife and it was the Countess who made it difficult, after Hermia had ceased to have lessons with Marilyn, for her to borrow the horses which filled the ample stables at the Hall and were usually under-exercised.

Her aunt was a plain woman and that partly accounted for her policy of more or less ostracising her husband's niece, besides her desire to protect her daughter from what she privately thought of as undesirable competition.

As it happened, Marilyn was quite pretty in a conventional way.

In fact, wearing gowns made by the most expensive

dress-makers in Bond Street, and having her hair arranged by a very competent lady's-maid, she would have stood out in any Ball-Room if her cousin had not been present.

It was therefore, as the Countess of Millbrooke saw only too clearly, unlikely that Marilyn would receive the compliments that were her due if Hermia was present.

The first time Hermia realised she was not to be asked to a Ball that was to be given at the Hall and to which she had looked forward excitedly, she wept bitterly.

"How can Marilyn leave me out, Mama?" she had sobbed. "We used to talk about what would happen when we were grown up and how we would share a Ball together."

She had given a little sob as she said:

"It all sounded such . . . f.fun, and we told each other how we would . . . count our . . . conquests and s.see who was the w.winner."

Her mother had put her arms around her and held her close.

"Now listen, my darling," she said. "You have to face the truth as I had to do when I married your father."

Hermia checked her tears and listened as her mother went on:

"You may have wondered sometimes," she began, "why your Aunt Edith, and sometimes even your Uncle John, are so condescending to me."

"I had noticed that they give themselves airs and graces, Mama."

"That is because your grandfather had planned that your father should marry a very rich young woman," her mother explained, "who lived near the Hall in those days, and who had made it very clear that she loved your father."

Hermia smiled.

"That is not surprising, Mama! He is so

good-looking that I can understand any woman thinking him fascinating."

"That is what I found," her mother said. "To me he
is the most attractive, charming man in the whole
world."

She spoke very softly and her eyes were tender as
she went on:

"But I was the daughter of a General who had
spent his life serving his country, and retired with only
a small pension which left him very little money for his
children."

Hermia sat up and wiped the tears from her cheeks.

"Now I understand, Mama," she said. "Papa married you because he loved you and he was not interested in the girl with lots of money."

"That is exactly what happened," her mother said.
"Your grandmother and your uncle pleaded with him
to be sensible and think of the future, but he told
them that was exactly what he was doing!"

"So you were married and lived happily ever after-
ward," Hermia said, her eyes shining.

"Very, very happy," her mother replied. "At the
same time, darling, you have had to suffer for it, not
only because you are my daughter, but also because
you are very lovely."

Hermia was startled. It was something her mother
had never said to her before.

"I am telling you the truth and not paying you a
compliment," her mother said. "I believe it was because your father and I were so happy and so very
much in love that both our children not only have
beautiful faces, but beautiful characters as well."

That was certainly true of Peter, Hermia thought.

He was outstandingly handsome and because she
resembled her mother she was aware that she was very
pretty.

When there had been any sort of parties at the Hall
all the male guests whatever their ages had always
seemed to want to talk to her.

"You know," her mother had gone on reflectively, "we always have to pay for everything in life. Nothing is free, and you, darling, while you may find it a great advantage to be beautiful, will have to pay for it by knowing that other women will be jealous of you and will often make things difficult in consequence."

That was exactly what Marilyn had done, Hermia thought, when the invitations no longer came from the Hall, and her aunt looked at her with an expression of hostility even when they were in Church.

Peter had come down from Oxford—they had made great sacrifices to send him there—and talked not only of the exciting things he did as a student, but also of the visits he made to London with some of his friends.

When he was alone with Hermia he told her how much he resented not being able to afford the clothes his friends had from the best tailors.

"The horses they own," he went on, "are so outstanding that I will never be able to own anything to equal them!"

He, like his father, was allowed to ride the horses in the Earl's stables, but he could not take one away with him, and all he had at Oxford was what he could borrow from his friends, or hire from some livery stable.

"How I hate being poor!" he said angrily the last time he had been at home.

"Do not say that to Papa and Mama," Hermia warned quickly. "It would hurt them."

"I know it would," Peter replied, "but when I go up to the Hall and find William, with all the money in the world, sniping at me not only behind my back but to my face, and making disparaging remarks about me to my friends, I want to even things up by giving him a good hiding!"

Hermia gave a cry of horror.

"You must not do that! It would infuriate Uncle John and he might no longer allow both you and Papa to ride his horses in future, and you know that I have been banned from the Hall."

"Papa told me," Peter replied, "but it is your own fault for being so ridiculously pretty!"

Hermia laughed.

"Are you paying me a compliment?"

"Of course I am!" Peter replied. "If you were dressed decently and allowed to go to London for a Season, you would be the toast of St. James's and I would be very proud of you!"

He was not only thinking of her, Hermia knew, but knowing that his richer friends, and especially his Cousin William, condescended to him and made it quite clear that he was "the poor man at their gates!"

Then because Peter was very like their father he said suddenly:

"To Hell with it! Why should I care? I intend to get the best out of life, and mark my words, Hermia, by hook or by crook, sooner or later I will have everything I want!"

"I believe you," Hermia replied, "if no one else does!"

Laughing they went down the stairs together hand-in-hand to eat the well-cooked but plain supper which was all their mother could afford from her housekeeping allowance which was a very modest one.

Now as Hermia walked in through the front door of the Vicarage she heard the clatter of pots and pans coming from the kitchen.

This meant that Nanny, who had looked after her when she was a child and now did the cooking, would be annoyed because she had taken so long in fetching the eggs.

She wondered if she should tell her the real reason, then as she walked in through the kitchen door Nanny said:

"It's about time! I suppose you've been day-dreaming as usual, and here am I trying to have a meal ready for your father before he sets out to see that Mrs. Grainger, who's sent for him!"

"I am sorry if I have been a long time, Nanny," Hermia said.

"Your head's always in the clouds!" Nanny snapped. "One of these days you'll forget your way home, that's what you'll do!"

She took the basket from Hermia, put it on the table, and started to break several eggs into a bowl preparatory to making an omelette.

"Why does Mrs. Grainger want to see Papa?" Hermia asked curiously.

"I expect she thinks she's dying again!" Nanny replied tartly. "Any excuse to have the Vicar holding her hand and telling her God's waiting for her with all His angels. I should have thought myself He had something better to do!"

Hermia laughed.

Nanny's caustic remarks were always different from what anybody else would say, but she knew it was because the old woman loved them all and resented their father, as she considered it, being 'put upon'.

"Now, go and lay the table, please, Miss Hermia," she said. "I'm not letting your father out of this house with an empty stomach, whatever he may say!"

Hermia ran to obey orders, and she had just laid the table in the Dining-Room for the three of them when she heard her mother come back from the village.

It always seemed extraordinary in such a small place that there was so much to do and so many people who wanted either her mother or her father to help them.

It resulted in there hardly being an hour in the day when they were all at home together.

Now as Mrs. Brooke came in through the front door and saw her daughter in the Dining-Room she exclaimed:

"Oh, darling, I am glad you are here! I have had

such a difficult time with poor Mrs. Burles, and I promised I would send her some of my special cough mixture. I wonder if, after luncheon, you would take it to her?"

"Of course, Mama," Hermia agreed.

Her mother paused at the open door and said:

"Did you fetch the eggs from Honeysuckle Farm? And has Mrs. Johnson any news of her son?"

"No, she has not heard from him," Hermia replied.

Her mother looked sad, and for the first time Hermia wondered how many people would take so much interest in the trouble and difficulties of those around them as her father and mother did.

If somebody's child was ill, an old person died, or there was no news of a boy in one of the Services, it became to them a personal problem.

In fact, Hermia often thought that the villagers' joy was their joy, their grief their grief.

It was like being part of an enormous family, she told herself, and knew that life was very different for other people who like her aunt and uncle were surrounded by a number of acquaintances, none of whom were really of any consequence to them.

Then she could not help feeling a little ache in her heart because Marilyn was no longer her friend, but only a relation who had no wish to see her any more.

It had been very different when they were children and competed with one another at their lessons.

They had found innumerable things to do, both within the huge rambling old house which had been in the Brooke family for generations, and outside in the well-kept gardens, but most of all in the stables.

The Earl had not married until he was older than was usual, with the result that his younger brother had a daughter almost the same age as his own, so that it was natural that the first cousins should be more or less brought up together.

This had been a great advantage to Hermia's mother and father.

At the same time, she thought, it had made her acutely conscious of the difference there was between her Uncle's position and their own.

She was not very old however, before she realised that the most important difference lay in the happiness which seemed to make the small Vicarage always full of sunshine, while at the Hall she was aware that there was an atmosphere which was gloomy and often oppressive.

A few years later she understood that her uncle and aunt did not get on together.

In public they put a very good face on it, and when entertaining guests referred to each other politely, and in a manner that only somebody perceptive would have been aware was insincere.

But when there was nobody there except for Marilyn and herself, it was quite obvious that the Countess found her husband extremely exasperating, while he, who was on the whole an easy-going man, disliked almost everything his wife suggested.

This meant there was a tension between them that was very obvious to anybody as sensitive and perceptive as Hermia.

When there were no guests in the house the two girls had luncheon downstairs.

But often Hermia would much rather have been at home eating the simple food that Nanny prepared rather than the rich, exotic dishes that were served by a Butler and three footmen at the Hall.

Then when she reached home in the evening, Hermia would fling her arms round her mother's neck and say with the spontaneity of a child:

"I love you, Mama, I love being with you, and I love this small, warm house when we are all here together."

Because Mrs. Brooke understood what her daughter was feeling, she went out of her way to explain how important it was that Hermia should study and learn everything she could from the experienced and expensive Governesses whom her uncle engaged.

"I am afraid, darling," she said, "if you did not go to the Hall for lessons, you would have to be taught some subjects by Papa, which would be very spasmodic because he would either forget or be too busy!"

Hermia laughed knowing that this was true.

"Or," her mother continued, "we should have to persuade poor old Miss Cunningham, who was a Governess once, but is now almost blind, to help you with the other things you must learn."

"I understand what you are saying to me, Mama," Hermia had replied, when she was fourteen, "and I am very grateful for everything Miss Wade can teach me. At the same time, I know it is more important even than my lessons that I am allowed to use the Library at the Hall."

She gave a little laugh before she added:

"Uncle John's Curator said that nobody else is interested in the books except me, and when he makes a list of what is required for the Library I am sure he includes books which he knows I will enjoy."

"Then you are very, very lucky," Mrs. Brooke smiled.

That was another privilege which Hermia was done out of.

It would not have been difficult for her to go to the Library, especially when her uncle and aunt were away.

But she felt it was wrong to make use of their books if they did not want her personally.

She told herself proudly that somehow she would manage, as Peter was going to do, to get what she wanted without relying on her relatives.

When luncheon was finished her father hurried off to keep his appointment, driving an old-fashioned gig, having between the shafts a spirited young horse he had recently bought cheaply from one of the farmers.

Hermia picked up the bottle of cough mixture her

mother had made and started to walk to the cottage where Mrs. Burles lived.

Her mother's healing herbs which she made into salves and lotions were famous in the village.

But Hermia suspected that the old gossips who talked about the Devil's revelries in the woods were sure the Vicar's wife was a White Witch.

"Yer mother's a miracle worker!" one of the villagers had said to Hermia last week, "or else her's got some special magic of her own!"

She had looked at Hermia with an expression in her eyes as she spoke which told her exactly what she was thinking.

"Mama believes that God gave us in nature the cure for every ill," she said firmly. "Just as a nettle stings us, so He made the dockleaf to take away the pain."

It was an argument she had used before, but she knew the woman to whom she was speaking did not want to hear it.

"Magic, that's what yer mother has," she said firmly, "and when I puts the salve her sent me on th' burn I had on me hand, an' very ugly it were, it disappeared overnight!"

Hermia smiled.

"I think you can thank the bees for that," she said, "because there was honey in the salve."

She knew even as she spoke what the woman was thinking, and nothing she could say would dispel the idea that it was super-natural magic which had cured her burn.

It was not surprising, Hermia told herself, that the people living in the small thatched cottages with their tiny gardens had nothing better to talk about.

The village green with the pond in the centre of it, the black and white Inn with its ancient clients drinking ale in pewter mugs, were the only centres of activity except for the small grey stone Church.

Nothing ever happened in Little Brookfield, which

of course had been named after the Brooke family
who lived at the 'Big House'.

The Earl owned the land, the farms, the cottages,
employed the young and healthy and of course, paid
the stipend of the Vicar who ministered to their spiritual needs.

"They want to believe in supernatural things,"
Hermia told herself.

If she was honest, she herself believed in the fairies,
goblins, nymphs, and elves which had all been part of
the stories her mother had told her when she was a
child.

She still thought about them, because they seemed
so real and so much part of the countryside.

When she was in the great woods it was easy to
think there were elves and goblins burrowing under
the trees.

She was sure there were nymphs like the morning
mist rising from the dark pond in the centre of one
wood where she would often go when she wanted to
be alone and think.

In the spring there would be a vision of bluebells
that were so lovely that she would feel they were en-
chanted, and after the bluebells would come primroses and violets.

Then the birds would begin to build their nests in
the trees overhead and the rabbits would move about
in the undergrowth.

Red squirrels would scurry away at her approach,
then stop to stare at her curiously, as if they wondered
how she dared to intrude on what was their secret
domain.

It was all so beautiful that she had no wish to believe
in anything ugly or frightening.

Then she thought of the man who had kissed her
this morning, and wondered if perhaps he had ridden
into the heart of the wood on his fine horse, and disappeared because he was not a human being.

To think of him made her anger well up inside her

as she remembered that in the pocket of her gown there was still the golden guinea he had given her.

She had forgotten about it when she had been laying the table for the luncheon and when they had laughed and talked while they had eaten.

Now after she had given old Mrs. Burles her 'magic cough lotion' she walked back towards the Church.

It was very near the Vicarage, in fact just on the other side of the road, and she slipped in through the porch that needed repairing and walked onto the ancient flagged floor.

The Church was very old, having stood there for nearly three hundred years.

Every time Hermia attended a Service she could feel the vibrations and prayers of those who had worshipped here and had left a part of themselves behind.

Her father believed the same.

"Thoughts are never wasted and never erased," he had said once.

"What do you mean by that, Papa?"

"When we think of something, and of course when we pray," the Vicar replied, "we send it out as if it had wings on the air. It is carried up by our vibrations, or perhaps by something stronger that we do not understand, into eternity."

"I think that is a terrifying idea!" Hermia protested. "I shall be very careful what I think in the future!"

Her father had laughed.

"You cannot stop thinking any more than you can stop breathing," he said, "and I am honestly convinced that wherever we have been, we leave our thoughts and the life force we give them."

Hermia had understood that he was thinking as he spoke of the atmosphere in the Church which she had always known was so vivid, so strong that she never felt as if she was alone there.

There were always other people with her, people whom she could not see, but who had lived in Little Brookfield.

They had taken their sorrows and their happiness into the Church, and their feelings had been bequeathed to the small building for ever.

They had given the Church, she thought, exactly the sanctity that people expected in a House of God, and she could feel it now as she walked in through the door.

It was there to welcome her and to make her feel that she was not alone, but enveloped by a love that could protect, help and inspire her whenever she had need of it.

As she drew the guinea from her pocket she felt as if there were unseen people around her who understood why she was putting it in the poor-box.

She knew what a lot of good her father would do with it.

She slipped it through the slit in the box and heard the sharp sound it made as it fell to the bottom.

Then as she knelt in one of the ancient oak pews to pray, she looked up at the altar.

The flowers which her mother had arranged the previous Saturday were still a brilliant patch of colour, and Hermia felt a strange joy sweep over her.

"Make something happen for me, God," she prayed. "I want to have a fuller life than what I am living at the moment."

As she prayed she almost felt as if she grew wings which would carry her away as her thoughts did, and she could visualise herself flying out into the great world outside of which she knew so little.

There would be mountains to climb like those in her stories, rivers to negotiate, and seas to sail over.

"Give me all that, please, God!" she finished.

Then as she rose to her feet she thought it was too demanding a request and God, like her father, would tell her to be content with her lot as it was.

"I am so lucky that I have . . . so much," she tried to tell herself philosophically.

But she knew it was not enough.

CHAPTER TWO

*W*hen Hermia arrived back at the Vicarage it was to find the house empty.

She knew that Nanny had gone shopping, and her father and mother were both visiting people who had asked for their help.

It was actually quite surprising that she had not been left a mass of instructions concerning other things to do.

With a feeling of delight she thought that this was an opportunity to continue reading a book that she was finding absorbingly interesting.

Usually the only time she had to read was when she went to bed at night, but as she was often too tired to do anything but sleep she had so far only read one chapter.

Now she brought her book down from her bedroom and curling herself up in the window-seat in the Sitting-Room she found her place and started to read.

She was concentrating so intently on the book on her knees that she started when the door of the Sitting-Room opened.

She turned her head impatiently thinking it was Nanny who would undoubtedly want her to fetch something like mint from the garden, or perhaps cut a lettuce for supper.

Then she saw to her astonishment her cousin Marilyn come into the room.

She was looking exceedingly smart in a gown which Hermia knew was in the very latest fashion.

Gowns during the war had been very plain and straight, and most people, however rich they might be, wore white muslins.

This material in fact sometimes verged on the indecent because it was inclined to cling to the figure, revealing not only the wearer's curves, but sometimes how little was being worn underneath.

Now far more luxurious materials were available and the bodice and sleeves of the gowns were either embroidered or trimmed with lace.

Marilyn's gown had three rows of lace round the hem.

Her bonnet had the high tilted brim which Hermia had seen illustrated in *The Ladies' Journal,* and the satin ribbons under her chin and round her high waist could only have come from Paris.

For a moment she could only stare at her cousin thinking it strange that she should call at the Vicarage herself rather than send a message, which was almost a command, for her to come to the Hall.

Then she scrambled to her feet saying:

"Marilyn! What a surprise! I have not seen you for such a long time!"

Marilyn did not look in the least embarrassed, although she was well aware she had not bothered to speak to Hermia since Christmas, and she merely replied:

"I have been very busy, but now I want your help."

"My help?" Hermia repeated in astonishment.

Of all the people who came to the Vicarage for help she would have thought the last person to ask the assistance of either her or her father or mother, would have been Marilyn.

The Countess had always made it very clear that she

29

thought that what she called 'slaving after the lower classes' was a waste of time.

"You do not suppose they are grateful to you," Hermia had heard her say once to her father. "From all I hear of such people they take everything for granted and complain that one does not do more for them."

"That is not true of my flock," Hermia heard her father object. "In fact, when Elizabeth was ill last year, we were both tremendously touched by the little presents brought her every day, and the way they prayed for her recovery."

The Countess had merely sniffed, but Hermia knew her mother had been deeply moved at the way the whole village had worried over her.

They had so little themselves, but they wanted to share what they could with her.

Sometimes it was only a fresh brown egg they thought she would like for her breakfast, a bunch of flowers from their gardens, or from those who were more practical, a comb of golden honey.

Hermia had known, though her father could never have made the Countess understand, that it was not the material things which mattered so much as the understanding and sympathy which came from the heart.

Now as she walked towards her cousin Hermia thought a little apprehensively that while Marilyn was looking very attractive in her elegant clothes, there was a contemptuous expression in her eyes.

She did not attempt to kiss Hermia, but merely looked around the room, selected the most comfortable chair, and sat down in it a little gingerly as if she felt its legs might be unsound and would collapse under her.

Hermia sat down on a stool that stood in front of the fireplace, moving as she did so some sewing her mother had been doing before she went out.

She knew that Marilyn thought it was untidy of her to have left it there.

Almost as if she was looking through her cousin's eyes Hermia was suddenly aware that the carpet was threadbare, the curtains were faded, and one of the brass handles which had come off the soft table in a corner of the room had not been replaced.

Then she lifted her chin proudly and told herself that whatever Marilyn might be thinking she would not exchange the shabby Vicarage which was filled with love and happiness for all the luxury of the Hall.

Then she looked at her cousin wondering what she had to say.

"I suppose I can trust you," Marilyn said, and her voice had a harsh note in it that Hermia did not miss.

"Trust me?" she questioned. "I do not know what you mean."

"I have to trust somebody to do what I want," Marilyn replied, "and I cannot believe that being a Parson's daughter you would do anything underhand or what Papa would call 'unsportsmanlike.'"

Hermia stiffened.

Then as she was about to defend herself she bit back the words to say quietly:

"We have known each other for eighteen years, Marilyn. If you do not know what I am like by this time, then there is nothing I can say to convince you I am anything but what I am!"

As if she did not wish to annoy her Marilyn said quickly:

"No, no, of course not! I am only a little apprehensive about what I want to ask you to do."

Hermia thought she could understand that.

She had not seen her cousin since five months ago, and then it had only been for the family Christmas dinner.

If there was one thing the household at the Vicarage all disliked it was the Christmas dinner which took place every year at the Hall.

31

Although it was the season of good will, Christmas Day celebrating the birth of Christ, was always a very busy one for the Vicar, involving a great number of Services in his Church.

He also visited several people in their homes if they were too ill or infirm to come to Church.

"I am dead tired," Hermia had heard her father say last Christmas when it was time to go out for dinner. "What I would like to do, my darling, is to sit with you and the children in front of the fire and drink a glass of port."

Her mother had laughed.

"There will be plenty to drink at the Hall."

"And plenty of snide remarks to listen to," her father replied.

Because of the way he spoke her mother had risen to sit on the arm of his chair and smooth his hair back from his square forehead.

"I know it is a bore, darling, that we have to go there, and Edith is certain to make things difficult for both of us, but I think in his heart your brother looks forward to seeing you."

"John is all right," the Vicar replied, "but I find his wife intolerable, his son a stuck-up young cock's comb, and although Marilyn was a sweet little girl of whom I was very fond, she has grown into a very conceited young woman!"

Because of the critical way he spoke which was so unlike him, his wife had laughed as if she could not help it.

Then she said:

" 'What cannot be cured must be endured,' as Nanny would say, and we will not stay long. But do not forget that you are hunting tomorrow and as it is on one of your brother's horses, you have to pay for the privilege."

"I love you!" the Vicar replied. "You always put things in the right perspective, and I will put up with a lot of disagreeableness from Edith so long as Peter and I can be mounted on those excellent horses of his."

As she went up to change for dinner Hermia had thought her mother had been right in saying one never got anything for nothing in the world.

Like her father she had found the Christmas dinner since she had grown up a very uncomfortable evening.

She knew that her aunt, and Marilyn for that matter, would look her up and down in her cheap evening-gown which was the best her father could afford.

They would contrive to make her feel as if she was the Goose-Girl who had got into the King's Palace by mistake.

Then as if Marilyn wished to impress upon her how important she was now that she had been to London, she had reeled off her successes one by one.

Like a child showing another how much bigger her toys were, she was determined Hermia should be suitable impressed.

Because she had never heard of the grand people of whom Marilyn spoke, it was not a particularly edifying conversation, and while she appeared to listen her attention was wandering to where she knew Peter was suffering in the same way from his Cousin William.

The Viscount, dressed as a very 'Tulip of Fashion,' would be endeavouring, as Peter had expressed it savagely on the way home, to turn him into a country yokel.

"The only consolation," he said to Hermia, "is that while I am absolutely certain I shall get my Degree at Oxford, William is so busy drinking at all the Clubs that he will undoubtedly fail. What is more, he was very nearly sent down last term."

Hermia slipped her hand into her brother's.

"You must not worry about what he says to you," she answered. "He is jealous because you look better and you ride better than he does, and if I were one of the Beauties he tells us he pursues in London, I should find him a dead bore!"

Peter threw back his head and laughed, but Hermia knew she had spoken nothing but the truth.

Compared with Peter, William was a plain young man with eyes too close together and a long upper lip which he had inherited from his mother's family.

He was not a particularly good horseman, and he found it distinctly annoying that when they were hunting his Cousin Peter was always in the front of the field and sailed over the highest hedges with ease.

William was often left behind despite the fact that he had the pick of his father's best horses.

Last Christmas Hermia remembered had been the least enjoyable of any dinner they had ever had at the Hall.

Because Marilyn had been particularly unpleasant towards her that evening, it was all the more surprising that she should be here at this moment asking for her help.

She sat on the stool waiting and had the idea that her cousin was finding it rather difficult to put what she wanted of her into words.

Then as if she felt that first she must make herself more pleasant than usual, she remarked:

"I can see, Hermia, that you have grown out of that gown you are wearing! It is too tight and too short! I suppose I might have thought of it before, but I have quite a number of gowns that I can no longer wear which I might as well pass on to you."

For a moment Hermia stiffened.

It flashed through her mind that she would rather wear rags and tatters than be an object of Marilyn's charity.

Then she told herself that was a very selfish attitude.

It was a struggle for her father and mother to afford the material for one new gown between them when any money that could be spared for clothes was spent on Peter.

Only last night Peter had said to her mother when her father was out of the room:

"Do you think there is any chance, Mama, of my having a new riding-coat? I am ashamed of the one I am wearing now, and since I have the chance to compete in the Steeple-Chase that is taking place at Blenheim Palace, I have no wish for you to be ashamed of me."

Her mother had smiled.

"You know I would never be that, and I noticed the other day how worn your coat was. I am sure Papa and I can manage to find enough money for a new one."

Peter put his arms round his mother and kissed her.

"You are a brick!" he said. "I know how little you and Papa spend on yourselves, and I feel rather like the Importunate Widow."

Her mother had laughed.

"You will have your riding-coat, dearest. We will find the money for it one way or another!"

Hermia had known that this meant the gown her mother had been planning for herself would not materialise, nor would the new bonnet she had been promised as soon as they could afford it.

It all flashed through her mind and she said quickly:

"It would be very, very kind of you, Marilyn, if you would send me anything you have no further use for. You know quite well it is always a struggle for Papa and Mama, even though they are as economical as possible."

"I will tell my lady's-maid to pack up everything I no longer want," Marilyn promised. "Now, Hermia, let me tell you what I want from you."

"What is it?"

"I must explain first that we have a very important guest staying with us."

Hermia's eyes were on her cousin's face as she went on:

"It is the Marquis of Deverille, and to express myself frankly—I intend to marry him!"

Hermia gave a little cry.

"Oh, Marilyn, how exciting! Are you very much in love with him?"

"It is not a question of whether I love him or not," Marilyn replied. "The Marquis of Deverille is without exception the most important matrimonial catch in the whole of London!"

"Why is he so important?" Hermia asked curiously.

"Because he is rich, and because of his position. He has houses and estates which, like his race-horses, are better than anybody else's."

"I think I have heard Papa speak of him," Hermia said wrinkling her brow.

"It is very unlikely that Uncle Stanton would know the Marquis," Marilyn said quickly. "He moves only in the most exalted circles, and his race-horses win all the Classic Races, so that he is acclaimed wherever he goes."

She gave a little sigh and said in a voice that sounded very human:

"As his wife I would have a position that would be almost Royal! Everybody would be extremely envious that I had managed to capture him."

"And do you think he would make you happy?" Hermia asked.

Marilyn hesitated before she replied:

"I would be very, very happy to be the Marchioness of Deverille, and that is what I am determined to be!"

There was a hard note in her voice which Hermia knew only too well.

When Marilyn made up her mind about anything it was always more comfortable for everybody concerned to let her have it immediately.

When she was a child she had found her tantrums would upset her Nurse and Governess to the point where they decided it was pointless not to give way to her.

Hermia knew only too well that behind a very pretty face there was a steel-like will.

This had meant, when they were in the School-Room together, that if Marilyn found the lessons boring she just refused to listen to anything the Governess said.

She would flounce out of the room leaving Hermia alone with a flustered teacher who had no idea how she could control such an obstreperous pupil.

Because Hermia had been anxious to learn everything she could even when she was quite young, she soothed down the elderly woman who had been insulted and coaxed her into continuing the lesson so that she could learn what she wanted to know.

She thought now that if Marilyn had made up her mind to marry the Marquis, or any other man, he would have great difficulty in escaping from her.

Then she thought that was rather an unkind thing to think and she said softly:

"If you marry the man you love, Marilyn, I can only wish you all the happiness in the world!"

"I thought you would say that," Marilyn replied, "and that means you will have to help me to win him."

"He has not proposed to you?"

"No, of course not! The minute he proposes to me I shall put it into the *Gazette* before he can change his mind, and every unmarried woman in London will be wanting to scratch my eyes out for succeeding where they have failed!"

"Is he very attractive, and do you love him very much?" Hermia asked softly.

"At this moment I find him extremely elusive and somewhat unresponsive," Marilyn said, almost as if she was speaking to herself. "He accepted Papa's invitation to stay, and while I know it was more to see the new mares that Papa has imported from the Continent than to be with me, I have made the very most of having him at the Hall."

Now Marilyn was speaking in the way she used to before they grew up, and as if once again she was thinking of her cousin as somebody very close to her, she said:

"I have to win him, Hermia! You do see I have to make him propose to me! But it is not going to be easy!"

"Why not?" Hermia asked. "You look very, very pretty, Marilyn, and I cannot believe that he would stay at the Hall and not be interested in you."

"That is what I would like to think," Marilyn confided. "At the same time, he is fawned on by all the most beautiful women in London."

She paused, then said as if she was speaking to herself:

"Of course they are all married, but the Marquis will have to marry some day in order to produce an heir. I have heard rumours that he bitterly dislikes his cousin who will inherit if he has no son."

"I am sure he will want to marry you," Hermia said reassuringly.

There was silence as if Marilyn was thinking it over before she said:

"I was told in confidence by one of his relatives that they have all been begging the Marquis on their knees for the last five years to marry and have a family."

"Does it matter if he does not?" Hermia asked.

"Do not be silly, Hermia! I have just told you that he hates the cousin who would succeed him, and so do his sisters, his aunts, his grandmother and everybody else in the Deverille family."

"What is wrong with his cousin that they hate him so much?" Hermia enquired curiously.

"I have never met him," Marilyn replied, "but they say he is always disgustingly drunk and spends his time hanging round very disreputable actresses."

She gave a little laugh.

"Nobody would ever expect the Marquis to behave like that, for he is very conscious of his own consequence! But he has been disillusioned through having a very unfortunate affair when he was a young man."

"What happened?" Hermia asked.

She felt this was almost like one of the stories she told herself and everything that Marilyn was telling her she found intensely interesting.

Marilyn shrugged her shoulders.

"I do not know all the details, but I gather it happened when he was very young, and it has given him a very poor opinion of women, and in consequence he is far more interested in his horses!"

She drew in her breath before she went on:

"But he has to marry, and I am determined that I shall be his wife!"

"And I am sure you will be, dearest," Hermia said, "but I do not see how I can help you."

"That is what I am going to tell you."

Marilyn's voice grew more intense as she said:

"The Marquis was talking to Papa at dinner last night and he was saying that he thought things had changed a great deal since the war. Noble families because they were hard-up or could not attend to their estates as they used to, were not looking after their people as his father had done when he was alive."

Marilyn glanced at her cousin to see that Hermia's blue eyes were fixed on her face with rapt attention and she continued:

" 'My father,' the Marquis said, 'knew the name of every man he employed, just as he knew the names of his fox-hounds, and my mother called at every cottage on our estate. If somebody was ill she took them soup and medicine, and when the children grew up she found them employment, either on our own land or with one of our relatives.' "

It flashed through Hermia's mind that was what her father and mother did in a very small way.

Marilyn continued:

"'Nobody appears to behave like that today,' the Marquis said, 'and I therefore understand why the labourers are dissatisfied in the North and there is a great deal of dissension, I am told, in the Southern Counties.'"

Marilyn paused and asked:

"Now do you understand what I want?"

She saw Hermia was looking bewildered, and the sharpness was back in her voice as she said:

"Do not be silly, Hermia! I have to convince him that, like his mother, I am interested in the people on the estate and help them."

"But, Marilyn . . ." Hermia began, then stopped.

She had been about to say that in all the years she had known her cousin she had never known her take the slightest interest in anybody on the estate.

What was more, the Countess had always sneered at the way her father and mother spent so much time looking after the people in the village.

Once when the Earl had had a man dismissed because his Agent had reported his work was shoddy and he was taking a long time over it, her father had pleaded with his brother to give the man a second chance.

"He is sick," he explained, "and cannot afford to stay at home and lose his wages. His wife is expecting another baby and there are three small children in the house."

The Earl had refused to listen.

"I leave all those things to my Farm Manager," he said. "I never interfere!"

It was her father, Hermia remembered, who had kept the man and his family alive out of his own pocket and had by some miracle found him another job with a wage that had at least saved them from starvation.

Hermia knew this was just one example of what

often happened on the estate and that her father, although he never said so, deplored his brother's in-
difference and lack of interest in the people he
employed.

"I cannot think what you want me to do for you,
Marilyn," she said apprehensively.

"I have thought it all out," Marilyn said, "and all
you have to do is exactly what I tell you."

"I will do it if it is possible," Hermia said.

"It is quite possible," Marilyn replied. "Now listen . . ."

She bent forward and lowered her voice almost as if
she was afraid of being overheard.

"I have decided that I will accompany the Earl tomorrow morning when he goes riding. I know neither
Papa nor William intend to ride early, but the Marquis
likes to ride before breakfast."

Hermia raised her eye-brows.

"I have never known you to be up before breakfast!" she said.

"I am quite prepared to get up at dawn if I have
good reason to!" Marilyn declared. "Now listen to
what I am saying . . ."

"I am listening."

"I shall join him in the stables and suggest we ride
towards Bluebell Wood. You know how pretty and romantic that is!"

"Yes . . . of course," Hermia agreed.

"I shall be there at about half after seven," Marilyn
went on, "and we will ride slowly through the wood.
Then I want you to come galloping in search of me."

"Me?" Hermia exclaimed.

"Just listen!" Marilyn snapped. "You will come riding as quickly as you can and say to me:

" 'Oh, Marilyn, I have been looking for you! Poor
old Mrs. "Thingumabob" is dying, but she says she
cannot die until she can say goodbye to you and thank
you for all your kindness to her!' "

Hermia stared at her cousin in disbelief.

It seemed a strange way for Marilyn to try to impress the Marquis and she did not think it would sound very plausible.

Almost as if her cousin read her thoughts Marilyn said:

"You can put it in your own words, but make it sound convincing and urgent as if the woman was really crying out for me."

"I . . . I will do my best," Hermia said, "but what happens . . . then?"

"I have thought it out carefully," Marilyn answered. "I shall exclaim: 'Oh, poor Mrs. "Thingumabob!" Of course I must go to her!' I shall start to ride away, but in case the Marquis should attempt to follow me I shall say to you:

" 'Show His Lordship the way home!' Then before he can accompany me, as he will obviously wish to do, I shall be almost out of sight."

"Supposing he insists upon following you?" Hermia asked.

"Then you must somehow prevent him from doing so," Marilyn said. "I shall ride towards the village, then go slowly back to the house by a different way so that no one will see me."

Her lips curved in a little smile as she said:

"Later I will tell the Marquis how a poor old woman died happily because I was holding her hand, and he will realise that I am just like his mother, and that I care about the people on the estate."

Now there was silence, and after a moment Marilyn said:

"Well, what do you think of my idea? It cannot be very difficult for you to play the part I have asked of you!"

"N.no . . . of course . . . not," Hermia said. "I am just . . . hoping that the Marquis will . . . believe you."

"Why should he doubt it?" Marilyn asked aggressively. "And if he does, it will be entirely your fault!"

"Please . . . do not say that," Hermia pleaded. "You know I will try in every way I can to sound as if somebody really is on their . . . death-bed, just as they always send for Mama . . . but . . ."

Her voice died away.

She knew she could not express in words that she felt it unlikely that any man, unless he was very stupid, would believe that Marilyn really cared for anybody except herself.

Then she was ashamed of being so ungenerous!

She told herself she would try very, very hard to persuade the Marquis that the people on the estate looked to her cousin for comfort and consolation in their troubles.

She still had a feeling it was not going to be easy, but because it was something she knew she could not put into words she merely said simply:

"I will do what you ask, Marilyn, but you are aware I have no horse to ride at the moment, and it might seem strange if I fetched one from your stables."

"I will send you a groom with a horse late this evening, so that your father will not be aware of it," Marilyn replied.

"I shall enjoy riding it," Hermia said with a smile.

She glanced at her cousin and now saw an expression in her eyes she had never seen before.

"There will be no reason for you to stay long with the Marquis," Marilyn said sharply. "You must give me just time enough to get out of sight, point the way back to the Hall, and then follow me."

"I will do that," Hermia agreed.

"And what is more, you need not doll yourself up because you are meeting the sort of gentleman you are never likely to see in Little Brookfield!"

"No . . . of course not," Hermia answered.

"If there were anybody else I could trust, I would not trust you."

"That is an unkind thing to say!"

"I cannot help it," her cousin answered. "You are too pretty, Hermia, and it has made me hate you ever since I knew that however expensively I were dressed you would always look better than I do."

Hermia made a little gesture with her hands before she said:

"We also used to have such happy times when we were young, and I miss them, Marilyn . . . I miss them very much!"

"If that is an attempt to coax me into asking you to the parties we give now that I am grown up," Marilyn replied, "I am not having you there! I have seen the expression in gentlemen's eyes when they look at you, and I am not so stupid as to want that sort of competition."

"I realise that," Hermia said, "and I cannot help my looks. But since you yourself are very, very pretty, Marilyn, I am quite certain you will capture your Marquis."

"That is what I intend to do."

Hermia was silent for a moment. Then she said:

"I do not believe love depends so much on people's looks. Mama said once that having a pretty face was only a good introduction! I think that when people begin to fall in love with each other, there must be many other factors to attract them, rather than just the outward appearance of the person in whom they are interested."

"If you are preaching to me about having a kind heart, a compassionate nature, and a love for old people and animals," Marilyn retorted, "I am not going to listen!"

Hermia laughed because she sounded just like the petulant little girl she had been when they used to quarrel in the Nursery.

Marilyn went on:

"I am quite content with myself as I am. The only

thing I am concerned with is getting married, and making sure that my husband is the most important man available."

"Papa always says that if you want something badly enough, with willpower and prayer you will get it."

Unexpectedly Marilyn laughed.

"I am sure Uncle Stanton would be delighted to know that I am in fact praying I will get the Marquis, and I shall be extremely angry if my prayers are not answered!"

"I am sure they will be," Hermia said soothingly. "And I can think of nobody, Marilyn, who would look lovelier wearing a coronet."

"That is what I intend to have," Marilyn said, "and the smartest wedding that has been seen in London for years!"

It flashed through Hermia's mind that the one person she would not ask to be a bride's-maid was herself.

Marilyn was however already rising to her feet, and pulling her elaborately decorated skirt into place.

"Now do not make any mistakes, Hermia, about what you have to do!" she admonished. "We should reach the Bluebell Wood at about twenty minutes to eight o'clock. I can make all sorts of excuses to linger in the centre of it, but you had better not keep me waiting too long!"

"I will be there, I promise you," Hermia said, "and do not forget the horse. It would not be so impressive if I arrived on foot, which is my only means of transport these days."

"I realise you are reproaching me in a very obvious manner for not allowing you to ride Papa's horses," Marilyn said. "The truth is, Hermia, you ride too well, and I am sick of hearing the grooms and everybody else say that I should ride like you."

There was nothing Hermia could say to this, and there was silence as her cousin walked towards the door.

"Be exactly on time," Marilyn said as she walked into the hall, "and I will repay you by remembering to send you the clothes I have promised you."

It was difficult for Hermia to refrain from saying proudly that she could keep them.

Instead she forced herself to answer gently and without the slightest note of sarcasm in her voice:

"It is very kind of you, Marilyn dear, and both Mama and I will be very, very grateful."

She walked to the front door with her cousin as she spoke, to see an elegant open carriage with a coachman and a footman on the box standing outside.

When they saw Hermia they both touched their cockaded hats and grinned at her.

She had known the coachman since she was a little girl, and the footman was a lad from the village.

He jumped down in order to open the door of the carriage for Marilyn and carefully placed a light rug over her knees.

As he clambered back up onto the box the horses started off and Marilyn raised her gloved hand with a graceful gesture of goodbye.

Hermia had a last glimpse of her pretty beribboned bonnet passing through the drive-gate which was sadly in need of a coat of paint.

Then she went back into the house thinking that Marilyn's visit was like one of her fairy-stories.

It was hard to believe it had happened or that she had been asked to take part in what seemed a ridiculous charade.

She could understand Marilyn's reasoning and her motive in working out what seemed a very complicated plot to capture the Marquis of Deverille, but privately she had her doubts as to whether she would be successful.

A great love, if that was what she was asking from the man who would want to marry her, should not be based on something that seemed on second thought rather theatrical and contrived.

Hermia had the uncomfortable suspicion that if the Marquis was at all intelligent and intuitive he would remember the conversation they had had at dinner about his mother.

Would he not therefore think it a strange coincidence that two days later Marilyn should be called to a dying woman's bedside?

Hermia felt sure that if she were in the Marquis's position she would certainly think it very strange.

But the Marquis might be different.

If he was a stupid man, beguiled by Marilyn's pretty face, the suggestion that she was like his mother might swing the scales in her favour.

She picked up her book again from where she had discarded it when Marilyn arrived.

She did not open it. Instead she looked out of the window at the beauty of the unkept garden with the shrubs just coming into bloom.

The blossom on the fruit-trees gave them a fairy-like appearance that swept her into one of the stories she had known as a child where the spirits of the trees danced at night under the stars.

Then she knew that if she ever fell in love, as she prayed she would one day, she would never stoop to scheming or intriguing to encourage the man on whom she had set her heart into proposing to her.

Either he would want her because he recognised her as the woman he loved, through time and space, or else whatever she might feel for him she would let him go.

Then she would hide her tears privately so that he would never be aware of how much she cared.

"It is humiliating and degrading to ensnare a man as if he were a wild animal," she told herself fiercely.

Then she found herself once again thinking of the man with a face like the Devil who had kissed her and pressed a guinea into her hand.

She told herself that the kisses she had dreamt of

and imagined in her stories were very different from the one he had given her.

She was sure that if ever she received them they would not be disappointing.

CHAPTER THREE

*H*ermia rose very early and put on the riding-skirt she had made herself.

She remembered Marilyn's instructions not to doll herself up, and decided it would be best not to wear her riding hat.

If she was supposed to have ridden off in a hurry to find her cousin she would not have bothered about herself but would have run out of the house as she was.

What was more, the Marquis, if he noticed her at all, would think she looked very countrified, and certainly not smart like the ladies with whom he usually rode.

As she dressed she thought how much her father and mother would disapprove of her acting a lie even to please her cousin.

However, it was the first time Marilyn had asked her to do anything for her for a very long time, and Hermia thought she must not only help her, but pray that if she was happy she would be much kinder to her and everybody else.

She had a feeling that Marilyn had changed a great deal since she grew up.

She was in fact becoming more and more like the Countess who always had something unpleasant to say, and looked down on most people as if they were dirt beneath her feet.

When Hermia was dressed and it was not much after six o'clock, she crept very softly down the stairs so that nobody should hear her.

Perhaps it was slightly reprehensible, but now that she had the chance of riding one of the fine horses from the Hall which she missed more and more every day, she did not want to ride straight to Bluebell Wood as Marilyn had instructed her to do, but to enjoy a good ride first while she had the opportunity.

When she reached the stable she found as she expected that late in the evening, without their hearing him, a groom from the Hall had put a horse in one of the many empty stalls.

The previous Vicar must have been very much richer than her father because he had extended the stables, and there was room for a dozen horses or more.

Now there was only the Vicar's new yearling which was only partly broken in.

He was training it not only to draw the gig in which he made his rounds in the Parish, but also the old-fashioned but comfortable chaise in which he drove his wife and daughter.

Rufus, as they had named him, being a chestnut, was excellent for the work he had to do, but he certainly looked outclassed by the horse in the next stall.

When she saw him Hermia felt her heart leap with excitement and she knew that for the next hour she was really going to enjoy herself as she had not been able to do for many a year.

She recognised the horse, for she had ridden him before, and knew he was called "Bracken."

She patted him and made a fuss of him while she

fetched her side-saddle which was hanging on the wall.

She was just tightening the girths when the old man who looked after her father's horse and worked in the large, untidy garden came shuffling through the stable-door.

"Be ye goin' ridin', Miss Hermia?" he asked. "Oi thinks as 'ow the 'orse had been sent for t'Reverend."

"No, I am riding this morning, Jake," Hermia replied, "and do not tell Papa, if you see him, that I have gone, as it is a secret."

Jake took sometime to digest this before he said:

"Oi'll keep me mouth shut, Miss Hermia, an' Oi 'spect ye'll enjoy yersel' wi' a fine animal loik 'e."

"I shall, Jake! It is a long time since I have had anything so magnificent to ride."

As she spoke Hermia led Bracken out of the stables and Jake held his bridle as she stepped onto a mounting-block.

She could manage to lift herself into the saddle without one, but she thought for Marilyn's sake that she should arrange her skirt tidily, although she was quite sure that whatever she did her cousin would find fault.

When she had settled herself in the saddle she smiled at Jake and said:

"Not a word now to anybody until I return!"

"Oi'll hold me tongue!" Jake promised and Hermia rode off.

She entered the Park and riding in the opposite direction from Bluebell Wood went past the wood nearest to the Vicarage which was marked on the maps as Brook Wood, but was known to everybody in the village as Witch Wood.

This was the wood in which they believed Satan's revels, which they whispered about amongst themselves, took place.

This morning Hermia was not interested in the

woods but in wanting the horse under her to gallop as swiftly as it was possible for him to do.

On the other side of Witch Wood there was a level piece of ground she had always hoped her Uncle would make into a miniature race-course, such as a number of race-horse owners had built on their own estates.

But he had refused, saying he found it boring to visit the same place day after day.

"As I own 10,000 acres I have plenty of room to ride where I wish," he explained, "which is good for my horse as well as for me."

Now as Hermia saw the flat grassland which extended for over a mile she drew in her breath with excitement and gave Bracken his head.

When she slowed him down to a trot after the wild gallop they had both enjoyed to the full, she felt anything she had to do for Marilyn in payment for this delight, was well worth while.

She rode on, seeing parts of the estate she had known ever since she was a child, but had not been able to visit for a long time.

Then knowing time was passing and she must not be late for Marilyn she rode Bracken back past Witch Wood and over the Park towards the wood where Marilyn would be riding with the Marquis.

Now Hermia had to go very much more slowly because the rabbit-holes were dangerous, and also because of the low branches on the trees.

It was as she had expected, getting warmer as the sun moved up the sky, and she was glad that she had not put on the jacket of her riding-habit.

Instead she was just wearing a white muslin blouse.

It was old and had been mended, darned and patched in places, but it was the best she had.

She thought once again that if the Marquis thought about her at all he would believe she had just come straight from the bed-room of the dying woman to fetch her cousin.

Now that the moment was upon her and she had to act the part that Marilyn had assigned to her, she rehearsed in her mind what she would say.

She hoped that if she spoke urgently and with a note of sincerity in her voice the story would be believed.

She entered the wood and moved slowly under the trees, along a path that led into the very centre of it.

The bluebells and primroses were over and the undergrowth was very much higher than it had been in the spring.

Occasionally Hermia would see the wild orchid called 'Lady's Slippers' growing under the trees, and there was also a profusion of small mushrooms which she had always believed showed where the fairies had danced the night before.

Because she could not help it she began to tell herself a fantasy story in which a Princess escaped from the goblins and was taken to safety by a wood-nymph.

She was just getting to the exciting part of the tale when she heard voices and realised that Marilyn and the Marquis were not far from her deep in the heart of the wood.

She drew in her breath, then having kicked her heel into Bracken to make him move faster she managed by the time she reached them to sound as if she was in a great hurry and almost breathless from the speed at which she had come.

Only when she had her first glimpse of Marilyn did she realise how untidy she herself must look.

Her hair had been blown about her forehead from the speed at which she had galloped, her cheeks were flushed, and although she was not aware of it her eyes were shining because it had all been so enjoyable.

Marilyn on the other hand, dressed in an exquisitely cut summer riding-habit of pale blue silk trimmed with white braid and with a jabot of lace at her chin, looked as if she had just stepped out of Rotten Row.

Her riding-hat was encircled with a gauze veil of the same colour as her habit and hung down her back.

As she turned to look at Hermia with well-simulated surprise her face was serene and lovely, and everything about her was neat and tidy to the zenith of perfection.

Hermia rode up to her at such a pace that she had to pull Bracken to a standstill so sharply that he reared up most effectively.

"Hermia!" Marilyn exclaimed. "What is the matter? Why are you here?"

"Oh, Marilyn, I have been looking for you everywhere!" Hermia replied. "Poor old Mrs. Burles is dying, but she says she cannot do so until she has said good-bye to you and thanked you for all your kindness to her."

Because she was feeling nervous Hermia had not attempted to alter the words that Marilyn had instructed her to say.

She thought as she said them, that they sounded somewhat contrived.

Marilyn gave a little cry that sounded very theatrical.

"Oh, poor Mrs. Burles!" she exclaimed. "Of course I must go to her!"

She turned her horse sharply as she spoke and passing Hermia gave it a sharp flick of the whip.

She had gone quite a way before as if she suddenly remembered what she had planned she turned her head to call out:

"Show His Lordship the way back to the Hall, and then follow me. I shall need you."

"I will do that," Hermia replied.

She thought as she spoke that Marilyn was making quite certain that she did not linger and ingratiate herself with the Marquis.

For the first time she looked at him.

He had turned his horse so that it was across the

path, and now he was nearer to her than Hermia expected.

Then she gave an audible gasp and realised simultaneously that she had been very stupid.

She might have guessed that the man who had kissed her and given her a guinea for helping him would turn out to be the Marquis of Deverille.

He was looking, she thought, as he had the other day, very much like the Devil, except that as she met his eyes she realised there was a slight twinkle in them and a decided twist to his lips.

For the moment she could only stare at him, wondering wildly what she should say.

"So you are not a milk-maid after all!"

He spoke with that dry, drawling voice which he had used before.

Then as she felt the colour come flooding into her face, Hermia in a voice which did not sound like her own, replied:

"No, . . . and you had no . . . right to . . . think I was!"

What she had meant was that he had had no right to kiss her and feeling shy and very embarrassed at meeting him again she could only wonder how she could make him realise how badly he had behaved.

"Do you want me to apologise?" the Marquis asked.

With an effort Hermia lifted her chin and looked at him defiantly.

"It is too late now for that! Were you able to find the Blacksmith without any . . . difficulty?"

"I rode back to where I was staying and left my grooms to cope with it."

"That is where you will wish to go now, and I will show you the way."

"There is no hurry. I am interested as to why at one moment you are pretending to be a milk-maid, and the next you appear as an Amazon on an exceedingly well-bred horse."

"I was not pretending to be a milk-maid!" Hermia retorted quickly. "And even if I was . . ."

She stopped because she thought what she was about to say would make the conversation even more embarrassing than it already was.

"What you are saying is that I had no right to kiss you," the Marquis said slowly. "Surely you must be aware that if you walk about alone looking as you do, you are a temptation to any man who sees you?"

"Not the sort of men I meet here in the country," Hermia replied, "but perhaps the Gentlemen who come from London have different ideas from ours about . . . respect and . . . propriety?"

She tried to speak defiantly, but because she was still feeling shy her voice sounded rather small, weak and ineffective.

"I stand rebuked!" the Marquis said and she knew he was laughing at her.

"If Your Lordship will ride on a little way," Hermia said, "I will show you a path which will lead you back into the Park. Then it will be easy for you to find your way to the Hall."

"I have already said," the Marquis replied, "I am in no hurry."

As his horse was across the path and the trees were close together it was impossible for her to go round him. Hermia could therefore only look at him help-lessly and wonder what she could do.

"Suppose you tell me who you are?" the Marquis asked. "And why do you make it your business, be-sides collecting eggs, to fetch young women to the death-beds of the villagers?"

Again Hermia was certain he was mocking at her, and she thought with a little flicker of anger that he was living up to his appearance.

"If you are interested," she said coldly, "my father is the Vicar of Little Brookfield, and when the old woman who is . . . dying asked for my . . . Cousin Marilyn I . . . naturally came in . . . search of her."

"And you were aware this was where she would be?"

Hermia drew in her breath.

She knew it was a very pertinent question and something Marilyn should have foreseen he might ask.

After a very short pause she replied:

"I was going up to the . . . Hall when . . . somebody told me they had seen you . . . riding in this . . . direction."

She tried to make the lie sound convincing.

At the same time, because the Marquis was looking at her closely she stumbled a little over her words.

"So Marilyn is your Cousin," the Marquis said slowly.

"Yes, as I have just told you," Hermia answered, "and she will be waiting for me. Please, My Lord, let me show you the way. Then I can hurry back to help her."

"Do you enjoy death-bed scenes?"

Again Hermia was aware he was mocking her, and now she was quite certain in her own mind that he did not believe that anybody was dying.

She hated him even more violently for being so perceptive and wanted to escape from him.

She had the feeling that his eyes, despite his drooping eye-lids, were sharp and penetrating and that he was well aware that she was becoming more and more involved in her lies and telling them very badly.

Then she hoped she was being needlessly apprehensive.

Yet because he was challenging her she wished that she could take him into the village and show him Mrs. Burles dying in her bed with Marilyn sitting beside her like an Angel of Mercy.

However, that being impossible she could only remain silent, her face turned away from him.

She was unaware that as she did so the sun flickering through the thick branches of the trees made her hair shine as if it were made of the same gold as the guinea he had pressed into her hand.

She was thinking of that, and of how he had insulted her, and also of the strange hardness and possessiveness of his lips when he kissed her.

Again as if he could read her thoughts he said:

"I appreciate that you are angry with me, and while I can only apologise again for mistaking your calling, I do not apologise for kissing you, because you are so unexpectedly beautiful!"

"It was an . . . intolerable way to . . . behave, My Lord, and I have no wish to . . . discuss it!"

"I imagine you have never been kissed before," the Marquis remarked reflectively.

"Of course not!" Hermia said angrily.

Then a sudden thought struck her and she turned her face towards him saying in a very different voice:

"Please . . . you will not tell . . . Marilyn or my uncle what . . . happened? If they spoke of it to Mama and Papa they would be very . . . upset."

There was something pathetic in the way she pleaded with him and after a moment the Marquis said:

"I have many faults, but I have never done anything so dishonourable as to talk about any woman I have kissed."

He saw the little sigh of relief Hermia gave and added quietly:

"Forget it! At the same time, because I am interested I would like to know what you did with the guinea I gave you."

"I wanted to throw it away!"

"But instead you kept it?"

"Certainly not! I put it in the Poor-Box. When Papa finds it he will be able to help a great number of people who at this moment are desperately in need of help."

"Why at this moment?"

Hermia looked at him in surprise.

"Surely you are aware of the suffering there is in the country as an aftermath of the War?"

He did not speak and she went on:

"The Farmers are having a desperate time after the bad harvest of last year, and because of the cheap food which is coming into the country from the Continent. They cannot afford to take on more labourers, and with so many men coming out of the Services there is terrible unemployment."

She thought the Marquis looked at her in surprise and he certainly raised his dark eye-brows before he replied:

"I should have thought your uncle was rich enough to see there was no unemployment on his estate."

Hermia was silent.

She knew that her uncle had refused, despite her father's pleading, to take on a number of young men in the village who had either returned from the war or who were now grown up and required work.

In fact, they had had several angry arguments about it quite recently and the last time the Earl had roared at his brother:

"Whatever you may think, I am not a Philanthropic Society, and the sooner you get that into your head the better."

Her father had come home very depressed and said:

"If only I could employ them all myself, but you know I cannot do that, and I hate to tell them I have failed to find them work."

"You have done your best, darling," her mother had said, "and no man could do more."

"I know, I know," her father replied, "but if I had the running of the estate, I could quite easily take on several dozen more men and give them work which would eventually pay for itself."

He had been depressed the whole evening, and it had taken her mother a long time to coax him back into his habitual good-humour.

Now it occurred to Hermia that if the Marquis was as rich as Marilyn had said he was, he could take on extra workmen on his estate and might even persuade her uncle to be more generous.

Without thinking, speaking in the same way as she talked to her father and mother as if she were their contemporary, she said:

"Surely you must be aware, as you too are a Landlord, that if you developed new industries it would create work for men who otherwise would starve, or take to stealing."

"What sort of industries are you thinking of?"

Hermia was sure he was sneering at her behind the drawling words, yet because she was determined to make him understand she said:

"I have no idea of what your land is like, but here, for instance, if Uncle John would only listen, there is so much timber ready to be felled that he could employ at least two dozen workmen in a new timber yard."

She knew the Marquis was listening and went on.

"There is also a gravel-pit which was not worked during the war which could be re-opened, and at the far end of the estate there is an ancient slate-quarry, and slate is always needed for the building of new houses."

"I see you are remarkably well informed," the Marquis remarked. "Are these your ideas or your father's?"

"They should be the ideas of great Landlords like yourself, My Lord," Hermia retorted.

Then because she felt it was a mistake to antagonise him she said:

"Please, if you get the chance, will you speak about such things to my uncle? I feel sure he would listen to you, even though he will not listen to Papa."

"I very much doubt if he would listen to me," the Marquis replied, "but if I do what you ask, will you forgive me my sins?"

"I think, My Lord, it would be best not to talk about them, but to let me show you the way to the Hall."

She thought as she spoke that she had spent far more time with the Marquis than she should have done, and if Marilyn was aware of it she would be very angry.

"Please . . ." she said. "I must go to my cousin. She will be . . . expecting me."

"Very well," the Marquis said, "but before you ride ahead to show me the way suppose you tell me your name?"

"It is Hermia!"

"I imagine when you were christened your parents were thinking of you as a female version of the Messenger of the Gods!"

For the first time since they had been talking Hermia gave a little laugh.

"It is clever of you to be aware of that. Most people merely exclaim: 'What a funny name!' and expect me to be called 'Jane,' 'Anne,' 'Sarah,' or 'Mary.' "

"Why those names in particular?" the Marquis enquired curiously.

"Because they are what is considered suitable for a Vicar's daughter," Hermia replied demurely.

"You mean it would be very much out of character for your parents to be thinking of Olympus! Well, shall I tell you that at the moment you look much more like Persephone, leaving Hades to bring Spring back to the world."

He spoke in his dry, sarcastic voice which did not make his words sound like a compliment, but again Hermia laughed and it was a very happy, spontaneous sound.

"Why are you laughing?"

He had drawn his horse up beside her on the path and as he did so she glanced at him.

Then without thinking she was being impertinent she replied:

"You must be aware who I thought you were after you left me!"

"Oh, now I understand!" the Marquis said. "Very well, lead the Devil out of Hades!"

Hermia did not reply, but she thought Bluebell Wood was not her idea of Hades.

She was riding ahead of the Marquis and she thought that if Marilyn was ever aware she had lingered and talked with him for so long she would be very, very angry.

Only when they reached the footpath which led out of the wood into the Park did she hesitate for a moment.

She had intended to go back the way she had come through Bluebell Wood, but that, she knew, would take longer than if she rode into the park with the Marquis.

While he went on to the Hall she would ride in the opposite direction towards the village.

She felt that he would not suggest accompanying her, but if he did she must try to find some excuse to prevent him from doing so.

As she made up her mind, she rode ahead, and a few minutes later they could see the Park in front of them and in the distance the Hall, looking very large and very impressive in the sunshine.

As the path came to an end Hermia drew Bracken to a standstill.

"You can find your way back from here, My Lord."

"I realise that," he replied, "and I should thank you for performing your task so efficiently."

The way he spoke made Hermia nervous that he was making it clear that he did not for one moment believe that she had summoned Marilyn to a death-bed.

Then she told herself she was being needlessly apprehensive.

Why should the Marquis not believe what he had been told? But even if he did, she had the feeling that it would not make him wish to marry Marilyn without having many other far better reasons for doing so.

He drew his horse alongside hers and sat looking at her with an expression on his face she did not understand.

It was as if he was appraising her in a manner that was vaguely insulting, and yet at the same time, because he was so cynical and bored, complimentary.

She did not know why she thought this, and yet she was sure it was true.

He did not move and after a moment Hermia said: "Good-bye . . . My Lord!"

"Good-bye, Hermia!" the Marquis replied. "I shall be looking forward, as of course the Devil expected, to seeing you again."

Hermia smiled and he saw the dimples in her cheeks.

"As I am not Persephone," she said, "that is very unlikely, unless of course the gods have a special message for you, which is again unlikely."

She did not wait for his reply, but started Bracken moving quickly away from him, at the same time being careful of the rabbit-holes and the low boughs of the trees.

She did not look back, but she had the feeling the Marquis was watching her go.

Only when she had reached the very end of the path and was nearing the gate which would take her out onto the road leading to the village did she look back towards the Hall.

She could see him in the distance riding slowly across the top of the path and felt glad he had not followed her.

She rode out onto the dusty road and trotted home, thinking it would be a very long time before she had the chance of riding Bracken or any horse like him again.

At the same time it had been an exciting morning,

and very different from the monotony of other mornings in which for months nothing unusual happened.

She put Bracken in the stable and Jake took off his bridle and saddle.

"If Bracken is not fetched before this evening," Hermia said, "I shall ride him again this afternoon."

"Ye do that, Miss Hermia," Jake agreed. " 't be a cryin' shame anyone as rides as well as ye do shouldn't 'ave a 'orse."

"I enjoyed myself this morning."

She reluctantly said good-bye to Bracken and left the stable to go into the house.

She was thinking quickly what she should say to her father and mother, and when she entered the Dining-Room where they were having breakfast her mother said:

"Nanny told me you went riding early this morning on a horse that came from the Hall. Surely that is a most unusual thing to happen?"

"Very unusual," Hermia agreed, kissing first her mother then her father, "but Marilyn wanted me to do something for her."

"Marilyn?" Mrs. Brooke exclaimed. "But you have not heard from her for months!"

Hermia sat down and started to eat a boiled egg which was waiting for her covered with a little woollen cap to keep it warm.

Instead of answering her mother she said to her father:

"Tell me, Papa, have you ever heard of the Marquis of Deverille?"

"Deverille?" her father replied. "Of course I have! 'Deverille the Devil' is famous in the sporting world."

Hermia stared at him in astonishment.

"What did you call him?" she asked.

"It is what they shout on the race-course when his horse wins," her father explained. "He is always said to have the Devil's own luck, so it is obvious that the racing crowd who never miss a trick should call him 'Deverille the Devil'!"

"That is exactly what he looks like!"

"I heard he was staying at the Hall," her father said. "When did you meet him?"

Hermia realised she had made a slip and said quickly:

"He was riding with Marilyn . . ."

"And she asked you to ride with them?" Mrs. Brooke asked with astonishment. "I cannot understand why she should do that!"

Hermia knew it was impossible to explain and she merely said:

"Marilyn came here yesterday, Mama, and she was very pleasant. She asked me to meet her this morning in the Bluebell Wood, and the Marquis was with her."

"I am astonished!" her mother answered. "Perhaps now, darling, they will ask you to the Hall."

Hermia knew this was very unlikely, but there was nothing she could reply except: "I hope so, Mama," and go on eating her egg.

"Deverille is an extraordinary chap!" her father remarked in a voice which told her he was following his own train of thought. "He is an exceptional rider. He is the foremost Corinthian in the 'Four-In-Hand Club,' and I have always heard that he is an exceptional Pugilist besides other accomplishments. Yet he always looks as if he has lost a florin and found a fourpenny bit!"

"Do you mean he looks bored, Papa?"

"Exactly!" her father replied. "Bored and cynical. There have been a lot of cartoons done of him, and they always depict him looking like the Devil who is down on his luck!"

He laughed before he went on:

"That certainly is untrue to life. Deverille is rich, important and as we used to say at Oxford 'riding high'! So there is nothing in his life to make him look so gloomy."

"There must be some reason for his attitude," Mrs. Brooke remarked.

"I heard John say once that he was crossed in love when he was a young man, and it turned him sour. I suppose if he is staying at the Hall the Countess has decided to try and marry him off to Marilyn."

"The Marquis does not sound as if he would make her happy," Hermia revealed.

She saw the expression on her father's face and knew he was thinking, as she did, that all the Countess was interested in was the position which Marilyn would occupy as the Marquis's wife.

Neither she nor the Earl would be concerned whether she would find him someone she could love and who would love her.

But it was not the sort of thing her father would say, and even while Hermia was sure he thought it, her mother gave a little sigh before she said:

"Perhaps once Marilyn is married your brother will allow Hermia to ride again. You know how she misses it."

"It was lovely riding this morning," Hermia said, "and I went for a long ride beyond Witch Wood before I joined Marilyn at the time she told me to."

"I am glad you enjoyed it, but you may be stiff tomorrow," her father said.

"If I am," Hermia replied, "Mama has concocted a new salve for stiff joints which all the village is begging her to give them."

"It is in such demand that I shall have to work for hours to make enough," Mrs. Brooke said. "And that reminds me, was Mrs. Burles pleased with the cough mixture you took her?"

"I think she was, Mama," Hermia replied. "At the same time she is growing very old and senile. She went rambling on about her son Ben and is obviously very fussed about him."

"A regular ne'er-do-well," the Vicar exclaimed, "and not quite right in the head. At the same time, the

65

boy is often hungry and nobody will give him any work when there are far better and stronger men in the village sitting about with idle hands."

He spoke bitterly and Hermia wished the Marquis could hear him and understand how depressing it was for strong and healthy men to be idle through no fault of their own.

"The trouble with Ben," Mrs. Brooke said in her soft voice, "is that he has never really grown up and he is into every sort of mischief that he can find. But of course that does not help his mother."

"She is very old," Hermia said. "Instead of giving her cough mixture, Mama, what she really needs is an elixir of youth!"

Mrs. Brooke did not laugh.

"I only wish I could find one! It is what half the people here in the village want, although I have a feeling if they had enough food a lot of them would look twenty years younger in a few days."

"I spoke to John about it the day before yesterday," the Vicar said getting up from the table, "but as usual, he would not listen to me!"

There was a note of disappointment and frustration in his voice which made his wife watch him with anxious eyes as he went from the Dining-Room.

Then she said to Hermia:

"I know what I will do, darling! I will make up a bottle of my soothing syrup and you shall take it to Mrs. Burles. Perhaps that will make her feel a little better."

"She was very depressed, Mama," Hermia replied, "and I know she will be delighted with anything you give her and believe that every spoonful is full of magic. In other words you are a Witch!"

Mrs. Brooke laughed and Hermia said jokingly:

"You will have to be careful, Mama, that they do not become frightened of you as they were of the poor old woman who lived in Witch Wood."

"You surely are not old enough to remember Mrs. Wombatt?" Mrs. Brooke asked.

"I do not remember ever seeing her," Hermia answered, "but of course in the village they believe she still haunts the wood, and that Satan dances with her ghost as he used to dance with her when she was alive!"

"I have never heard such nonsense!" her mother said. "The poor old thing was about ninety when she died and too old to dance with anybody, let alone Satan!"

"They make it sound exciting when they tell me stories of how when she cursed people they withered away or some terrible accident happened to them, or when she gave them one of her magic charms everything went right."

"Then I wish she could give you one," Mrs. Brooke smiled. "For I would love you, my darling, to have a magical horse, some magical gowns, and a wonderful magical Ball at which everybody would admire you!"

"Thank you, Mama, that is just what I want for myself," Hermia said, "and if I tell myself stories in which all that happens, perhaps it will come true."

She was laughing as she carried the empty plates from the Dining-Room into the kitchen and she did not see the look of pain on her mother's face.

Mrs. Brooke knew that loving and sweet though her daughter was, there was nothing for her in the future except a very restricted life in Little Brookfield.

She was barred from the parties which took place at the Hall and even from riding her Uncle's horses.

"It is not fair!" Mrs. Brooke said to herself.

Then because she could never be parted long from the husband she loved so deeply, she hurried from the Dining-Room to find him in the small Study where he had started work on the sermon he would preach on Sunday to the few villagers who came to Church to listen to him.

CHAPTER FOUR

*R*eluctantly Hermia walked towards Mrs. Burles' cottage which was at the end of the village carrying the tonic her mother had made.

She always found Mrs. Burles exhausting.

Sometimes she was more or less sensible, but at other times her mind wandered and she talked on and on, really not making sense.

There had been quite a lot of things to do in the house after luncheon, and Hermia had then hurried to the stables to see if there was a chance of having one more ride on Bracken.

To her disappointment he had already gone and she realised that one of the grooms must have come while they were having their meal and taken him home.

For a moment she felt her disappointment turn to anger that she should have been deprived of something she wanted so much.

Then she told herself that she was very lucky to have been able to ride this morning, and it was greedy to expect to have the same joy again in the afternoon.

She also suspected that Marilyn might have realised how long she had talked to the Marquis and had deliberately sent for Bracken to punish her.

Then she told herself that once again she was being over-imaginative and Marilyn could have no idea that she had not hurried after her immediately as she had been told to do.

At the same time she did not regret it.

It had been exciting to talk to somebody like the Marquis, even though she was hating him.

He might look cynical, he might behave in what she thought was a very reprehensible manner. Nevertheless he was obviously intelligent and she thought he was without exception one of the smartest men she had ever seen or could imagine.

The way he held himself, the way he sat his horse, and the almost blinding shine of his polished boots was something, she thought, which would colour her fantasy stories in the future, even though she cast him in the role of the villain.

She found herself thinking of him all the time she was walking towards Mrs. Burles' cottage.

When she was within sight of it she saw Ben Burles come running out of the low door.

He looked down the road and she thought he must have seen her, because he scuttled off in the opposite direction in a surreptitious manner as if he had something to hide.

'I expect he is up to some mischief,' she thought, thinking of her father's words.

She reached the cottage door and knocked loudly because Mrs. Burles was inclined to be deaf.

It took sometime for her to rise out of the armchair in which she habitually sat in front of the stove and come to the door.

She opened it a few inches, peered round it to see who was standing there, then said:

"Come in, Miss, come in! Oi were hopin' ye'd remember Oi were in pain, an' a real pain it be!"

Hermia entered the cottage, thinking as she had often thought before that it needed a lot of repair. It was something her Uncle should order to be done for his tenants even though they paid only a shilling or two a week.

She knew her father had spoken about the state of the cottages and had told his brother that many of those occupied by aged pensioners leaked when it rained.

The Earl had replied that he had no money to waste on a lot of old people, especially those who had sons who could do the repairs themselves.

The room however was clean, and as Mrs. Burles lowered herself very carefully into the armchair Hermia sat down in a high-backed one near her so that she could hear what she had to say.

"I have brought you a tonic to make you better," she said. "My mother says you are to take a spoonful every morning, one after your midday meal, and one when you go to bed at night."

"It be good of ye, Miss, very good," Mrs. Burles said. "Oi needs somethin', not only fer me body, but fer me mind."

"This will soon make you feel better," Hermia said optimistically.

"It's worried Oi be, worried all the time, an' Ben shouldn't do it, he shouldn't!"

"Do what?" Hermia asked curiously.

"She'll cast a spell on 'e, she will," Mrs. Burles went on as though Hermia had not spoken. "Oi've warned 'e, time after time, not to go near that old Witch, but 'e'll never listen to me!"

Hermia realised she was talking of old Mrs. Wombatt, who used to live in Witch Wood, and who the villagers still believed haunted it.

Because she could see Mrs. Burles' puckered face and the fear in her eyes, she leaned forward to put her hand on the old woman's and said quietly:

"Listen, Mrs. Burles, Mrs. Wombatt is dead. She has been dead for a long time, and she cannot hurt anybody now, so that you need not be afraid for Ben."

"She'll put a curse on 'e!" Mrs. Burles repeated. "He's no right to go there, as Oi tells him. An' they says that Satan heself has been seen with her."

The way she spoke told Hermia there was no use arguing.

This was one of her bad days, and she knew that Mrs. Burles would never believe that not only the poor old woman who had lived in Witch Wood was dead, but her magic had died with her.

She was quite certain if Mrs. Wombatt had been a Witch, she was a White one.

Hermia thought she had magic powers because she used herbs when she cooked, told the fortunes of the village girls, and gave the older folk cures for rheumatism and colic which they believed healed them.

'It is no use arguing with her about a woman who has been dead for such a long time,' Hermia thought.

Instead she went to the table, found a spoon and poured a little of her mother's tonic into it.

"Swallow this," she said to Mrs. Burles, "and you will soon feel better, and I am sure it will help you to sleep."

She knew her mother had added camomile and a little verlain to the other herbs the tonic contained. Although she disapproved of giving those who were hale and hearty any form of sedative, it was different for those who were very old and whose minds wandered.

The old woman swallowed what was in the spoon and said:

"That be good! Give Oi some more."

"No, that is enough for the moment," Hermia said, "but you must remember to take another spoonful before you go to bed."

She put the tonic in the centre of the table and said:

"Goodbye, Mrs. Burles. I know you would like me to thank my mother for what she has sent you."

She walked towards the door as she spoke and as she reached it Mrs. Burles said:

"Ye'll not tell Ben Oi talked to ye? He said everythin' he tell Oi be a secret."

"No, of course not," Hermia said soothingly. "Shut

your eyes and forget about him. I expect he will be back soon to look after you."

Mrs. Burles did not seem to understand, and as Hermia opened the door she heard the old woman mutter to herself:

" 'E shouldn't have gone there! Oi says to him, Oi says: 'Her'll curse ye, that's what her'll do!' "

"Poor old thing, she really gets madder and madder!" Hermia thought as she walked back through the village.

By now the sun had lost its heat and she longed to ride as she had done in the past over the fields and through the woods just as the birds were going to roost.

It had been an enchantment when the last rays of the sun made the tree-trunks look like burnished brass, and the shadows full of mystery which increased as the dusk came bringing with it the night.

"Now that I have to walk it is not the same," she thought, "but I suppose it is better than nothing."

There were so many parts of the estate that she now never saw and yet she could conjure them up like pictures in her mind and knew their beauty could never be forgotten.

When she was nearly home she found herself again thinking of the strange conversation she had had with the Marquis.

He might be cynical and sarcastic, but her father had said how successful he was on the race-course and always won the big races.

"That means he will be at Royal Ascot next week," Hermia told herself, remembering it started on Monday.

Because her father was interested in horses he always read the Racing News in *The Morning Post* which was the only newspaper they had at the Vicarage, and in fact, the only one they could afford.

When Peter was at home they would have long discussions on the merits of the horses they read about.

After Peter had been to the Derby with some of his friends he had described to his father exactly what had happened and how thrilling it had been.

"What is more," he said boastfully, "I won £5!"

"You might have lost it," the Vicar replied warn-ingly.

"I know, Papa, and I was very nervous that might happen," Peter said honestly. "However I won, and that paid all my expenses for the day and left me a little in hand."

His father smiled as if he understood what a satis-faction it had been.

From the way he talked Hermia was sure her father would have liked to be at Epsom with Peter, and she wondered if her brother would have the chance of going to Ascot.

It must be very frustrating for him, she thought, to know that his rich friends could afford to attend all the race-meetings, either travelling from Oxford for the day, or staying the night with some generous host or if they had no invitation, at an Hotel which was invariably very expensive.

And yet Peter, although she felt sorry for him, was seeing a great deal more of life than she was.

She wondered if there would ever be a chance of her going to a race-meeting, attending one of the Balls which took place after every big meeting, or even just travelling to London to see the shops.

Then she laughed.

Those things were out of reach so it was no use troubling about them.

" 'If wishes were horses, beggars could ride,' " she quoted to herself and hurried into the Vicarage to tell her mother about Mrs. Burles.

They had waited for the Vicar for nearly a quarter-of-an-hour and Nanny was complaining crossly that her food was getting spoilt, when the Vicar arrived home.

Hermia heard old Jake taking the gig round to the stables, and when she opened the front door and her father came in to the hall, her mother came hurrying out of the Sitting-Room to exclaim:

"Darling, I have been so worried! What kept you so long?"

The Vicar kissed his wife affectionately and said:

"I have told you not to worry. As a matter of fact I would have been home in plenty of time if I had not been delayed when I reached the village."

"The village?" Hermia exclaimed. "What has happened in the village?"

As if the Vicar was aware he ought not to keep Nanny waiting any longer he walked into the Dining-Room and sat down at the head of the table.

"You will hardly believe what has happened," he said, "in fact, I do not believe it myself."

"What is it?" Mrs. Burles asked.

"The Marquis of Deverille has disappeared!"

Hermia stared at her father as if she felt she could not have heard correctly what he said.

"What do you mean disappeared, Papa?"

"Exactly what I say," the Vicar replied. "The whole village is agog with it. Apparently everybody on the estate is out looking for him."

Hermia's eyes were very wide in her face, but it was her mother who exclaimed:

"Tell us everything, darling, from the beginning. I am trying to understand what you are saying."

"I find it difficult to understand it myself!" the Vicar said. "But when I was coming home half-a-dozen people stopped me all chattering like parrots."

He smiled before he went on:

"Before I could stop them from all talking at once, half the village was clustered round the gig."

He stopped speaking to help first his wife, then his

daughter from the soup tureen that Nanny had put in front of him on the table.

It was a soup made with celery which always tasted delicious and was in fact, one of the Vicar's favourites.

He filled his own plate, then as he drank a spoonful Hermia begged:

"Please go on, Papa. We must know what happened!"

"Yes, of course," the Vicar replied. "Well, it appears that immediately after luncheon at the Hall my brother had arranged to take the Marquis to see his yearlings which he has in a field on the North side of the Park."

Hermia knew where this was, but she did not interrupt as her father went on:

"The two gentlemen were apparently not hurrying themselves but talking as they rode when a groom came galloping after them to say that a visitor had arrived at the Hall asking to see the Earl urgently and saying that he could not wait."

The Vicar paused and took another spoonful of soup before he continued:

"My brother was obviously annoyed at having to go back, but as they had not gone very far he told the Marquis to go on alone. He then rode back to the Hall."

"Who did he find waiting for him?" Mrs. Brooke asked.

"The village did not seem to know this," the Vicar replied, "but they say that John was only a few minutes at the house before he rode off again to catch up with the Marquis."

"Then what . . . happened?" Hermia asked breathlessly.

"He could not find him!"

"What do you mean—could not find him?" Mrs. Brooke enquired.

"Exactly what I say," her husband answered. "There was no sign of the Marquis and at a loss to understand what could have happened, John rode back to the stables."

He paused dramatically, almost as if he enjoyed keeping his audience in suspense as he drank some more soup.

"My brother had only just arrived in the stables when to his consternation the horse the Marquis had been riding came galloping in, his stirrups flapping at his sides, and his saddle empty!"

Hermia gave a little gasp.

"I thought he was a good rider!"

"He is!" the Vicar said. "In fact I have always been told that the Marquis has boasted that the horse has never been bred that can throw him!"

"On this occasion he must have been thrown!" Mrs. Brooke exclaimed.

"That of course, is what I gather John and everybody else thought," the Vicar said.

"What happened then?" Hermia asked.

"Naturally your Uncle told all the grooms to get mounted and find the Marquis as quickly as possible."

There was a little pause before Mrs. Brooke asked:

"Are you saying that they have not found him?"

"There is no sign of him!" her husband replied.

"That is impossible!" Hermia exclaimed. "He must be somewhere not very far away!"

The Vicar finished his soup and as Nanny took away the tureen and came back with the next course he said:

"As soon as I have finished eating I am going up to the Hall to see if I can help in any way. According to Wade, who is a sensible man, everybody on the estate has been searching all the afternoon and evening, but there is not a sign of the Marquis anywhere."

Hermia and her mother both knew that Wade was the Head Keeper and had been at the Hall for many years.

He was a man who did not speak much, but what he said could be believed and they could understand that the mystery of the Marquis's disappearance was, if Wade had said so, unexaggerated.

"Yes, of course you must go to see if you can help, darling," Mrs. Brooke said, "but it does seem incredible that they cannot find him."

"I quite agree with you, but Wade told me they have searched everywhere."

He smiled as he added:

"It is a pity his horse cannot talk, because he in fact, must know where he left his distinguished rider."

Hermia was silent.

It flashed through her mind that perhaps after all, as she had thought the first time she met him, the Marquis was the Devil and he had now returned to the Underworld from which he came and they would never see him again.

"I should have thought the only thing any of us can do," Mrs. Brooke replied, "is somehow to find the Marquis."

"Well, for one place he is not here in the Vicarage!" her husband said.

He put his arms around his wife and held her close against him as he said:

"I was looking forward to our having a quiet evening, but I will not be any longer than I can help. I suppose it would be a mistake for me to take Hermia with me?"

"She had better stay with me," Mrs. Brooke replied.

Hermia knew that her mother was thinking that if, as she suspected, the Marquis was being thought of as a suitable husband, for Marilyn, they would certainly not want her.

After her father had left, Hermia and her mother sat in the Sitting-Room discussing what could have happened. Then Mrs. Brooke said:

"You must have spoken to the Marquis this morning when he was with Marilyn. What is he like?"

"The best way I can describe him, Mama, is bored, cynical and very sarcastic!"

Mrs. Brooke looked surprised.

"Why should he be like that?"

"I expect he has been spoilt, Mama, through being so successful at everything he undertakes."

"Do you think that Marilyn is in love with him?" her mother enquired.

"She is very anxious to marry him, Mama, and of course it is something that would please Aunt Edith."

"Of course," her mother agreed, and there was no need for Hermia to explain herself any further.

It was nearly eleven o'clock when her father returned, and as he came into the hall his wife and daughter sprang to their feet eagerly.

"Is there any news, Papa?" Hermia asked before her mother could speak.

"None at all," the Vicar said. "It seems quite unexplicable, and I have never known John to be so agitated."

"And Edith?" Mrs. Brooke enquired.

"She had no time for me, as you can imagine," the Vicar replied, "and I was informed that Marilyn is so distressed that she has taken to her bed."

"I must say it is a terrible thing to happen when one is entertaining a guest, whoever he may be," Mrs. Brooke remarked. "I suppose there is nothing we can do to help?"

"Nothing," the Vicar replied, "except pray he has not been murdered for any money he might have been carrying."

He paused before he said:

"I suppose I should not tell you this, but John is sure this could be the work of the Marquis's heir presumptive—Roxford de Ville."

"What a strange name!" Hermia murmured.

Her father sat down in his usual chair near the fireplace.

"De Ville is spelt the French way and is his family name," he explained. "I believe they originally came from Normandy at the time of William the Conqueror."

"And you think that this man Roxford de Ville has murdered the Marquis?" Mrs. Brooke asked with an incredulous note in her voice.

"Personally I cannot believe it," the Vicar answered. "It would be too obvious. But there is no doubt, according to John, that there is a great deal of animosity between the two of them. The Marquis has paid de Ville's debts dozens of times and recently refused to do any more for him."

"So if he disposes of the Marquis he will inherit the title and his fortune?" Hermia asked.

"If he is not arrested for murder and hanged for it," her father replied.

"But surely if he was bound to be the chief suspect, that would be a very silly thing to do?" Hermia persisted.

"You are quite right, my dearest," her father agreed, "and that is why I do not believe the Marquis has been murdered. He must have fallen somewhere and so far they have not been able to find him. John will be sending everybody out to search for him again as soon as it is dawn."

He rose from his chair as he spoke saying:

"I imagine I shall be expected to go with them, so I am now going to bed, and thank you, my darlings, for waiting up for me."

They all went up the stairs together and Hermia kissed her father and mother an affectionate goodnight and went to her own bedroom.

It was small but her mother had made it very pretty, and she had around her all her special treasures which she had collected ever since she had been a child.

Some of the china ornaments had been given to her by Marilyn, and as she looked at them she thought she was sorry for her cousin.

"She must be anxious that she may have lost the man she wants to marry," Hermia murmured.

At the same time some intuition that she could not deny told her that the Marquis had had no intention of marrying Marilyn, and was quite aware that she was trying to trick him into proposing to her.

She did not know how she knew this, but it was just as clear to her as if somebody had proved to her that was the truth.

"Poor Marilyn," she thought sympathetically, "she will be very disappointed. But doubtless when she is in London and looking so pretty there will be heaps of other men to offer her marriage."

They might not be as important or as rich as the Marquis, but there was every chance that she would be happier with a man who was not so contemptuous of everything in life.

Hermia got into bed having pulled back the curtains from the window before she did so, and lay watching the stars come out and the moon creeping up the sky.

The moon was full, and she remembered that the villagers thought that was the time of the Witches' Sabbat when they flew towards it on their broomsticks.

The moment she thought of it she imagined she could see one silhouetted for a moment against the moon overhead.

Then suddenly she gave a little cry and sat up in bed.

If her uncle was right and the Marquis's wicked heir had murdered him, she knew where those who were employed to do anything so evil would have hidden the body.

Nobody who lived in the village and on the estate would, she knew, dare to search old Mrs. Wombatt's cottage which was situated in the centre of Witch Wood.

They were so frightened of their own tales about it that they believed that although she was dead and buried her ghost haunted the place where she had lived.

What was more, on moonlit nights she could still be seen revelling with Satan.

Even somebody as sensible as Wade the Head Keeper would not go near the cottage in the wood.

"That is where he will be!" Hermia told herself.

Although she was so sure she was right, she knew that she would have to find out for certain.

She thought perhaps she should tell her father, but if she did so he would insist on coming with her, and she would look very silly if she was proved wrong. He might then question her as to why she was so interested in the Marquis.

It would be much easier to suggest in the morning that he should look there.

But for some reason Hermia could not explain to herself she felt she must look for him now, at this moment, and it was important not to wait.

She got out of bed and dressed herself, putting on the first gown that came to hand.

She tied back her hair with a bow of ribbon, and slipped round her shoulders a little woollen shawl in case she felt cold when she got outside.

In fact, that was unlikely because it had been so hot all day, and now it was still warm and there was no wind.

When she was ready Hermia very cautiously opened the door of her bedroom and crept down the stairs in her stockinged feet holding her shoes in her hands.

She let herself out through the kitchen-door at the back, so that she would not be heard by her father and mother who slept in the big bedroom overlooking the front of the house.

Putting on her shoes she started to walk through the garden which adjoined the main road where she was out of sight of the windows.

It was not likely that anybody would see her.

At the same time she knew that Nanny as well as her father and mother would have been astonished had they known she was walking about at this time of the night.

There was no need to use one of the entrances which led into her Uncle's Park.

Instead, as she had done often before, she climbed over the wall and dropping down onto the soft ground started off in the direction of Witch Wood.

The wood was the nearest one to the village which was why, Hermia thought, all those years ago Mrs. Wombatt had built herself a house there.

It had been in her grandfather's time, who from all she had heard had been very much like her father, good-natured and kind to everyone who lived on his land.

He had made no objection when Mrs. Wombatt, with the help of two young men she had bewitched, built a house partly of bricks, partly with the trunks of trees, and lived there alone.

Now as Hermia entered the lower end of Witch Wood she wondered if the tales the villagers told were true.

Perhaps in the moonlight she would see strange sights and hear the music to which the Witches danced echoing among the trees.

Then she told herself that even if they were there they would not hurt her, while the elves and fairies who had been her friends ever since she first learnt about them would protect her from coming to any harm.

The wood itself was very beautiful in the moonlight, and it was impossible to believe that any evil could mar such loveliness.

The moon shone silver through the branches of the trees and made strange patterns on the path along which Hermia walked.

She could see the stars brilliant as diamonds in the

heavens above her, and if there was music it came from her heart and from the trees.

She had always believed as a little girl that if she listened against the trunk of a tree she would hear it breathing, and sometimes singing a little song to itself.

Any other sounds she imagined were made by the goblins who lived under the roots or by the squirrels who built their nests high up in its branches and were afraid of nothing except human beings.

It was a long way to the centre of the wood, but even as she drew nearer to Mrs. Wombatt's cottage she was not afraid.

She saw first the forest pool in which she knew the old woman had washed, and also drank the water.

It was a very beautiful pool surrounded by irises and the kingcups and the still surface of the water looked in the moonlight as if it held mystical secrets.

Then just beyond it, half-hidden by the bushes that had grown up over the years, she saw Mrs. Wombatt's house.

It was in surprisingly good repair considering it had not been lived in for so long. The roof was intact and the chimney was still there.

Then as she reached it Hermia could see quite clearly that the two small windows on each side of the door had been boarded up and she wondered who had taken the trouble to do this.

She stood looking at them, thinking that somebody who had not been afraid of the Witch's Curse must have come here since her death and protected the house against intruders.

There were not likely to be any, and she could only imagine it had been done on her Uncle's instructions, then thought that was unlikely.

She was quite sure, knowing him, that he would merely say that as far as he was concerned the house could fall down, and the sooner the better.

Then because the same instinct which had brought her here told her now she must look inside, she put out her hands towards a heavy wooden bar that lay across the centre of the door.

It was lodged firmly into two iron cradles, which looked, although it was difficult to see clearly, as if they had been added recently.

The bar of wood was heavy and it took all Hermia's strength to lift it, but she managed at last to do so, and dropped it down onto the ground.

Then as she was ready to pull the door open she felt for the first time, afraid.

Suppose she found something horrible inside?

She felt a tremor of fear strike through her. Then as she trembled, she heard the soft hoot of an owl in one of the trees.

It was such a familiar sound and so much part of her life that it was reassuring, just as if her father or somebody she trusted was with her.

If the creatures of the forest were not afraid, then she had nothing to fear either.

She half opened the door and for a moment she could see nothing.

Then as her eyes grew accustomed to the darkness she could see something lying on the floor in the centre of the small room.

At first she thought it was just a pile of clothing, or perhaps some leaves.

Then her intuition told her it was a man and she knew that she had found the Marquis.

She opened the door as wide as it would go, and now the moonlight made it easy to see she was not mistaken.

There was a man's body lying still on the floor, and the first thing Hermia saw was the shine on his boots and then the white of his breeches.

She knelt down beside him, thinking with a sudden constriction of her heart that he was dead.

But as she put her hand on his forehead, feeling for it rather than seeing exactly where it was, she knew he was alive but unconscious.

To be quite certain she was not mistaken, she undid the buttons of his waist-coat and put her hand inside to feel his heart.

Through his fine linen shirt she could feel it beating faintly and now as she began to see more clearly in the darkness she saw his eyes were closed and there was blood on his forehead and on the side of his cheek.

It flashed through her mind that he had fought against those who must have brought him here!

Perhaps finally they had either shot him, or hit him with something heavy which had rendered him unconscious as he was now.

She took her hand from his heart and very gently felt his head.

She thought there was blood congealed in his hair and she was certain, although she dared not investigate further, that there was an open wound where he had been hit perhaps with a blunderbuss or a heavy stick.

"I must go and fetch help," she thought.

Then as she would have risen to her feet the Marquis opened his eyes.

As he did so he made a movement with his hands and she was aware that he was struggling back to reality.

"What—has—happened?" he asked.

"You are all right and quite safe," Hermia replied, "but I think somebody has struck you on the head."

She was not certain if he had understood or not, but he made an effort as though he would sit up and she helped him.

She realized as she did so how big and heavy he was, but somehow she managed to assist him into a sitting position.

He groaned and tried to put his hand up to his forehead as if he felt dizzy.

"You are all right," she said again, "but I want, if possible, to get you away from here."

She had a sudden fear that whoever had brought

him to the Witch's house and flung him down on the ground might return to finish him off, or to make sure he was still imprisoned and nobody had rescued him.

Now as he was sitting up she could see that the sleeve of his riding-jacket had been torn away from the shoulder and his cravat was untied and crumpled.

She looked at the hand he was attempting to put to his forehead and saw that the knuckles of his fingers were bleeding.

It was obvious he had put up a tremendous fight against his assailants, whoever they were, but the blow from a heavy weapon was what had finally defeated him.

She let him rest for a moment. Then she said softly:

"Will you try to get to your feet while I help you? I do not want to leave you here alone while I fetch help."

The Marquis did not reply but she felt he understood what she had said to him, for he reached out his hand to try to find something by which he could pull himself up to his feet.

Putting her hand under his arm and straining every muscle in her body to assist him, Hermia thought it was only by a miracle and what she knew was his indomitable willpower that finally he stood upright.

She placed one of his arms over her shoulder so that he could use her as a crutch, and put her other arm round his waist.

Then step by step, afraid every moment he would fall down, she got him to the doorway.

She put her free hand up to prevent him from hitting his head on the lintel of the door, and he winced as if the part of his head that had been struck felt very tender.

But still he did not speak.

Then they were outside in the moonlight and moving at a snail's pace down the path by which she had come through the wood.

Afterwards Hermia asked herself how she had ever managed to take the Marquis so far, when she had all his weight leaning on her and only by directing his every step was she able to keep him on the path.

She felt at times he must have shut his eyes and just let her lead him as if he were blind.

Because of the way she was supporting him, she could not look at his face, but could only drag him to safety, knowing that if the men who had left him imprisoned in the cottage returned there was nothing she could do to save him.

It must have been over an hour before they reached the point in the wall where she had climbed into the Park.

There they stopped and when at last she was able to look up at the Marquis he collapsed onto the ground.

As she released her hold on him he lay stretched out with his eyes closed, and once again for one terrifying moment she felt he might be dead.

Then she knew he had just willed himself to follow her lead and was now too utterly exhausted to go on any further.

She felt very much the same herself, but she knew it would be easier now to fetch her father and it was also unlikely that anybody who was looking for the Marquis, would find him here while she hurried home.

She climbed over the wall, feeling that the Marquis's weight on her had left her almost crippled.

But because she was frightened that he might disappear again while she was gone, she ran back the way she had come through the overgrown garden to the kitchen-door.

Inside the house she hurried up the stairs and without knocking burst into her parents' room.

They were both asleep, and as Hermia stood there gasping for breath her mother awoke first to ask:

"What is it, darling? What is the matter?"

"P.Papa . . . I want Papa!" Hermia gasped in a voice that did not sound like her own.

Her father sat up.

"What has happened? Who wants me?"

"I . . . I have found the . . . Marquis!"

For no reason she could understand tears began to run down her cheeks as she spoke.

"You have found the Marquis?" the Vicar repeated in astonishment. "Where was he?"

"He was in . . . Witch Wood, Papa, and I have . . . brought him . . . along the path as far as the wall . . . but he is badly . . . injured."

"In Witch Wood?" her father said. "I cannot understand why he should be there."

"He was put there by men who must have . . . attacked him. He has been hit on the head . . . but he is . . . alive!"

As if her father understood the urgency of what she was saying he started to get out of bed.

"Go and fetch Nanny," her mother said, "while Papa and I dress. If His Lordship is wounded, tell her we shall need hot water and bandages."

Hermia disappeared to do what she was told and by the time she had woken Nanny and explained what had happened her father was coming down the stairs.

"Show me where you have left him," he said. "I suppose I can manage to bring him back on my own?"

For the first time Hermia smiled.

"I brought him from the Witch's house to the wall."

"Obviously by magic," her father replied, "but I shall have to manage by more human means!"

They both laughed, then Hermia was running ahead of her father back to where she had left the Marquis.

It took both of them to carry him back through the Park gates and into the Vicarage.

He was unconscious and Hermia thought

afterwards it was only because her father was so strong that with her help he could manage.

By the time they arrived at the Vicarage her mother and Nanny had made up the bed in Peter's room.

They also had the kettle boiling, fresh bandages ready torn from old sheets, and her mother's salves made from herbs and honey to treat the Marquis's wounds.

Hermia was sent away while they undressed him and got him into bed.

Then when she was allowed to see him he looked very different from how he had appeared to her before.

Wearing one of her father's nightshirts, with his eyes closed and a bandage round his head, he looked very much younger and neither cynical nor bored.

He might in fact have been one of Peter's contemporaries.

Looking down at him Hermia thought he was not the grand, much-acclaimed Marquis, but merely a young man who had been hurt and who would doubtless tomorrow suffer a great deal of pain.

"There is nothing more we can do for him tonight," she heard her mother say.

"Then you go to bed, my darling," her father answered, "and I will sit up with His Lordship in case he wakes. As soon as it is light I will go to the Hall, send a groom for the Doctor, and tell John that his visitor is safe, but somewhat the worse for wear!"

Mrs. Brooke moved towards the armchair—an old and dilapidated one—and put on it a spare pillow which she had taken from the bed and she arranged it so that her husband could rest his head.

"I will get a stool for your feet," she said, "and a blanket to cover you. I do not expect he will recover consciousness for several hours."

"You are spoiling me," the Vicar teased.

"You know I hate you to be uncomfortable, darling," his wife replied, "and as I have a feeling that tomorrow will be a busy day, you will need all the sleep you can get."

"You are quite right, as you always are," the Vicar said. "I will fetch the stool. Where is it?"

"In front of my dressing-table, where it always is!"

The Vicar smiled as he went into the next room to fetch it.

Her mother put her arm around Hermia's shoulders.

"What made you look in old Mrs. Wombatt's house?" she asked.

"I was quite sure no one would dare to look for him there," Hermia replied, "and something told me that that was where the men who had attacked him would hide his body."

As she spoke she gave a little cry.

"Mama!" she exclaimed. "I know now who told them where to hide the Marquis!"

As she spoke Mrs. Burles' conversation came back to her.

"It was Ben!" she said aloud. "Ben knew that no one in the village would go into the Witch's cottage for fear of being cursed!"

She was quite certain this was true and she added:

"But why should Ben be involved in this. And why should the Marquis be attacked in such a horrible manner, even if Papa is right, and it was his heir who hates him?"

"I do not understand it either," her mother replied, "but if you are right and Ben is mixed up in this it will not only get him into trouble, but will make things very uncomfortable for your Uncle John because one of his people is involved."

"Perhaps I had better say nothing about it."

"I think that would be wise, dearest," her mother answered, "at least until the Marquis himself can tell us what happened."

"Yes, of course, Mama, the best thing we can do is to wait," Hermia agreed.

She kissed her mother and went to her own room.

She thought as she undressed, her arms and shoulders aching from the weight of the Marquis's body, that tomorrow they would be able to learn the truth of the whole mystery.

In a way it would be very exciting.

Then she realized that when Marilyn learnt that the Marquis was in the Vicarage and that she had saved him she would be very angry.

"It is not my fault!" Hermia said aloud, as if Marilyn was accusing her.

Then she could almost see the anger in her cousin's eyes, and knew that whatever she might say in her own defense she would not be forgiven for interfering.

CHAPTER FIVE

*I*t was strange, Hermia thought, what a difference it had made to the Vicarage having the Marquis there.

For two days he lay unconscious, only occasionally murmuring nonsense and turning restlessly from side to side.

The Doctor, who was an old friend and came from the nearby market town, said:

"Let him rest, and Mrs. Brooke's magic potions are far better than anything I can prescribe."

He laughed as he spoke and Hermia was aware that her mother's fame for the herbs and natural ingredients she put together to cure almost every ill had spread all over the County.

He confirmed what Hermia already suspected, that the Marquis had fought violently against his assailants, only succumbing when they had hit him on the head with a heavy stick or perhaps a piece of wood.

Her mother's salve and the skilful way she bandaged him ensured that every day the wound got better.

That also applied to the Marquis's broken knuckles, the huge bruises on his body and, as the Doctor suspected, a fractured rib.

The Marquis's valet had come from the Hall, and although Nanny had exclaimed disagreeably that if they housed any more people the house would burst at the seams, Hickson had proved to be a real asset.

As he had the same original but somewhat caustic outlook on life as Nanny they got on famously.

He also demanded things for his master which neither the Vicar nor his wife would have thought of asking for and could not afford.

Legs of lamb, beef steaks, chickens and fat pigeons came into the house every day.

Although the Marquis at first could not eat them, Hermia thought even her father looked less harassed and her mother more beautiful because the food they were eating was so good.

Mrs. Brooke had at first remonstrated with Hickson saying:

"I cannot accept all these things from the Hall."

"Now you leave it to me, Ma'am," Hickson replied. "It's what 'Is Lordship's used to, an' if he was a stayin' there 'e'd have the best."

Mrs. Brookes knew this was true and when Hermia saw the huge peaches from the greenhouse and large bunches of Muscat grapes, she thought the Earl might occasionally have remembered how poor his brother was.

Her uncle came in and out of the Vicarage like a fussy hen who had lost a particularly prized chick.

Hermia suspected that it was Marilyn who urged her father to insist that the Marquis come back to the Hall, but when he recovered enough to think and talk he refused point-blank to be moved.

"I am very comfortable here," he said, "and Dr. Grayson has made it quite clear that I am to move as little as possible in case it affects my head and I become a lunatic!"

It seemed strange that he should prefer Peter's small bed-room to the very grand State Room in which Hermia knew he would be sleeping in her uncle's home.

He lay looking at Peter's trophies, many of which were hung on the wall, and appeared to find everything to his liking.

In fact he did not complain about anything.

When he was well enough to talk he told the Earl and the Vicar exactly what had happened to him.

The Vicar related it to his wife and daughter that same evening.

"It seems even more incredible than we had imagined," he said, "except that it fits in with the despicable reputation enjoyed by de Ville."

"We are filled with curiosity, darling," Mrs. Brooke smiled.

"I will tell you everything," the Vicar replied, "but of course it took some time to extract it all from His Lordship because he had lapses of memory and we had to wait until he could think clearly again."

What Hermia and her mother learnt was that after the Earl had been summoned back to the Hall on what he now knew to be a pretext to inveigle him away, the Marquis had ridden on alone.

He rounded the end of Witch Wood to go in the direction where his host had told him the yearlings were to be found.

He was not hurrying, and it was therefore easy for

three men to spring out at him from the bushes and before he realised what was happening to drag him off his horse.

Thinking they were footpads he fought violently, until they over-powered him and dragged him just inside the wood.

There was another man there who looked younger than the other three, but he did not see him very clearly before they forced him down onto the trunk of a fallen tree.

"Two of the men," he related to the Vicar, "might have been foreigners or gypsies, the third seemed a superior type and better educated."

It was that man who produced a letter written on a piece of the Marquis's own writing-paper stolen from his house in London.

Because he had already been knocked about quite considerably the Marquis had a little difficulty in reading it, but he soon found it consisted of instructions to his trainer to withdraw his horse from the Gold Cup race at Royal Ascot.

Knowing his horse 'Firefly' was the favourite and having no doubt that with his usual luck he would win the Cup, he refused to sign the letter.

However, the men then began to punch him systematically until, knowing he had no chance against three of them, he agreed to do what they wanted, and wrote his signature at the bottom of the letter.

The minute he did so he felt something strike him on the back of his head, there was a blinding pain and he knew no more.

"There was no doubt," the Vicar said as he related the story, "the whole plot was set up by Roxford de Ville for the simple reason that he owned a half-share in the horse that won the Gold Cup quite easily when the Marquis's did not run."

"I suppose he had it backed for a large sum," Hermia remarked.

"Of course!" the Vicar replied. "But in fact the plot

was even more crooked than it appears, because the owners ran also another horse which they told everybody was better than the one that actually won!"

"Surely that is illegal?" Mrs. Brooke exclaimed.

"No, only unsportsmanlike," the Vicar replied. "The horse they tipped to all and sundry was unplaced, while the one that did win romped home at 16-1!"

"They must have made a fortune!" Hermia exclaimed.

"That is exactly what Roxford de Ville intended," the Vicar said, "but he was not so stupid as to give instructions that the Marquis should be murdered outright."

"Murdered!" Mrs. Brooke cried.

"Instead," the Vicar continued, "they carried him into what they had been told was the Witch's cottage and flung him down on the floor!"

He paused then he said slowly:

"They had already learnt that nobody from the village or the estate ever dared to visit old Mrs. Wombatt's cottage."

"I suppose anyone could tell them that," his wife exclaimed.

"It was murder by intent—a very difficult charge to prove," the Vicar said sternly, "for if Hermia had not been clever enough to think that was where the Marquis would be, he might easily have died during that night or would certainly have done so in two or three days time!"

Mrs. Brooke gave a cry of horror.

"It was a diabolical plot! What will the Marquis do about it?"

"John has been talking to the Chief Constable and they are considering if any charges can be brought against Roxford de Ville. Unfortunately it will be very difficult to prove that he was actually involved with the three men who have of course disappeared, having doubtless been well paid for their services."

"But if Mr. de Ville has failed . . . to murder the Marquis . . . this time," Hermia said, "he will surely . . . try again?"

"That is a possibility," her father agreed. "But in the meantime we must be concerned with getting the Marquis back on his feet. He is so healthy that I do not think it will take very long."

Having learnt from Hickson that the Marquis was not only better, but in the Valet's words: "Bored to his 'igh teeth, Miss, if I may say so," Hermia went to seen him.

It was late in the morning and her father and mother were both out, and Nanny had also gone shopping in the village.

She knocked tentatively on the bed-room door and when there was no answer went in.

The Marquis was in bed, propped up against several pillows.

Although the bandage had been removed from his forehead there was still a pad at the back of his head.

He looked thinner and somewhat paler than she had last seen him.

But she thought when he glanced towards her that his eyes were still as penetrating as they had been before and made her feel shy.

"Come in, Hermia!" he said. "I was wondering when you would have time to visit me."

"Of course I had time, and I wanted to do so before," Hermia replied walking towards the bed, "but you had to be kept quiet and you were not supposed to talk to anybody."

"I am sick of being quiet!" the Marquis said petulantly. "And I want to talk to you!"

"I am here," Hermia smiled sitting down on a chair by the bedside, "and I thought perhaps you would like me to read to you."

"Later," the Marquis replied. "At the moment I should first thank you for saving my life."

She did not speak and after a minute he went on:

"Your father told me how in the middle of the night you went to what is called Witch's Wood and looked for me where nobody else would have dared to go. Why did you do that?"

"It . . . is difficult to explain," Hermia replied, "but I was sure with a feeling which could not be . . . denied that it was where I would find . . . you."

"I am very grateful."

He spoke rather dryly, and she felt somehow that he was being cynical until he asked:

"Hickson tells me the whole village speaks of 'Witch Wood', as they call it, with horror. Were you not frightened of going there alone at night?"

Hermia shook her head.

"I have loved the woods ever since I was a child, and I did not at all believe the stories that Mrs. Wombatt, who built the little cottage, really used to dance with the Devil."

"But you thought it was an appropriate place for me!" the Marquis remarked again in his mocking voice.

"I did not think of your nickname at the time." Hermia replied, "and I was not frightened until just before I opened the door!"

"Then what did you do?"

Because she thought the conversation sounded so serious and almost as if he was interrogating her she replied lightly:

"If I had thought of it, which actually I did not, I would have repeated the Cornish Litany which Mama taught me when I was a little girl."

She saw that the Marquis was listening and she therefore recited:

"From Witches, Warlocks and Wurricoes,
From Ghoulies, Ghosties and Long-leggity Beasties,
From all Things that go bump in the night—
Good Lord deliver us!"

When she finished the Marquis laughed.

"I can see that would be very effective, but as you did not say it, I presume you prayed that you would be safe and not shocked by what you found?"

"What really happened," Hermia said, "was that when I finally managed to remove the bar across the door, I put out my hand to open it and suddenly I felt frightened of what I would find inside."

She gave a little shudder as she remembered what she had felt.

"It was a nasty feeling, but then I heard an owl hoot in the trees and I knew there was no reason to be afraid for the animals in the wood would not be there if there was anything evil about."

She was silent for a second before she added:

"Also the fairies and elves have always protected me ever since I was a little girl."

She spoke naturally without thinking to whom she was speaking, then because she thought he would think her foolish she felt herself blush and said quickly;

"I found you and now you are safe."

"I can hardly believe what your father tells me, that you supported me all the way through the wood to the wall which borders the road!"

"You were very heavy," Hermia replied, "and if I have a crooked shoulder for the rest of my life, it will be all your fault!"

Again she was trying to speak lightly but the Marquis unexpectedly put out his hand towards her, laying it palm upwards on the white cover on the bed.

"Give me your hand, Hermia," he ordered.

Obediently she did so.

As his fingers closed over hers he said:

"Words are very inadequate with which to thank anybody for saving one's life and I am wondering how best I can express what I feel."

Because there was a deep note in his voice which Hermia had not heard before she felt a strange feeling she did not understand and her eye-lashes flickered as she said:

"Please . . . it would only make me very embarrassed, and really it is Mama you should thank for using her herbs and honey on you so cleverly that in . . . a day or two you will be as good as new."

Once again, because the Marquis was making her feel so shy, she was trying not to sound serious.

His hand tightened on hers, then he released her.

"Now," he said in a different tone, "tell me what happened when they first realised I was missing."

Because she thought it would amuse him, Hermia described what a flap there was at the Hall, her uncle's agitation and how Marilyn had retired to bed.

"When Papa came home at eleven o'clock that night," she said, "Uncle John was planning a Military Operation to search for you, and I think, if the truth were known, rather fancying himself as a strategist!"

"But Marilyn retired to bed," the Marquis observed slowly.

"She was very upset," Hermia said quickly, "and I know she hopes you will go back to the Hall as soon as you are well enough to be moved."

"I am sure she does!" the Marquis remarked.

There was a little silence as Hermia wondered what to say next. Then he asked:

"How fond are you of your cousin?"

"I had a lovely time with her when we were young," Hermia answered. "We shared the same Governess, the same teachers, and of course it was marvellous for me to be able to . . . ride Uncle John's horses and use the . . . Library at the Hall."

She had no idea how wistful her eyes looked as she remembered what those two activities had meant to her.

"Then what happened?"

It flashed through Hermia's mind that he was perceptive enough to guess that she had been exiled as soon as Marilyn was grown up.

Because she thought even to talk of it would be humiliating she said quickly:

"I am sure you are talking too much. Let me read to you. It may be upsetting for you to hear what happened last week, but I have kept Wednesday's newspapers in case you wanted to hear about The Gold Cup."

"I am more interested at the moment in what has been happening here," the Marquis replied, "and I am trying to understand why your father and mother are so poor and have to skimp and save every penny when your Uncle is so rich."

Hermia stared at him. Then she said:

"You have been listening to Hickson who has been talking to Nanny! You must not believe everything he tells you."

"I use my eyes," the Marquis said, "and one thing is quite obvious: your Cousin Marilyn does not share her gowns with you!"

His words made Hermia immediately conscious that the gown she was wearing was very much the same as the one in which he had first seen her.

It was three years old and in consequence too tight, too short, and the colour had been almost washed out of it.

Because she thought it was not only tactless but impertinent of him to speak in such a way, her chin went up and she said:

"You may criticise, My Lord, but I promise you I would not change anything in my home for all the comforts at the Hall which are entirely material!"

"Is what you are seeking more important than the luxuries of this world?" the Marquis asked.

Hermia felt she might have guessed he would not let such a statement pass and she replied:

"You will laugh, and because you are so rich you will not understand, when I say completely truthfully that money cannot buy happiness!"

There was silence as the Marquis stared at her and

she felt once again that he was looking deep into her heart.

"Yet I suppose that being a woman," he said, "you would like pretty gowns, Balls at which to wear them, and of course a number of charming young men to pay you compliments."

Hermia laughed, and it seemed to echo round the small room.

"You are talking like Mama," she said, "who said she was wishing I could have magical gowns, magical Balls, and of course magical horses to ride."

She paused and there was a dimple in both her cheeks as she said:

"And actually that is exactly what I do have!"

Only for a second did the Marquis look puzzled. Then he said:

"You mean in your imagination!"

Hermia thought it was quite clever of him to know that was what she meant, and she gave another little laugh before she replied:

"None of the magical things I have can be spoilt or taken away from me, and they never, never disappoint me. Also, My Lord, I should add they are very much cheaper!"

The Marquis smiled and now it was more than a twist of his lips.

"If I stay here very much longer," he said, "I have a feeling I shall be caught up in these magical spells and find it impossible ever to escape."

"You can always run away," Hermia said provocatively.

She paused before she went on more seriously:

"Perhaps a magical spell is what we must somehow give you before you leave, so that you will be safe . . . in case the wicked men who . . . attacked you once should do so . . . again."

She bent a little towards him as she added:

"Please . . . please, be very careful! The next time

they might be more successful . . . in their . . . attempt to . . . destroy you!"

"If I were destroyed, I doubt if anybody would mourn me particularly," the Marquis said, "or miss me if I were no longer there."

Hermia sat upright.

"That is a ridiculous thing to say!" she said sharply. "Of course a great number of people would mourn you because they admire you for your sportsmanship, and even if they are envious, it makes them strive to better themselves."

She felt from the Marquis's expression that he did not believe what she was saying and after a minute she continued:

"I can tell you who would really miss you."

"Who?" the Marquis asked in an uncompromising voice.

Hermia had not the slightest idea that he was expecting her to say, as any other woman he had ever known would have said, that she would miss him.

"Your horses!" Hermia replied. "Nobody who rides as well as you do, could fail to love animals, and perhaps it is because your horses know you love them that they win so many races."

The Marquis did not speak and she went on reflectively:

"That was why I was quite certain the horse you were riding when you were attacked would not have thrown you!"

"It is certainly something I had never thought of before," the Marquis said quietly.

"Well, think about it," Hermia insisted, "and be careful if for nobody else's sake for the horses who are waiting in your stables and longing for you to visit them again."

The Marquis was just about to reply when the door of the bed-room opened and the Earl came in.

He seemed very large and overpowering in the

102

small room, and as Hermia hastily rose to her feet he looked at her, she thought, somewhat critically.

"Good-morning, Uncle John!" she said, and kissed him on the cheek.

"Good-morning, Hermia!" the Earl replied. "And how is your patient today?"

"As you can see he is very much better," Hermia said, "and Mama is very pleased with him."

"Good!" the Earl exclaimed. "That means with the Doctor's permission we can take him back to the Hall."

Hermia wanted to expostulate but quickly bit back the words.

Instead she said:

"I expect you would like to talk to His Lordship alone, and Dr. Grayson has insisted that he should not have more than one visitor at a time."

She went towards the door. When she reached it she turned to ask:

"Is there anything I can bring you, Uncle John? A cup of coffee, or perhaps a glass of port?"

As she mentioned the port she suddenly felt afraid her uncle would be aware that it was his own port she was offering him.

Only last night when Hickson was serving their dinner in the Dining-Room as he poured some excellent Claret into the Vicar's glass he had said:

"I thought, Sir, you'd like a glass of port tonight, and I've filled the decanter."

"That sounds an excellent idea, Hickson!" the Vicar replied.

Then as he saw the expression on his wife's face he added:

"But I hope you had His Lordship's permission to bring the wines from the Hall."

"I'm sure 'Is Lordship would want my Master to have what he's used to, an' what he'd be drinking if he were there," Hickson answered. "But he doesn't like drinkin' alone and tells me while he were having his meal, I was to serve it to you, Sir."

Hickson spoke somewhat aggressively and Hermia suspected that in fact the Marquis had said nothing of the kind.

He had probably assumed that the Vicar would have wine with his meals just as he did.

He would have no idea that as far as the Vicarage was concerned wine was a treat they could only afford on special occasions, such as Christmas, birthdays, or when they entertained which was practically never.

However the Earl replied:

"I want nothing, thank you, Hermia."

She shut the door and ran downstairs hoping fervently that her Uncle would not say anything to upset her father.

She knew however that her father did enjoy such luxuries.

Because she was thinking of him, almost as if she had conjured him up he came through the front door, shaking his hat because it had been raining.

"I see John is here!" he remarked.

Hermia was aware that the Earl's smart Phaeton, drawn by two well-bred horses with two men on the box, was waiting on the drive outside.

"Yes, he is talking to the Marquis, Papa, and has only been here a short while. So I should wait a minute or two before you join them, because Dr. Grayson said His Lordship was still to be kept as quiet as possible."

"I shall miss him when he goes," the Vicar remarked, walking into the Sitting-Room. "When I was talking to him yesterday, I realised he is a very intelligent man."

"I thought so too," Hermia replied.

It came into her mind that as the Marquis was intelligent he would find Marilyn if he married her, a bore.

She never read a book, was not interested in the

political situation nor in anything that did not concern
her Social Life.

Then Hermia told herself she was being unkind,
and that Marilyn would make the Marquis a most
agreeable wife, and would certainly look very pretty
and graceful at the head of his table.

"I am sure they are well suited to each other," she
tried to convince herself, but knew it was not the
truth.

"Where is your mother?" the Vicar asked.

It was a very familiar question to Hermia because
her father and mother missed each other if they were
apart for even an hour or so during the day.

It was therefore the first thing each of them asked
as soon as they returned home.

"Amongst other people, she has gone to see Mrs.
Burles," Hermia answered. "She has been very bad
the last few days because she is worrying over Ben."

"He is always a worry," the Vicar remarked, "but
that is nothing unusual."

Hermia was aware that Mrs. Burles was terrified in
her muddled mind that Ben would be in trouble because he had helped the men who had assaulted the
Marquis.

She had said nothing to her father, and now changing the subject, she asked:

"Who have you seen today, Papa?"

"As usual the men, who are getting more and more
desperate because they cannot find work," the Vicar
replied. "I shall have to speak again to John, but God
knows if he will listen to me!"

As he spoke he heard the Earl coming heavily down
the stairs.

The Vicar walked from the Sitting-Room out into
the hall to say:

"Nice to see you, John! As you see our patient is
perking up and looking like his old self again."

"He certainly seems to be full of new ideas," the
Earl remarked.

He did not go out through the open front-door as Hermia would have expected, but walked into the Sitting-Room and the Vicar followed him.

The Earl stood with his back to the fireplace and there was a frown between his eyes before he said:

"Deverille and I were discussing the unemployment problem before I left him to be half-murdered at the instigation of his cousin."

"The Unemployment problem?" the Vicar repeated in surprise.

"He was speaking about it again just now," the Earl went on, "and he is convinced that I should build a new Timber-Yard, because there is a great demand for wood now that the war is over."

Hermia listening, held her breath.

She could hardly believe she was actually hearing what her Uncle was saying.

"I find it difficult," the Earl continued, "not to follow up his suggestion. But as I have no time, and as this is something which will employ a lot of those layabouts with whom you are so concerned, Stanton, I am going to leave it to you!"

"Leave it to me?" the Vicar ejaculated.

Hermia knew that her father was as stunned as she was by what the Earl had just said.

"That is what I said," the Earl answered, "and you had better get on with it. Employ whom you like and as many as you like, but I shall expect the place to show a profit, or at least to break even within two or three years. Then we shall decide whether it is worth keeping it going."

The Vicar gave a deep sigh before he said:

"I can only thank you, John, from the bottom of my heart."

"Well, do not trouble me with the details," the Earl answered, "and make all the financial arrangements with my accountant. I will tell him to come down from London to see you."

With that, and as if he resented his own generosity,

the Earl walked from the Sitting-Room, while his brother finding it hard to believe he was not dreaming, followed him.

Hermia clasped her hands together and knew that this was the Marquis's way of showing his gratitude.

Then, feeling she must tell him what it meant and how amazing it was, she ran from the room up the stairs to his bedroom.

She went in, shut the door behind her and stood for a moment just looking at him lying in the bed.

He did not appear for the moment to be either cynical or bored, and this in a way made her feel shy.

Nor for that matter did he seem like the stranger who looking like the Devil had dared to kiss her and whom she had hated!

As she did not speak, the Marquis turned his head, and she ran forward to kneel down beside the bed.

"How can you have done . . . anything so . . . marvellous as to persuade Uncle John to open a Timber-Yard?" she gasped. "It was wonderful . . . wonderful of you! And it will make Papa so . . . very happy!"

"And you," the Marquis questioned. "I see it has made you happy too."

"Of course it has, and I know Mama will go down on her knees and thank God, as I am . . . thanking you."

There were tears in her eyes as she looked at him and after a moment the Marquis said in his usual mocking manner:

"As you are so effusive over a Timber-Yard, I wonder what you would say if I offered you a diamond necklace?"

Because his remark was so unexpected Hermia sat back on her heels and laughed.

"At the moment I would rather have a Timber-Yard for Papa than anything in the world! Although I cannot wear it round my neck, I feel very, very proud that . . . perhaps what I . . . said to you made you

107

. . . persuade Uncle John to do something for the men who . . . cannot find work."

The Marquis looked at Hermia, but he did not speak.

Then the door opened and Mrs. Brooke came into the room.

She was looking very pretty with her hair, which was nearly the same colour as her daughter's, a little untidy because she must have taken off her bonnet as she came upstairs.

She was holding it in her hand and now her cheeks were flushed and her eyes were shining as she said:

"I expect Hermia has already thanked you, as I am going to do."

"I think your husband should do that," the Marquis replied. "But please sit down, Mrs. Brooke, I want to talk to you."

Hermia rose to her feet as if she felt she should go away, but the Marquis said:

"You must stay, Hermia, because this concerns you."

He sounded serious and Hermia looked at him apprehensively wondering what he might be going to say.

A little nervously, in case he revealed something that her mother did not already know, she sat down on a chair.

Pushing himself up higher against his pillows the Marquis said:

"I have been thinking since I have been lying here what present I could give you as a family for all your kindness."

"We want nothing," Mrs. Brooke said quietly.

"That is what I might have expected you to say," the Marquis replied, "but I have a fixed rule in my life that I always pay my debts."

He paused, then added sourly:

"Unlike some people!"

108

Hermia thought he was referring to Roxford de Ville.

"I am only so glad that we have been able to do anything to help you," Mrs. Brooke said.

"I still, as it happens, value my life very highly," the Marquis answered, "and as Hermia is responsible for my being alive I would of course in normal circumstances have sent her a very expensive piece of jewellery to express my gratitude."

Mrs. Brooke would have spoken but he went on quickly:

"Instead I have another idea which I hope will meet with your approval, and as it happens, I know it will mean that one of your wishes will come true."

Hermia who was watching him as he spoke felt it hard to breathe as he continued:

"I have decided that what I will give Hermia is a few weeks in London until the Season ends."

Mrs. Brooke gave a little gasp and stared at the Marquis increduously as he continued:

"I have a sister, Lady Langdon, who is a widow and who has been alone and unhappy since her husband was killed at the Battle of Waterloo. I know it would give her great pleasure to chaperone Hermia and introduce her to the Social World."

He gave a twisted smile before he added:

"She also, I believe, has very good taste in gowns, and would be delighted to find herself in the role of Hermia's Fairy Godmother!"

"It is . . . impossible!" Mrs. Brooke gasped. "Something we could not accept!"

"Nothing is impossible," the Marquis contradicted, "except that you should refuse to let your daughter have what is best for her. And this is an opportunity that should not be missed."

Because this was undoubtedly true, Mrs. Brooke could not reply and the Marquis went on:

"I will give a small Ball for Hermia at my house in London and my sister will make sure that she is invited to all those which take place before the Season ends. So there is only one thing we must do now."

"And what is that?" Mrs. Brooke asked and her voice seemed to come from very far away.

"We must get Hermia to London by the beginning of the week," the Marquis said. "There is not much of the Season left because the Regent will soon be leaving for Brighton, and after that a great number of people will shut up their houses and go to the country."

Again he smiled as he added:

"Therefore it is now up to your magic to get me on my feet, Mrs. Brooke, and then the Fairy Story, as far as Hermia is concerned, can start immediately!"

"I do not . . . believe what I am . . . hearing!" Mrs. Brooke said in a strange voice, and Hermia was aware that there were tears running down her mother's cheeks.

Only when Hermia went to bed that night, after she had talked over what the Marquis had planned with her father and mother until there seemed nothing left to say on the subject, did she go to her bedroom window and look out at the moon and the stars.

She had thought ever since the Marquis had told them his plan that she was living in a dream, and it was impossible to believe she was hearing that her prayers were about to come true.

And yet, just as if he had in fact waved a magic wand, the curtain was rising on a future so sparkling and so glorious that she felt as if she was being carried across the sky on a shooting-star.

The only thing that frightened her was what Marilyn would say, and whether when they heard what was happening her Uncle and Aunt would be angry.

Then she thought of the Timber Yard which had pleased her father so much, and knew that the Earl had accepted the Marquis's suggestion simply because he believed it came from the man he anticipated would be his son-in-law.

As she thought of it, it was as if a cold hand swept away the shining gossamer veil from her eyes and the stars were no longer shining so brightly.

Perhaps before he left the Marquis would propose to Marilyn, in which case it would not upset them that he was arranging for his sister to chaperone her.

"He is grateful . . . of course he is grateful to me," Hermia told herself, "and, as he says, he wishes to pay his debts."

She was working everything out in her mind in a practical manner, but somehow that spoilt the rapture she felt.

Although it was something she seldom did, she pulled the curtain to and shut out the glory of the night, and got into bed in the dark.

As she lay sleepless she found herself wondering what the Marquis would say to Marilyn when he asked her to marry him, and what she would feel when he kissed her.

At the thought of it she could feel his lips hard, demanding and insistent on her own mouth.

She knew although he would never kiss her again, she would never forget he was the first man who had ever done so.

CHAPTER SIX

*H*ermia followed Lady Langdon into the large marble hall, and asked a footman:

"Is His Lordship back yet?"

"His Lordship came back a few minutes ago, Miss, and he's in the Study."

Hermia waited until Lady Langdon had set one foot on the stairs before she said:

"I wanted to speak to your brother, if you do not want me."

"No, we have finished all we had to do this morning, so go and talk to Favian," Lady Langdon replied with a smile, and walked up the exquisitely carved staircase which led to the State Rooms on the First Floor.

The Marquis's house was different from what Hermia had expected.

It was one of the largest mansions in Piccadilly, and even more magnificent and awe-inspiring than its owner.

On the Ground Floor there was the Dining-Room, the Library, the Breakfast and Writing Rooms, and the Study where the Marquis sat when he was alone.

All the Reception rooms were on the First Floor, and the top of the double staircase seemed to have been designed for a hostess glittering in diamonds to receive her guests.

There were two Drawing Rooms adjoining each other which could be converted into a Ball-Room, large enough to hold at least two hundred guests, and beyond that were a Card-Room, a Music-Room, and to Hermia's delight a Picture Gallery.

It was all so well designed and decorated with exquisite taste that it seemed incredible that accustomed to living in such style the Marquis had seemed content with the small and shabby Vicarage.

The disadvantage of living in such a grand house was, as Lady Langdon pointed out, that all the bedrooms were on the Second Floor, and it was a long climb up and down unless one flew on wings—which Hermia felt she did.

Every day since she had arrived in London she had woken expecting to find herself in her small bedroom at home, and could hardly believe that what was happening to her was not just one of her fantasies that was more vivid than usual.

When the Marquis's carriage drawn by four horses had arrived at the Vicarage to take her to London she found he had also sent his elderly and very respectable Housekeeper to look after her during the journey.

At the last moment she had clung to her mother and said:

"I do wish you were coming with me, Mama. It would be so much more fun if you were chaperoning me instead of the Marquis's sister."

"I would enjoy it too," her mother answered, "but you know I could not leave Papa, and I am very, very happy that you are having a Season in London which I always imagined would be impossible."

To Hermia it had seemed impossible too! Moreover she was frightened that it would be overwhelming and that she would feel insignificant and make many mistakes in the world of which she knew nothing.

The welcome she received from Lady Langdon however warmed her heart.

"This is very exciting!" she exclaimed, as soon as she and Hermia were alone. "I have been so depressed and so lonely this last year that I could hardly believe it was true when I received an urgent note from my brother telling me what he had planned."

She had not waited for Hermia to reply, but continued:

"The first thing we have to do is to buy you a whole wardrobe of glorious gowns in which I know you will be the Belle of every Ball."

Because she was speaking sincerely and there was no doubt that she was genuinely delighted at the idea, she swept away all Hermia's nervousness and apprehensions.

The next morning they started very early to visit the shops in Bond Street.

Because it was near the end of the Season and the dressmakers were not so busy as they had been, Lady Langdon easily persuaded them to create gowns for Hermia in record time.

One of the dressmakers actually switched the dresses they had made for a bride so that Hermia could have them at once, and they could repeat the model in time for the wedding.

By the time they had bought gowns, bonnets, shoes, gloves, shawls, pelisses, and reticules, Hermia felt as if her head was spinning.

She could no longer count what had been acquired and was actually, although it seemed ridiculous, feeling tired.

She found the fittings the following day more exhausting than riding, or indeed dancing.

Yet at her first Ball she knew she was the success her mother had wanted and she had many more partners than there were dances.

In the last five days she had been to three Balls, two Receptions, and there had been luncheon-parties either given by Lady Langdon or to which they had been invited as guests.

There had also been two dinner-parties given by other hostesses and Hermia felt she had lived through a lifetime of experience, and yet none of it seemed completely real.

Now as she walked down the passage decorated by some very fine pictures and exceptionally beautiful furniture, she thought that since she had arrived in London she had never had a conversation alone with the Marquis.

When they dined at home he sat as host at the top of the table, which invariably meant that he had two extremely attractive, sophisticated distinguished married women on either side of him.

When he accompanied his sister and Hermia to a Ball, he either retired almost immediately into the Card-Room or else, as had happened last night, he left early.

As Lady Langdon and Hermia drove home alone, she had asked curiously:

"Where do you think His Lordship has gone?"

Lady Langdon had given a little laugh.

"That is the sort of question you must not ask, dear Child," she replied. "As you can imagine, my brother has a great many lovely women praying and hoping that he will spend a little time with them."

Then as if she thought she had been indiscreet she said quickly:

"Unfortunately Favian soon becomes bored, and he is always looking for somebody new to amuse and entertain him."

She spoke lightly, but Hermia thought it was what she might have expected.

Yet if the Marquis was not particularly amused at this moment it was a good thing as far as Marilyn was concerned.

Marilyn had called to see the Marquis the day before he left the Vicarage, and as soon as she came through the front door Hermia was aware how angry her cousin was.

She was looking very attractive in a sprigged muslin that was made in the very latest fashion, and her bonnet, trimmed with pink roses, had a tipped up brim edged with lace.

She greeted Hermia in a frozen manner that could not be misunderstood.

Hermia opened the door of the Sitting-Room where the Marquis having dressed and come downstairs was resting in a chair by the window.

Marilyn had swept past her with a disdainful air which told her cousin more clearly than words what she thought of the Vicarage. Also how much she commiserated with anybody especially the Marquis, who had been forced to stay in such a shabby and uncomfortable place.

Hermia shut the door behind her, then ran upstairs to her own room.

She wondered if the Marquis would take this opportunity to ask Marilyn to marry him, or perhaps make it clear that when he was in better health he would return.

Marilyn was with him for quite a long time and Hermia did not see her go. But the next day after the Marquis had left, she was quite certain from the way he said goodby to her parents that he intended to come back.

That undoubtedly meant he wished to marry Marilyn.

"A nicer, more generous Gentleman I've never known in all me born days!" Nanny said positively after the Marquis had gone.

Hermia knew that she had received a sum of money for her services which had left her gasping.

She had learnt too from Nanny that there was still a great deal of wine in the cellar which had come not from the Hall, but from the Marquis's house.

It had been brought to the Vicarage by his secretary when he arrived to take instructions about her visit to London.

"It was very kind of the Marquis to think of it," she said to Nanny.

"Very kind," Nanny agreed, "but there's no reason for you to go chattering about it to your father. Let him think it was left over from His Lordship's visit. Them as asks no questions are told no lies!"

In the days before she departed for London Hermia guessed the Marquis had made some other arrangements too, for the food remained as excellent as it had been when he was staying with them.

She thought this was due to some intrigue on the part of Nanny and Hickson.

But because she realised how much better her father looked and that the worried lines had disappeared from her Mother's face, she took Nanny's advice and said nothing.

Now as she neared the Study door there was an expression in her eyes that would have told anybody who knew her well that she was feeling nervous and apprehensive.

She opened the door and saw that the Marquis was sitting at his desk writing.

"May I . . . speak to you for a minute? Or are you . . . too busy?" she asked.

There was a little tremor in her voice that he did not miss. He put down his pen and rose to his feet saying:

"How are you, Hermia? I must congratulate you on the gown you are wearing."

"I wanted to . . . ask how you are," Hermia replied, "and make quite certain you are not doing too much."

"If you fuss over me in the same way that Hickson is doing, I think I shall pack my boxes and leave England!"

"You cannot expect us . . . not to worry . . . about you!" Hermia answered.

The Marquis walked across the room to stand with

his back to the fireplace which because it was summer was filled with flowers.

Hermia stood looking at him until he said:

"I can see you are upset about something. Suppose you sit down and tell me about it?"

Hermia sat as he told her to do on the edge of a chair, her hands clasped together. She did not look at the Marquis, but at the flowers behind him.

After a moment he said pointedly:

"I am waiting!"

"I . . . I do not know how to . . . put what I . . . want to say into . . . words," Hermia stammered.

There was a little pause before the Marquis said:

"In which case I imagine you are about to tell me that you are in love. Who is the happy man?"

He was drawling the words. At the same time, there was the dry, cynical note in his voice which she had not heard for sometime.

"No . . . no," she said quickly, "it is nothing like . . . that! It does not concern me . . . at least not in the way you are . . . suggesting."

"Then I must apologise. I thought perhaps you wished me to give you my permission, in your father's absence, to marry one of the young men who were making love to you so ardently last night."

Because he was mocking her, and because it hurt her in a way she could not understand, Hermia clasped her fingers even tighter and said in a voice he could hardly hear:

"P.please . . . you are making it . . . very difficult for me . . . to say what I want to . . . say."

"Again my apologies," the Marquis said. "I will listen without guessing what it is you want to tell me."

"I am sure that you will think it . . . terrible of me . . ." Hermia faltered, "and therefore . . . I am . . . afraid."

"It is unlike you to be afraid, Hermia," the Marquis replied. "In fact, I have always thought you exceptionally brave."

He gave one of his twisted smiles before he added:

"After all, if 'Witches, Devils and Things that go bump in the night' do not scare you, I cannot believe you are afraid of me!"

"I . . . I am afraid of what you will . . . think."

"Why should that be so terrible?" the Marquis enquired.

She did not answer him, and after a moment he said in a softer and quieter voice:

"I hoped you would be happy here, not worried and frightened as you are now."

"I am happy!" Hermia said. "It has been so marvellous, so glorious to be able to dance at the Balls with new and fascinating people and to have such beautiful gowns!"

"Then what is wrong?"

"Your . . . sister who has been . . . kindness itself . . . has just said to me that she wants to buy me two more Ball gowns to wear at the end of next week."

As she finished speaking Hermia seemed to draw in her breath before she said.

"Please . . . please . . . do not think it . . . ungrateful of me . . . but could you . . . instead of spending any more money on gowns for me give . . . Peter some new c.clothes?"

She did not dare to look at the Marquis in case he was scowling.

Instead she said pleadingly:

"It would not cost you any more, and I . . . can manage perfectly with the gowns I already have . . . but Peter would give . . . anything to be dressed like . . . you."

Still the Marquis did not reply, and now Hermia raised her eyes and he could see how desperately she was beseeching him to understand.

There was also the flicker of fear in their depths in case he should think her ungrateful and importunate.

"And you have been worrying about asking me this?" the Marquis enquired.

"Of course . . . I have." Hermia replied. "It . . . seems so greedy and ungrateful when you have done so much . . . but I do not wish Peter to feel . . . left out and as it is a terrible struggle for Papa to send him to Oxford . . . he can never afford any of the things his friends take for granted."

"I too was at Oxford," the Marquis remarked, "and I understand. You can leave Peter to me."

Hermia gave a little cry and jumped to her feet.

"You mean that . . . you really mean it?" she cried. "Oh . . . thank you . . . thank you!"

She paused before she asked in a very small voice: "You . . . you do not think I am . . . imposing on you?"

"Shall I tell you," the Marquis replied, "that I am still deeply in your debt, and of course your mother's? The Doctor has told me this morning that there is nothing wrong with me, except that it would be a mistake to be hit in the same place again."

"Then you must be careful!" Hermia said quickly. "Promise me you will take care of yourself."

"First Hickson, and now you!" the Marquis remarked, but he was smiling.

"I keep thinking," Hermia said in a worried voice, "that you could be attacked perhaps in the Park when you are out riding, or when you come home late at night."

"I shall be all right," the Marquis said, "and all you have to do, Hermia, is to enjoy yourself and look as beautiful as you do now."

Hermia looked at him wondering whether he meant it or was just flattering her.

As if he read her thoughts he said:

"Good Heavens! You must be aware that you have been an overnight sensation in the *Beau Monde* and my sister is delighted!"

"She has been very, very kind, but you will not forget to tell her I do not . . . require any more . . . gowns?"

"I doubt if she would listen to me," the Marquis replied, "and I have already told you that I will look after Peter."

"But . . . I do not mean it like that," Hermia cried. "He is not to be . . . an *extra* expense."

"I seem to remember your telling me," the Marquis said, "that money does not buy happiness, and material things are not important."

"Now you are quoting my own words at me, in a different sense from what I meant them," Hermia said. "When you have done so much for me and my family I feel . . . ashamed of taking . . . anything more, and I know Papa and Mama would feel the same."

"I suppose what you are telling me is that you feel too proud," the Marquis said, "but I have my pride too, and I refuse to value my life at the cost of a few gowns, and a Ball which I might have given anyway, had I thought about it."

Hermia did not speak. She merely looked up at him and the Marquis said sharply:

"Stop trying to interfere! I enjoy making plans, and I cannot have them disrupted by rebellious young women who have other ideas than mine."

Hermia laughed.

"Now you are trying to frighten me again! But I refuse to be frightened! I was thinking last night that the Devil was originally an Archangel who fell from Heaven and now quite obviously he is climbing up Jacob's ladder to be there again."

"I am no angel," the Marquis retorted, "and I am quite content as I am. So stop trying to canonise me!"

"There is no need for me to do that," Hermia said. "I have a feeling that without my doing anything about it, there is already a halo firmly round your head, and wings sprouting from your shoulders."

"If there is," the Marquis said quickly, "it is some of the magic you are weaving around me until I am certain everything I drink contains a magic potion and there is witchcraft creeping into every corner of the house!"

"What a lovely idea!" Hermia exclaimed. "That is the right sort of magic, the magic which will bring you happiness and give you everything you wish for yourself!"

"I wonder!" the Marquis remarked reflectively.

Because there seemed to be nothing more to say, Hermia thanked him again, then ran up to her room to write a letter to Peter.

The Marquis, she thought, had been very kind, and now she felt as if she was enveloped in a golden light for the rest of the day.

Only when she came downstairs dressed in an exquisitely beautiful gown which she hoped he would admire, did she see Hickson coming from the Hall with the Marquis's evening-cape over his arm.

It seemed strange that he should be bringing it up the stairs now, and she stopped to say:

"Good-evening, Hickson. Is His Lordship in the Drawing-Room?"

"No, Miss," Hickson replied. "I thought 'Is Lordship would have told you he's not dining here tonight."

"Not dining here?" Hermia asked. "But there is a party."

"Yes, I know, Miss, but His Lordship promised a long time ago to dine at Carlton House before 'Is Royal 'Ighness leaves for Brighton tomorrow."

"I understand," Hermia said, "but I hope he will come on later to the Ball I am attending."

"If 'e does, I think it would be a mistake for 'Is Lordship to stay up late and as he won't wear his cape he may catch a chill," Hickson spoke in exactly the same tone that Nanny might have used.

Hermia smiled.

"His Lordship is very much better," she said. "In fact he told me so today."

"All the same, 'e should take more care of 'imself," Hickson persisted.

Because the valet seemed as worried as she was, Hermia said:

"I am desperately afraid that the men who attacked him last time might try to do so again."

"That's right, Miss," Hickson agreed. "But 'Is Lordship never 'as a thought for 'imself, and when I tells him Mr. de Ville will murder 'im before 'e's finished, he just laughs."

Hermia gave a little exclamation.

"Do you really think that?"

"I does, Miss," Hickson said. "Mr. Roxford's tried it once, and he'll try again, you mark me words!"

"H.how can we . . . stop him?" Hermia stammered.

"You try speakin' to 'Is Lordship, Miss. He won't listen to me, says I'm an old 'fuss-pot', but it's no use fussing after a man's dead. You has to do something about it before that happens."

"Yes, of course," Hermia agreed, "but what can I do?"

Hickson gave a deep sigh.

"I don't know, Miss, an' that's a fact! I puts a loaded pistol beside the Master's bed at night, but he tells me anyone who attacks him in his bedroom would have to be a spider, or else fly through his window."

Hickson spoke in an aggrieved voice, but Hermia knew how fond he was of the Marquis. If he was apprehensive, so was she, feeling that the attack, having failed last time, would be repeated sooner or later.

"Does His Lordship carry a pistol with him when he is out riding?" she asked.

"I suggested it, but His Lordship says it spoils the shape of his coat!" Hickson replied. "However there's always one in the Phaeton, when His Lordship travels any long distance."

Hickson paused before he added:

"But the men who're attacking His Lordship don't want 'is money, but 'is life!"

Hermia gave a cry of horror, but there was no chance of saying any more because from where they were standing she could see the guests arriving for dinner.

Then as she walked into the Drawing-Room where Lady Langdon was waiting, Hermia felt that with the Marquis not there all the excitement had gone out of the evening.

She found this surprising, for she had been looking forward to it so much.

Then as she moved over the soft carpet she knew, although it seemed incredible, that unmistakably, irrefutably, she loved him.

Afterwards Hermia could never remember what she said at dinner or even who had sat on either side of her.

All she could think of was that she had fallen in love as she had always wished to do, but with a man who was as far out of reach as the moon.

She had hated him when he kissed her, she had thought him to be the villain in her fantasies, and she had been afraid of his sarcastic remarks and the way he looked at her.

Now she knew that only love could have guided her to the Witch's cottage, so that she could save his life.

Only love could have made it possible for her to support a man of the Marquis's size and weight back through the wood to safety.

She thought she had been very stupid not to realise why it had felt so exciting to have the Marquis, even though he was injured, at the Vicarage.

Then when he had persuaded the Earl to build a Timber-Yard, because it was what she had suggested to him, she should have known that what she felt for him was not only gratitude but love.

How could she have been so foolish as not to understand that beneath a disdainful facade he was warm-hearted, generous, compassionate and understanding?

It was not just magic that had changed everything and made the atmosphere in the Vicarage seem even happier and more exciting than it had ever been before, but her love for the man whose life she had saved.

"Of course I love him!" Hermia thought.

She knew that the men she had met and the compliments they had paid her had never seemed quite real. They were but cardboard figures stepping out from the pages of a book rather than flesh and blood.

The Marquis was real, so real that he had filled her thoughts, her mind, and her heart ever since she had known him.

However she tried to use her common sense and tell herself she could never mean anything to him and that he was going to marry Marilyn.

She had thought at first it was unlikely, but when he had persuaded her Uncle to open a Timber-Yard, she was quite certain it had been understood between them, even if it was not put into words, that the Marquis had got his way simply because the Earl wished to placate such an important son-in-law.

"I love him!" Hermia said to herself when they arrived at the Ball which was taking place in one of the most splendid and important houses in London.

Again there was all the glitter of jewels and decorations that she had found so entrancing and about which she had written pages and pages of description to her mother.

But tonight the chandeliers did not seem to shine and she found the decorations tawdry.

Although she had no shortage of partners, she had

the greatest difficulty in showing any interest in what they said to her or listening to them.

She was wondering how soon it would be possible for her to go home, and if Lady Langdon would think it strange that she should not wish to dance until the early hours of the morning, when two men appeared in the doorway of the Ball-Room.

Hermia was dancing with Lord Wilchester, a young man who was paying her the most fulsome compliments.

"When may I see you alone? he asked. "Can I call on you tomorrow?"

"I am not sure what we are doing," she replied vaguely.

"That is the same answer you gave me last night and the night before," he said. "I have something to say to you that I can only say when we are alone."

His fingers tightened on hers until his clasp was painful and Hermia realised that he intended to offer her marriage.

It flashed through her mind that as he was very rich and very important, it would be a marriage which would delight her father and mother and, of course, Lady Langdon.

But when she looked up into his eyes Hermia knew that if he pleaded with her for a hundred years she had no wish to be his wife.

"Lord Wilchester was paying a lot of attention to you," Lady Langdon had said last night as they drove home. "You have certainly made a conquest. I wish I could think that he might propose to you, but I am afraid that is aiming too high."

Hermia had not replied and Lady Langdon went on:

"Lord Wilchester is one of the most charming young men I have met for a long time. He has a large estate in Oxfordshire, besides owning Wilchester House in London which is quite exceptional."

She had sighed before she added:

"But it is expecting too much! Every ambitious mother in London has been trying to capture him for their daughters, and I think if he marries anybody it will be one of the Duke of Bedford's daughters."

Hermia had not thought about it again, but now she knew without Lord Wilchester saying any more what he intended.

"I should accept him to please Papa and Mama," she thought.

She looked up to see the Prince Regent coming into the Ball-Room, and behind him the Marquis.

Because she was so glad to see him and because everything else faded away from her mind she forgot Lord Wilchester and what he was saying to her until as if his voice came from a long way away she heard him say:

"I asked you a question!"

"I . . . I am sorry," she said quickly. "I did not . . . hear what you said."

Again she was watching the Marquis talking to their hostess, and she saw as he did so that his eyes were searching the Ball-Room as if he was looking for her.

Then she told herself that if Lady Langdon thought Lord Wilchester was out of reach, even more so was the Marquis.

She did not miss the innuendos she had heard almost every evening at dinner, or at any luncheon party she attended.

"You are staying at Deverille House?" her partners always exclaimed. "Good gracious, you must be a very important person!"

"Why should you think that?" Hermia had asked, knowing the answer.

"Deverille is never seen with young women. In fact, it is always said in the Clubs that he would not know a young woman if he saw one!"

Then usually the man who had thus spoken would look embarrassed and say quickly:

"Perhaps I am being rude. Of course, as Lady

Langdon is chaperoning you, that means you are a relative."

Hermia had not troubled to contradict that idea.

She did not miss either the disagreeable and jealous looks she received from the beautiful women who clustered round the Marquis when he introduced her to them.

"Miss Brooke is my guest," he would explain, and a look of curiosity would be replaced by one of incredulity or of unconcealed antagonism.

Hermia thought she could not imagine women could look so beautiful or so alluring and not hold every man irresistibly captivated by their charms.

There was no doubt they set out to entice the Marquis, and watching them Hermia thought for the first time that she could understand what the temptations of St. Anthony had been like.

Or to put it in a more familiar way, she thought that the lovely Sirens who surrounded the Marquis pictured the villager's imagination of the Witches who revelled with Satan in Witch Wood.

They fluttered their long, dark eye-lashes at the Marquis, pouted at him with reddened lips and the gowns they wore seemed almost indecently *décolleté*.

It told Hermia quite clearly that despite the beautiful gowns she had been given, she was no more than the stupid, inconsequential village-girl whom the Marquis had once mistaken for a milk-maid.

"That is how he thinks of me," she thought.

Then she felt as if she went down into a little Hell of her own, where there was no requited love, only the frustrations of yearning and wanting what was out of reach and unobtainable.

Although the Marquis smiled in her direction at the Ball he made no move to speak to her and when the Prince Regent left he left with him.

Later Lady Langdon and Hermia drove home alone, and as the two horses drew the comfortable carriage swiftly down Piccadilly Lady Langdon said:

"You looked very lovely tonight, and the Duchess said you were undoubtedly the prettiest girl in the room! I noticed too that Lord Wilchester was very attentive."

"He asked if he could call and see me tomorrow," Hermia said without thinking.

Lady Langdon gave a little exclamation.

"He asked to see you alone?"

"Yes, but I do not wish to be alone with him!"

"My dear child, do not be so ridiculous! Can you not understand that he is going to propose to you? He would never ask to see you alone otherwise."

"I thought perhaps he was thinking of something like that," Hermia said in a low voice, "but . . . I do not wish . . . to . . . marry him."

"Not wish to marry Lord Wilchester?" Lady Langdon cried in amazement. "But my dearest Hermia, you must be off your head! Of course you must marry him! It would be the most marvellous, brilliant marriage to which you could aspire! In fact I will be honest and say that I had no idea you could capture the heart of the most elusive bachelor in the whole of the *Beau Monde!*"

She paused, then added almost as if it was a joke:

"With, of course, the exception of my brother, who has sworn he will never marry!"

"Why should he do that?" Hermia asked with a different note in her voice from what there had been before.

"Has no one told you that poor Favian was abominably treated by a girl to whom he lost his heart the year after he came down from Oxford?"

"What happened?"

"It was quite an ordinary story, but had consequences we never envisaged at the time."

"What were they?"

"Favian fell in love with the Duke of Dorset's daughter. She was lovely, quite lovely, but I always thought she was not quite what she appeared."

"I do not understand," Hermia murmured.

"Caroline was very beautiful, looked magnificent on a horse, which of course pleased Favian, and appeared to be as much in love with him as he was with her."

Lady Langdon gave a little sigh.

"The whole family was delighted because Favian had just come into the title and being so rich and so attractive was being pursued by every woman he met."

She paused before she went on:

"We all thought if he settled down and spent more time in the country than in London it would be excellent for him, and perhaps prevent him from going into the Army, as he wished to do."

"Did they become engaged?" Hermia asked.

"Not officially. The families of both sides knew it was an understanding, and in fact the announcement was due to go into the *Gazette* when Favian discovered that Caroline was behaving in an outrageous manner with the man with whom she was really in love!"

Hermia made a murmured exclamation, and Lady Langdon continued:

"I could hardly believe that any well-bred girl would stoop to having a love-affair with a man of a different class all together, and disgrace herself by meeting him surreptitiously on the ground of her father's estate."

"Who was he?"

"He was her father's horse-trainer and of course Caroline had often been escorted by him when she went riding."

Hermia could see what had happened and Lady Langdon said in a tone of the most utter contempt:

"It was disgraceful, absolutely disgraceful that any Lady should behave in such a manner! I learnt, although Favian could never talk about it, that he had received an anonymous letter from somebody who was jealous of him, and he surprised Caroline and the man she loved in very unfortunate circumstances."

"It must have hurt him very much," Hermia murmured.

"It made him extremely cynical, and he immediately joined the Army and fought in the Peninsula and France until Wellington was victorious at Waterloo."

"I had no idea he was a soldier."

"The Duke of Wellington told he was an excellent officer in every way, but although he came back to enjoy the good things of life that were waiting for him, I have always felt he was somewhat contemptuous of them."

It was what Hermia had thought herself. Then she said, because she could not help asking the question:

"Has the Marquis never fallen in love with anybody else?"

"There have been many women in his life," Lady Langdon replied. "In fact, they never leave him alone! We have been hoping and praying that he will marry, if only to prevent that ghastly cousin of ours Roxford de Ville, from borrowing money as Favian's heir presumptive."

There was a pause before Lady Langdon said:

"I rather hoped he might marry that pretty cousin of yours. In fact, when he told me he was going to stay with her father I hoped it was she who attracted him rather than your Uncle's horses, of which Favian has quite enough already!"

There was no need for Hermia to reply, because at that moment the horses drew up outside the Marquis's house.

"We are home," Lady Langdon announced, "and I must admit I am ready for bed."

They walked up the staircase together and climbed the next flight to the Second Floor.

The rooms there were equally impressive with high ceilings and, as was to be expected, exquisite decoration.

When she reached her own bedroom Hermia felt that for all the pleasure it gave her it might as well have been an attic with nothing in it but an iron bed-stead.

All she could think of was the Marquis being disillu-sioned and disgusted by the girl with whom he had fallen in love and in consequence swearing that he would never marry anybody.

When her maid who had waited up to undo her gown had left her, Hermia went to the window to pull back the curtains.

Once again, as she had done before she looked at the new moon that was just rising up in the sky and thought that just as it was out of reach, so was the Marquis.

"I may love him, but he will never love me!" she thought.

Then she thought that Lord Wilchester was coming tomorrow to propose to her and felt herself shudder.

"I cannot marry him, I cannot!" she told herself passionately.

Then she saw herself back at the Vicarage spend-ing the rest of her life carrying soothing syrups and salves to Mrs. Burles and a dozen other women like her.

Or waiting for her mother or her father to come home in the evening, knowing that while they both loved her and she meant a great deal to them, they would rather be alone with each other.

"I should marry him," she thought.

Then she looked at the sky through the un-curtained window and thought that she could see the Marquis's face amongst the stars.

"Out of reach!"

She could almost hear him saying the words mock-ingly in that dry voice of his that made her feel shy.

"Out of reach! Out of reach!"

CHAPTER SEVEN

$\mathcal{H}$ermia found it impossible to sleep.

She twisted and turned, and all she could think of was the Marquis and that if she married somebody else or returned to the Vicarage she would never see him again.

She was also afraid for him, and although he might laugh at Hickson's concern she kept thinking of how every hour of every day he was in danger from his cousin.

Because she had been thinking about him the previous night she had said to an elderly man who was at the Ball she was attending:

"Is Roxford de Ville here by any chance?"

He looked at her in surprise before he answered:

"I cannot imagine our hostess would contemplate having such a disreputable character as one of her guests!"

Hermia did not speak and after a moment he laughed and said:

"Anyway, this is not the sort of company in which de Ville feels at home."

She looked at him for explanation and he explained:

"He spends his entire life in low Night Clubs, with the gypsies on Hampstead Heath, or I have heard recently with the trapeze artists who perform at Vauxhall Gardens."

"Why does he like those sort of people?" Hermia enquired.

Her companion went into a long explanation of how disreputable the Marquis's cousin was and how much he was disliked.

But Hermia was remembering that the Marquis had told her father that two of the men who had knocked him about were swarthy and might have been foreigners or gypsies.

She wondered if she should warn the Marquis that it would be a mistake to go anywhere near Hampstead Heath, but she doubted if he would listen to her.

She was sure he would merely laugh and say he could look after himself.

"If Roxford de Ville is determined to murder him, he will do so," she thought.

The idea made her want to cry because she felt so helpless.

Throwing off the sheets because it was hot she climbed out of bed and went to the open window.

She told herself it was because she needed air, but actually she wanted to look at the moon and think about the Marquis.

She had to force herself to accept the fact that he was out of reach.

Then as she leaned out of the window she looked along the back-wall of the house towards the far end where she knew the Marquis was sleeping.

She had learnt that when he had inherited he had not altered the front of the house which faced onto Piccadilly and was very impressive.

The back was rather featureless, but he had added to it the wrought iron balconies which had just come into fashion.

Hermia had learnt that all the houses that were being built in Brighton, and there were a great many because the *Beau Monde* followed the Prince Regent there, had wrought iron balconies.

Those the Marquis had added were all of beautiful workmanship and the windows of the State Rooms on the First Floor now had large balconies with elaborate designs rising to about three feet around them.

Those on the second floor where she was sleeping were only half as big, but equally as elaborate.

On the floor above there was only a token surround outside each window.

The effect from the garden was very impressive.

But as Hermia leaned out of the window she thought the Marquis had been very clever to improve his London house so outstandingly.

Then as she looked at his bedroom, which was on the same level as her own, she raised her eyes and thought that a chimney had fallen forward onto the balustrade of the roof.

She wondered vaguely if anybody was aware of it, and determined in the morning, to tell the servants to make investigations.

Then what had appeared to be a heap of stone moved, and she realised it was not a fallen chimney as she had thought, but a man leaning over from the roof to look down below him.

For a moment she thought it might be workmen, but it was a strange time of night for men to be working on the roof.

Then she saw in the moonlight there was not one man, but two.

'Something must have happened,' she thought.

Then as she stared, finding it hard to see clearly from the angle at which she was looking, she suddenly remembered what her partner had said last night.

"Trapeze artists at Vauxhall Gardens!"

She started and felt a streak of fear run through her as she knew that this constituted a danger for the Marquis.

She could hear Hickson saying to her that his

master had said that no one could enter his bedroom unless they were a spider, or flew in through the window.

"That is what his cousin intends to do!" Hermia told herself in terror.

She took one last look and now she could see that one man was on the very edge of the balustrade and she thought that there were ropes around his shoulders.

It was obvious that the other man was beginning to let him down slowly towards the Marquis's bedroom window.

With a cry that was stifled in her throat, she turned and pulling open her bedroom door lifted up her nightgown and started to run down the passage which led to the other end of the house.

It was quite a long way, and as she ran she felt frantically that if she should be too late either Roxford de Ville, or whoever he had hired to kill the Marquis, would have performed his evil task before she was able to save him.

She thought the murderer was most likely to enter the bedroom and stab the Marquis because that would make no noise.

And yet she could not be sure. It would be quicker and perhaps easier, to shoot him from the balcony.

Then the criminal would immediately be hauled back up onto the roof before anybody would think of looking for him in such an unlikely place.

It all flashed through her mind as she ran with her heart thumping violently against her breast over the soft carpet, past Lady Langdon's room, past the empty spare rooms which came before the Marquis's Suite.

She knew where his bedroom was because Lady Langdon had taken her round the house and had shown her the Marquis's room saying:

"This is the Master Suite where my father, my grandfather and my great-grandfather all slept. It is the one place in the house that Favian has not changed, but left very much as it was, and I love it because it brings back so many memories of my childhood."

She remembered it was a large, very impressive room with one window looking onto the garden, and another on the side of the house from which there was a glimpse of Green Park.

What had impressed Hermia most was the huge four-poster bed curtained with crimson velvet, the back embellished with an enormous replica of the Marquis's coat-of-arms in colour.

It seemed almost regal and a most fitting background for him, and now as she ran faster and even faster she thought it might be his death-bed.

She opened the door.

The room was in darkness except for the moonlight coming through one open window.

It was the window which looked onto the garden, and even as Hermia moved towards the bed to awaken the Marquis she saw the stars outside being obscured by a dark form which she knew was a man's legs coming down onto the balcony.

Because she was so breathless it was almost impossible to speak.

"My . . . Lord!" she whispered and because she was so frightened she could not even hear herself.

Then as he did not answer she knew with a terror that seemed to strike into her body like the point of a dagger that the light from the window was now almost completely blocked out and she whispered again:

"My . . . Lord! My . . . Lord! Wake . . . up!"

She put out her hand as she spoke to shake him because he must be sleeping so heavily.

Instead of touching his shoulder, however, as she had intended to do, she found her hand was touching something hard and cold that was lying on a low table by the bedside.

Her fingers closed over it almost before her mind

told her that it was the loaded pistol which Hickson had told her was always there.

As she took it up in her hand looking frantically towards the window, she realised the man outside had shaken off the ropes by which he had descended.

She saw something glint in his hand and knew it was a dagger.

It was all happening so swiftly that she hardly had time to think but only to be aware of the danger coming towards the Marquis whom she could not waken.

Lifting up the pistol she pointed it towards the intruder and just as he stepped forward to enter the room she pulled the trigger.

There was a resounding explosion that seemed almost to break her ear-drums. Then the man in the window gave a shrill cry, and Hermia shut her eyes.

Trembling she opened them and there was only the moonlight once again coming into the room.

It was then, with her ears still ringing from the explosion, that she looked towards the bed and saw a door on the other side of it was open and silhouetted against the golden light in the room behind him was the Marquis.

For a moment she could hardly believe that he was there and not asleep as she had expected him to be.

Then she threw the pistol down on the bed and ran towards him, to fling herself against him.

"He was going to . . . kill you," she cried. "He was . . . going to . . . kill you!"

The Marquis put his arms around her and as she felt the strength of them and knew he was safe, Hermia burst into tears.

She hid her face against his shoulder sobbing:

"He was . . . let down by a . . . rope from the . . . r . . . roof . . . I saw him and thought I would never get . . . here in time . . . and he would kill you . . . while you . . . slept."

Her words seemed to fall over each other and they

were broken by sobs which made her whole body tremble beneath her thin nightgown.

"But you were in time," the Marquis said quietly, "and once again, Hermia, you have saved my life."

He held her close for a moment. Then he said:

"I must go to see what has happened, but do not move until I tell you to do so."

He sat her down gently on the side of the bed and while she still cried he walked away from her to look out of the window.

He did not speak and she suddenly thought the whole thing had been a dream and there had been no man there, that she had just imagined it.

She was afraid the Marquis would think she was very foolish and hysterical to behave in such a manner.

Then she remembered that if it was real and she had killed a man the repercussions would be frightful.

She stopped crying, but the tears were still on her cheeks as the Marquis came from the window.

She saw that he was wearing a dark robe which reached the ground, making him somehow more impressive than usual.

She looked up at him beseechingly and now he could see her face clearly in the light which came from his Sitting-Room.

"It was very brave of you, Hermia," he said quietly. "My Cousin Roxford is dead. No one could fall from such a height and not break his neck."

"I . . . I have . . . killed him!" Hermia whispered.

"No," the Marquis answered. "You surprised him but your bullet went into the side of the window-frame and actually did not touch him."

She stared at the Marquis as if she could not believe what she had heard.

Because she could not speak he put his arm around her and drew her gently to the window.

She could see the rope which Roxford de Ville had

shrugged from his shoulders before he was ready to enter the bedroom.

Then the Marquis pointed a little above her head, and Hermia could see quite clearly in the moonlight that the wooden lintel was splintered where the bullet she had fired had entered it.

Because she was so relieved that she had not actually killed anybody, even if it was a man with murder in his heart, she turned her face once again towards the Marquis's shoulder.

He knew she was thinking that now she would not have to stand trial or explain what had happened and his arms tightened around her as he said:

"I want you to understand that you must not be involved in any way."

He looked out of the window before he went on:

"They will find my cousin in the morning, and the ropes from the balcony outside this room. The story I shall tell is that he must have lost his balance coming down from the roof."

Hermia lifted her face to look up at him.

"Everybody will . . . know he intended to . . . kill you."

"Officially nobody must know that," the Marquis said sharply. "The Magistrates will be told that it amused him to climb over roofs and play pranks on people at night, and having had too much to drink he slipped and fell."

"They will . . . believe that?"

"I will make sure they do so."

"Now . . . you are safe . . . and nobody will . . . try to kill you?"

"I hope not," the Marquis answered, "but as I do not wish you to be questioned you are to go back to bed and forget what has happened. We will talk about it again in the morning."

"But . . . you will be . . . safe?" Hermia said almost beneath her breath.

"I shall be safe," the Marquis repeated, "because you have saved me."

He looked down at her. Then as she stared up at him in the moonlight his lips came down on hers.

For a moment she could hardly believe what was happening.

Then as the Marquis kissed her for the second time she knew this was very different from the kiss he had given her before.

Because she loved him her lips were very soft and warm as she felt his mouth take possession of hers she knew that it was what she wanted more than anything else in the whole world.

It was what she had yearned for, prayed for, and now as he kissed her she felt as if she surrendered herself to him completely and gave him not only her heart, but her soul.

It was so perfect, so exactly as she had felt a kiss should be, and yet a million times more wonderful than she had ever imagined.

She at the same time, felt as if the moonlight moved through her body in a silver stream and the stars fell out of the sky to shine in her breast and join her lips with the Marquis's.

It was so perfect, so ecstatic, so unbelievably rapturous, that she felt if she died at this moment, she would be in Heaven and never have to return to earth.

Then as she moved closer and still closer to the Marquis he raised his head and said in a voice which seemed strangely unlike his:

"Go to bed! Forget what has happened and nobody must know that you have been in my room tonight."

Because what she felt when he kissed her made Hermia speechless and in a daze she could not answer him.

She was only aware that he drew her across the room to open the door and very gently push her outside.

"Do as I have told you," he commanded.

Then almost before she could realise what was happening his door had shut behind her and she was alone in the corridor.

It was difficult to think, difficult to be aware of anything but the emotions pulsating through her and feeling that her lips were still held captive by the Marquis.

Somehow she walked back along the corridor finding her way now by the light of the candles guttering low in the silver sconces which she had not noticed when she had run to save the Marquis.

She reached her bedroom and only the open window and the moonlight coming through it told her that what she had seen when she had looked along the wall of the house, had been real.

Even though the Marquis had not been in his bed his cousin could have stabbed him in the other room when he was weaponless.

Quickly Hermia got into bed, then as she shut her eyes she could only think that the Marquis had kissed her and nothing else was of any importance.

Hermia was awoken as usual by the maid who looked after her.

She came in and set down by the bedside the hot chocolate she always brought Hermia before she rose.

As she did so she said as if she could not prevent herself from speaking about it:

"Oh, Miss, there's such a to-do downstairs! Everybody's in a turmoil!"

"What has happened?" Hermia asked and managed to speak quite naturally.

"It's His Lordship's cousin, Miss. He's been found dead in the garden after falling off the roof!"

"How terrible!" Hermia exclaimed. "But why was he on the roof?"

"Mr. Hickson says it's all them tricks them trapeze

people 'as taught him. Them as performs in Vauxhall Gardens."

Hermia smiled a little as the maid chatted on, feeling sure that Hickson would be the only person who might guess what was the real truth, even though he would not know she was involved in it.

Lady Langdon insisted that after they had a late night neither of them had breakfast until late in the morning.

Now as Hermia waited for the maid to tell her her bath was ready, she said:

"Oh, I almost forgot to tell you, Miss—His Lordship says neither Her Ladyship nor you are to come downstairs before luncheon. Mr. de Ville's body is being taken away as soon as the Undertakers arrive. Until then he wants you to stay upstairs."

As she finished speaking she went to the door saying:

"I'll bring your breakfast, Miss, as soon as it's ready, but I thinks as 'ow Her Ladyship's still asleep."

Hermia lay back amongst the pillows with a little sigh of relief.

In spite of what the Marquis had said, she had been afraid that Roxford de Ville might be injured and not dead, and would live to try to kill again.

Now the Marquis was safe, and it suddenly came into her mind that there would now be no pressure on him to marry, and he could continue to enjoy his freedom as he had before.

She thought Marilyn would be disappointed, but she knew that while the Marquis need not marry Marilyn, he would also not think of marrying her.

He had kissed her, and she was quite certain that if he had loved her, he would have said so.

Instead he had sent her to bed and told her never to think or speak of what had happened again.

"I will never speak of it," Hermia said to herself, "but I will never . . . forget that he . . . kissed me

143

. . . and how could I ever feel the same for . . . another man?"

Then with a little feeling of apprehension she remembered that Lord Wilchester was coming today to propose to her.

She thought in the circumstances it would be reasonable to say that no visitors should be admitted to the house.

Then a frightening thought struck her.

However disreputable he might be, Roxford de Ville was a member of the Marquis's family, and he and his sister would now be in mourning.

This meant that it would be impossible for Lady Langdon to take her to any more Balls or parties, at least until after the Funeral.

"I shall have to go home!" Hermia thought and felt her spirits drop.

It was as if the sun was eclipsed and there was only darkness outside.

She would say goodbye to the Marquis and go home, and that would be the end.

"I cannot bear it! How can I . . . leave him?" she asked, but knew she had no alternative.

When she came downstairs just before luncheon it was to find, as she had expected that Lady Langdon had cancelled the luncheon party they were to have had, and she and Hermia ate alone.

There was no sign of the Marquis and as she and Lady Langdon sat in the big Dining-Room and for the first time since her arrival there was nobody else with them, Hermia felt as if she was already on her way back to the Vicarage.

Lady Langdon could talk of nothing but the strange behaviour of Roxford de Ville which had made him climb over the roof at night.

It never seemed to strike her that he might have had a sinister motive for doing so.

"He has always been unpredicatable," she chatted in her usual manner, "but who but Roxford would

144

wish to associate with trapeze artists and the gypsies of whom most people are afraid?"

"It certainly seems strange," Hermia murmured.

"When I saw Favian this morning he said it was obvious Roxford had had too much to drink and was therefore unsteady on his feet, and considering the way he has behaved recently he might easily have died in far more disreputable circumstances! We can only be thankful that it was no worse than it was."

"Yes . . . of course," Hermia agreed.

"It has certainly upset our plans for today," Lady Langdon said. "But we must find out what Favian thinks we can do tonight. I have no intention of cancelling more parties than is absolutely necessary for propriety's sake. No one will mourn Roxford, least of all his relatives."

Lady Langdon rose to leave the Dining-Room as she spoke and when they reached the Hall she said to the Butler:

"When His Lordship returns tell him Miss Brooke and I will be in the Library."

"Very good, M'Lady," the Butler replied.

They went to the Library, and another time Hermia would have been happy to browse amongst the books and find a new one to read.

But she could only wonder what the Marquis would have to say when he returned and hoped he would not be long.

She desperately wanted to see him but at the same time she felt shy.

Then she told herself that while his kiss had taken her into the sky and she had touched the Divine, to him it had been just an expression of gratitude.

"I must not behave towards him," she told herself, "in any way which would make him feel embarrassed."

She went on reasoning it all out:

"If I cling to him, if I show that I love him, I will

just be like all those other women who fawn on him
and with whom he is quickly bored."

But she knew it was going to be very difficult.

Lady Langdon put down the magazine she had
been reading.

"As I have nothing particular to do," she said, "and
because as we got to bed so late I am rather tired, I
think I will go and lie down. Tell Favian when he
comes that if he has anything important to tell me he
can wake me up. If not, I will be down in time for tea."

"I will tell him," Hermia replied.

She opened the door for her hostess and Lady
Langdon said:

"You have not forgotten that Lord Wilchester will
be calling on you? I do not expect he will arrive before
three o'clock, which is the correct time for such visits."

She walked away before Hermia could ask her to
tell the servants she was not at home.

Quite suddenly she was frightened.

"I cannot see him," she thought. "If he asks me to
marry him and I refuse it will be very embarrassing,
and it would be much better to prevent him from
speaking to me."

She waited until she thought Lady Langdon would
have reached her bedroom, then rang the bell.

The Butler answered it and she said to him:

"I am expecting Lord Wilchester to call at about
three o'clock. If he does, will you tell him that in the
circumstances I am not at home to any visitors?"

"Yes, I'll tell him, Miss," the Butler replied.

As he spoke, through the open door behind him
came the Marquis.

He was looking very elegant and Hermia thought
more exquisitely dressed than usual.

But it might have been because just to look at him
made her heart turn several somersaults in her breast,
and she felt as if the room was suddenly lit by a thousand lights.

"What is this?" he asked. "Who are you refusing to see?"

It was somehow impossible for Hermia to answer him, and the Butler replied for her:

"Miss Brooke understood Lord Wilchester was calling, M'Lord, but I'll inform His Lordship she's not receiving."

"Yes, do that," the Marquis agreed.

The Butler shut the door and the Marquis walked towards Hermia. She watched him, her eyes filling her face.

Then as he reached her he said:

"You are all right?"

"Y.yes . . . of course."

"But you have no wish to see Wilchester! Why?"

She felt his eyes looking at her in the penetrating manner which always made her feel shy, and she looked away from him.

Then as she realised the Marquis was waiting for an answer to his question she said:

"I . . . I thought it was . . . correct."

"Is that the only reason?"

As if he compelled her to reply she said:

"I . . . I did not . . . wish to . . . see him alone."

"Why not?"

It was difficult to find an answer. Then as she was silent after a moment the Marquis said:

"Last night when I returned after you had gone to bed, my sister left me a note to say that Wilchester had asked to see you alone today and she was sure he intended to propose marriage. Is that what you expect?"

"Y.yes."

The monosyllable seemed to be drawn through lips that trembled, but still Hermia dared not look at the Marquis.

"He is very important in the Social World and a

man whom other men admire. I doubt if you will have a much better offer."

The way the Marquis spoke made Hermia feel as if every word was a blow that hurt her most unbearably.

She also realised he was drawling his words and speaking in the same, dry, cynical manner as he had done when they first met.

When she did not speak the Marquis said:

"Well? Are you going to accept him? I am interested to know."

"I.it is what your sister thinks I should do," Hermia answered, ". . . but it is . . . impossible."

"Why impossible?"

Hermia drew in her breath.

"Because . . . I do not . . . love him."

"And you think that is more important than all he can give you? Security, money, a position which most women would fight frantically to attain?"

Hermia clenched her fingers together until her knuckles dug into the palms of her hands.

"I know you will . . . think me . . . very foolish," she said, "but . . . I could not marry anybody . . . unless I . . . loved them."

"What do you know about love?" the Marquis asked. "When I was in the country I was sure it was something of which you were very ignorant. I am equally certain that I am the only man who has ever kissed you!"

His words made the colour flood into Hermia's cheeks and she wanted to run away before she could be questioned any further.

At the same time, she wanted to stay simply because she was with him.

"Now, strangely," the Marquis went on, "you know . . . you do not love one of the most charming young men in the whole of the *Beau Monde!* How can you be so sure?"

There was a very easy answer to that, Hermia thought, but it was something she could not say.

She could only feel herself tremble and hope the Marquis was not aware of it.

Then in a voice that she had never heard him use before he said:

"Last night, Hermia, when I kissed you I thought it was very different from the first time, even though to me that was an unexpected enchantment which I have found it impossible to forget."

Because she was so surprised Hermia looked up at him for the first time.

As her eyes met his it was impossible to look away and she felt as though he was looking deep down into her soul and knew how much she loved him.

"After last night," the Marquis went on, "I might have been mistaken, Hermia, but I was sure you loved somebody, even though you are afraid to admit it."

She could only stare at him, her lips slightly parted, her heart pounding in a manner that made it impossible to speak, or even to breathe.

The Marquis stepped nearer to her as he said:

"Then we were both carried away by the drama of what had just occurred, so shall we see today if what we feel is any different, or perhaps even more wonderful?"

As he finished speaking his arms went round her and his lips were on hers.

He held her against him, then he was kissing her not gently or tenderly but demandingly, as if he wanted to be sure of her, as if he wanted to conquer her and possess her completely.

It was like being swept from the despair of thinking she must leave him, into an unbelievably glorious Heaven, and Hermia could only give him her heart and soul as she had given them to him last night.

He kissed her until they were both breathless, until Hermia felt she was no longer herself, but part of him and they were one person.

Then as the Marquis raised his head he said in a voice that sounded strange and a little unsteady:

"You are mine! How could you dare to let another man think you might marry him when you belong to me and have done so ever since the first moment I saw you?"

"I . . . I love you!" Hermia said. "I love you . . . until there is no other man in the world but you!"

The Marquis kissed her again.

Now she knew that he wanted to conquer her and dominate her and make her his, so that as she had said there was no other man in the world except him.

Because the sensations he aroused in her were so overwhelming and fantastic, when his lips released her she hid her face against him and he could feel her quivering.

But it was with happiness, not fear.

"What have you done to me, my darling?" he asked.

He laughed.

"I know the answer to that. You have bewitched me and I am in your spell from which I can never escape. I believe now in all the magic with which you have enveloped me from the moment you removed the shoe from my horse's hoof, when I was unable to do so myself."

Hermia gave a little laugh that was almost like a sob.

"It was not magic . . . it was only that being so rich you never have to do such menial tasks for yourself."

"It was magic!" the Marquis averred. "And when I looked at you I thought you had stepped out of a dream."

"You thought I was a milk-maid!"

"I was trying to pretend that you were," he replied, "but I should have realised that you had bewitched me, and I could never escape."

Hermia put her head on his shoulder.

"If I am a witch, I only became one when you kissed me, and I want you to go on kissing me for ever and ever."

The Marquis did not answer.

He merely kissed her and she thought that nothing

could be more rapturous, more wonderful than the feelings he evoked in her, or which she realised she was arousing in him.

Only when she could speak did she say:

"I do not believe this is . . . true. I never thought for a moment that you could . . . love me as I . . . love you."

"When you came riding into the wood to perform very badly that piece of play-acting to impress me," the Marquis said, "I knew you were what I had been looking for all my life, and I would never lose you."

Hermia flushed.

"You guessed I was . . . lying?"

"There was no doubt in my mind," the Marquis replied, "even if I had not already been aware that your cousin would no more sit at a dying villager's bedside than carry a wounded man back from a Devil-infested wood!"

"She . . . she is very anxious to . . . marry you."

"I would never have married her!" the Marquis replied. "In fact I had determined never to marry any-body!"

"That is what your sister has told me."

"But, of course, I have no defence against magic."

"You are not to say that," Hermia said quickly. "I could not bear you to think that I tried to catch you or forced you into doing something you did not really wish to do."

The Marquis pulled her against him.

"I am marrying you because I want you," he said, "and I will kill any man who tries to take you away from me."

Hermia thought for a moment, then she said:

"But . . . you brought me to London to . . . meet other men."

The Marquis's arms tightened around her.

"I knew I loved you," he said, "I knew you be-longed to me, but I was giving you a sporting chance in case you should prefer somebody else not for your sake, but for mine."

He realised Hermia looked puzzled.

"You see, my darling, having been so disillusioned I thought all women were the same: ready to sell themselves to the highest bidder, wanting only the position in life I could give them, and not me as a man."

"I want you . . . as you!" Hermia said quickly. "I only wish you were not a Marquis, but just an ordinary man . . . then I could show you how I would look after you and love you."

She moved a little closer to him as she added:

"You would know then that my love is the same that Mama has for Papa and nothing else is of any importance."

The Marquis smiled.

"I realised that when I stayed at the Vicarage," he said. "I have never seen two people as happy as your father and mother, and when I saw how poor you were and how few luxuries you enjoyed, I was almost certain you would feel the same, but I had to be sure."

"But supposing . . . just supposing I had promised to marry Lord Wilchester . . . or somebody . . . like him?"

"Then I should have lost you," the Marquis replied, "because I would have known that to you, thinking I would not marry you, money and position meant more than love."

"And you . . . knew already that I . . . loved you?" Hermia whispered.

"My precious, your eyes are very expressive," the Marquis said, "and I saw when I came into a room how they seemed to light up, and you looked at me in a different way from how you looked at anybody else."

"I . . . I did not realise at first that I . . . loved you," Hermia said honestly, "but then I knew it was . . . love which enabled me to find you in the Witch's Cottage, and . . . love which made it possible for me to bring you back to safety."

"And it was love again that made you save me last night," the Marquis added.

"I was so terribly afraid that he would . . . kill you."

"I am alive," the Marquis said, "and now there are no more dangers to threaten us, and only the elves, the fairies and the water-nymphs in which you believe to give us their blessing and to show us how to live happily ever afterwards."

The way he spoke told Hermia he was not laughing at her and she raised her lips to his with a gesture of delight which brought the fire into the Marquis's eyes.

He looked down at her for a long moment before he said:

"I adore you! I love everything about you, your kind, compassionate little heart, the way you think of everybody except yourself, and most of all because you love me! You do love me?"

"I love you until you fill the whole world . . . the sky, the moon and the stars and there is . . . nothing else but you . . . and you . . . and you . . ."

Now there was a note of passion in Hermia's voice that had not been there before and the Marquis's lips sought hers.

He kissed her until she felt as if instead of moonlight there were little flames of fire flickering within her breasts, and he was drawing them up into her lips until they burned against the fire on his.

Some time later Hermia found herself sitting on the sofa, the Marquis's arms around her and her head on his shoulder.

"Now what we have to decide, my precious one," he said, "is how soon we can be married with the least possible fuss."

Hermia gave a little sigh of relief before she said:

"Do you . . . really mean that?"

153

"I suppose you want a grand wedding," he said, "with all the paraphernalia of bridesmaids and an indefinite number of so-called 'friends'."

"I should hate it!" Hermia said quickly. "I should like to be married very quietly with nobody else there except for Papa, Mama and Peter and because we really love each other, I want no one to snigger or be envious."

The Marquis put his cheek against hers.

"How can you be so perfect? I know of nobody else who would say that to me."

"It is true," Hermia said. "I could not bear to have anybody there hating me or being furious because you had married anybody so insignificant."

She was thinking of Marilyn.

"Then I tell you what we will do," the Marquis said. "We will be married secretly and nobody, except your family, shall know what we have done until we are far away on our honeymoon."

"Do you really mean that?"

"Of course," he replied.

"That would be the most . . . wonderful thing that could ever happen!" Hermia said. "And . . . please . . . can it be very soon?"

The Marquis laughed before he said:

"Tonight, tomorrow or at the very latest two days from now."

Then when Hermia wanted to tell him she was sure it was impossible, she had no chance to do so.

He was kissing her again and his kisses swept her up into a Heaven of happiness where there was only love and him.

The Church had been decorated by her mother with every white flower that the garden possessed.

As Hermia came in through the door on Peter's arm she knew, although the pews were empty, that the whole building was filled with those who had once prayed there, and were now wishing her happiness.

She had not seen the Marquis since she had left London two days earlier with the excuse that because they were all in mourning it was only right for her to return home.

"I am so disappointed, dear child," Lady Langdon said, "but I am sure I can persuade my brother to invite you back again as soon as the summer is over and people return to London for the winter."

She sighed before she continued:

"It will not be as gay as it is now, but there will be Balls and Assemblies, and I should love to chaperone you again."

"You have been very, very kind," Hermia murmured, feeling a little ashamed that Lady Langdon should not know the truth.

But she knew the Marquis was right in saying that if he invited one of his relatives to his wedding the rest would take umbrage for the rest of their lives, and it was therefore best to have all or none.

"The same applies to me," Hermia said. "I am quite sure that Uncle John and Aunt Edith will be absolutely furious, and not only because they were not asked to the wedding."

"Forget what they are feeling," the Marquis said. "I am quite certain your cousin will find an eligible husband sooner or later because she is a very determined young woman."

Hermia did not answer this, as she did not want to seem unkind.

She thought it would be impossible for Marilyn to find anybody as wonderful as the Marquis, and if she had lost him, she knew how miserable she would be feeling.

But it was difficult to think of anything except the happiness of knowing that she would be his wife and they would be together for ever and ever.

"You are quite certain that once you marry me you

will not be . . . bored and . . . cynical again?" she asked.

"If as a Witch you cannot prevent me from being bored," he answered, "I shall not think much of your magic."

"Now you are frightening me."

"I love you," he answered. "I love you so much that I know that what we know about each other at the moment is only the tip of the iceberg, and there is so much more for us both to explore and discover which will take at least a century."

Hermia laughed, but she knew it was the truth.

"What is more," the Marquis went on, "I have so much to teach you, my darling one, and love is a very big subject."

The way he spoke made Hermia feel shy, but it was not the shyness she had felt before.

It was something warm and exciting which seemed to pulsate through her so that she wanted him to kiss her and go on kissing her, and for them to be closer and closer to each other.

"I love you . . . I love . . ." she whispered and then could say no more.

When she returned home and told her father and mother that she was to marry the Marquis, they were at first astounded.

Then when they realised how much she loved him they were happy in a way which made the Vicarage seem to vibrate with joy.

"It is what I have always prayed would happen to you my darling!" Mrs. Brooke said. "I suppose it was foolish of me not to realise that God would answer my prayers, and I should never have doubted for a moment that you would find the same love that your father and I found."

Her mother understood, Hermia thought, as

nobody else could have done, how very important it was that her marriage should not be spoilt in any way and must therefore be very secret.

The day after she returned home her wedding-gown arrived from London, and she knew only the Marquis could have chosen something so exquisitely beautiful which was exactly what she would have wished to wear to marry him.

It was white and embroidered all over with tiny diamante which looked like flowers with raindrops on them.

There was a diamond wreath for her hair fashioned in the form of wild flowers that was so beautiful that Hermia thought it must have been made with fairy hands.

When Nanny put the white veil over her face there were tears in the old woman's eyes.

"You don't look real," she said, "and that's the truth! It's just as if you'd come out of the garden or the woods like one of them fanciful creatures you were always talking about when you were a child."

"That is what I hope I look like," Hermia said.

She knew strangely enough it was what the Marquis wanted too, as no other man would have done.

Peter dressed in the clothes the Marquis had given him was so pleased with his own appearance that Hermia thought he hardly had time to notice her at all.

"What do you think?" he had said to her when he arrived. "Your Marquis sent a Phaeton and four horses to bring me home, and there was also a letter!"

He drew in his breath as if he could hardly believe what he had read.

"It told me that next term I can have two horses at Oxford of my own, besides a large credit at my new brother-in-law's tailors, which will ensure I can look very nearly as smart as he does!"

"He is so wonderful!" Hermia said softly.

"I think you are wonderful too," Peter said, "and

you deserve everything you have and a lot more besides!"

The way he spoke made Hermia smile, and as she walked up the aisle on his arm and saw her father waiting in front of the altar, and her mother sitting in the front pew she thought nobody could be blessed with a more marvellous family.

Then as she saw the Marquis waiting for her she felt as if he was enveloped by a dazzling celestial light.

The angels were singing overhead and the whole church was filled with the music of love.

After they had cut the cake which Nanny had baked and iced for them and everybody had drunk the excellent champagne the Marquis had brought down with him from London, her father had made a very small speech.

He wished that the happiness they felt at the moment would grow and deepen every year they were together.

Then Hermia had changed into her going-away gown which matched the colour of her eyes and had a light cloak over it, a bonnet trimmed with ribbons and flowers of the same colour.

There were very few people awake in the village as they drove through it. The Marquis had been staying only two miles away and there had been no one to notice his arrival at the Church.

Only as they passed Mrs. Burles' cottage did Hermia see Ben peeping out through one of the windows, and she knew that as usual he would be the first to carry the news around the village that something unusual had occurred.

But now it did not matter.

She was married, she was going away with the man she loved, and the Marquis had already planned a long honeymoon, starting first with a few nights at his country house which Hermia had never seen.

He had already told her that he wanted to show her not only all his treasures, inside it, but also the places outside which he had loved as a child.

"The woods meant something to me also," he said, "which I have never confided to anybody except you, and of course, ordinary people would not understand."

"Only witches, fairies and elves!" Hermia smiled.

"And Devils?" he questioned.

"You are not to call yourself that again," she answered. "Now you are back to being the Archangel you were before you fell from grace, and I shall be very angry if anybody calls you a Devil again."

"Except on the race-course," he said, "and my darling, no man in the world could have so much luck as to have you!"

Because it was impossible for Hermia to find words to express how lucky she was she could only press her lips against his.

Later that night as Hermia lay in the great State Bed in which the Marquises of Deverille had slept for generations she moved a little closer to the man beside her.

"Are you awake, my precious?" he asked.

"It is impossible to sleep when I am so happy."

His arms held her to him as he said:

"You are quite certain I have not hurt you? You are so precious and so like a flower that I am afraid of spoiling something which is too perfect to be human."

"I adore you," Hermia said, "and when you loved me it was the most glorious . . . magical thing that ever happened . . . I felt as if we had wings and flew through the sky towards the . . . moon."

There was a little pause before she said the last word.

Then as she felt the Marquis was curious she explained:

"When I was in London I looked at the moon and felt you were as far out of reach as it was, and that I could never . . . never mean . . . anything to you, except somebody to whom you felt you . . . owed a debit."

The Marquis turned so that he could look down at her.

The only light came from a candle that was beside the bed, but he thought that no one could look lovelier or more ethereal.

"How can I tell you what you mean to me?" he asked, "or explain that you have given me back the dreams, the ambitions and ideals that were mine when I was young?"

"That is what I want you to have," Hermia said. "I could not bear you ever again to be bored or cynical. And, darling, because I love you I feel I have so much to give you."

She knew the Marquis would understand that she was talking about spiritual rather than material things and he said:

"That is what I want to receive and, what we will one day give our children—an understanding of the real value of things, not the tawdry luxuries which can only be counted up in cash."

Hermia gave a little sigh.

"And yet if we spend money in the right way we can do so much to make people happy. Papa told me last night that he has already started on the Timber-Yard and is employing twenty-five men and hopes to be able to employ more."

She knew that her husband smiled and she went on:

"I also have a suspicion that you and Nanny have come to some special arrangement, which is why Papa and Mama are looking so well. There are a great many delicious things in the larder that I have never seen there before!"

"You should not go poking your nose into other people's business!" the Marquis said.

"I did not believe anybody as . . . important as you could be so human . . . so understanding, so very, very . . . wonderful," Hermia said with a little break in her voice, "and that is why I say you are now an Archangel! And you make me love you more every moment of the day and night."

The Marquis kissed her eyes and said:

"I find you not only irresistible, but an enchantment from which no man could escape."

"Do you . . . want to?"

"You know the answer to that," he said, "and, my precious, how can I ever have thought I was happy before I found you?"

"You did not look happy!"

"I suspected everybody of having ulterior motives, for everything they did and everything they said. Then you came along like a star which had dropped from the sky, and everything changed."

"I want you always to feel like that," Hermia murmured. "But supposing I had . . . lost you?"

The horror she had felt when she found him lying on the floor of the Witch's cottage and the memory of his cousin descending from the roof to kill him swept over her.

Instinctively she put out her arms to draw him closer to her as if she would protect him against any danger, any evil.

As if he read her thoughts he said:

"I am safe now and with your love to encircle me, nothing can hurt me. It is love, my precious, that is the magic spell that holds us both enthralled from now until eternity."

"And I love you, my wonderful, kind, marvellous husband," Hermia said, "until there are no words to tell you how much you mean to me."

"I do not need words."

His lips held hers captive, and as she felt his hand touching the softness of her body and his heart beating against hers she knew the fire was rising in him and felt flames flickering within herself.

Then as he carried her up into the sky, they were inside the moon, coveted by the stars, and there was only love—the love that would hold them spellbound until the end of time.

A SONG
OF LOVE

Author's Note

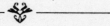

"I am going with my Soul betwitched
For I have dreamed my life away . . ."

When I visited Provence this year, for the second time, I found it just as mystical, magical and entrancing as I have described it in this novel.

The beauty of the women of Arles, the wonder of the barren rocks of Les Baux, the eeriness of the Gorges of Verdon were exactly what I expected but I did not hear the nightingales.

In 1938 an author wrote:

"I have never known such a place for nightingales and I acquired the habit of writing to their voices. In the Cypress trees and in the thickets there are nightingales . . . I had never imagined that so many could be got together for the nightingale is a solitary bird and does not like the propinquity of its own species."

And what should the nightingale sing about except love, especially in Provence? Like the song of Uc de St. Cinc, a 13th century Troubadour:

"To be in love is to stretch towards
heaven through a woman."

CHAPTER ONE

1889

*L*ady Sherington gazed out of the window onto the very formal garden at the back of the *Duc* d'Aubergue's house in the Champs Élysées.

She was thinking that Paris was far more exciting than she had expected it to be, especially in one particular.

As the sun shone on her fair hair she looked very young, in fact, far younger than she actually was and very beautiful.

It had been amazingly fortunate, she thought, that the *Duchesse* d'Aubergue had been a friend for so many years.

They had met the first time when Lord Sherington had taken her to a formal party at the French Embassy and she had been afraid that neither her gown nor her jewels would compete with those of the other guests.

The *Duchesse* had, however, singled her out and they had been friends all through the succeeding years. Now when she had specially wanted to come to Paris, Lorraine d'Aubergue had invited her to stay as long as she wished.

"How lucky I am!" Lady Sherington said to herself. "So very, very lucky!"

The door of the Salon opened and she turned

167

quickly with an expectant look in her eyes to see the woman of whom she had been thinking.

Lorraine d'Aubergue certainly looked extremely *chic* as only a Frenchwoman could, and the elegance of her gown with its satin bustle and the touches of lace under her chin made Lady Sherington know once again that she could not compete with her French friend.

"Ah, here you are, Susi!" the *Duchesse* exclaimed in English with the merest trace of an accent. "I just wanted to say good-bye. I suppose you would not wish to change your mind and come with me to the Prince's luncheon? It will be a very impressive gathering."

"I am sorry, Lorraine," Lady Sherington replied, "but you know I promised . . ."

"I know, dearest, I am only teasing, although I cannot say that I approve of what you are doing."

Susi Sherington looked worried.

"Is it—wrong of—me?" she asked hesitatingly.

"Not exactly wrong," her friend replied, "shall I say a trifle indiscreet?"

She laughed and threw up her hands in a typically French gesture.

"But, *ma Cherie* why should you not be indiscreet in Paris when the sun is shining, you are unattached and —in love?"

Lady Sherington gave a little cry of protest.

"Lorraine!"

Even as she spoke the colour flooded up her pink-and-white cheeks.

"Of course you are," the *Duchesse* insisted, "and Jean de Girone is very much in love with you! But be careful, Susi, that he does not break your heart!"

"Why should you—say that?"

Lady Sherington had turned away to stand once again looking out onto the garden, now with unseeing eyes.

"My dear, I have known Jean for many years, as I

have known you. He is the most attractive man in France, but the most unpredictable and undependable."

The *Duchesse* paused, then said in a different tone which was one of concern:

"You are not serious, Susi, in what you feel for him?"

Lady Sherington did not answer and after a moment the *Duchesse* continued:

"I blame myself, I should have made it clear when he first met you that he is a heart-breaker; a man who plucks the most beautiful flowers by the wayside and when they fade, throws them away."

Still Lady Sherington did not speak and the *Duchesse* went on:

"It is not only that. Now that Jean is free of his tiresome wife, he has to marry money."

"He—behaves as if he is—very rich!"

Lady Sherington spoke almost as if she was startled.

"He was," the *Duchesse* replied. "As long as the *Comtesse* was alive. But her father made sure that as there were no children of the marriage, Marie-Thérèse's enormous dowry should return, on her death, to her family."

The *Duchesse* made an expressive gesture as she added:

"*Hélas!* For Jean this was a cruel twist of fate! To have the handling of a huge fortune and then to lose it because his wife loved God and not him!"

"What do you mean?" Susi Sherington asked.

Because she was curious she turned her face towards her friend again.

The *Duchesse* sat down in a chair by the window.

"It is very remiss of me not to have told you this before," she said, "but I had wanted you to have a wonderful time in Paris. So when Jean singled you out and danced with you all night the first time you met I knew how amusing you would find him. He is the best dancer I have ever known."

Lady Sherington moved towards a chair opposite her friend.

"Go on," she pleaded.

"I thought," Lorraine d'Aubergue continued, "that Jean would give you the fun you have missed for so long, could thrill you with compliments which he can pay more skilfully than any other man I know, and make you look as beautiful as you were when we first met."

She smiled a little wryly before she added:

"He has certainly done that! But, Susi, dearest Susi, I shall never forgive myself if, when it is all over, you are left unhappy and heart-broken as so many other women have been."

"I have not said that I am—in love with—the *Comte*," Susi Sherington said a little defiantly.

"You do not have to tell me in words anything that is so obvious," the *Duchesse* replied. "I saw it by the look in your eyes as I came into the Salon just now when you thought it was Jean arriving."

"Now you are—making me embarrassed."

"I just want you to be sensible," the *Duchesse* replied. "Flirt with Jean, let him make you feel that you are the only woman in the world, as he will do! But remember that to Jean love is like a very good meal: it is delicious, but when it is finished, it is very easy to forget when you have eaten!"

It was now Susi who made a gesture and it was one of protest.

"You make him sound—horrible."

"I have no wish to do that," the *Duchesse* said quickly. "I want you to enjoy your little flirtation, but remember that is all it must be."

She looked at the expression on her friend's face and went on quickly:

"Already Jean's relatives, and there are a number of them, all very distinguished, are thumbing through the *Almanach de Gotha* to find him a suitable and rich bride. She will have to be very rich to be able to keep up the Castle Girone, which is the most imposing in the whole of Provence, and the most historical. Jean has told you about it?"

"He has not said—much about it."

"Good!" the *Duchesse* exclaimed. "That means that he is not as serious as I feared, because let me tell you that the one great love in Jean's life is his home, his estates and the history of the Girones which makes them one of the greatest families in France."

"I remember reading about Provence," Susi said. "The Troubadours, the battles, the Sieges by the invading hordes."

"That is all in Jean's blood," Lorraine d'Aubergue replied, "and part of his mystique which attracts all women like a magnet."

"I can—see," Susi said hesitatingly after a moment, "that I have been—very foolish even to—listen to him."

"*Non, non!* You must not feel like that!" the *Duchesse* cried. "Of course you must listen to Jean, of course you must enjoy being with him! There is no-one in the whole of Paris who can be more enthralling and more entertaining. I am only telling you this, Susi, because of the position you are in."

"I—understand," Susi said in a low voice. "Thank you for—telling me."

The *Duchesse* sighed.

"How I hate to be a spoil-sport! But when you told me of the conditions your husband laid down in his Will, I knew it would be impossible for you to marry a Frenchman."

She paused for a moment before she said:

"Not that I am suggesting for one moment that Jean's intentions would be honourable, even if you could remain as rich as you are now. When he marries it must be to a member of the *Ancien régime* and of course somebody young who can give him children."

She sighed before she continued:

"The children he should have had long ago, if his

171

wife had not been abnormal, a woman who should never have been married, who should have gone into a Convent as soon as she was old enough to take her vows."

"Then—why did she marry him!" Lady Sherington cried.

"Because Jean's father wanted a daughter-in-law rich enough to keep up the Castle, and Marie Thé-rèse's family wanted the prestige of her being the *Comtesse* de Girone."

"I—I suppose I had forgotten that the French always have arranged marriages."

"But of course!" the *Duchesse* answered. "It is a very sensible arrangement and works out in most cases extremely well. It is just that poor Jean was unlucky. Or perhaps the wicked Fairy at his Christening was determined that his life should not be entirely a bed of roses."

"It certainly sounds as if she cursed him!"

"That is exactly what she did," the *Duchesse* agreed. "Jean had good looks, charm, intelligence, a family history which goes back to the Princes of Provence— and a wife who hated him from the moment that she walked down the aisle on his arm!"

"Is that—really true?" Susi asked softly. "I feel so sorry for him."

"So do I," Lorraine d'Aubergue said. "But remember, Susi dearest, he will marry again very shortly, and it will be to somebody rich and young who will adore him and because she is the *Comtesse* de Girone, will turn a 'blind eye' on the many other women who will succeed those who have been captivating his heart since he was old enough to know he had one."

The clock on the mantelshelf chimed the hour and the *Duchesse* gave an exclamation of horror.

"I shall be late!" she cried, "and the *Duc* will be furious! I promised to pick him up on my way to the luncheon."

She rose to her feet with a rustle of her silk gown, then she put her arms around Susi and kissed her.

"Forgive me, dearest, if I have cast a shadow on the sunshine of your day, but I have to look after you and although I am younger than you, I feel immeasurably older and, if it does not sound conceited, immeasurably wiser."

"I know you mean to be kind," Susi replied in her soft voice, "and I am very—very grateful for your—affection."

The *Duchesse* kissed her again, then hurried from the room giving a despairing glance at the clock on the mantelpiece as if she thought she had perhaps been mistaken when the hour had chimed.

As the door closed behind her Susi Sherington rose once again to her feet to stand looking into the garden.

The *Duchesse* had been right when she said she had cast a shadow on the sunshine. Something now was missing; something which had been there before.

"Lorraine is right—I must be—sensible," she admonished herself.

At the same time she knew that never in her whole life had she felt as she had these last few days since she had met the *Comte* de Girone.

From the moment she had been introduced to him and had seen an expression in his dark eyes, something strange had happened within her breast.

It was a feeling that had intensified during the evening when they had danced together, then sat talking in a manner which made words seem unnecessary as they could understand each other without them.

'I suppose,' Susi thought now, 'it is only because I am so unsophisticated, so countrified, that I not only —believed everything he said, but felt he was different —very—very different from any man in the whole world.'

As if the very thought of the *Comte* conjured him up,

the door of the Salon opened and a servant announced:

"*Monsieur le Comte* de Girone, *Madame!*"

In spite of her resolve to be sensible, despite everything she had heard the *Duchesse* say, Susi Sherington felt her heart leap in her breast and an uncontrollable excitement sweep through her whole body as she turned round.

Just for a moment the *Comte* stood looking at her across the Salon. Then as the servant shut the door behind him, he moved towards her with an unmistakable delight.

He was the most handsome, attractive man Susi had ever seen, and the expression in his eyes drew hers so that she could not look away from him, but could only watch him drawing nearer as if she was mesmerised.

Automatically she put out her hand and as he took it and she felt his lips on the softness of her skin, a little quiver ran through her.

"Is it possible that you can be more beautiful than the last time I saw you?" the *Comte* asked in his deep voice. "You are so lovely that I cannot believe you are real and not part of the dream I dreamt all night."

With an effort Susi took her hand from his.

"It is very—kind of you to—ask me to have—luncheon with you in the—Bois," she said in a tense little voice, "but—I think perhaps it is an—invitation I should have—refused."

The *Comte* was still, his eyes searching her face.

"What has happened?"

"Nothing—I—I was just thinking . . ."

"Somebody has been talking to you," he said. "When I left you last night you were looking forward to our little expedition as much as I was."

Susi did not reply. Now she was looking away from him, and his eyes flickered over her straight little nose and the curve of her lips before he said softly:

"Have you really changed your mind about me? Or

are you trying, when it is much, much too late, to be sensible?"

This was the very word Lorraine had used and as Susi started the *Comte* laughed softly.

"It is as I suspected," he said. "Lorraine has been giving you a lecture on propriety and of course, on getting too involved with me."

"Lorraine—loves me," Susi said quickly, feeling she must defend the *Duchesse*.

"As I do."

Susi drew in her breath. It was impossible not to know when he spoke in that way, that something very strange swept through her body to make every nerve vibrate to the fascination of him.

"Yes, I love you!" the *Comte* said, "and we both knew what we felt last night. But I told myself it was too soon to put it into words and because, my darling, you were very innocent and unspoilt, I must not rush you."

Susi's lips moved, but no words would come from them and the *Comte* went on:

"Why should we waste our time in pretending and trying to hide what we both know is the truth? I loved you from the very moment I saw you, and I think I am not mistaken in believing that you love me too."

The soft and caressing way in which he spoke made it very difficult to reply, and yet with a little cry Susi managed to ejaculate:

"We—must not—you know—we must—not!"

"Why not?"

"Because . . ."

It was impossible to finish the sentence.

How could she speak of marriage to him when he had not mentioned it to her?

"Because we come from—different—worlds," she forced herself to say. "Lorraine says we must only have a—light amusing—flirtation."

"And do you think that is what it is?"

"I—I have never had many flirtations, but—I feel

175

that we should—not be talking as if what we—felt was
—serious."

The *Comte* laughed and when Susi looked surprised
he explained:

"I am laughing, my precious, because you are so
ridiculous, so utterly and completely absurd!"

Susi glanced at him, saw the expression in his eyes
and looked away again.

"Do you really think this is a flirtation between two
people who have met at a dance and just want to have
fun for a few hours, a few days, a few weeks?" the
Comte asked.

"That is—what it—has to be."

"Because Lorraine says so? My dearest dear, can
you really control the beat of your heart, the throb in
your voice, the expression in your eyes?"

She did not answer and he went on:

"Last night we talked to each other and it did not
really matter what we said because my heart was
speaking to your heart of love, real love, Susi! We both
knew it was something very different from what either
of us had ever felt before."

"It was—different for me, but not—for you."

"Who is to know that except myself?" the *Comte*
asked.

She did not answer and after a long moment he
said:

"Look at me, Susi. I want you to look at me."

Slowly, as if she was afraid to obey him and yet was
compelled to do so, she turned her head towards him
and he saw her eyes as they looked up at him were
very blue, worried and afraid.

For a moment they were both very still. Then almost as if they did not move but melted into each
other, his arms went round her and his lips were on
hers.

At first his mouth was very gentle, feeling the softness of hers, then he became more possessive, more

demanding and instinctively they both drew closer, and still closer as their kiss became more passionate.

Only when the world seemed to have stopped breathing and there was nothing in the whole Universe but the strength of his arms and the wonder of his kiss did Susi free herself to hide her face against his neck.

"Je t'adore, ma Cherie, I love you! I swear that no kiss I have ever given has been so perfect, so absolutely wonderful!"

His voice was a little hoarse and unsteady.

"Please—please . . ." Susi whispered, "do not make me feel—like this."

His arms tightened and he smiled.

"Like what, my lovely one? There is no need for you to answer, because I feel the same."

"It is—not possible," Susi tried to say.

But even as she spoke the *Comte* put his hand under her chin and turned her face up to his.

"You are so beautiful," he said, "so incredibly breathtakingly beautiful, but it is more than that. It is something I have looked for, longed for and begun to believe did not exist until I saw you."

Then he was kissing her again, fiercely, demandingly, until she felt the fire on his lips awaken a flame within herself.

It seemed as if her whole body was alight with a fire that burnt its way through them both, and came from the very heart of the sun . . .

An hour later, sitting under the trees in a Restaurant in the Bois, the *Comte* said:

"Now we can talk."

They had driven in his chaise saying hardly a word to each other but Susi knew her whole body was tinglingly aware of him.

Now at the small table she was aware that his

personality vibrating from him made it impossible to escape his magnetism.

'He is so handsome, so overwhelmingly masculine,' she thought, and blushed at her very thoughts.

His eyes were watching her and because through shyness she could not meet them she busied herself with taking off her long white gloves. As she did so, she saw the sunshine glittering on the gold of her wedding-ring and felt as if the very brightness of it reproached her.

Although after a year of mourning for her husband Susi had laid aside the mauve and grey gowns that she had worn for the last three months, something sensitive in her nature had hesitated at immediately reverting to bright colours.

Instead today everything she wore was white, her chiffon gown trimmed with a heavy Valenciennes lace which also covered the crown of her hat and decorated the white chiffon sunshade she carried.

With her fair hair, her blue eyes and her pink-and-white skin, it made her look very young and, the *Comte* thought, untouched.

He corrected himself and changed the word to 'unawakened.' He knew it would be the most exciting thing he had ever done to awaken to an awareness of love, this enchanting creature, who had done something very strange to his heart from the moment they had met.

"Now," he said aloud, "you can tell me all the unkind and untrue things Lorraine has told you about me."

"They were not unkind," Susi said quickly. "She was only worrying about me because, as you know already, I am very—out of—place in Paris."

The *Comte* smiled.

"If you believe that," he said, "then you have never looked in your mirror!"

Before Susi could speak he added:

"Yet I agree that in a way you are out of place, not

A Song of Love

because you are unsophisticated as you were thinking, but because you are so different from the women we met last night at dinner, and all the friends with whom Lorraine fills her hours and finds amusing."

"Why—am I different?" Susi enquired.

"Because, my darling," the *Comte* replied, "you are someone out of a fairy-tale, a 'Sleeping Beauty,' unawakened and waiting for a kiss to bring you to life."

He saw the colour creep up over her face as he spoke of a kiss and thought it was the most beautiful thing he had ever seen.

"If you blush like that," he said, "I shall take you away this moment among the trees and kiss you until neither of us can breathe or think of anything except each other!"

For a moment Susi could not take her eyes from his. Then she glanced around saying in a frightened little voice:

"P.please—you must not say such—things to me— here—not when there are people listening—and watching us."

"They are all very intent upon themselves," the *Comte* replied, "and we have to talk about ourselves, Susi, as you well know."

"Then we must talk—sensibly!" she said firmly, "and I think Lorraine would be—shocked that after we have known each other for such a short time, you should call me by my—Christian name."

The *Comte* laughed.

"It is impossible for us to explain to Lorraine or anybody else that we have known each other since the beginning of time, and all through the years we have been journeying towards each other until finally fate allowed us to meet."

"Do you—really believe that?"

Her eyes were like a child's listening to a fairy-story and the *Comte* said:

"I swear to you that I believe that because it is true.

179

I have been looking for you all my life, and if you imagine that now I have found you I will ever let you go, you are very much mistaken!"

"B.but—we have to . . ." Susi tried to say, "I mean . . ."

Once again it was difficult to put what she was thinking into words and the *Comte* put his hand over hers that lay on the table.

As he felt her quiver at his touch, he said:

"You must know that we will be married as soon as it is possible!"

Susi's eyes widened.

"M.married?" she whispered.

Then she took her hand away from his and said in a very different voice:

"You must—forget you—said that."

"Why?"

"Because there is—something I must tell you."

"I am listening."

It seemed for a moment as if the words would not come. Then at last, not looking at him but blindly across the Restaurant, Susi said:

"My husband—was a very—rich man—as I expect —Lorraine has told you. I was—married when I was very young—and he was—very much—older than I."

There was a note in her voice which told the *Comte* what the discrepancy in their ages had meant, but he did not interrupt and Susi went on:

"My family—who were not well off—were delighted that anyone so—important and so—wealthy as Lord Sherington should have wished to—marry me. He was very kind and—generous to them—as he was to me—but when he—died last year his—Will was somewhat different from what—everyone had expected."

Now Susi clenched her hands together in her lap and for a moment it seemed as if it was impossible for her to go on.

Then with an effort she said:

"My husband—left me a very large income—but if I

remarried I was only to have an allowance of £200 a year!"

Her voice died away and Susi wished that she could get up and leave before the *Comte* spoke.

She dared not look at him.

She could not bear to see that the expression on his face had changed, that the love which he had said was so real had gone and in its place there was something else; something she dreaded.

She had the feeling, because he was so understanding and sympathetic where women were concerned, that he would continue to compliment her, to flirt with her and he would try not to let her feel embarrassed by what she had told him.

At the same time an ecstasy and a rapture beyond anything she had ever imagined would have gone.

There was a little pause before Susi said:

"You must have the children—you were unable to have with your first wife."

The *Comte* smiled.

"I have thought of that too. Lorraine told me you were married when you were seventeen and your daughter was born when you were eighteen. As she is eighteen, that means that you are now thirty-six. We are the same age, my lovely one."

Susi looked at him wide-eyed as he went on:

"I have calculated that we can have two sons before I refuse to allow you to have any more children."

"Two—sons?"

It was difficult to say the words.

"It is a tradition of the Girones to produce sons, but if one is a daughter, then if she looks like you, I shall love her overwhelmingly."

Susi gave a little choking laugh that was half a sob.

"How can you—talk like this? How can you have—worked it all—out?"

"My precious darling, I told you that I love you."

"But Frenchmen do not marry in such a way, Lorraine said . . ."

"Forget Lorraine and listen to me," the *Comte* interposed. "You belong to me, and nothing and nobody is going to stop us from being married. Because we have taken so many years to find each other, it is going to be very soon, and I have already written home to tell my grandmother that we shall be arriving to stay with her in two or three days time."

"How can we—I mean . . ."

Susi's almost incoherent voice stopped suddenly. Then she exclaimed:

"Trina! You have forgotten Trina!"

"No, I have not forgotten," the *Comte* said, "and she, of course, can come with us. I realise the reason you came to Paris was to collect her from School."

"But what will Trina think about you—and me?"

"If she is anything like as sweet and adorable as her mother, she will want you to be happy," the *Comte* replied, "and I think, my precious, we both know that I can give you a happiness you have never known in your life so far."

That was true, Susi thought wildly. At the same time she felt as if everything was swimming round her and it was difficult to think clearly.

Because the *Comte* had everything mapped out, because she seemed to have no say in what she should do or not do, he had made everything seem inevitable and yet at the same time frightening.

When she had come to Paris to stay with Lorraine she had made the excuse that she intended to collect Trina from the Convent.

At the same time, she was aware that she wanted to live a very different life from what she had done so far, but she had never envisaged for a moment that she might find another husband.

She had always seen herself as living in the Sherington Mansion in Hampshire with the Sherington ancestors frowning down upon her from almost every wall, and continuing in her position as 'Lady

Bountiful' until Trina married and she moved to the Dower House.

Because Lord Sherington had no sons and there was no heir to the title, the house and estate had been left to his daughter with a proviso in his Will that unless Trina's husband had an ancestral name of greater importance than Sherington, her husband must hyphen his name with hers.

It was the sort of rather complex, pompous idea that only her husband could have conceived, Susi had thought, then felt ashamed of being disloyal.

The whole Will had been filled with instructions that people should or should not do so and so, legacies to relations and retired servants, gifts to old friends, and quite generous contributions to charities and organisations in which Lord Sherington had been interested.

The only person who had been harshly treated was Susi herself, and it seemed inconceivable when the Will was read by the Solicitor that he could have made it a condition of her marrying again, that she would go to her new husband almost as penniless as she had come to him.

She knew this had been laid down because he had been jealous not of her behaviour with other men, but of her youth.

During the last ten years of their marriage he had been crippled with arthritis, unable to move about except in a wheel-chair, and he had almost hated her because she could walk, ride and when the occasion demanded, dance.

They had gone to the Hunt Balls because he was Lord Lieutenant of the County.

Susi had known as she danced with those who asked her as a matter of politeness because of her position that her husband followed her around the dance-floor with his eyes, not admiringly, as some of the younger men did, but angrily and resentfully.

He was always particularly disagreeable on the

drive home and the following days until he could forget that he had watched her dance while he had been
unable to get on his feet.

It was this resentment and envy which had made
him determined that if it was possible she would remain unmarried until she was too old to want another
man in her life.

As Susi had listened to the Will she could almost
hear him pointing out to her the advantages of re-
maining Lady Sherington—the grandeur, the comfort
of the big house, the luxuries she would still enjoy
when she lived on the estate, the horses she could
ride.

And there would be carriages at her disposal, an
army of servants, besides a very large income which
she could spend as she wished, entertaining in London, travelling, having anything she wanted, as long
as she did not share it with another man.

"I am still young," Susi had told herself the night
after the funeral.

When she got into the huge comfortable double-
bed in which she had slept alone for so many years,
she quite unaccountably cried herself to sleep.

Looking back, she had forgotten for the moment
that the *Comte* was beside her, his eyes watching her.

Then at last when she felt the silence between them
was full of things that must be said, she managed to
whisper:

"You know it is—impossible from—your point of
view."

"That is for me to decide."

"No—it must be—my decision."

"Why yours?"

"Because I—have to think about—you."

"If you are thinking of me, you will want me to be
happy."

"That is what I want you to be, and that means that
your Castle which Lorraine says you love more than

anything else, must be properly maintained, so you must have money."

"You think that is more important than love?"

"You—you have—loved many—times."

"I am not denying that there have been many women in my life, but do you imagine that what I felt for them was anything like the love I have for you?"

She did not answer but glanced up at him for a moment and he saw the bewilderment in her eyes.

"Oh, my precious darling," he said, "you are so unworldly, so innocent in so many ways. How can I make you understand that what I feel for you is completely and absolutely different from anything I have known in the past? There are no words in which to explain it, I can only show you, so that is why we must be married very quickly."

"And supposing," Susi murmured, "supposing when we are—married—and I am not agreeing that we should be—you find me—disappointing. You will have lost—everything."

The *Comte* smiled.

"I shall not be disappointed."

"How—can you be sure?"

"I am sure in the same way that I was sure when I saw you that you are the woman for whom I have been searching through all eternity."

There was something in his voice that made Susi's heart beat so quickly that she could not reply.

Then their food arrived and they tried to eat what the *Comte* had ordered.

After luncheon was over they did not immediately step into his chaise which was waiting for them outside, but instead they wandered away under the trees in the Bois until they found a secluded spot by a small stream and sat down on a bench.

Then the *Comte*, turning so that he was half-facing Susi, put out his hand and after a few seconds' hesitation she gave him hers. Very gently he unbuttoned and drew off her glove.

He kissed her fingers one by one, then her palm, making little thrills run through her so that her breath came quickly from between her lips and she felt her heart thumping in her breast.

"I love you!" he said softly, speaking both in French and in English.

Then as he kissed her hand again he said:

"You will come to Provence with me the day after tomorrow?"

"You are—sure that is—something I—should do?"

"I want you to see our future home."

"I am not agreeing that is what it will be. How can we—afford it?"

"As I have told you, we will manage, and as it happens I already have an idea."

"An idea?" Susi queried.

"When I knew I meant to marry you, I began to think what we could do about the Castle, which is very big and entails a lot of money being spent on it. But it is so beautiful that I want it always to look its best, especially when it belongs to you."

There was a note in his voice which told Susi that Lorraine had been right when she said that the Castle was his great love.

She asked herself frantically how she could take it from him.

'If I do so, he will hate me,' she thought, 'because he will blame me!'

In her imagination she saw the ceilings falling in neglect, the stonework crumbling, the rugs becoming threadbare, the curtains torn and faded.

Could their love, wonderful though it seemed at the moment, survive the years when he would reproach her for having caused him to be unfaithful to something which was part of himself?

'I cannot—do it,' Susi thought.

Then taking her hand from his because it was difficult to think while he was touching her, she said, using his Christian name for the first time:

"Jean—I have something to say to you."

"What is it?" he asked.

He knew before she spoke from the tension of her body, the way her fingers were linked together, that what she was about to say was something immensely important at least to her.

There was a long pause before Susi said in a voice he could hardly hear:

"I—love you—but because I—love you I know that I—cannot hurt you—so I have—something to—suggest."

The *Comte* knew by the way her voice trembled that she was finding it hard to say the words that came to her lips.

He waited and after a moment she went on:

"It may be—wrong and wicked of me—but because you must not—spoil your home—or your future—perhaps we could be—together—without being—married."

The last words were spoken in a rush and now Susi's face, which had been very pale while she was speaking, was suffused with colour.

For a moment there was only silence. Then the *Comte* said in a voice she had never heard before:

"Oh, my darling, my precious, wonderful little love, now I know what you feel for me."

He knew as he spoke that her suggestion was one which his smart Parisian friends would have expected him to have made. But that Susi with her conventional background and her intrinsic purity, should have suggested it, made him know exactly what it meant for her to put it into words.

He took both her hands in his and feeling them tremble beneath his fingers, he said softly:

"Look at me, Susi!"

She obeyed him, her eye-lashes fluttering, and he knew how shy and at the same time, ashamed she was of what she had suggested.

"I adore you! I worship you!" he said very quietly.

187

"I want to kneel at your feet and kiss the ground on which you stand. Now I know that your love, my darling, equals mine, and it would be impossible for us ever to be separated from each other!"

He bent and kissed her hands one after the other and said:

"I shall always remember what you offered me, and I must refuse simply because while I want you and need you with my whole body, my soul tells me what we feel for each other comes from God and without His blessing we would both feel incomplete."

"Oh—Jean . . . !"

There were tears in Susi's eyes and they ran down her cheeks.

Then regardless that someone might see them, the *Comte* put his arms around her and kissed away her tears before his lips found hers.

CHAPTER TWO

"*I* am very excited, Sister Antoinette!" Trina said as they drove away from the station in the Duc's magnificent carriage drawn by two horses.

"I am sure you are, Trina," Sister Antoinette agreed in her calm, quiet voice. "But as the Mother Superior has always said, we must learn to control our emotions."

Trina flashed her a little smile and replied:

"That is difficult to do when I have not seen Mama

for over a year. I am sure she will think that I have altered."

"I expect she will," Sister Antoinette said. "You are much taller for one thing, and you are certainly not as thin as you were when you first came to us."

Trina laughed.

"I was 'all skin and bone,' my Governess used to say, and especially just before I left England, because I had Whooping Cough that winter. What I needed was the sunshine which I found in France."

She spoke with a warm affection in her voice, then leaned forward to stare at the high houses they were passing. With their grey shutters she thought they were so characteristically French that she would have recognized them anywhere in the world.

"Is it really a year since you have seen Lady Sherington?" Sister Antoinette asked as if she was working it out in her own mind.

"Yes, a year and nearly two months," Trina replied. "If you remember, during the Christmas holidays after Papa died, Mama let me go to Spain to stay with Perdita and in the Easter holidays I was in Rome with my friend Veronica Borghese."

"Of course! I recall that now," Sister Antoinette exclaimed. "You are really a much-travelled young woman, are you not, Trina?"

"I wonder if, as the Mother Superior hoped, it has made me wiser," Trina replied with a touch of mischief in her voice, "but it has certainly made me appreciate the world that I have seen so far. But I still think I love England the best."

"That is as it should be," the Nun answered. "After all, England is your home."

With a smile Trina sat thinking of the huge house in Hampshire in which she had been brought up.

Sometimes she thought it seemed rather gloomy and she could understand why her mother had pressed her to stay with her friends immediately after her father had died.

But there had been horses to ride, her dogs to follow her everywhere she went, and a hundred other things to do on the big estate that she had never found anywhere else.

"Now Mama and I will be together," she told herself, "and that will be wonderful!"

She felt a warm happiness sweep over her at the thought that now her mother could be with her far more than she had been in the past.

Then Papa had always wanted her to be with him, and Trina knew, even though he did not say so, that he disapproved of the way in which she and her mother would ride alone without a groom, go boating on the lake, or skating when it was covered with ice.

Mama was such fun, far more fun than any of the girls at the Convent even though she had many friends amongst them.

Now as they approached the Champs Élysées where Trina knew the *Duc's* house was situated, she found herself sending up a little prayer that her mother would be pleased with her.

'I want her to love me, and I want to be just like her,' Trina thought.

The carriage drew up outside the front door and even as Trina stepped into the Hall a door at the other end of it opened and there was her mother.

"Trina!"

"Mama!"

As the two voices spoke together, Trina was running towards her mother and their arms were around each other.

"Darling Mama! I have been longing, simply longing to see you!" Trina cried.

"And I have been counting the hours," Susi Sherington replied.

She drew her daughter into the Salon, then as the sun coming through the window illuminated her face under the small bonnet she gave an exclamation.

Trina looked at her apprehensively, as Lady Sherington exclaimed:

"But you have changed, you have altered! Why, Trina, you are exactly like me!"

It was true. Trina had grown to the same height as her mother and the thin, angular body of the adolescent had developed until their figures were almost identical.

They had the same fair, corn-gold hair, the same gentian blue eyes, that seemed almost too large for their small faces.

Looking at her daughter Susi began to laugh.

"It is absurd! Ridiculous! We might be twins!"

"I cannot imagine anyone I would rather have as a twin than you, Mama."

Susi sat down suddenly on a chair.

"I am a little bewildered. I was expecting a child, but I find instead that you are very grown up, a young woman, and a very beautiful one!"

"You are paying compliments to yourself, Mama!" Trina teased.

Susi looked startled for a moment, then she laughed too.

"Oh, Trina, I have missed you so terribly all the time you have been in France, but it was rather sad and gloomy at home after dear Papa died."

"I knew that was why you told me to stay with my friends in the holidays," Trina said. "It is so like you, Mama, to be so unselfish. But I would really like to have been with you."

"I had Aunt Dorothy and Aunt Agnes to keep me company."

"Poor, poor Mama!" Trina said, making a grimace, and they both laughed.

"They vied with each other at disapproving everything I did," Susi said, "and that was why I came to France to meet you! They disapproved of that too!"

"I am sure they would disapprove of the *Duchesse*," Trina said. "Her niece who was at School with me told me how smart and witty she is, and how the invitations to her parties are sought by everyone in Paris."

"That is true," Susi agreed, "and she is giving a party for you tonight. All sorts of exciting young men have been invited to meet you, and I am only hoping that you have a suitable gown to wear."

"Do not worry, Mama," Trina replied. "When you told me to buy some clothes in Rome at Easter, I spent an absolute fortune!"

"I am glad," Susi said simply. "I like what you are wearing now. It is very becoming."

Trina jumped up to slip off her travelling-cape, then twirled round and round to let her mother see the very elegant bustle and the waist which the girls at School had said enviously could be spanned by a man's two hands.

"You have always had very good taste, Trina," Susi said, "but of course, I have been imagining you in little girl's dresses."

"I have a whole wardrobe with which to dazzle you, Mama, but we must still go shopping together. There are lots of things I want to buy."

Susi hesitated, then she said:

"There will not be much—time for—shopping."

"Why not?"

"Because we are leaving—here the day after tomorrow."

"Where are we going?"

Again there was a little hesitation before Susi replied:

"I have—promised to go and stay in—Provence with the *Comtesse* Astrid de Girone."

The way Susi spoke and the way she did not look at her daughter brought a questioning expression to Trina's blue eyes.

"Who is she? I seem to know the name."

"You will find the *Comtes* de Girone mentioned in your history books."

"I will look them up," Trina decided. "But tell me

about the present *Comte*. Is he a friend of yours, Mama?"

At the mention of the *Comte* the colour deepened in Susi's cheeks and Trina gave a little exclamation.

"Oh, Mama, he is your Beau? How exciting!"

"You must not say such things," Susi said quickly. "This is not something I can discuss with you, Trina."

She rose as she spoke in an agitated way and walked across the room to the window as if she would avoid her daughter seeing her face.

Trina gave a little laugh.

"It is no use, Mama," she said. "You could never hide anything from me. Tell me about the *Comte*. Is he fascinating, and is he madly in love with you?"

"Trina!"

Susi looked shocked and at the same time, embarrassed.

Trina went to her side and slipped her arm through hers.

"Dearest Mama, I am not a baby, and although you sent me to be educated at a Convent I have been staying both in Madrid and in Rome where no-one talks of anything but love."

"You are—too young," Susi murmured.

"Nonsense!" Trina retorted. "You were married when you were my age and if you want the truth, I have already had a proposal of marriage!"

"Oh, Trina! Why did you not tell me?"

"It was not a very exciting one. In fact, I would not have married him if he had been the last man in the world! But at least I was one up on most of the girls at School who have not got further than receiving Valentines!"

"You did not tell them?" Susi asked in a horrified voice.

"Of course I told them," Trina answered. "It was a distinct feather in my cap and, as they had not seen him, they did not know how repulsive he was."

Susi looked at her daughter and shook her head.

"I do not know whether to laugh or cry," she said. "I was expecting to look after my baby daughter—to protect her—against the world . . ."

Trina hugged her mother.

"But, Mama, dearest, you have always been the one who needed protecting and looking after. I think I have known that ever since I was about eight."

Susi took a tiny handkerchief and wiped the tears from her eyes.

"Now, Mama," her daughter said firmly. "Tell me about the *Comte* de Girone and the real truth as to why we are going to stay with him in Provence."

Trina took a last look at herself in the long mirror in her bedroom.

"M'mselle est ravissante!" the maid who had been attending her exclaimed.

"Merci," Trina answered. "I do not think I need be afraid in this gown, of feeling completely eclipsed by the Parisian creations."

It was certainly very attractive and exceedingly becoming to Trina.

It was white, because she had been told that as a débutante that was the colour she must wear, the tulle which encircled her shoulders and cascaded from her tiny waist was like clouds touched with rain-drops.

Thousands of diamanté-pieces were sewn on the transparent material which glittered and shimmered with every move she made.

The gown was a perfect foil for her mother's: tonight Susi wished, as she said, to look like a Dowager chaperoning her débutante daughter, she was wearing mauve.

Of all the gowns she had chosen when she was in mourning this had been too elaborate for her to wear and brave the disapproval of her late husband's sisters.

But now she had brought it to Paris and she had known that worn with the diamonds that were part of the Sherington collection, it made her look like a violet greeting the spring after the dark, cold days of winter.

"You look lovely, Mama, perfectly lovely!" Trina exclaimed.

"So do you, my dearest," Susi replied. "Oh, Trina, I am so proud of you, and the *Duchesse* says you will take Paris by storm!"

"I hope so!" Trina said complacently. "After all the polish I have been getting for myself this past year, it will be very lowering if nobody notices me."

"Polish?" Susi queried.

"That is what you told me I should acquire when we discussed my going to a French School."

Susi laughed.

"I though it was a ridiculous word, yet now I think it is the right one."

"Of course it is the right one," Trina agreed, "and I feel exactly like a door-knocker that has been polished until it is gleaming, bright and inviting. But the question is who will raise it and knock?"

"Trina!"

Susi was half-shocked, half-amused by the things her daughter said.

Then they had reached the Salon and she knew that she was tense as they walked together into the room.

All the time she had been dressing Susi had been wondering what Jean would think of Trina and Trina of Jean.

She had, she told herself, so stupidly thought of her daughter as the child she had been when she last saw her, but she could not help wondering if things would be changed now that Trina was obviously a grown up, somewhat self-assured young woman.

There seemed to be a great number of people in the Salon and for the moment their faces swam in front of Susi's eyes.

Then the *Comte* was beside her and at the sound of his voice her heart, as usual, turned a dozen somersaults.

He lifted her hand to his lips.

"I have never seen you in that colour before," he said in a voice that only she could hear. "It enchants me!"

Because it was difficult to think of anything but the touch of his hand on hers and his closeness which made her quiver, it was an effort for Susi to say:

"I—want you to—meet Trina."

She turned towards her daughter saying in what she tried to make a conventional tone:

"Trina, may I present the *Comte* de Girone."

As she spoke she saw the surprise in the *Comte's* eyes and the flashing smile with which Trina greeted him.

"But it is incredible!" he said, looking first at Trina, then at Susi. "Completely incredible! You might be twins!"

"That is exactly what I said to Mama when I arrived," Trina laughed.

It was then that another thought came to Susi; a thought that was so painful it was as if a dagger pierced her breast and she told herself she had been extremely stupid not to have thought of it before.

But of course, that would be the solution to the problems that concerned Jean . . .

"It was absurdly extravagant of you," Susi said.

"What was?" the *Comte* enquired.

"To have your own special carriage attached to the train."

"But I always have one when I go from Paris to Arles."

He spoke casually but they both knew they were thinking that in the past it would have been easy because such luxuries were paid for by his wife's money which was no longer there.

"Besides," the *Comte* went on, "I want you and Trina to enjoy every moment of your visit to my home, and first impressions are very important."

"Yes, very," Susi agreed.

She was thinking of the surprise and what she thought was an expression of delight in his eyes when he had first seen Trina, and she thought that perhaps as time went by, it would be easier to think of them together and not so excruciatingly painful as it was at the moment.

Every instinct in her mind and body had told her the night after the *Duchesse's* party that she would be wise to leave immediately for England and take Trina with her.

It would be difficult for Jean to follow them unless she specially invited him, but if they went anywhere in Europe she was sure he would turn up whatever she might say to try to prevent it.

Then she told herself she must not run away and, if he loved Trina as she was sure he would, then she must be content with his happiness because love was worth the sacrifice of self.

At the same time, it was something she had never envisaged that Trina should look exactly as she had done when Lord Sherington had seen her at her first Ball and three days later asked for her hand in marriage.

She had been astonished when her father told her that he was not only delighted at the idea of her marrying anyone so distinguished but had already given his consent.

If Susi made any protests they had not been listened to. Besides she was not really certain what she felt herself about marrying Lord Sherington or anyone else.

She only knew that he seemed very awe-inspiring and very old.

After all, at fifty, he had lived more than half his life while hers, she felt, had only just begun.

There had been letters, flowers, expensive presents. In fact, as her mother had said: "He is completely enamoured of you."

She had always been kept strictly in the School-Room and had enjoyed no social life until this moment, so it was fascinating to realise that she was looked at with envy by her friends and told over and over again that she was making an oustandingly brilliant marriage.

Once they were married she met very few men and women of her own age.

It was Lord Sherington's contemporaries who were entertained at dinner, who came to stay for the big pheasant shoots at Sherington Park and who would then ask them back to house-parties in Yorkshire and Scotland, and invite them to stay for the classic race-meetings like Ascot and the Derby.

Although the men complimented her and called her a 'pretty little thing' and squeezed her hand when they said goodnight, their wives treated her as if she was still in the School-Room.

When Trina was born Lord Sherington began to talk incessantly about having a son, but then he began to suffer from ill-health.

First it was bronchitis which made him little better than an invalid during the winter months, then arthritis prevented him from enjoying the sports that had been so much a part of his life.

Susi became nurse to a fretful and often disagreeable invalid, but worse than anything else, entertainment of any sort became more and more rare.

It was then Susi found she could escape from her husband's querulous, complaining voice only in the Nursery where she could laugh and play with Trina.

As soon as she was old enough Susi took her away on her own from Nanny's disapproving eyes and they

A SONG OF LOVE

would go for walks in the woods or drive in a pony-cart without a groom.

As the years passed there were a thousand other things which were fun simply because they were both young, could laugh and talk nonsense, when there was no-one else there to look down their noses at Susi for not being more dignified.

Of course there had been no question of her ever thinking of love until a few days ago—or was it a few centuries—when she had first met Jean de Girone.

"Why should he have this strange effect on me?" Susi asked herself.

She looked at him sitting opposite her in the comfortable armchair in the travelling Drawing-Room, so debonair and at the same time, so masterful.

She met his eyes and felt the usual quiver run through her, while every nerve responded to him and she longed in what she thought was a very reprehensible manner to be close in his arms.

Because she felt shy she looked to where on the other side of the compartment Trina was reading a magazine.

"Why are you sitting so far away, Trina?" Susi asked. "Come and talk to the *Comte*."

"I am quite happy where I am," Trina replied, "and I promise to be a most self-effacing gooseberry!"

"I do not want you to be anything of the sort!" Susi said almost crossly, "and you are not to say things like that!"

"Why not, when they are true?"

Trina buried herself once again in her magazine and the *Comte* with a smile in his eyes, said quietly:

"Your daughter has tact."

"But I want you to get to know each other."

"There is plenty of time for that, and at the moment I want to talk to you."

"What about?"

The *Comte* moved to sit next to Susi so as to make it impossible for Trina to hear what he said.

"You have told her about us?" he asked.

Susi did not answer and he waited. She felt that he was willing her to reply whether she wished to do so or not.

"N.not—exactly," she said at length, "but she—guessed."

"She would have been very obtuse not to realise that I love you," the *Comte* said, "and that you love me."

Susi made a little gesture as if she would repudiate the idea, and after a moment he said:

"You have not changed your mind, have you, Susi? I thought last night that somehow there was a barrier between us. I was not certain what it was, but I felt it was there."

"I have—told you that what you have—suggested is —impossible."

"We cannot go over that again," the *Comte* said. "Stop thinking about me and think about yourself. I know what your life has been like until now, and I intend to change it, and completely."

Susi thought if that was possible it would be the most wonderful thing that could ever happen, but she told herself she had to be strong, she had to save him from himself.

If he married Trina, then at least she could see him and hear his voice.

Somewhere, far away at the back of her mind there was a question of whether that would be enough, but she refused to consider it.

Trina, with her great fortune and being so young, was exactly what Jean needed in a wife, and what Castle Girone needed too.

Then as if he knew she was thinking of his home the *Comte* began to talk about it.

"I have been thinking all night of how exciting it will be to show you where I was brought up and where much of the history of Provence was enacted."

He had raised his voice, and now Trina was listening too.

"Is your Castle very old?" she asked.

"Parts of it were there at the time of the Romans," the *Comte* replied, "but what will amuse you most are the strange innovations introduced by my great, great, great-grandfather."

"Who was he?"

"He was *Comte* Bernhard, one of the legendary characters of Provence, an eccentric, a man who will never be forgotten, mostly because magical powers were attributed to him."

"Magical!" Trina exclaimed. "In what way?"

The *Comte* smiled.

"When you have been in Provence for some time you will find that they speak of some people as *fadas*."

"What are they?" Trina enquired.

"They are really visionaries, the painters, the poets, the bewitched who believe in fairies, who see the Virgin in a tree's foliage, and who can predict the future."

"Like the Scottish who are fey," Trina remarked.

"Exactly!" the *Comte* agreed, "and actually the word *fada* comes from *fata*—the fay!"

"And that was what your ancestor was?"

"What everybody believed him to be. But I think, as a matter of fact, he was a bit of a hypocrite."

"Why?" Trina enquired.

She had crossed the carriage now and was sitting as Susi had wanted near to them, a rapt expression on her face, as she listened to the *Comte*.

"My great, great, great-grandfather was an inventor very much ahead of his time," the *Comte* explained. "During his life there was a great deal of strife amongst the different families of Provence and they were continually engaged in battles with the rest of France."

"I remember that their armies were always crossing the Var," Trina cried.

"Exactly!" the *Comte* agreed, "and it was then Bernhard, who knew of the secret passages which were already in the Castle, contrived some more ingenious ones of his own."

"What were they like?" Trina asked.

"There was hardly a main room in the whole building in which it was not possible for him to disappear at a moment's notice."

"How thrilling!" Trina exclaimed, and the *Comte* realised that Susi too was listening with shining eyes.

"He brought craftsmen from Italy, men who were past-masters at that sort of work. You can touch a mantelpiece and it turns round completely, a lever moves a stone in the wall and in a moment it is impossible for anyone to know that you have ever been in the room you have just left."

"Go on," Trina cried as the *Comte* paused.

"There are small staircases hidden in turrets," he continued, "by which you can go from the roof to dungeons without ever setting foot in any other part of the Castle."

"It is the most exciting thing I have ever heard," Trina cried. "Will you show them to us?"

"I will show you those I know about," the *Comte* replied. "As a matter of fact, I am told there are a great many still undiscovered, or rather forgotten over the ages."

"And the people thought," Susi said, "that the *Comte* Bernhard was a magician."

"They thought he had the wings of angels and the cunning of the Devil," the *Comte* replied. "Time after time his enemies stormed the Castle certain he was inside, and yet although they searched it with a whole army of soldiers, they never discovered him."

He laughed as he went on:

"Sometimes he would taunt them from the battlements, and when a hundred archers aimed their arrows at him, they would hear him laughing from lower down near the moat."

"Is there a moat?" Trina enquired.

"In the front of the Castle," the *Comte* replied, "and a draw-bridge."

"It is the sort of Castle I have always dreamt of visiting," she said, "and I am sure it is like the ones Mama described in the fairy-stories she used to tell me when I was a little girl."

"I have already told your mother that she looks as if she belongs in a fairy-story," the *Comte* said.

Susi knew he was thinking of the kiss that had awakened 'The Sleeping Beauty', and she blushed.

"Why are we not staying in the Castle?" Trina asked.

"For two reasons," the *Comte* answered. "First, because my grandmother who lives in the Dower House will chaperone you both, and secondly, for a reason I have not yet told your mother."

"What is it?" Susi asked a little apprehensively.

"I have let the Castle!"

"Let the—Castle?"

Susi repeated the words in a tone of sheer astonishment.

"Only for the summer months, but the sum I was offered was too good to refuse."

The *Comte* paused before he said:

"It will mean I can live there all through the winter without worrying about the expense."

Susi knew this explanation had a special meaning for her, but she said a little incoherently:

"But you—must not do—such a thing. I am—sure it will upset you and be horrible for you to think of having—tenants in the place you love so much."

"When the suggestion was made to me," the *Comte* said, "it seemed as if once again fate had taken a hand in my life and it was something I could not refuse."

Susi knew what he meant, but she could not look at him and it was left to Trina to ask:

"Who are your—tenants? Are they very rich?"

"Immensely so," the Comte replied. "And they are English."

"English?"

"I do not know if you have ever heard of them," the *Comte* said, addressing Susi. "The Dowager Marchioness of Clevedon was, I believe, a very great beauty about ten or fifteen years ago."

"Of course I have heard of her," Susi answered. "I remember my father saying she was the loveliest woman he had ever seen in his life, and there were pictures of her in all the illustrated papers for years."

"That is what I understood," the *Comte* said. "Well, she wishes to rent Castle Girone because she believes by coming to Provence she will be able to regain her beauty."

Both Susi and Trina looked at him in astonishment.

"How can she do that?"

The *Comte* shrugged his shoulders.

"Provence has a reputation not only for restoring sick people to good health and having magic cures for almost every sort of disease, but most especially for retarding old age and restoring lost youth."

"Can that be true?" Susi asked.

"It is certainly one of the legends that is repeated and re-repeated especially around Arles."

"Why especially there?"

"The women in Arles," the *Comte* replied, "are reputed, on which they pride themselves, as being the handsomest women in France. They attribute it to all sorts of herbs and potions of which apparently the Marchioness has heard rumours as far away as England."

"Do you believe in them?"

"To be quite truthful," the *Comte* replied, "I think their beauty comes from their combination of Roman blood mingled with Greek."

He smiled as he said:

"It is very obvious in their straight brows and beautifully chiselled noses, in their black eyes and hair which forms a dark misty halo round their rather haughty, often noble faces."

"I shall look forward to seeing them," Trina said.

"To make quite certain you notice them, they walk like Queens," the *Comte* smiled, "and they certainly do appear to remain looking young longer than women in other parts of the country."

"And are you also providing your tenants with the requisite ingredients?" Trina enquired.

"Actually when I saw the Marchioness two days ago, it was the one thing she wanted to talk about."

"I suppose everybody who is beautiful minds growing old," Susi said in her soft voice.

She was looking at Trina as she spoke, thinking it must be impossible for the *Comte* not to realise how lovely she looked as she listened to him attentively, her blue eyes raised to his.

"What I have promised to do," the *Comte* said ruefully, "is to find the Elixirs of Youth which have been written about in ancient books and manuscripts and which are somewhere in the Library of the Castle."

"I will help you find them," Trina offered, "and Mama who can read French as easily as she reads English, will be another able assistant."

"We ought to find something between us to make the Marchioness feel that her money has not been wasted," the *Comte* laughed.

"Is she going to stay alone in the Castle?" Susi asked.

"No, I believe her son is coming with her for at least part of the time, and she talked about having a few guests to stay. I think as a matter of fact, she is intent only on keeping away the dreaded hands of Old Age."

"Perhaps that is what I shall be trying to do in a few years," Susi said in a low voice.

"Considering at the moment you look as young as Trina," the *Comte* said, "it will be at least another thirty years before you need begin to worry about your wrinkles and lines, and by that time I shall doubtless look like an octogenarian."

"Supposing we really find the Elixir of Youth," Trina said, following her own thoughts, "perhaps we could bottle it and sell it for enormous sums all over the world. The mothers of the girls who were at the Convent with me spent astronomical sums on creams and lotions to make themselves look beautiful."

"It is certainly an idea," the *Comte* remarked.

"We should make it compulsory, if they wish to buy it, to spend a month at an enormous rent, at the Castle," Trina went on, "and you would soon be so rich that you would never have to take another tenant."

"You are so full of ideas," the *Comte* said, "that I am going to insist that you and your mother concoct this Elixir of Youth for the Marchioness. I must say when she asked me to procure it for her, I thought she was rather a bore and only agreed because I wanted her money. Now I find the idea rather entertaining."

"But of course it is," Trina said, "especially if you have the right prescription hidden away in some musty old manuscript which nobody has looked at for years. Think of it, Mama, we can distil the herbs and mix them together!"

"We had better try it on ourselves first," Susi said, "to make certain our patient does not fall dead through some obscure poison!"

The *Comte* was smiling as he said:

"We must obviously go into partnership, but of course it will have to be a family business."

He looked at Susi as he spoke, but she was thinking how much more helpful Trina could be to him than she was.

She had young ideas, the enthusiasm of youth and the kind of vitality which she thought the *Comte* should have in a wife.

'I am too old to make any enterprise a success,' she thought.

She wondered as she looked out of the window, why

the sun did not seem to be shining as brightly as it had done before.

When they reached Arles there were two carriages waiting for them, the first a very impressive open carriage drawn by four well-bred horses, the other a Landau to carry the luggage and the servants.

"This is exciting!" Trina exclaimed as they set off. "I keep remembering that Provence is said to be one of the most beautiful parts of France."

"I think so," the *Comte* said simply and looking at Susi he added:

"It is a land for lovers because everywhere you will hear the nightingales."

Susi looked surprised and he went on:

"You will hear them before you go to sleep, singing to you of the love and romance which to those who live here, is part of the very air they breathe."

He spoke in a deep voice which always gave Susi strange sensations which she found difficult to hide.

Because she felt shy she said quickly:

"I am glad there are nightingales. I have always been told that there are not so many birds in France as in England because they are shot."

"You will find plenty of birds in Provence," the *Comte* replied. "On my own land the hills are alive with hares and boars, and there are also thousands of partridges and ortolan."

"We must not forget," Trina said, "that we have to concentrate on the herbs."

"I will show you where you can find plenty of those," the *Comte* smiled, "but I want you now particularly to notice that the air of Provence is scented with the fragrance of rosemary, lavender, thyme and orange blossom."

"I can see the spires of enough churches to supply the bells for the latter," Trina said.

"Of course," the *Comte* agreed, and once again he was looking meaningfully at Susi.

They drove on and now both Susi and Trina began to grow excited as they had their first glimpse of the rock formation which they knew was characteristic of Provence.

White, glistening like sugar, it made everything look strange and pagan, at the same time, wildly romantic.

On some of the bare rocks rising high against the skyline, there were the ruins of impregnable citadels which had never fallen to an enemy, while below them were eerie gorges that might have been the haunts of demons and supernatural beings.

It was all fascinating until suddenly the *Comte* bent forward to say:

"There is the Castle!"

It stood high above a silver river with the bare rocks rising behind it and its towers peaking towards the blue sky.

It looked strong and as if the centuries had made little mark upon it, and yet it had a beauty that made it part of the landscape, part of the mystery of the country itself.

"It is beautiful," Trina cried.

Susi knew the *Comte* was waiting for her to say what she thought, but for the moment she could only stare at the great building ahead of them.

Then because she knew that she must tell him what she felt, she said in a voice hardly above a whisper:

"It is exactly the—background you should—have and what—you must—keep."

He smiled as if he knew what she was thinking, and she knew too that he was pleased because his instinct told him that it meant something to her, as it did to him.

They crossed the river over an ancient bridge, then they were driving between trees, nearer and nearer to the Castle.

Trina was leaning out of the side of the carriage to see it more easily and the *Comte* put his hand over Susi's to say very softly so that only she could hear:

"Welcome to our home, my darling!"

She tried to look at him with an expression of warning in her eyes in case Trina should hear him, but all she managed was an expression of so much love that he felt almost as if she kissed him.

Then they passed the Castle and drove on to where perhaps less than a quarter-of-a-mile away behind some formal gardens was a Château built in the 18th Century.

The exquisite architecture which had been fashionable at the time was traditional of so many lovely French buildings of the period.

As the carriage drew up at the front door and the servants hurried down the steps to greet them, several small dogs came tumbling down too, to jump up at the *Comte* yelping with excitement.

There were some elderly servants whom he introduced to Susi and Trina, and then they walked through an exquisitely proportioned Hall into a Salon which overlooked a flower-filled garden and beyond it the river.

In a chair was a woman who might have sat for a picture by Fragonard. Her hair beautifully arranged on top of her head was dead white, and although her face was old and lined it still held traces of the aristocratic beauty she had once possessed.

Her hands laden with rings were blue-veined as she held them out in welcome and there was no mistaking that she was delighted to see her grandson.

He kissed her hands, then both her cheeks.

"How are you, dearest boy?" she asked, speaking in English because their guests were English and it was only polite to speak their language rather than her own.

"I am happy to see you, *Grand'mère*," the *Comte* replied, "and now I wish to introduce my friends: First

Lady Sherington, whom I am very anxious for you to meet, then her daughter Trina."

The *Comtesse* held out her hand, then said:

"Are my eyes deceiving me or perhaps in old age I have developed double vision."

The *Comte* laughed.

"It is extraordinary, is it not, *Gránd'mère*, not one beautiful woman, but two exactly similar!"

"C'est extraordinaire!" the Comtesse agreed. "And now let me offer you some refreshment. You must be fatigued after such a long journey."

The servants brought them wine and delicious little pâtisseries that Trina found irresistible.

Then because there was still an hour before they must change for dinner, both Susi and Trina insisted they must see the Castle.

"How can we wait after all you have told us?" Trina said to the *Comte*. "Please, let us go there at once! Otherwise I am sure you will find me walking towards it in my sleep."

"Come along then," he said good-humouredly. "You know there is nothing I want more than to show the Castle to you both."

He included Trina in what he said, but he looked at Susi and she tried to tell herself he was only being polite and kind to her.

The Castle was in fact, fantastic and Susi realised how much money had been spent in making its ancient walls the perfect background for the magnificent tapestries, pictures and furniture which had been collected down the ages.

There were Persian carpets that had been woven hundreds of years previously. There were gold-framed mirrors designed by the great masters of art, there were carved and gilded tables which matched them.

There were huge mediaeval fireplaces in which the trunk of a tree could smoulder every day and many carved in marble by craftsmen who were as great in their own way as the master painters who had decorated the ceilings with goddesses and cupids.

In every room they went Susi and Trina enthused until they had run out of admiring adjectives. Then they reached the Library.

There were thousands of books, most of them bound in coloured leather tooled in gold and they stretched from floor to ceiling.

Trina looked around almost with an expression of despair.

"Have you any idea," she asked the *Comte*, "where the books on herbs we are seeking are likely to be?"

"Not at the moment," he replied, "but there is an old Librarian who comes twice a week to keep everything in order, and I am sure he will be able to tell us what we want to know."

"Thank goodness!" Trina replied. "Otherwise poor Mama and I will have to stay here for a hundred years to find what we require."

"That is what I want you to do," the *Comte* said.

Then with a change of mood, he said lightly:

"Look out of the window, there is something I want you to see."

They obeyed him, seeing only another magnificent view of the surrounding country.

"What particularly do you want us to look at?" Susi asked.

She turned as she spoke to find the room was empty.

"Jean!"

The door through which they had entered was still closed and there was no sign of him in the Library.

"Jean!" she cried again, feeling suddenly afraid because he had left her.

Then a portion of the bookcase flew open and there he was!

Trina gave a shriek of delight.

"That is one of the secret hiding-places! Oh, show me how to disappear, please, show me!"

The *Comte* explained to her that there was a little catch concealed in the ornamentation on the bookcase. He pressed it and the whole panel flew open.

Trina insisted on doing it for herself and as the bookcase shut behind her the *Comte* turned to Susi.

"Well, my precious?" he asked. "Will you be happy to live here with me?"

"You are—not to ask me that—question," Susi said quickly. "You know it is—something to which I must not—give you an—answer."

"I have already had my answer," the *Comte* retorted. "You told me you loved me and that was all I wanted to hear. This is to be our home, my lovely darling, and we will bring up our sons to love it and be as happy as we are."

"Oh—please—please—you must be—sensible," Susi pleaded.

He bent forward and just for one moment his lips rested on hers.

"That is being sensible!" he said quietly as the door of the bookcase opened and Trina came back into the Library.

CHAPTER THREE

"*H*ere is something fascinating!" Trina exclaimed. "It says in very difficult old French that *Comte* Bernhard not only magicked himself away but his weapons, his treasures, and his women. I wonder how many he had!"

She looked up as she spoke, then exclaimed:

"Mama, you are not listening!"

"I am—sorry," Susi answered, "what were you saying, dearest?"

She had been thinking of the *Comte* and of the trouble and difficulties she was making in his life.

Last night after dinner, just as the *Comtesse* was thinking of retiring to bed, the *Comte* had said:

"I hope, *Grand'mère* you will not mind if I move in here tomorrow."

"Move here!" the *Comtesse* had exclaimed in surprise, "but why should you wish to do that? What is wrong with the Castle?"

"There is nothing wrong," the *Comte* replied, "I have not had time to tell you before, but I have let it for the next three months."

There was a moment's silence as the old lady looked at him incredulously. Then she said:

"Let it? What do you mean—you have let it?"

"My tenant is the Marchioness of Clevedon," the *Comte* replied, "she and her son are, I believe, of great importance in England and they are very rich. Quite frankly, *Grand'mère* I need the money."

"Never have I heard anything so extraordinary!" the *Comtesse* replied.

Then she was so agitated that she could only express herself in her own language and lapsed into French.

"*C'est incroyable!* Unbelievable that the *Comte* de Girone should stoop to taking money for his personal possessions from strangers! We may not be rich, but we are at least proud!"

"It is no use being proud without money," her grandson replied quietly.

"Money, money! Is that all you think about?" the Dowager cried. "If that is what you need, the remedy is very easy without your resorting to lowering yourself to the position of a shop-keeper with goods to sell."

"I do not think there is anything particularly degrading in letting the Castle to someone who will appreciate its beauty, and would not do anything to spoil its contents," the *Comte* remarked mildly.

"You think like an imbecile!" the old lady flared. "I know you are slightly embarrassed financially at the moment, but you are aware that it is only a question of time before you can take a wife and one who has the same dowry or perhaps a greater one, than Marie-Thérèse."

Her blue-veined hands were shaking with the intensity of her feelings. Then as the *Comte* did not speak, she added:

"I had a letter from your cousin Josephine only this morning. She tells me that the *Duc* de Soisson has already intimated that he would be proud for one of his daughters to be associated with the de Girones."

"When I want to marry the *Duc* de Soisson's daughter I will say so," the *Comte* said coldly. "I am not a young boy, *Grand'mère*, to have my marriage arranged for me as it was when I was twenty. Now I will decide whom I marry and I wish for no interference, however well meant, from any of my relatives."

His grandmother pressed her lips together and rang a silver bell which stood beside her.

When the servant came in answer to the summons, she merely indicated with a gesture of her hand that she wished to be wheeled from the room.

Without saying a word, gazing stonily in front of her, she left leaving an awkward silence behind.

The *Comte* poured himself a glass of brandy and after a moment Susi said in a small, frightened voice:

"I am—sorry your Grandmother is—upset—but she is right—of course it is upsetting and degrading for you to—let the home of your ancestors."

The *Comte* smiled.

"I assure you they have done far worse things in their time."

"That is—not the—point . . ." Susi began hesitatingly.

"I see no reason to discuss it," the *Comte* said quietly. "The Marchioness is arriving tomorrow."

They talked of other things, but it was an uncomfortable evening and when Susi went to bed she could not sleep but lay tossing and turning in the darkness.

She knew that it was her fault that the *Comte* was not prepared to marry the *Duc* de Soisson's daughter or any other girl with a huge dowry which would keep up the Castle in the way his first wife had been able to do.

"I must go away—I must—leave him," she told herself as she had done before.

But she knew that he would prevent her from doing so, or if she insisted, would follow her to England or where-ever else she and Trina went.

"I must talk to him about it tomorrow," she decided.

But when the morning came, there seemed no opportunity for an intimate conversation.

As the Marchioness was arriving late in the afternoon, Trina insisted that they explore the Castle once again and immediately after luncheon they collected all the books they needed from the Library and had them carried to the Château.

They had already discovered quite a number of manuscripts which spoke of the efficacy of the local herbs, but Trina kept saying they still had not enough.

"Whatever we prepare for the Marchioness, it must have a dramatic effect the moment she drinks it," she insisted.

"It may make her feel well," Susi said, "but I cannot believe we can hope any herbs to be potent enough to perform miracles on her face."

Trina, however, was optimistic. She had found a

number of references to the *Vinaigre des Quatres Voleurs* which was a potion containing an elixir of youth.

This was an extract which had been used at one time as a safeguard against contagious diseases, but the septuagenarian Queen of Hungary, who married the King of Poland when he was a very young man, attributed her attraction for him entirely to the elixir.

"It certainly contained wild thyme, fennel, and rosemary, which every writer says retard old age," Trina said. "But there may be other things as well, and I am determined to find them."

She had realised ever since breakfast-time that her mother was only giving her half her attention, and now when she had not listened to what she had to say about Count Bernhard, she looked across the table and realised that Susi was looking very tired.

There were blue shadows under her eyes, and Trina thought for the first time since she had arrived from the Convent that her mother looked her age.

"What is the matter, Mama?" she asked coaxingly. "You look exhausted."

"I did not—sleep well," Susi admitted.

"Was it the *Comtesse* who upset you?" Trina asked. "Of course she is old, and to her the only thing that matters is the pomp and glory of the *Comtes* de Girone. But she is not prepared for them to be human."

"She believes they have a—responsibility for what has been—handed down to them—through the ages," Susi said in a low voice, "and which has to be—handed on to future—generations."

"Now you are siding with her. If the *Comte* does not want to marry some stupid young girl just because she is rich, why should he?"

"It is his—duty."

"That is nonsense, and very old-fashioned," Trina retorted.

At the same time, she was aware that she had not convinced her mother, and she wondered what she could say to make Susi realise how fortunate she was to have anyone so attractive and charming as the *Comte* in love with her.

'Poor Mama,' she thought, 'she has had a miserable time all these years, looking after Papa when he was ill and so disagreeable. I want her to enjoy herself, I want her to be happy.'

At the same time, because Susi had said nothing to her about the *Comte*'s intentions, Trina hesitated to broach the subject first.

She was sure Susi believed 'her little daughter' was quite unaware that he was passionately in love with her or that anyone, unless they were blind and deaf, would not have noticed the love in his eyes.

'If Mama wants me to appear half-witted I will act as she wishes,' Trina said to herself, 'but sooner or later I must prevent her from throwing away her happiness.'

As she realised that Susi did not want to talk now she went on reading, quickly turning over the pages of a book.

Then the door opened and the *Comte* came in.

"She has—arrived?" Susi asked.

There was a note of anxiety in her voice, as if she felt something might have happened to disappoint him at the last moment.

"The Marchioness has arrived," he replied, "together with her retinue of lady's-maids, coachmen, her own special footman, and a secretary!"

Trina laughed.

"She certainly travels in luxury."

"You should see her luggage!" the *Comte* answered. "I thought when I first saw it that she must be intending to stay for three years rather than three months!"

"Perhaps the trunks are full of beauty-creams," Trina suggested.

"The moment I met her," the *Comte* said, "she started to talk of the youth-giving herbs she expects me to find for her. I only hope you have discovered something which will keep her happy, otherwise she intends to leave almost immediately."

"Leave?" Trina exclaimed.

The *Comte* sat down.

"It is hard to believe it," he said looking at Susi, "but I think the Marchioness is mad."

"Why should you think that?"

"She is utterly obsessed with this idea that somewhere in the world there is someone who will restore her beauty to what it was. She is nearly sixty and she expects some magician to make her look like Trina."

"Have you told her it is impossible?"

"I was trying to put some sense into her head," the *Comte* said, "and what do you think she said to me?"

"What?" Trina asked.

"That if the herbs and the magic of Provence cannot help her, then she intends to go immediately to Rome where Antonio di Casapellio has offered to perform the miracle she requires."

"Who is he and how can he do that?" Trina asked.

"By hypnotism."

Susi gave a little cry.

"But, surely that is dangerous?"

"Of course it is," the *Comte* replied, "I know all about Casapellio. He is a charlatan, a quack, and a crook!"

"Have you told the Marchioness so?"

"It would be useless if I did. She is convinced he can do what he says. She told me she is prepared to pay £10,000 to the man who will give her the Elixir of Youth!"

There was silence for a moment. Then Trina said:

"Did you say 10,000 pounds or francs?"

"Pounds," the *Comte* answered. "We were talking in English."

"It is unbelievable!" Susi exclaimed. "That is an enormous sum of money!"

"Yes, I know," the *Comte* agreed, "and I doubt if

however hard you and Trina research you will find an elixir worth that sum."

There was another silence, then Trina asked:

"Is she prepared to pay *before* she tries it?"

"She is so stupid," the *Comte* said scornfully, "that she would pay anything to anyone who told her enough lies, which is exactly what Casapellio will do!"

"By hypnotising her into believing him?"

"The man is actually dangerous," the *Comte* replied, "but I do not see what I have to gain by maligning him. Besides, I am quite certain she will not believe a word I say against him."

"If she is so stupid she deserves everything she gets!" Trina said.

"It is not only that," the *Comte* said, in a worried tone.

"What else?" Susi enquired.

"A certain woman who went to Casapellio," the *Comte* replied, "and who was as rich as the Marchioness, was not only hypnotised by him, but he also doped her. He kept her in a twilight world under drugs and she died only after he had extracted from her every penny she possessed."

Susi gave a little cry of horror and Trina said:

"You must tell her the truth! However stupid she may be, she must realise what dangers she will encounter from such a charlatan."

The *Comte* did not reply and after a moment Susi said in a soft voice:

"You must—make her believe you."

She thought as she spoke that she herself could be persuaded by the *Comte* to believe anything he wished, and as if he knew what she was thinking, he smiled a little mockingly and said:

"You had better come and see for yourself. You will then know that the Marchioness is a typical example of a pretty face that has nothing behind it."

"I would like to—convince—her."

"When she sees you, all she will want is to look exactly like you," the *Comte* said.

There was a caressing note in his voice which sent a little quiver through Susi and which made Trina smile secretly to herself.

Because she was tactful she looked down at the book she had been reading and saw the reference to *Comte* Bernhard.

She gave a sudden scream which made both the *Comte* and Susi look at her in astonishment.

"I have an idea!" she cried. "I have a wonderful idea!"

"What is it?" Susi asked.

"Wait a minute, I have to think it out," Trina replied.

They waited and after a moment she said:

"It came to me when the *Comte* said the Marchioness would want to look like you, Mama. You will remember—or rather you will not, because you were not listening—what I told you about *Comte* Bernhard. Let me read it again."

Trina picked up the book and read slowly from the ancient French with its strange spelling:

"Monsieur le Comte with his wizardry and powerful sense of magic could not only disappear himself without sound or trace, but contrived by powers beyond mortal men to hide his weapons, his treasures and his women from the eyes of those who sought them."

Trina's voice seemed to vibrate round the Salon. Then as she finished speaking she looked at her mother and the *Comte* and realised they did not understand what she was trying to say.

"You are being very slow," she said to the *Comte*, "I am trying to get you £10,000 and surely you see how easy it would be to make the Marchioness hand it over to you rather than to the Italian quack."

"I am trying to follow your line of reasoning," the *Comte* said, "but I do not see . . ."

"It is quite simple," Trina interrupted, as if she was impatient to give him time to think it out.

"You introduce Mama to her and first you tell the Marchioness how old she is. If she doubts your word she can look it up in Debrett. Then when Mama has drunk the Elixir, she will immediately look even younger because in her place there will be . . . me!"

Trina saw by the sudden glint in the *Comte*'s eye that he understood what she was trying to explain, but before he could speak Susi cried:

"But that would be deception—it would be—wrong!"

"It would be much more wrong," Trina objected, "for us to let this wretched woman go to Italy, to be doped by the Italian crook until she dies. Be sensible, Mama! We shall not only be doing her a favour, but we shall be collecting £10,000 for the *Comte,* to keep the Castle going for quite a long time."

"It is certainly an idea," the *Comte* said slowly. "But Susi is right. It is a deception."

"What does that matter?" Trina asked angrily. "Surely this is a case of the end justifying the means, as the Jesuits have preached for years?"

The *Comte*'s eyes twinkled.

"You are beginning to persuade me."

"All I can say," Trina said, "is that you will be extremely stupid if you allow the £10,000 to slip through your hands."

She glanced at her mother as she spoke and saw that Susi was looking worried.

"It may seem shocking to you, Mama," she said, "and I know how you hate lies and deceit. But what is the alternative? Suppose we cannot dissuade the Marchioness from trusting this Italian and she dies under his treatment. Are you prepared to have that on your conscience?"

"Surely you can make her see sense?" Susi said to the *Comte*.

"Quite honestly I doubt it," he said. "When women are obsessed by one idea and can think of nothing else, all the wisdom of Solomon, combined with the eloquence of Demosthenes would not move them in another direction."

"But supposing," Susi said hesitatingly, "she—gives you the £10,000—and finds the elixir is no good—she will still go to Rome after all."

The *Comte* made a gesture with his hands.

"That is a chance we have to take. At the same time, rich though she is, I cannot believe the Marchioness will be able to find another £10,000 so quickly. Perhaps she will wait a year and in that time grow not only older, but a little wiser."

Trina clapped her hands.

"I know you have accepted my idea," she said, "and now we must plan it very carefully. You must tell the Marchioness that you are not only procuring the Elixir of Youth for her, but in a day or two, you will be prepared to give her a demonstration of how it works."

She smiled before she added:

"The only difficulty is going to be that Mama does not look old enough, except perhaps today. She has lines under her eyes I have never seen before."

As if the *Comte* noticed them for the first time, he turned quickly towards Susi, putting out his hand towards her.

"What have you been doing to yourself?" he asked. "What has upset you?"

Trina got up from the table to walk to the far window as if she wanted more light to read the book she had in her hands.

"I am all—right," Susi replied.

Then as if she could not help herself, she put her hand in the *Comte*'s.

His fingers tightened on hers.

"I know why you are worrying, my precious darling," he said in a low voice that only she could hear, "but leave everything to me, and of course, to your very intelligent daughter."

"We—should—go away."

"If you do, I shall come with you and I can promise you there is no place in Heaven or on earth where you can hide from me."

She raised her eyes, dark with worry, to his, and he said very softly:

"I worship and adore you! If it meant I had to pull the Castle down brick by brick, I would not lose you now."

He spoke with so much sincerity that Susi felt the tears come into her eyes.

"How can you—say such—wonderful things to me?" she asked with a little sob in her voice.

"I will answer that question when we are alone," the *Comte* promised.

He raised her hand to his lips. As he kissed it, he saw a sudden radiance that seemed to transform her face and said very softly:

"I feel the same, and that is something neither of us can fight."

Trina came back to the table.

"I think we have enough material now to make the Elixir," she said in a practical tone. "It will be full of herbs which all through the ages, if your books are to be believed, have special properties, if not for actually rejuvenating the body, then at least, making it strong and well."

"I expect you have found the book written by Abbé Tisserand nearly thirty years ago. He came to Provence to die, but because of the air and our herbs, he lived to a remarkable old age," the *Comte* remarked.

"There are much older books than that," Trina said, "and every one of them says that rosemary has a rejuvenating effect on anyone who takes it."

"Here that is the easiest herb in the world to obtain," the *Comte* replied.

"We shall want thyme and basil," Trina said. "I will make a full list and the moment we have all the herbs Mama and I will begin distilling and mixing them until I am sure we shall begin to believe in the Elixir of Youth, as well as the Marchioness."

"Then—what do you—intend to do?" Susi asked nervously.

"That is where you have to play your part, Mama," Trina said firmly. "When you meet the Marchioness, talk to her and establish in her mind that you too, are interested in being again as young as you once were."

"I shall be too—frightened to say anything," Susi said quickly.

"I shall be with you," the *Comte* remarked quietly.

"All you have to do is be yourself," Trina said. "Then when the *Comte* says he can obtain the Elixir of Youth from some Provencal witch who lives in a gorge or a cave in the rocks, you offer to take it and see what effect it has on you."

Trina looked at the *Comte*.

"You must make up your mind which room in the Castle we should use for this experiment."

"We have a considerable choice."

"Yes, of course," Trina agreed, "but I think the most dramatic one would be where the chair slides down through the floor."

"Perhaps you are right," he agreed. "The only trouble is that however carefully we oil the machinery, the Marchioness might hear the slight noise that it makes."

"Unless I am mistaken, there is a piano in that room."

"Trina, you are a genius!" the *Comte* exclaimed. "I will say that the patient, who is Susi, must be in the dark while the Elixir works. We can surround her with screens or curtains, whichever is the most convenient.

Then while I play, she sinks through to the floor below, and you take her place."

"That is exactly what we will do!" Trina cried. "And if you ask me, the whole thing will be a brilliant performance!"

"Supposing I—let you—down?" Susi faltered.

Once again the *Comte* took her hand in his.

"Leave everything to me," he said. "All you have to do is to look beautiful, and not quite as young as your daughter."

"I think we should make Mama when she meets the Marchioness," Trina said, "look a little older than she usually does."

"That will be difficult," the *Comte* replied.

"Not really," Trina answered. "Today with those shadows under her eyes she looks older, but tomorrow they may be gone unless we make certain they stay."

"What—do you—mean?" Susi asked apprehensively.

"I have my paint-box and crayons with me. You forget I have studied painting and drawing amongst other things at the Convent."

"And apparently Drama as well!" the *Comte* smiled.

"As it happens," Trina said, "I have read a lot of plays and I often think that were I a man I would like to be a producer."

"And not be an actress?" the *Comte* enquired.

Trina laughed.

"Can you imagine Mama's face if I suggested going on the stage?"

"I was only thinking of it in an amateurish capacity," the *Comte* replied. "I had one ancestor who had his own Theatre, not here, but in Paris. Of course he was emulating King Louis XIV because Madame de Pompadour produced the most amusing Comedies for him at the Theatre in Versailles."

"Now you are giving me ideas of what I can do in the future," Trina said.

Susi gave a little cry of protest.

"Do not encourage her!" she begged the *Comte*. "Can you imagine how shocked all our relations, especially my late husband's sisters will be, if Trina goes back to England with such ideas? As it is, they are certain that everything in France is the invention of the Devil!"

"Forget England and your relatives for the moment," the *Comte* said. "This is going to be amusing, Susi, and I promise you that although it may seem reprehensible, as far as the Marchioness is concerned, it is the better of two evils."

Trina laughed.

"Think that over, Mama, and know that you are really doing that stupid woman a good turn and saving her from herself."

"I do not—really know—what to—think," Susi faltered.

She looked at the *Comte* and added:

"But—if it will help you, I will do—anything you ask of me."

The expression in his eyes made her blush and Trina said:

"Let us get to work. The sooner we have that £10,000 in our hands the better!"

That night they dined alone because the *Comtesse* had not been seen all day.

When Susi enquired after her anxiously, the *Comte* replied:

"She is punishing us. All her life when *Grand'mère* is upset, she retires to bed to make those who have offended her feel guilty."

"What a funny idea!" Trina exclaimed.

"She realised it upset my grandfather when she was not there. He adored her because, as you can imagine, she was exceedingly beautiful, and although their marriage was arranged, they fell in love with each other the moment they met."

"Do tell me about your grandparents," Trina begged.

"*Grand-père* was extremely handsome and had been a roué until he married. But he and *Grand'mère* settled down at the Castle and I remember when I was a very small child realising how happy they were together."

The *Comte* smiled as he went on:

"But *Grand'mère*, despite her soft and feminine appearance, was a very determined person and she always got her own way. When *Grand-père* opposed her, she used to go to her bedroom and lock herself in. My father used to tell me how *Grand-père* would knock and knock without receiving an answer, until he apologised abjectly for something he had done."

The *Comte* laughed and went on:

"Then they would make it up and look radiantly happy in a way that made their love for each other very noticeable to everyone who saw them."

"No wonder you—wanted to be happy in the—same way," Susi said in a low voice.

Then she blushed as the *Comte* said quietly:

"I am!"

Trina walked out through the open window into the garden.

She knew from the way they were looking at each other that they would barely notice she had gone, except for being aware that they could now say things they prevented themselves from saying in her presence.

'I am sure the *Comte* wants to marry Mama, but she is being difficult about it,' she reasoned. 'If he has the £10,000 it will help them to live fairly comfortably until I come into my father's fortune when I am twenty-one. Then I can give Mama what she should have had if Papa had not made that horrible and unfair will.'

It was impossible for Trina to give her mother anything at the moment, for her father had appointed

227

Trustees who had complete control of her fortune until she came of age.

She had every intention then of giving her mother everything to which she believed she was entitled, but she knew it would be a mistake to say so now, in case they took steps, she was not certain how, to hinder her from circumventing her father's Will.

'I will keep quiet until it is too late for them to do anything or interfere in any way,' she had told herself as soon as she heard what the Will laid down.

Now, however, she thought that if she told Susi exactly what she intended to do, then perhaps she would agree to marry the *Comte*, and they could all be very happy.

At the same time, she was astute enough to realise that he was humiliated by the knowledge that the money that had been expended on the Castle had come from the wife he had not loved and with whom he had been extremely unhappy.

Trina was as perceptive in her way as Susi was.

She noticed as they went round the Castle how every time they admired some new acquisition, a piece of tapestry, a fine oil-painting or some newly decorated room, there would be a defensive note in the *Comte*'s voice when he had to say: "My wife bought that," or "That was a gift from my late father-in-law."

'Because he has spent years being beholden to a woman,' Trina reasoned, 'it is obvious why he has no wish to be in the same position again.'

But it was undeniable that the Castle cost an enormous amount of money to keep up, as well as the grounds with their beautiful gardens descending from flower-filled terraces to the river.

'Somehow I must find a solution,' Trina told herself.

She had been walking all the time she was thinking out the problem, and now she found herself among the cypress trees which stood high above the river pointing like fingers towards the darkening sky.

The sun had sunk but there was still a faint glow far

away on the horizon, the first stars were coming out overhead and a half-moon was throwing its beams down onto the moving water.

It was very lovely, at the same time it had a strange, almost unreal mystery about it that she could not remember having experienced before.

It was almost as if the stories of the magic and enchantment of Provence being different from anywhere else in France, were true. Even as she thought of it she heard the nightingales.

They were not very near, and yet in the silence of the deepening dusk they seemed first to attract her attention, then to come nearer and still nearer so that she listened entranced to the music made by what she knew were two birds.

One sang to the other and would then wait for the reply, after which they sang in unison and Trina felt as if her heart sang with them.

She heard a quiet step behind her and she thought the *Comte* had come in search of her, and held up her hand so that he should not speak or break the spell.

The nightingales trilled on, until still singing their voices grew fainter and Trina knew they were flying up towards the stars.

She felt almost as if she could see them and follow them, but as she threw back her head to search the sky, she could see only the glimmer of the stars and the light from the moon.

For a moment she felt as if she too could fly. Then remembering that the *Comte* was beside her, she gave a little sigh and came back to reality.

"That was a song of love," she said softly and turned her head.

To her astonishment, it was not the *Comte* who stood there, but a man she had never seen before.

He was very tall and broad-shouldered, and it was light enough for her to see he was handsome, but in a very different way from the *Comte,* in fact in a manner that was peculiarly English.

For a moment they stared at each other as the light from the moon haloed Trina's fair hair. Then as the man beside her did not speak, she said:

"I think you must be the Marquis of Clevedon."

He smiled.

"And I am sure you are Lady Sherington. The *Comte* told me you were staying here."

Trina was just about to say that she was in fact Lady Sherington's daughter when she remembered that it was important that the Marchioness should not know of her existence.

Just in time she replied:

"That is clever of you."

"Not really," the Marquis replied. "Our host told my mother what a very lovely guest he had staying with him, and may I tell you he did not exaggerate?"

"Thank you."

Trina did not blush or feel embarrassed by the compliment because, unlike Susi, she had received so many when she was in Rome.

She looked away from the Marquis down at the river and towards the distant, darkening horizon.

"So you were listening to the song of love," the Marquis said. "I was not told that nightingales were a part of the attractions of Provence."

He spoke with a slightly mocking note in his voice which told Trina without words that he was rather dubious about what he had heard of this part of France, and that doubtless included the Elixir of Youth which his mother was seeking.

As he spoke she was thinking with surprise that the *Comte* had not mentioned his arrival at the same time as the Marchioness.

"When I was driving here this evening from where I have been staying," he said, almost in answer to her unspoken question, "I thought how beautiful and unusual the countryside was. I have not visited this part of France before."

"Neither have I, and I find it very exciting."

"I should have thought 'romantic' was a better word," the Marquis remarked. "When I saw you silhouetted against the cypress trees I thought you must be a nymph from the river, or perhaps a ghost from the past."

"You are certainly entering into the spirit of the place," Trina said, "and surely you find the Castle different from any building you have ever seen before."

"It is certainly very magnificent."

Again there was that slightly mocking note in his voice, as if he was determined to be cynical about everything, and perhaps everybody.

"I think perhaps I should return to the Château," Trina remarked.

"Must you leave me alone with my thoughts?" the Marquis asked.

"Are you afraid of them?"

"Not in the least, but I would rather you stayed with me."

"I am of course honoured," Trina said, "but I have a feeling that your anxiety for my company is because it is me or no-one!'

The Marquis laughed.

"Perhaps I am not as eloquent as a Frenchman would be in the circumstances, but shall I say in plain English that I would like to talk to you. Why do we not sit down?"

He indicated as he spoke, a stone seat which Trina had not noticed before, placed a little to the side of them and protected at the back by two tall cypress trees.

Without arguing Trina moved towards it, aware that Susi and the *Comte* would not be anxious for her to rejoin them and if she was honest she was rather interested in the Marquis.

She had a feeling that it would be a mistake to underestimate his intelligence and, however foolish and gullible his mother might be, he would be very different.

Trina seated herself on the stone seat and the frills
of her bustle swept the ground very elegantly beside
her. Her waist silhouetted against the cypress trees
looked very tiny, while her bare neck and shoulders
glowed white in the light from the moon.

The Marquis sat beside her and turned so that he
was almost facing her.

Trina knew that his eyes were on her face and she
wondered what he was thinking.

"I still feel," he said after a moment, "that you are
not real. The Castle, the moonlight, the nightingales
are a fantasy, and even if I find them here in the
morning, you will have disappeared."

"I hope I shall sleep most of the night comfortably
in my bed."

"Now I know that you are English," the Marquis
remarked. "Only an Englishwoman would sweep
away the poetry of the moment with such a practical
remark!"

"Only an Englishman would be uncouth enough to
point out to her where she had failed him!" Trina
flashed.

The Marquis laughed and answered:

"I have been staying in a French household, and I
am trying to emulate the ease with which a Frenchman can pay compliments. But I know now it is the
result of a lifetime of endeavour and practice."

"While a Frenchman is learning the art," Trina said,
"an Englishman is studying how to bowl a cricket-ball,
or how to punch another boy on the nose!"

"I have an uncomfortable feeling that is true, because I remember going through a phase of disliking
women, and wondering what possible use they could
be in the world."

"A Frenchman knows the answer to that when he
first opens his eyes!" Trina smiled.

"You do not believe everything a Frenchman says to
you?" the Marquis asked.

"Of course I want to do so! It is just that some

critical, very English part of my brain warns me I should not believe a word they say!"

The Marquis laughed again.

"I think we will agree and disagree on quite a number of subjects, one way or another," he said, "but I shall be hoping, and I say this with a very English sincerity, that you will not leave before I return."

"You are going away?"

"I only came tonight to see that my mother was safely installed in the Castle," he replied. "Tomorrow I go to Monte Carlo, but only for a week or so."

"Then I expect I shall be here, My Lord, when you return."

"That is exactly what I wanted to hear."

Trina rose to her feet.

"May I wish you *Bon Voyage* and *Bonne Chance* at the card-tables?"

"I have a feeling I shall find them very dull and prosaic after the magic of the nightingales and of course, you!"

"Now that is very flattering and very French!"

Trina held out her hand as she spoke and the Marquis took it in his.

"Good-night, Lady Sherington!"

He seemed to hesitate for a moment, then he bent his head.

As she felt his lips on her hand she had a feeling that it was not a perfunctory kiss of politeness and she told herself it was a very good thing he was going away.

Too late she thought that this had been the type of conversation in which Susi would never have taken part, and it would be difficult to explain to her exactly what had been said or how she must carry it on when the Marquis returned.

Quickly Trina took her hand from his and moving through the cypress trees she hurried over the lawns back towards the Château.

He made no move to follow her and she had the

feeling that he thought perhaps it might embarrass her and also that he might be encroaching on the *Comte*'s preserves.

"He is intelligent and perceptive," Trina told herself.

She thought that when the *Comte* had spoken of her mother he would not have been able to prevent the warmth in his voice and the expression in his eyes that Susi always evoked in him.

She also guessed that the Marquis, being convinced that she was Lady Sherington, a married woman and a widow, had flirted with her as he would not have attempted to do with a young girl.

He had a definite fascination of his own. He was very different from the *Comte* and yet in his own way he was extremely attractive.

Trina told herself regretfully that in other circumstances it would have been fun to meet him again and talk to him. In a strange way she could not quite determine, he made her feel provocative.

She had not met many Englishmen. There had been some in Rome, but she had spent most of the time with the older brothers and their friends of the Italian girl with whom she was at the Convent, and who had invited her to stay.

They had been prepared to flatter her from first thing in the morning until last thing at night, but she had always kept them at arm's length, laughing at their eloquence and not taking anything they said seriously.

It had been an experience that had given her a sophistication she had not had before, even though her time in Spain had taught her a great deal about men and their approach to women.

Of all the men Trina had met, the Marquis was different. Perhaps it was because he was English, or maybe because he was older. She guessed him to be twenty-nine or thirty.

Although she had no reason for thinking so, she

had the feeling that he was slightly rakish, and perhaps as much a heart-breaker in his own way, as the *Comte* was in his.

Whatever he might be, as she reached the Château she told herself this was the last time she would be able to see him.

It was a dispiriting thought, and she wished it was not so imperative to play a trick on the Marchioness and extract £10,000 from her.

Chapter Four

*W*hen Trina got back to the Château she decided to go straight to bed.

As she passed the Salon she could hear the voices of her mother and the *Comte* and was certain they did not want to be interrupted.

When she was undressing it struck her again that it was really very strange that the *Comte* had not said the Marquis was at the Castle.

They had obviously met and talked together, and it would have been natural for him to mention his presence when he returned to the Château for dinner.

Then on thinking it over, she decided the reason he had not done so was that he was well aware that the Marquis with his cynical, slightly sceptical attitude towards everything, would frighten Susi.

'He is sensible in that,' Trina thought, 'because Mama is very easily frightened, and I am sure of one thing, she would never have been able to talk to the Marquis as I did tonight.'

It was extremely lucky that he was leaving tomorrow morning, and she decided that once they had the £10,000 they must all leave.

She had the uncomfortable feeling that however easy the Marchioness might be to deceive, it would be very hard to do the same where the Marquis was concerned.

Then she told herself she was being unnecessarily apprehensive.

Who would imagine in their wildest dreams that there would be two women, mother and daughter, who looked so much alike as she and Susi?

At the same time Trina was aware that, while there was a superficial likeness in that their hair, their skin and their eyes were the same colour, inevitably to any observer who was searching deeper and was suspicious, there were obvious differences.

Susi, despite her youthful appearance, had given birth to a child and in consequence her breasts were a little fuller than Trina's, her waist not quite so small.

Also the way she moved did not have the spontaneous buoyancy of a girl of eighteen, while her face had a slight sharpness about its outline, unlike the softness of Trina's.

Apart, it would be easy for them to impersonate each other, but if they stood together, Trina was astute enough to guess that someone like the Marquis would be able without hesitation, to pick out who was the elder of the two.

'We shall have to leave,' she told herself again, but that did not mean they would have to return to England.

They could stay in Paris where the *Duchesse* would be only too pleased to act as hostess.

"It has been such a short visit, Susi dearest," she had said as they were leaving. "I quite understand that you want to see Jean's Castle, but when you are tired of country life, come back to Paris, and I will make you and Trina the most sought after young women in the whole city."

She was speaking sincerely and Trina had thought at the time that she would love to accept such a generous invitation.

'It would be very good for Mama to be a success,' she thought, thinking more of her mother than of herself. 'She has always been crushed and snubbed by those horrible old sisters of Papa, and when she was nursing him she never thought of doing anything of which he would not approve.'

As she got into bed, Trina thought once again of how she could help her mother financially once she was twenty-one.

"In the meantime," she decided, "I can pay for her clothes, pretending they are mine, and if the Trustees complain I am extravagant, I will make myself so objectionable that they will give me all the money I want."

She wanted to go on thinking about her mother, but somehow insidiously she found herself going over her conversation with the Marquis.

"I suppose, if I am honest, he is the most attractive man I have ever seen," she told herself before she fell asleep.

With the morning came the first difficulties of making sure that neither the Marchioness nor any member of her household was aware of Trina's existence.

"It means we cannot all ride together," the *Comte* said. "I am sorry, Trina, but when we made our plans, I did not realise how restricting this would be for you."

"I can put up with a good deal of discomfort as long as you get the £10,000," Trina smiled. "It would be best for you to take Mama riding while I begin work in the Still-room. When I peeped in before breakfast, I saw great bundles of rosemary."

"There is also thyme and fennel," the *Comte* said, "and I have told the gardeners to bring in a number of other herbs which grow in the Castle gardens and which I am sure you will find useful. There is comfrey for one, and French tarragon, which I am sure should be added to the Elixir."

"Of course they must!" Trina agreed, "and if the lilies-of-the-valley are not over, I would like to have a few of those as well."

"You may have anything you wish," the *Comte* said. "How long do you think it will take you to make this magic potion?"

"I want to do it quickly and get it over with," Trina replied. "You know until the drama has taken place Mama will worry! If we take too long she will actually look so old that the contrast between us will make the transformation seem very necessary!"

"You can leave your mother to me," the *Comte* said to Trina.

She had the feeling, although he had not said so, that he too was thinking that everything must be done and finished with before the Marquis returned.

She went to the Still-room which fortunately was not used by the *Comtesse*'s staff, and with the ancient manuscripts and books to guide her, she started to chop up the herbs.

She soaked the juices from them, mixed them with each other one by one, until she had achieved a fairly palatable flavour.

Herbs are never very appetising at the best of times, and Trina decided it would be wise to add honey to the potion to sweeten it.

Her Nanny had told her when she was a child, that honey had special 'magical' qualities because the Queen Bee lived for twenty years, and there had always been a comb of fresh honey from the bees on her father's estate on the Nursery table.

At luncheon-time she asked the *Comte* if there was a special honey to be found in Provence.

"Of course there is," he said, "in fact, quite a number of them. There is thyme-honey, lavender-honey, and a very special one which the bees make from the spring flowers . . ."

"Which of course must go into our Elixir of Youth," Trina finished.

The *Comte* promised to order some to be brought to the Château. Then he said:

"This afternoon I am taking your mother to call on the Marchioness. I think, Trina, this is where you must apply the little touches of old age that she does not possess naturally."

Because she had been so happy on her ride with the *Comte,* Susi looked young and very lovely.

"I think really," Trina said jokingly, "it is I who should pretend to be Lady Sherington and Mama can come up in the chair as me!"

"It is certainly an idea," the *Comte* laughed, but Susi cried:

"You are both making me feel shy! If I do look young it is only because I am so happy."

"That is what I want you to be," the *Comte* said in his deep voice.

They looked into each other's eyes, and Trina was forgotten.

Later she went to her mother's bedroom where Susi was changing into an elegant afternoon-gown, one which made her look older than the comparatively simple white dresses did, which constituted the main part of her wardrobe.

It was another of the gowns she had worn when she was in mourning, of pale parma violet, the skirt having frill upon frill of pleated chiffon edged with lace, which was echoed on the bodice and on the sleeves.

There was a sash of mauve velvet around her waist, and Trina decided her mother must wear a necklace of amethysts with ear-rings and bracelet to match.

"I have always thought this set old-fashioned and stuffy," she said, "and I am quite certain Aunt Dorothy influenced Papa into buying it for you! But it is just what you want at the moment."

"He gave me so many beautiful jewels," Susi said, "that I would be very ungrateful if I complained."

"You never complained, Mama, but you know as well as I do the amethyst is a dull stone, but I love your diamonds and of course, the turquoises."

"You may wear anything I possess," Susi said.

"And that applies the other way round, Mama," Trina replied. "When you marry the *Comte* and no longer have a lot of money to spend on such frivolities as clothes, I intend to buy all your gowns for you and they will be a present from me to you."

"You must do nothing of the sort!" Susi said automatically.

Then she added quickly:

"What makes you—think I will—marry the *Comte?*"

"But of course you will marry him, Mama," Trina said. "He is so attractive, charming, and very much in love with you."

"How can I—allow him to—give up so—much for—me?" Susi asked in a low voice.

As she spoke Trina knew without her mother telling her so, that the *Comte* did want to marry her and had already said so.

"He has been very unhappy with one wife whom he married for money," Trina said in a practical tone. "You can hardly condemn him to spend the rest of his life being unhappy with another one."

"But suppose," Susi said in a very small voice, "after we are—married he—regrets that he—cannot spend so much money on the—Castle?"

"If you think like that, Mama," Trina said, "then I can only believe you are not really in love."

Susi looked at her in a startled fashion as she went on:

"I am sure the *Comte* loves you as he has never loved

anyone before in his whole life, and although you are making difficulties, Mama, you are well aware that you love him in the same way."

Susi's eyes filled with tears.

"Oh, Trina—I am so worried—what am I to do?"

"Marry him, and let him do all the worrying!"

Trina put her arms round her mother as she spoke and kissed her cheek.

"How can you be so foolish?" she asked. "You have the most attractive man one could imagine madly in love with you, and offering you an exciting life away from England and all those disagreeable relatives of Papa's. Personally, I would not hesitate for a second to snap him up before somebody else does!"

"Oh, Trina—you do say such—terrible things!" Susi complained.

But her tears had turned to laughter.

"I am so lucky, so very, very lucky," she said, a sob still in her voice, "to have you and—Jean, and I have not known for years what it is like to laugh, to feel as if I could dance, or fly in the sky."

"That is love!" Trina said.

As she spoke she remembered how last night, the nightingales had flown away towards the stars singing their song of love.

She made Susi wipe her eyes and very delicately she drew in a soft shadow underneath them and added what appeared to be several faint wrinkles at the corners.

She stood back to see the effect of what she had done.

"Look at me, Mama," she ordered and as Susi did so, said:

"I suppose it does make you look a little older, but you are still absolutely lovely. I am not surprised that the *Comte* was bowled over the first moment he saw you."

It flashed through her mind that the Marquis might have felt exactly the same about her.

Then she told herself that he was much more cynical than the *Comte* and it would take a great deal more than a pretty face to upset his well established equilibrium.

Trying not to think about herself or the Marquis, Trina concentrated on arranging her mother's hair in a slightly different style, then placed on it a very elaborate bonnet of mauve flowers and velvet ribbons which matched the gown.

"You look as though you might be going to Ascot or a Reception at Marlborough House rather than making a simple afternoon call in the country," she smiled.

"Do you think Jean will—think I am—overdressed?" Susi enquired anxiously.

"It will not matter what the *Comte* thinks," Trina replied. "You have to concentrate, Mama, on the Marchioness. Do not forget to sympathise about her search for the Elixir of Youth and say it is something you have always wanted to find yourself."

Finally Susi was ready and, when they went downstairs together, Trina knew that the *Comte* was delighted with her efforts.

To make Susi feel at ease he talked to her in a way which brought the colour to her cheeks which were rather pale and made her eyes shine.

"He is just the sort of husband Mama should have," Trina told herself, as she watched them drive away in the open carriage.

It was to take them the long way round so that they could arrive in style, entering the Castle by the drawbridge which spanned the moat, to drive into the courtyard in the centre of the building.

At the back of the Castle there were green lawns right up to the ancient walls and, the *Comte* had told Susi, formal gardens laid out in the reign of Louis XIV.

Trina, however, wasted no time in watching them but ran upstairs to the Still-room.

When, over an hour later Susi and the *Comte*

returned, a servant came to tell Trina that *Monsieur le Comte* and *Madame* were waiting for her in the Salon.

She pulled off the apron with which she had covered her gown while she was working, washed her hands and ran downstairs.

Susi had already taken off her bonnet and placed it beside her long kid gloves and her hand-bag on a chair.

"What happened? Tell me!" Trina exclaimed as she hurried across the room.

The *Comte* deliberately waited for Susi to speak first.

"The Marchioness must have been very beautiful," she said in her soft voice, "but, Trina, she is really rather pathetic."

"In what way?"

"She obviously cares for nothing and nobody except her lost looks! Oh, dearest, I hope I shall never be like that!"

"How could you be?" Trina asked. "You never think of yourself, but spend your time in worrying over other people."

"I can see the Marchioness is going to be added to the list," the *Comte* said, "but your mother is right—she is pathetic."

"She looked—quite wild," Susi said, "when she insisted she must find—the Elixir of Youth."

"Did you tell her there was one?" Trina asked.

"Jean—did that."

"What your mother is trying to tell you is that she is not a good liar," the *Comte* smiled. "I told the Marchioness that a wonderful age-old secret Elixir would be here in two days. Was that too soon?"

"No, I think I can have it ready by then," Trina replied, "but I wish we had taken a little time in rehearsing going up and down through the floor in the moving chair."

"I suppose we could use one of the other secret entrances," the *Comte* said, "but you are right in thinking it is far more convincing if somebody disappears from the centre of the room than if they sat near to a wall or a book-case which could be immediately suspect."

"We will manage," Trina said, "but I meant to ask you to find a very ancient-looking apothecary's bottle in which to put the Elixir, once it is ready."

"I know exactly what you want," the *Comte* replied.

"But for the moment, go on telling me what the Marchioness said," Trina begged.

"She is still beautiful in a somewhat faded manner," Susi answered, "but the dye she has used on her hair is rather bright and it gives her an unreal look, as if she was a painted doll."

"I know what you mean," Trina said. "Perhaps we could make her a different kind of dye. Some of the books give details about which herbs to use and how to dye the hair, including one which says that the blood of a hare is very efficacious in helping it to grow."

Susi looked shocked.

"I can think of nothing more unpleasant!"

"There are much worse prescriptions than that!" Trina said. "But you were telling me about the Marchioness. What did she talk about?"

Susi smiled.

"She talked, but only about her looks and how many different treatments she has tried. She went to Paris last year."

"I am sure they made her pay something horrifying for what she required," the *Comte* remarked.

"According to her they promised all sorts of improvements," Susi answered, "but when she went back to England she thought the massage they had given her on her face had made the skin loose."

"I should think that was quite likely to happen," Trina said.

"That was what made her decide," Susi went on, "that external treatments were useless and that somehow, somewhere, she would find the Elixir of Youth."

"Did she say again what she would pay for it?" Trina enquired.

"She actually said," Susi replied, "that she would give every penny she possessed if she could look as she did in the days when people stood on chairs in the Park to watch her pass and her carriage was mobbed when she attended the Opera or went to the Theatre."

"In a way I can understand what she feels now."

"It has made me determined to grow old gracefully," Susi said. "Please, if you ever see me fussing about my face, tell me I am being a fool and that there is nothing that can make time stand still."

She spoke to Trina, but she looked at the *Comte* and he said quietly:

"I think every age has its attractions. To me, *Grand'mère* is still very lovely, and I admire her more every time I see her."

"Have you seen her today?" Trina asked.

The *Comte* nodded.

"She has forgiven me enough to grant me an audience! At the same time, she intends to keep to her own room until she feels she can face a world in which her grandson would demean himself for mere money!"

He spoke in a way which made Trina laugh at what he said, but Susi remarked:

"If only you did not—have to—upset her."

"One thing she said firmly and in a manner in which I know she means it," the *Comte* said, "and that is that she will never meet my tenant."

He paused to add:

"It is the best thing that could happen. I was wondering how we could tell *Grand'mère* on no account to mention Trina's existence."

"Everything is working out for the best," Trina said, "and that will be achieved when you receive the sum of £10,000 and we can all leave."

"Do you think—that is what we—must do?" Susi enquired.

"But of course," Trina said. "We do not want to be

245

here when the Marchioness finds the Elixir does not work in the way she expects it to. But I promise you one thing, she will certainly feel better in health."

"She does not look well," Susi said. "I think, although I may be mistaken, that she diets to excess to keep her figure. She would not eat anything at tea-time, although she gave us a large and delicious English tea."

"When you have time, Mama," Trina said, "I want you to come and sample the Elixir I have concocted so far. It tastes rather nice, but I want to be quite certain it does not give you indigestion or make you feel dizzy."

"You are not to upset your mother," the *Comte* said quickly. "Let me try the Elixir."

"Of course you can," Trina replied, "but I doubt if your reactions would be as sensitive as Mama's."

"We will both try it," Susi said firmly.

She and the *Comte* each drank a wine-glassful before they went to change for dinner and when they came down to the Salon Susi said:

"I am trying to decide whether I feel any different. I feel so well anyway that it is difficult to know what effect the Elixir could have on me."

"What about you?" Trina enquired of the *Comte*.

"I feel as if I could push the world over, swim the Channel and fly to the moon!" he replied.

"It is not the Elixir that makes you feel like that!"

"I know," he answered, "but your mother will not believe me when I tell her she is the only Elixir I need!"

"Then make her believe you," Trina said and they smiled at each other in a conspiratorial fashion.

They laughed a lot during dinner which was a delicious meal, and when it was over Trina thought that once again she should leave her mother and the *Comte* alone.

Without their even noticing what she was doing she

walked out of the window as she had done the night before and onto the lawn.

The moon was fuller and when she reached the place where she had heard the nightingales the moonbeams were already rippling on the river touching it with silver as it twisted away between the high banks.

She could not hear the nightingales, so she moved towards the stone seat where she had sat with the Marquis and wondered what he was doing.

Had he thought of her today as she had thought of him?

She was sure that in Monte Carlo he would find innumerable glamorous and sophisticated women who would be only too willing to flirt with him and make his stay there extremely entertaining.

She wondered why he was not married, and thought perhaps he was one of the fashionable men who she heard danced attendance on the much acclaimed social beauties and in the words of one cynic: "Spent their time going from Boudoir to Boudoir."

Trina knew, as it happened, quite a lot about London Society although there had been few English girls at the Convent.

When she had been first in Madrid and then in Rome, she had listened to the gossip which was the main topic of conversation amongst the grown-ups and found she learned not only about the amorous intrigues of the country she was in, but also about her own.

It was obvious that the Prince of Wales was not only greatly admired on the Continent, but that his love-affairs—there were a great number of them—were known and talked about from Bordeaux to Warsaw and from Madrid to the shores of the Adriatic.

Because she was curious she had written home to her mother to ask her to send her every week the *Illustrated London News,* the *Graphic,* and the *Ladies Journal.*

She found in them pictures of all the Society

Celebrities she had heard about and studied them with interest.

It was a world in which Susi had taken a small part before her husband became ill and incapable of leaving his home.

Trina could remember when she was a little girl how lovely her mother had looked wearing a diamond tiara which was part of the Sherington collection, a diamond necklace which had always seemed to be too heavy for her neck, and the bracelets, rings and brooches which would really have suited a much older woman.

"You look like the Fairy Princess, Mama!" she had said. "Perhaps the Prince will be waiting for you at the Ball."

Susi had smiled.

"Papa is my Prince, dearest."

At the time Trina had thought that her Papa, distinguished though he appeared, was really too old to be the Prince in a fairy-story.

It struck her now that the sort of Prince she had been envisaging for her mother would have looked very much like the Marquis.

As she thought of him, almost as if she had conjured him up out of her thoughts, someone sat down beside her on the stone seat.

She gave a little exclamation of sheer astonishment.

It was the Marquis, and with the moonlight on his face he seemed even more handsome, more broad-shouldered and more over-powering than he had the night before.

"Good-evening, Lady Sherington," he said. "It is obvious you are surprised to see me."

"I . . . thought you had . . . left for Monte Carlo," Trina replied, finding it somehow difficult to speak.

"I did," he answered, "but when I reached Arles I was told that the trains were late owing to a landslip of some sort, on the line. I waited for several hours, then decided I had no intention of staying in an uncomfortable Hotel and came back here for the night."

Trina gave a little sigh of relief.

This meant he had not seen her mother although for one perplexing moment, she had thought perhaps Susi and the *Comte* had entered into a conspiracy not to tell her that the Marquis was at the Castle.

"You will be leaving tomorrow?" she asked aloud.

"Are you in such a hurry to get rid of me?" he enquired.

"No, of course not! I was only interested. It must be upsetting for you to have your plans altered at the last moment."

"Shall I confess that I was glad to have the opportunity of seeing you again?"

"You can hardly expect me to believe that."

"Then shall we say I was feeling romantic and hoped that the nightingales were in good voice."

"Have you noticed that they have decided not to give a performance tonight?"

"How disobliging of them. I shall have to make do with you. Will you sing me a song of love?"

"I doubt my voice would be as beguiling."

"Then we must talk instead," the Marquis said. "And now that we know each other so much better, I suggest you tell me about yourself."

"That would be very dull," Trina replied. "As it happens when you suddenly appeared I was thinking about you."

"You were thinking of me?" he asked quizzically.

Trina realised he was not likely to let such an opening pass and she replied:

"Not particularly personally, but of the social life in which I am sure you play a prominent role."

"I can tell by your tone of voice that it does not particularly impress you."

"I am not prepared to criticise, except that it is a world of which I know nothing except what I have read and heard."

"Which I am convinced, was not only inaccurate, but slanderous!"

Trina gave a little laugh.

"How can you be sure of that?"

"Tell me to whom you have listened on the subject. I am sure I can tell you exactly what they said."

"I think that would be very indiscreet," Trina retorted, "but you are well aware that Europe as a whole is fascinated by the Prince of Wales and those who are considered his friends."

"I understood from my mother," the Marquis said, "that this was your first visit to France."

Too late Trina realised she had for the moment forgotten she was supposed to be Susi for she had been thinking of her own visits to Madrid and to Rome.

"I stayed in Paris on my way here, My Lord."

She hoped, by improvising thus on the spur of the moment, she had covered up any slip she might have made.

"Then I expect you found the gossip of the Parisians very informative," the Marquis said.

"I found them very fascinating," Trina replied, hoping to change the subject.

"Actually we were talking about me," the Marquis reminded her, "and I was flattered when you admitted to thinking about me, as I have thought about you."

"Why?" Trina asked.

"Because you are not only different from what I expected, but in a way, different from anybody I have ever met before."

"I am not going to ask in what way," Trina said defensively.

"Then I will tell you," the Marquis replied. "You are beautiful, as you are well aware, but there is something else: a kind of vibration that comes from you which I have never encountered before, but which I find definitely intriguing."

"Once again you are speaking in a very un-English manner."

If she wished to divert him from making too intimate observations about herself, she was unsuccessful.

"It may seem to you un-English," the Marquis replied, "but I suppose the majority of us consider only the words which we hear and seldom look deeper for the motives or feelings or truth which underline them."

What he said immediately intrigued Trina.

"I am sure you are right," she said in a very different voice from what she had used before. "Words are only a vehicle and often very inadequate to express emotions. That is why I believe all the great teachers of mankind used an esoteric language when they spoke to their pupils which so far has never been adequately interpreted by the uninitiated."

"Who told you that?" the Marquis asked.

"It does not matter . . . but it is true, is it not?"

"So you think that the disciples of whatever Messiah they were following, sensed what they were taught more than simply by hearing with their ears?"

"Of course," Trina replied. "That is exactly what I wanted to say to you, but you have expressed it better than I could."

"I think you express it very ably, by just being yourself."

Trina gave a little sigh.

"Now you are making everything personal again. I was enjoying talking to you because we were both using our brains and that I am sure is unusual."

She was thinking as she spoke, that this was just the type of conversation she had always wanted to have with somebody cleverer than herself.

The teachers at the Convent, even the best of them, had been unable to answer the questions which she had put to them and she had found only some of the answers she sought in the books which she read.

Many of these, however, were so erudite that the

Mother Superior of the Convent had told her scornfully they were far beyond her comprehension.

But Trina had always wanted to seek the unattain-
able.

She thought now that the Marquis quite unexpectedly was someone she had always sought not because
he was an attractive man, but because he had obviously been thinking along the same lines as herself.

"I suppose," the Marquis said, as if he was reasoning it out for himself, "while nursing your husband
during the years he was sick, you had nothing else to
do but read."

Again Trina was startled to realise that she was supposed to be Susi.

"Yes . . . of course," she said quickly. "I had . . .
plenty of time for that."

"Are you surprised I find you different?" the Marquis asked. "Most women who are as beautiful as you
are, worry about their looks, seldom about their
minds."

Trina was aware he was thinking of his mother and
she said lightly:

"They should have had a Nanny like mine who always said: 'Beauty's only skin-deep and looks don't
last, so make the best of them while you can!' "

The Marquis laughed.

"I am sure my Nanny said equally deflating things
but with a masculine slant to them."

"Nannies are always practical and down-to-earth,"
Trina smiled, "and now I must be going. They will be
wondering at the Château what has happened to me."

"Why are you alone?" the Marquis enquired.
"Surely the *Comte* should be accompanying you, both
last night and tonight."

"He is with his grandmother who is not well."

"Then his loss is my gain!" the Marquis observed. "I
should have been very disappointed if I had not found
you here, and very piqued, if that is the right word, if
you had not been alone."

"Then perhaps I have been some compensation for the fact that you are not sitting at the green-baize tables, as I imagined you would be, with a lovely lady on either side, helping you challenge the Goddess of Fortune."

"Your imagination runs away with you, Lady Sherington," the Marquis said dryly. "I seldom gamble, and actually, although it may surprise you, I am going to Monte Carlo to visit a friend who is in ill-health, and who particularly desires my company."

"Then I hope she is also very pretty," Trina said before she could prevent herself.

Once again she was sparring with the Marquis as she had done the night before, and as she put it to herself, some devil within her wanted to provoke him.

She had risen as she spoke and the Marquis rose too.

"I see," he said in an amused voice, "that you are determined to turn me into a rake. Very well, Lady Sherington, I am only too prepared to play the part you have assigned to me."

Trina looked up at him, wondering how she could reply to this assertion and wanting to say something witty.

Then to her astonishment before she could speak, the Marquis's arms went round her and he pulled her against him.

Before she could realise what was happening, before she had time even to raise her hands to ward him off, his lips came down on hers and held her captive.

She was so astounded that for a moment she did not even struggle against him.

She was so astounded that for a moment she no longer seemed to function.

Then as she thought his lips were hard and being kissed was not what she had expected it to be, his arms tightened and it was impossible to fight herself free.

Suddenly she found herself surrendering to his mastery in a manner she could not explain.

Something strange and very wonderful seemed to move up through her breasts, into her throat, and to vibrate from her lips against his.

It gave her sensations she had never known she was capable of feeling.

It was also so wonderful, so perfect that she knew it was what she had heard in the song of the nightingales.

She felt as if the Marquis carried her up into the sky towards the stars, and they were one with the moonlight rippling on the river, the trees, the flowers and the view that stretched in the darkness away into the horizon.

She vibrated to a rapture for which he had said there were no words. It was a wonder and a glory which moved from the sky onto his lips and made her a part of him.

Only when it seemed that time had ceased to exist and a few minutes or several centuries had passed the Marquis raised his head.

With a little cry that was hardly audible, and yet came from the very depths of her being, Trina fought herself free of his arms.

Then she was running from him, speeding across the lawn with a swiftness that would have been impossible in anyone who was not very young.

She reached the Château.

Without thinking she ran to the open window by which she had left the Salon and only then was she conscious that her heart was thumping so violently in her breast that she could not breathe.

To her relief the lights were still glowing, but the room was empty. Susi must have gone to bed.

Because she was exhausted by her headlong flight, Trina sank down into a chair. Her breath was coming in uneven gasps from between her lips and she tried to control it.

Yet she knew what she had felt when the Marquis

kissed her was something from which she could never
escape, even if she never saw him again.

He had captured a part of her which she could
never regain.

CHAPTER FIVE

Trina awoke in the morning to think: 'How dare he
kiss me!' Then because she could not help it, she whispered: "It was wonderful!"

Although quite a number of young men had tried
to kiss her in Rome, she had kept them at arms' length
and decided firmly in her own mind that she would
never be kissed on the lips until she was in love.

The Marquis had taken her by surprise and she
thought that ordinarily she would have not only strug-
gled against him, but been extremely angry at his impertinence.

But she could not forget the wonder he had evoked
in her and the way he made her feel as if he carried
her towards the stars and that with his lips he drew
her heart from her body and she became a part of
him.

"I shall never see him again," she told herself.

She felt it was true that she had lost a rapture and
enchantment that was his and his alone.

Because she was afraid of her own thoughts, she
dressed quickly and ran downstairs to find her mother
and the *Comte* were already having breakfast.

"You did not come to say goodnight to me," Susi said reproachfully.

"I thought you might be asleep," Trina replied.

She knew the truth was that after what she had felt with the Marquis, it would have been impossible to talk to anybody or to discuss any subject except him.

"Today, after we have been riding," the *Comte* said, "I am going to tell the Marchioness that the Elixir is arriving tonight and we can demonstrate its powers tomorrow."

Susi looked at him as if she was surprised at the urgency in his voice.

"If you want the truth," he said, "I wish we had not embarked on this particular adventure."

"I feel that too," Susi said. "At the same time, I know how much it means to you."

"I suppose it is necessary," the *Comte* said, "but even the Castle seems to have shrunk in importance."

Trina was well aware what he was trying to say: that the only thing which mattered was his love for Susi, and that he wanted her for his wife.

At the same time she could understand her mother's reluctance to allow him to sacrifice so much.

Trina was sure she was right in thinking that the *Comte* had never in his whole life been in love as he was now, and she knew that happiness would be a compensation for almost everything else.

Yet she understood too how much the history of their forebears meant to the noblemen both of France and Italy. It was part of their blood, and part too of the very air they breathed.

The *Comte* had been brought up to believe that his background was interwoven with his character and his personality, and it would be as difficult to divorce him from the Castle as it would be from a wife.

'If only I could find a solution,' Trina thought, 'then everything would be perfect.'

Perfection was, however, something few people found in this world, and she told herself she had no magic wand to make her mother and the *Comte* live happily ever after.

At the same time, the sun was shining and they were both very much in love.

Trina watched them ride away on two of the *Comte's* superb horses and felt, as she was left behind, rather like Cinderella.

But there was still a great deal for her to do, if the Elixir was to be ready by tomorrow and she ran up the steps and into the Still-room to find that the *Comte* had left the apothecary's bottle which she had asked him for.

In fact, there were two of them, both very old, one of a deep amber glass which seemed to hold a faint touch of the sun in it, and the other made of the black crystal that she knew was used for the special products produced in Grasse.

She had found in the *Comte's* Library, a *Catalogue de Parfumerie de la Fabrique,* 'furnished to the principal foreign Courts.'

In it were listed pots made of faience, pipeclay, porcelain, glass and crystal which contained pomades extracted from flowers, creams for the complexion made from snails, cucumber and alabaster, and wax for the moustache.

There were also flasks made of crystal or black glass which contained hazelnuts, Macassar water, Russian leather water and of course, lavender water.

Trina had thought that perhaps they should procure some of these age-old recipes for beauty to please the Marchioness.

There had, however, been no time to concentrate on anything except the Elixir and she decided the amber bottle would be most suitable, especially as it had an amusing little silver top which depicted a fawn dancing.

There were just one or two more ingredients that Trina wanted to introduce into what she had already distilled.

Two of them were very ancient herbs which the *Comte* had told her had been planted in the garden of the Castle at the time of Catherine di Medici.

There had been then a great interest in beauty products because Queen Catherine was so desperately jealous of the King's mistress, Diane de Poitiers.

Her beauty and the fact that she never appeared to grow older were attributed to witchcraft, but the real reason was that she bathed in cold water and preferred plain food and fresh vegetables to the heavy, over-rich meals that were fashionable at the Court.

'I wonder what the Marchioness eats?' Trina thought, and suspected, as Susi had said she was slimming, that it was not the right things.

"Perhaps we could include suggestions for a health-giving and beautifying diet with the Elixir," she ruminated as she chopped up the herbs.

Then she smiled because she was concentrating on the Marchioness's beauty as if she had a personal interest in effecting for her what she craved.

"If we make her feel better, that automatically will improve her appearance, and we will not feel so guilty about the money," Trina told herself.

She knew, although Susi had not said so, that it went against her intrinsic honesty and frankness to deceive anyone, even a woman as stupid as the Marchioness.

"We are saving her from worse things," Trina said firmly, "and that is a good deed, whatever anyone might think."

The herbs were prepared and ready to be added to the rest of the Elixir by the time Susi and the *Comte* returned, and Trina tidied herself and went to the Salon to join them.

She began to open the door and as she did so, she heard her own name and instinctively stood still.

"I have not mentioned it before," she heard her mother say in a low voice, "because I thought when you—saw Trina as she looked so like—me that you would fall in love—with her."

"Do you really believe that I love you only because of your looks—breathtaking though they are?" the *Comte* asked.

"I thought," Susi said as if he had not spoken, "that you would—realise that Trina can—give you—everything that I am unable to do."

"By that you mean money."

"Yes. Trina will be rich—very rich, and there would be no—difficulty about—keeping up the Castle, the grounds and all the other properties you—own."

There was silence for a moment. Then the *Comte* said:

"Look at me, Susi!"

"You are not attending to what I am saying to you," Susi cried.

"You have not said anything that you have not hinted at a dozen times, my darling. But as I know everything you think, everything you feel, I have known this was in your mind ever since Trina arrived in Paris."

"Then if you knew what I was—thinking, why can you not—understand that is what would be—best for you? That is what will—ultimately make you—happy."

The *Comte* laughed.

"I adore you!" he said. "In many ways you are incredibly foolish, and I think actually that is another reason why I love you so much. Do you really believe, my precious, that a man of my age does not know his mind or can transfer his heart from one woman to another because it is more expedient for him to do so?"

"There have been—many women—in your—life," Susi faltered.

"Many!" the *Comte* agreed, "but they have always disappointed me. I imagined it was because I expected too much; demanded that they should match the ideal which lies in a special shrine in my heart."

He paused for a moment before he added very softly:

"That was until I met you."

"Oh, Jean, why do you say such—perfect things to me?" Susi cried.

"Because I love you," he replied, "and because you love me. Because also, my adorable little goose, your daughter to me is only a pale reflection of you, and I am not prepared to accept second best!"

"I am—trying to—help you."

"I know, my sweetest, but it is a very amateur effort and from my point of view very ineffective."

"You are laughing at me!" Susi protested.

"Only because I love you so much for thinking of me rather than yourself. Can you imagine what it would be like if I did what you wanted, and you had to watch me loving Trina and doing all the things with her I have planned that you and I would do together?"

"I should—try to be—glad for—your sake."

"You know that would be impossible, and when you were alone at night, you would want me as I want you. Oh, my lovely one, I adore you for thinking of me, but I am selfish enough to want to think of myself, and I know you are the only woman in the world who could possibly make me happy."

"Is that true? Really—true?"

"Of course it is true!"

"Oh, darling—I love—you so—much!"

There was silence and Trina knew that the *Comte* was kissing her mother.

She shut the door quietly and moved away with a smile on her face.

She too, had been aware that Susi had planned that she and the *Comte* should be married so that he could share her fortune.

'Dearest Mama, is so unworldly,' Trina told herself, 'and of course, she has never been in love before now, so she knows so little about it, and less about men.'

She thought perhaps that was Susi's attraction for the *Comte*.

He would have been bored with a very young girl, but Susi intrigued him as a woman, and at the same time, her unsophistication and her purity was something he had never found previously in the life of gaiety and amusement he had led in Paris.

"They are perfectly suited!" Trina said to herself. "But Mama will never understand that much as I like him, I am not the least in love with Jean de Girone."

A little voice inside her asked her if there was not someone else she loved—a very different type of man —but she had no answer and was only sure that when they reached Paris there would be plenty of men provided by the *Duchesse* who would both amuse and interest her.

After dinner that evening she found herself wondering if she should go to the place where she had heard the nightingales. Then she thought it would be an anti-climax to be alone there after the two nights when she had talked with the Marquis.

She drew in her breath as she remembered how last night he had kissed her and it was agonising to think that perhaps tonight he was kissing someone else on the Riviera.

She told herself severely that she would be very foolish if she attached too much importance to his kiss.

She had teased and provoked him and he had retaliated in a manner she had not expected, merely because she was not as experienced in the art of flirtation as he thought her to be.

She was quite certain that the sophisticated women with whom he usually associated would have expected to be kissed if they were alone with such an attractive man, and would have thought it was merely a compliment to their beauty and their attractions.

How could the Marquis guess it was the first time she had ever been kissed or that it had made her feel a thousand wonderful emotions she had never even imagined?

She imagined that as he journeyed towards Monte Carlo early today he perhaps had thought with a cynical smile on his lips that he had scored off the *Comte* by kissing the woman of whom at the moment, he was obviously enamoured.

The particular social set in London to which the Marquis belonged doubtless spent their time in this way when they were not watching their horses race each other's, or attempting to kill more pheasants than their friends.

'I mean nothing to him,' Trina thought, 'and by now he will already have forgotten me.'

She left the Salon but she did not go out into the garden.

Instead she went up to bed and quite unaccountably, after Susi had come to say goodnight to her looking so radiantly happy that her eyes seemed to light the room, Trina cried herself to sleep.

The following morning the *Comte* was very business-like in his plans for the day.

"I have arranged with the Marchioness," he said, "that she will meet us in the Music Room at three o'clock. Until then there is a lot to do."

He saw that both Susi and Trina were listening to him and he went on:

"I have found several heavy and very beautiful tapestry screens with which I intend to encirle the chair in which Susi and you will sit."

"If they are heavy, that should prevent them from falling over by mistake, which would be disastrous!" Trina said.

"Exactly!" the *Comte* agreed. "Over the top to make a kind of box in which you will be enclosed there will be a Chinese shawl."

"I am—feeling rather frightened," Susi said. "You must tell me exactly what I have to do."

"I will seat you in the chair," the *Comte* said, "which, although it will not be obvious to anyone else, will be fastened to the floor so that you will not be frightened when it moves."

He smiled at her and went on:

"*Comte* Bernhard had a special spring by which he made the chair descend, but it will be quite easy for Trina waiting below to wind you down without your doing anything. Then when she seats herself in your place, you turn the handle which lifts the chair back into place."

"Supposing—it sticks—and I am not—strong enough?" Susi asked.

"I promise you it is very easy," the *Comte* replied, "and so that you will not be worried, I am going to take you there this morning and show you exactly what to do."

"I have been wondering about one thing," Trina said, "when we have finished you and I will be in the Music Room but Mama will be down below. How will you get both of us away from the Castle and back here?"

"I have thought of that," the *Comte* said. "You will stay with the Marchioness, telling her what effect the Elixir has had on you and how young you feel."

"I am sure I can be very eloquent on the subject," Trina said dryly.

"While you are doing that," the *Comte* said, "I will slip away and go to the room below. Susi and I will leave the Castle by the same way that you will enter it."

"How is that?" Trina asked.

"My magical ancestor thought of everything," the *Comte* replied. "When he disappeared from the Music Room through the floor, he wound the chair back into place, then left the Castle by an underground passage which comes out near the stables."

Trina's eyes sparkled.

"I want to see it."

"It is a very ingenious route of escape," the *Comte* said, "because even in those days, as now, the exit was concealed by shrubs. We can walk back to the Château through shrubberies where it will be impossible for anyone to see us from the Castle."

"It grows more and more exciting!" Trina exclaimed.

Only Susi made no effort to enthuse about the plans.

The *Comte* then took Susi off to show her the way into the Castle and how to work the moving chair.

"I shall have time to show you, Trina," he said before he left, "when I put you in the room immediately after luncheon. Susi and I will arrive at the front door at about a quarter to three."

Trina understood that he was enjoying the plot, treating it as she had done at the beginning as a theatrical performance where everything must be on time and everybody have their right cue.

"What music are you going to play?" she enquired.

"Something loud to begin with," the *Comte* answered, "because as you anticipated the machinery might squeak a little. Then something soft and soothing while presumably the Elixir works and Susi is transformed into a young and beautiful maiden!"

Trina had found among her gowns two that were identical.

"I cannot imagine now why I ordered two exactly the same," she said. "But it was such a pretty model for the summer, that I suppose I got carried away, or else I thought it would save me the trouble of choosing something else."

"It is certainly exactly what we need," Susi said, "and they will require little alteration."

Actually Susi's lady's-maid had to let out for her the waist of Trina's gown by nearly two inches, but as there was a sash it did not show and if it was a little tight in the bodice she did not complain.

Trina made sure before luncheon that their hair was arranged in exactly the same way, and even the *Comte,* regarding them with a critical eye, could not find fault.

"Do you really—believe that no-one could—tell us apart?" Susi asked him.

"I should always know you," he answered, "but then, as you know, I am *fada* where you are concerned."

"Let us hope the Marchioness will not have the same powers," Susi said.

"How could she have?" the *Comte* answered. "They are exclusive to a Provençal and we are very zealous to make sure that outsiders do not encroach on our special magic."

They laughed, but Trina was sure it was very unlikely that anyone, especially a woman as stupid as the Marchioness, would notice any difference between her and Susi.

'The Marquis might be different,' she thought.

Then she told herself that he had believed her to be a married woman eighteen years older than she actually was!

"He is certainly not *fada!*" she said scornfully.

At the same time, she was glad he was not to be present at the afternoon's performance.

Although Trina had told herself she did not suffer from nerves, she found her heart beating a little faster when after she and the *Comte* had reached the place beneath the Music Room, he left her there alone.

It had been an excitement walking through the shrubs, finding the entrance to the underground passage and creeping along it in a crouching position.

They entered the room through a secret place in

the panelling. This too, was very low as it was really only a space between two floors and not intended to be occupied.

In the centre of it was a strange contraption consisting of a wheel with iron struts stretching to the ceiling.

"It is quite easy to turn," the *Comte* said.

To demonstrate he rolled the wheel with his hands and the chair came down from above firmly fixed to a piece of the parquet flooring.

Trina watched fascinated, then said:

"You are quite sure there is nobody in the room above?"

"I locked the door after I had arranged the screens and the Chinese shawl over them."

"You think of everything!"

She peeped upwards but all she could see was darkness.

The *Comte* then made her sit in the chair while he turned the wheel that would lift her to the Music Room.

It was so well contrived that even after so many years, now that it had been oiled, it moved with very little effort.

There was just a slight click as the floor fitted into place, then the *Comte* wound her down again and Trina cried:

"How could *Comte* Bernhard have thought of anything so clever?"

"He was well in advance of his time and had a very inventive mind," the *Comte* answered, "and remember he was always propelled by an ardent desire to survive."

"There were so many enemies to be afraid of in those days!"

"Now we have only one," the *Comte* remarked wryly, "poverty!"

Trina thought for a moment. Then she said:

"I heard what Mama said to you last night. I knew it was in her mind, but she did not say anything to me."

"I have never known a woman as unselfish and with such a sweet character as your mother," the *Comte* said. "Are you surprised that having found her, I intend never to let her go?"

"I should be very angry if you did," Trina remarked. "And now that we can talk openly, I want to tell you that you are exactly the person she should marry."

"I am glad you approve of your future Step-father!" the *Comte* smiled.

Trina laughed.

"You do not really seem old enough, but I accept you in that position with the greatest of pleasure!"

They both laughed without bothering to say in words that neither of them had any desire for any other kind of relationship.

Then they hurried back to Susi.

Waiting for the music above to tell her that she must wind down the chair, Trina found herself offering up a little prayer that everything would be successful.

The *Comte* was so charming, she thought. He deserved happiness just as her mother did.

"I will help him, I will help him in every way I can," she vowed.

The *Comte* was aware as they drove over the drawbridge which would lead them to the centre of the Castle, that Susi was trembling.

"Please do not be frightened, my darling," he said. "If you are, I shall call the whole thing off. I cannot bear you to be upset or worried."

He could not have said anything which would have made Susi more resolute in her desire to help him.

"I am only—afraid that I may—fail you," she answered, "but I—want to help you—I want to do everything you ask of me."

"That is easy," the *Comte* replied. "I want you to love me!"

He saw the light come into her eyes and knew as she stepped out of the carriage, that she had a new confidence in herself.

The Marchioness was waiting for them in the Hall and was looking excited except that her face was so plastered with cosmetics that it was almost impossible to see what she really did look like.

Her hair was a glaring, rather hard gold that in contrast made Susi's look like the sunshine in the spring, and her eye-lashes were heavily mascaraed.

"You have brought the Elixir?" she asked, although she was well aware of what the *Comte* carried in his hand, carefully wrapped in paper.

"I have it here," he replied.

They walked towards the Music Room and Susi saw that the *Comte* had drawn the curtains slightly so as not to admit too much sunlight.

The room was also decorated with great vases of flowers which scented the air.

"How pretty this room is!" the Marchioness exclaimed. "I do not think I have been in it before."

"Today it is the right atmosphere for the experiment we are about to make," the *Comte* said. "As I have already told you, Lady Sherington will sit in the chair surrounded by screens. She will drink the Elixir and we must have perfect quiet and peace for it to work. The only sound will be the music I shall play."

"You think that is important?" the Marchioness asked.

"Very!" the *Comte* replied seriously. "Any shock or disturbance might have the opposite effect to what we intend."

"I understand!" the Marchioness said.

Susi looked at her and thought that in her eagerness she was even more pathetic than she had been when they had first met.

There was still a great deal of beauty in her face, but

there was no character and very little personality behind it.

'It must be terrible,' Susi thought, 'to spend the last years of one's life only looking back at one's youth. There must be things to do which will help, even things to learn, however old we become. How can she be so foolish as to waste her life on a wild goose-chase?'

But she knew that was something she could not say.

Then as the *Comte* unwrapped the amber-coloured glass flask, the Marchioness gave a shrill cry of delight and excitement.

"So that is the Elixir of Youth! The Elixir I have been seeking for so long! Why do we waste time. Let me drink it now!"

"No," the *Comte* said firmly. "That would be a mistake. I want to prove to you what it should do, although of course, I must tell you that as you are older than Lady Sherington you cannot expect one glass to work as quickly where you are concerned."

"Of course, I understand that," the Marchioness said.

"Come and sit here," the *Comte* suggested indicating the chair he had chosen where the Marchioness was facing the light while Susi, when she was not sitting in the chair, had her back to it.

"Yes, of course, I will do exactly what you tell me," the Marchioness agreed. "And as you have the Elixir for me, *Comte*, I have something for you."

As she spoke she drew from her bag a cheque made out for £10,000 and held it out towards him.

For a moment the *Comte* hesitated, and Susi knew that his instinct was to refuse it, to be honest and say that after all what they offered her would not work as the Marchioness wished it to do, and tell her to keep her money.

But even as she held her breath she knew the *Comte* had remembered Antonio di Casapellio waiting in Italy to hypnotise and rob the poor, foolish woman.

"Thank you," he said.

The abrupt way he spoke told Susi just how much he disliked now, at the very last moment, what he was doing.

He put the flask down on a table where there was already a crystal wine glass on a silver tray, then he took the cheque and thrust it into his pocket.

"You are ready to drink the Elixir, Lady Sherington?" he asked Susi.

"I am—longing to do so," Susi replied. "I am thirty-six and afraid that old age is already beginning to creep towards me. It will be wonderful to be really—young again."

The Marchioness gave a deep sigh.

"That is what I am longing for; to know one can look in a mirror without shuddering, to see a man's eyes light up when I appear, and know that every woman who looks at me, is envious."

Her voice throbbed with emotion as she went on:

"I can still hear the cheers of the crowd whenever I appeared in London. There were always a hundred people or more waiting outside Clevedon House when I left in the morning, and riding down Rotten Row was like a Royal procession."

Susi had heard her say this before, but she listened wondering if the Marchioness ever thought of anything else but her triumphs of many years ago.

"Do you know what the Emperor of France, Louis Napoleon, said to me the first time I went to Paris . . . ?" the Marchioness began, then she stopped. "I can tell you all this later. Please, *Comte,* do not let us waste any more time. Give Lady Sherington the Elixir."

The *Comte* poured from the amber flask, then with the glass in his hands he said to Susi:

"You must sit in the chair and compose yourself. Keep your eyes closed."

Susi walked to the chair set between the screens and when she was seated she took the glass from the

Comte's hands and drank it. He immediately closed the screen around her and pulled the embroidered shawl into place.

Then without speaking he walked very quietly across the room and sat down at the piano.

As he struck the first chords he knew that Trina would know what she had to do.

She had, in fact, put her hands some minutes earlier on the wheel.

Although they were very faint, she could hear the sound of voices above and the slight scrape which she knew meant that the *Comte* had put the screen in place.

Now slowly, without hurry, as he had instructed her, she turned the wheel and immediately the chair came down from above with Susi sitting in it.

They smiled at each other, but the *Comte* had told them very firmly that they must not speak.

Trina took Susi's place and immediately the chair began to rise.

She held her breath in case something should go wrong until it fitted, as *Comte* Bernhard, those centuries ago, had intended, precisely and accurately into its place in the floor above.

She felt the agitation which had made her hold her breath subside as she listened to the music the *Comte* was playing on the piano.

It made her think of the nightingales and the song of love they had sung to her that first night when to her astonishment she had found the Marquis standing behind her.

She was thinking of how handsome he was, how broad-shouldered and in a way, overpowering, when the music stopped and she heard the *Comte's* footsteps coming towards her across the room.

She kept her eyes shut and now he was moving away the screens and she knew that he was standing in front of her.

"Wake up, Lady Sherington!" he said quietly.

Trina blinked her eyes as if she had actually been sleeping, and the *Comte* put out his hand and drew her from the chair.

"Let us look at you," he said, "and you must also tell us what you are feeling."

He drew her from between the screens and Trina saw the Marchioness staring at her with a rapt expression on her face.

Then she felt as if her heart stopped beating, for standing a little distance behind the Marchioness in the entrance to the room where the *Comte* had been unable to see him from the piano, was the Marquis!

It seemed to Trina as if everything turned a somersault including her heart and she had no idea what she should do about it.

Quite unaware that the Marquis was there, the *Comte* was leading her towards his mother.

"Now we shall know, Your Ladyship," he said, "how successful the Elixir has been."

He thought as he spoke that even anyone as stupid as the Marchioness could not fail to see the difference between Susi and Trina.

The purple shadows and the little wrinkles at the corners of her eyes which Trina had put in so painstakingly were, of course, missing.

But it was obvious to him that there was something very young and spring-like about Trina that made her seem for the moment, as if she was Persephone come back from the darkness of Hades.

"There *is* a difference," the Marchioness said, in an ecstatic voice. "I can see it! The lines have gone from her face. They have really disappeared!"

"How do you feel?" the *Comte* enquired of Trina.

She had while she had been waiting below, rehearsed what she was to say, but now because the Marquis was listening, she found it difficult to speak.

"At first I . . . felt strange . . . a little dizzy," she said after a moment's hesitation, "but then . . . it was as if . . . something alive was moving within me . . .

it was . . . strange . . . and yet exciting . . . and now I feel as if . . . I . . . could dance and sing . . . because I am . . . happy."

"That is exactly what I was told you would feel," the *Comte* said.

"It works! It really works!" the Marchioness cried. "Shall I take it now or wait?"

"I think it would be wise in your case, to wait," the *Comte* replied, "at least until tonight. It would perhaps work better if you slept longer, to give the Elixir a chance to work."

"I will take it tonight," the Marchioness agreed.

"But only one wine-glassful each day," the *Comte* said. "What is in the flask should last for a week or longer."

"Yes, yes," the Marchioness cried. "One glass—but I shall be impatient if it does not work at once."

"Too much might do more harm than good."

"Then it shall be just one glass," the Marchioness said meekly.

"I am sure you would like Lady Sherington to sit down and talk to you for a little while," the *Comte* said. "There must be many questions you will want to ask her, and so I shall leave you."

He kissed the Marchioness's hand, then as he walked towards the door, Trina stole a glance in the same direction.

To her inexpressible relief the Marquis was no longer there.

'Perhaps I dreamed it,' she thought, 'but he seemed real, so very real.'

Nevertheless she was afraid.

The Marchioness, however, was ready to begin her questions.

"Tell me what you feel," she begged. "I am so intrigued to learn how it works."

Trina explained, and the Marchioness asked:

"Did you have a creeping feeling under your skin, as if it was more active than it had been before?"

273

"It is very difficult to put into words," Trina replied.

She knew as she spoke, that the real difficulty was that the Marquis had upset her by his sudden appearance.

Why had he come back?

Surely there cannot have been another fall of stones on the railway line? It could not be to see her—she was certain of that. Then, why? Why?

All the time the Marchioness was talking, going over and over the same ground, but she found it impossible to concentrate on anything.

It gave her a feeling of unutterable relief when about ten minutes later the Marchioness, as if she was aware there was nothing more to discuss, rose to her feet.

"I am going to take the Elixir of Youth very carefully to my bedroom," she said. "It would be disastrous if the servants knocked it over by mistake. Thank you, Lady Sherington. Will you come and see me tomorrow? Then we can compare notes, and you will be able to see what this wonderful potion has done for me!"

"Yes, of course," Trina agreed.

"Thank you again, from the bottom of my heart," the Marchioness said, "and tomorrow morning, if I look like you, I shall be the happiest woman in the world."

Clutching the amber bottle closely against her breast, she went from the room without waiting for her guest.

Trina was aware that although the *Comte* had said he would return for her, it would be impossible for him to do so quickly.

It would take him nearly a quarter-of-an-hour to drive away so that the servants would see him go and then another fifteen minutes at least, to walk back through the shrubs to the hidden passage and take Susi back to the Château.

"I will walk," Trina told herself. "After all, if I go through the gardens no-one will be surprised."

She had almost reached the door of the Music-Room when she remembered that Susi would have left her gloves and her hand-bag on a chair before she had been enclosed by the screen.

Trina retrieved them and holding them in her hand, walked from the Music Room. Only as she reached the passage outside did she start and draw in her breath.

Waiting for her, looking very large and overpowering, was the Marquis!

Chapter Six

*F*or a moment Trina could only stand looking at the Marquis, and she knew that he was angry.

"I want to speak to you, Lady Sherington."

"I was just . . . going home."

He did not answer but they walked away down the passage and he opened the door into the Library.

Because there was nothing else she could do, she walked in ahead of him and moved towards the fire-place.

She thought as she did so, how many hours she and her mother had spent poring over the books on herbs in their efforts to make the Elixir of Youth for the Marchioness.

Then she could think of nothing but that the

Marquis seemed very large and overpowering as he walked slowly to join her on the hearth-rug.

"I want an explanation," he said, "and it had better be a good one!"

"I do not know what you mean," Trina replied. "I thought you had gone away."

"I had," he answered, "but when I arrived in Nice yesterday it was to learn from the newspapers that the friend I was to see in Monte Carlo had died, so I returned—obviously at an inopportune moment."

The way he spoke made Trina aware that he was not only suspicious of what had been happening while he was away, but also extremely annoyed.

Because she was nervous, she said quickly:

"I want to . . . return to the Château and I am sure the *Comte* will answer all your . . . questions if you wish to . . . put them to him."

"I prefer to put them to you."

"I have nothing to tell you."

"That is not true, and you know it!"

Trina did not answer and after a moment he said:

"I was aware that my mother came to Provence to find herbs which she thought would make her young again, and I imagine that is what she was carrying when I saw her leaving the Music Room."

He paused then continued:

"But I should be interested to know, Lady Sherington, what she paid for the flask she carried in her hand and how you were deceiving her in coming out of that contraption which was obviously a part of some conjurer's magic trick."

Trina thought he had come uncomfortably near the truth and lifting her chin a little, she replied:

"I think your mother can give you a very adequate explanation."

"First, the *Comte,* then my mother," the Marquis said. "I am asking you, Lady Sherington."

"I have nothing to tell you."

"Why? Are you ashamed of what you have done?"

"Not in the slightest, and I only took part in the experiment . . ."

"An experiment?" the Marquis interrupted. "Now we are getting somewhere! What sort of experiment? And why were you hidden behind those screens?"

He had raised his voice to speak in an unmistakably aggressive tone.

"I think, My Lord," Trina said quietly, "I have every right to refuse to be cross-examined by you, and I therefore repeat that I am going back to the Château. If you wish to come with me, you are of course, at liberty to do so."

As she spoke she glanced at the Marquis and saw his eyes narrow. Then she looked away again, conscious that her heart was beating uncomfortably in her breast.

"My mother has been duped by one charlatan after another," the Marquis said, "but I was not expecting the *Comte* de Girone, and least of all you, to be added to the list of those who have extracted money from her, under false pretences."

Trina longed to reply that neither she nor the *Comte* had done anything of the sort, but she was uncomfortably aware there was a cheque for £10,000 in his pocket.

"Who are you?" the Marquis demanded unexpectedly, "and what are you getting out of this?"

Trina looked at him in surprise and he went on:

"I do not believe you are Lady Sherington. My mother told me she was thirty-six and a widow. It is completely impossible for you to be that age."

"What makes you so . . . sure of that?"

"Now that I see you in the daylight," the Marquis replied, "I would be prepared to wager a very large sum that you are half the age you pretend to be."

It flashed through Trina's mind that when she had thought he was perceptive, she had been right.

Because she knew she had annoyed him, she said with what she hoped was almost a simper:

"Your Lordship is very . . . complimentary."

"And I would also be prepared," the Marquis said slowly, "to swear that when I kissed you, it was for the first time."

Now the colour flooded over Trina's face and because she wanted only to escape from the penetrating expression in his eyes, she turned towards the door.

"I refuse to go on with this . . . conversation."

She meant to sound proud and dignified, but instead her words came out in a soft, shy little voice.

She was already moving when the Marquis seized hold of her wrist and brought her to an abrupt stop.

"Answer me!" he commanded. "Who are you? Are you some actress the *Comte* has engaged to play a part in defrauding my mother?"

"Let me go!"

The Marquis's fingers only tightened.

"You will go when you have answered me, and not before!"

"Then you may have to wait here all night," Trina retorted.

"Doubtless like when you were waiting for the nightingales, you will prove yourself a very skilled performer."

His voice was so cynical and bitter that Trina longed to reply that she had not been acting then.

The wonder of his kiss, the strange sensations he had evoked in her, swept over her to make her feel that she could not go on prevaricating. She must tell him the truth and ask him to forgive her.

Then she knew she could not be so disloyal to the *Comte*. She knew also that once the Marquis knew she had in fact, been deceiving his mother, he would never speak to her again.

Because she was upset, she tried once again to free herself, saying:

"Let me go! You have no right to keep me here."

"I think I have every right," the Marquis contradicted. "You have conspired to make a fool of my mother and therefore you will either tell me the truth now or I shall keep you here until you do!"

"Do not be so ridiculous!" Trina exclaimed. "Those sort of threats are only empty words!"

"I will prove that they are meaningful, unless you tell me what I want to hear."

"Which I have no intention of doing," Trina replied. "When the *Comte* returns for me, which he will do in a very short time, you can hardly tell him that you are keeping me as a hostage."

"You sound as if you are certain he will not wish to lose you. Is he your lover?"

Trina did not stop to think before she flared furiously:

"No, of course not! How can you . . . suggest such a thing?"

"From the way he spoke about you to my mother, there was no doubt he was enamoured of you. I therefore presumed that he has had to let his Castle since he needs the money, and you are assisting him to get it."

"You have a very active imagination, My Lord," Trina said in a voice which she hoped was as sarcastic as his.

"You certainly stimulate it," he replied. "It is not hard to see the way you have been plotting."

He paused and Trina was wondering how she could get away from him.

He still held her wrist in what was almost a vice-like grip, and she knew that, even if she was free, long before she could reach the door and open it, he would be able to stop her.

"I think really all I need to know," the Marquis went on, "is how much my mother paid you to produce that herbal rubbish and to deceive her by some mumbo-jumbo which took place in a make-shift magician's cabinet."

He was getting nearer and nearer to the truth, Trina thought.

But for the *Comte*'s sake she must not let him know the existence of Susi or indeed the enormous sum of money his mother had paid for what she believed to be an Elixir of Youth.

"If you are determined not to let me go," she said coldly, "we . . . might sit down. I am finding it extremely tiring standing here arguing for no reason."

"There is plenty of reason," the Marquis answered, "but I have a better idea."

Pulling her by the wrist he walked towards the door, opened it and drawing her with him, started to walk down the passage.

Trina hoped he was taking her to the front door, perhaps to throw her out.

But she could feel the waves of anger emanating from him which did not give her any real hope of escape.

They walked some way along the passage which she knew led to the back of the Castle, and while she was puzzling as to where they were heading the Marquis seemed sure of himself.

She thought if they met any of the servants they would think it strange that the Marquis should be dragging her by the wrist, but they met no-one.

Trina had the idea, although she was not sure, that they were in a part of the Castle that was not often in use.

Soon they came to a stairway leading downwards, which was wide enough for two people to walk side by side and the Marquis started down it.

Only as they descended lower and still lower, did Trina ask:

"Where are you taking me? This is ridiculous! The *Comte* will be expecting me at the Château."

"Then he will be disappointed," the Marquis snapped.

It struck Trina that the air was cooler, in fact almost cold, after the heat of the rooms they had just left.

There were still a few steps ahead, when she stopped dead.

"I am going no further!" she said. "Let me go back, or I will scream for help!"

The Marquis looked around as if he would draw her attention to the ancient stone walls which Trina suddenly realised were bare and not decorated with tapestries or pictures, as in other parts of the Castle.

Quite suddenly she remembered that she had seen this particular staircase before, when the *Comte* had been showing Susi and her around the Castle the first afternoon they had arrived.

"That is the way to the dungeons," he had said. "I will show them to you sometime, but not now. There are so many other things to see."

Now she was afraid.

"Why are you . . . bringing me . . . here?" she asked and her voice trembled.

"You will see," the Marquis said ominously.

Although she tried to resist him, he pulled her down the last few steps.

Now as they moved forward with the light coming only through arrow-slits in the walls, she saw ahead, as she had half-expected, a huge oak door with iron hinges and an enormous square lock.

"This is the . . . way to the . . . dungeons," she said.

"I am aware of that," the Marquis retorted, "and I think you will find it a salutary experience to be incarcerated in one until you are prepared to tell me what I intend to hear."

"You are mad!" Trina exclaimed. "You cannot really be behaving in such a crazy manner!"

"It may seem crazy to you," the Marquis replied, "but if you use mediaeval methods yourself, then you must expect mediaeval punishments!"

He stopped, still holding her by the wrist, turned the key in the lock, and she saw ahead of her more steps going down to a lower floor.

The dim light coming through the arrow-slits revealed chains fastened at intervals along the walls
which must once have been used to tether prisoners.

She gave a little gasp, and the Marquis said:

"I am afraid you will not find it very comfortable,
but when you are ready to tell me the truth you will
see there is a bell attached to a rope on the right-hand
side of the door. Ring it, and I will come and set you
free."

Completely bemused by what he was saying, Trina
looked towards the rope, and she was about to speak
when the Marquis added:

"If you think to attract attention by ringing it or by
shouting, let me inform you it is quite impossible for
anyone who is not in this part of the Castle, to hear
you. I hope you enjoy your solitude, Lady Sherington!"

He took a step backwards as he spoke, and almost
before Trina could realise what was happening, he
had moved back through the heavy oak door and shut
it behind him.

She heard the key turn in the lock, then his footsteps crossing the stone floor and walking up the
stairs.

She could hardly believe he had actually gone or
had locked her in the dungeon. It must be some horrible dream from which she could not awaken.

Then there was a damp smell that was inescapable,
and she felt cold on her face and hands.

The ceiling in the dungeon was quite high and the
arrow-slits were at the very top of the walls which she
told herself must be just at ground level.

For a moment she contemplated beating on the
door and screaming. Then she knew it would not only
be undignified but useless.

From what she had seen of the Castle, she was sure
that the part in which she was now imprisoned was at
the back.

It was also beyond the stables where the *Comte* and

Susi would have emerged from the hidden passage, to walk home through the shrubberies.

There would, therefore, be no-one to hear her, however loudly she screamed and, as the Marquis had said, no-one inside would suspect for one moment where she was.

"I will not give in to him!" Trina told herself defiantly.

She wanted to hate him for what he had done to her —yet at the same time, she could not help feeling a sneaking respect for the man who was so determined and so dominating.

In a way, although she hated to admit it, he was perfectly right. They were defrauding his mother, and he was protecting her as only a good son would do.

"I am making excuses for him," Trina murmured.

Even so, just as she had sparred provocatively with him ever since they had met, she wanted now to defy him and, if it was humanly possible, to beat him at his own game.

The question was how?

She was quite certain he was determined not to let her out until she told him the truth and it would be impossible to lie convincingly enough to deceive him.

And yet, Trina asked herself, how could she give in tamely? How could she ring the bell and say:

"I am sorry. I helped the *Comte* take £10,000 off your foolish mother, for some herbs we told her were the Elixir of Youth, and which she thinks have changed me from the appearance of a woman of thirty-six, to how I look now!"

"I will not do it! I will not!" Trina told herself defiantly. "If I do he will be more sure of himself than he is already, and even more overpowering."

Because she felt cold, she walked down the steps and crossed the stone floor.

She looked at the heavy, rusty chains and thought perhaps she was lucky he had not used them to fasten her to the wall.

She could not help thinking of the prisoners who had sat here year after year in abject despair, gradually losing their hope of being rescued.

Vaguely at the back of her mind she thought she had once heard that the only time they were allowed to ring the bell was when one of their number had died.

She shuddered at the thought of it.

Then she told herself the Marquis was only frightening her because he was angry and because he was determined to get his own way.

'I shall not die,' she thought, 'but I shall catch a cold which will be extremely unbecoming.'

As she walked the whole length of the dungeon and back again she thought imaginatively that the prisoners who had once been incarcerated there were telling her that it was hopeless to try to fight against the inevitable.

She would have to do what the Marquis said even though doubtless he would gloat over her helplessness and his victory, in what had really been an unequal contest.

"How could we have anticipated for one moment," Trina asked, "that his friend would die, and he would come back when he was not wanted?"

At the same time, she could not help remembering that if he had not done so, she would never have seen him again.

She was sure that now the *Comte* had the £10,000 and was anxious that no-one should realise that she existed, he would arrange for her to leave for Paris immediately.

She wondered what he would think when he returned to the Castle to find she was not there.

She had a feeling that the Marquis would tell him that he had no idea where she had gone. It would be the obvious thing to say.

"Lady Sherington? Oh, I think she walked home

some time ago. You will doubtless find her in the garden."

The *Comte* would believe him and it would certainly never enter his mind that she was locked in the dungeon of the Castle.

There was obviously no hope of being rescued that way.

"I shall have to give in," she sighed.

Then it suddenly struck her that *Comte* Bernhard might have imagined a day might come when he would be a prisoner in his own Castle.

In which case, surely, as he had escape routes everywhere else he would have put one here?

There was a light in Trina's eyes that had not been there before! When first she had moved slowly and rather hopelessly, she now walked quickly around the walls, noting every detail.

The arrow-slits were all on the West side, which meant that the East wall was doubtless an interior wall of the building, while the North wall which was opposite the door, was blank.

She stared at it wondering if there was any place where *Comte* Bernhard could have concealed a catch or lever such as she had seen in other parts of the Castle.

But there had always been ornamentation of some sort to hide his clever contraptions, a carving in a panel, a marble fireplace, or a place on the floor like they had just used in the Music Room.

Trina touched one or two of the bricks. They were cold and slightly damp and she thought that if there was mechanism of any sort, it would have rusted hopelessly by now.

She however looked at everything, scrutinising every detail carefully and trying to think where a secret passage could be hidden.

She found herself almost praying that she would find an escape because it would discomfit the Marquis and he would be astonished when he came back, expecting her to be penitent and apologetic, to find the dungeon empty.

'Perhaps then he will believe not only in the Elixir, but that I am Lady Sherington, and that I am thirty-six years of age,' she thought with a smile.

She went on searching only to feel as helpless as the prisoners must have felt years ago. She tried the West wall, and that too was damp.

'I shall have to give in,' she thought despairingly.

But some obstinacy made her refuse to acknowledge defeat until she absolutely had to.

Defiantly she crossed the dungeon floor.

As she touched the East wall she found it was dry. That at least gave her the hope that if there was any mechanism there it might still be in working order.

There seemed to be no reason to think any of the bricks were different from any others, but she moved along the wall methodically, looking for a crack or anything that might suggest a hidden spring or lever.

She had almost reached the end and was back again at the North wall when her foot caught in one of the chains. She stumbled over it, only preventing herself with an effort, from falling on her knees.

'It is no use,' she thought, 'I am cold, and when it grows dark I shall be frightened if I am here alone.'

To save herself from falling she had caught at the chain where it was attached to the wall, and now she felt as if it gave a little.

An idea struck her. She pulled.

It seemed loose and because she was curious and it was a last forlorn hope, she pulled as hard as she could with both her hands.

Then she gave a little cry of excitement. The chain came towards her and with it part of the wall to which it was attached.

It moved slowly and then there was a space about three feet high and two feet wide.

"A secret passage!" Trina cried. "This is what I have

been looking for, and now the Marquis will look foolish."

She sank down on her knees and stared inside.

She expected it to be dark, but strangely enough she saw a faint light in the distance.

She was well aware that any passage that had not been used for a long time might be dangerous not only because it might collapse on top of her, but also because the air could be poisonous.

However she told herself that she was prepared to risk almost anything rather than surrender to the Marquis as she had thought she would have to do.

She began to crawl through the opening, conscious that there was very little air, but telling herself if it was too foul she would go back.

The passage was wider than she had thought it would be. In fact, once she was inside there was plenty of room to move except that its height was no more than about three feet.

She crawled on, finding the earth on which she was moving was dry, and all the time there was a faint light ahead.

It was only a distance of perhaps twelve feet but it seemed a long way and she was, in fact, rather frightened, although she would not admit it, of becoming unconscious due to the bad air.

Suddenly she found herself in a high circular cave, for it could be nothing else, and the light in it came from an arrow-slit high up near the roof.

Trina's first feeling was one of disappointment. This was not a passage leading her outside by which she could escape as she had hoped, but ending in another part of the Castle from which there seemed to be no exit.

It was however difficult to be certain because there had been a fall of stones in the centre of the cave, and if there was, in fact, an exit on the other side, she would have to crawl over or round the rubbish to reach it.

Then as she looked at what lay in her way she saw it was not a pile of stones as she had first thought, but some material which had over the ages crumbled to become nothing but dust.

She pushed it with her fingers and as she did so, discovered there was something hard underneath:

Again she thought it must be stones or earth from the ceiling, until she saw something glitter.

She stared, moved a little more of the dust and saw that what she was looking at was a plate, round but dark, and yet there was no doubt that it was made of some substance which, old though it was, could still glitter in the light from the arrow-slit.

Then an idea struck her and the words she had read to her mother when she had not been listening, about *Comte* Bernhard came back to her:

"... *has contrived by powers beyond mortal men to hide his weapons, his treasures, and his women from the eyes of those who sought them!*"

Trina gave a little cry, then she was urgently pushing away the dust of the pile in front of her with both her hands.

It took her a little time to realise the magnitude of what she had found, and by that time her hands were filthy, the front of her white gown was grey from the dust, and her cheeks were smudged.

But her eyes were shining like stars and with some difficulty she turned and crawled back the way she had come.

Only when she reached the dungeon did the excitement of her discovery make her feel weak and she sat for a moment on the floor, propped against the secret opening, gasping for breath, at the same time, saying a prayer of thankfulness which seemed to come spontaneously to her lips.

"Thank You . . . God. Thank You . . . thank

You! Now Mama can marry the *Comte* and there will be no more problems, no more worries."

She felt curiously near to tears from the very wonder of it.

Then she started to her feet and running down the dungeon she grasped the rope attached to the bell and pealed it again and again.

She was impatient, and when the Marquis did not appear immediately she thought perhaps he had changed his mind and was determined to leave her alone until she was as humble and compliant as he wanted her to be.

Then with a leap of her heart she heard his footsteps coming down the stairs, and a moment later the key was turning in the lock.

As he opened the door Trina pushed her way through the opening as if she could not wait.

"Take me back . . . take me back," she cried before he could speak, "and I will tell you everything . . . everything! But I must go to the Château . . . first."

Only as she saw him staring at her in astonishment did she realise what she must look like.

"It does not matter!" she said impatiently as if he had asked a question. "Just take me back. You shall have an . . . explanation of everything, and the money! It is all wonderful! Wonderful! But I must tell the *Comte* first."

"What must you tell him?" the Marquis asked.

Because he was not holding onto her, Trina was already halfway up the stairs.

"Come on!" she urged. "We cannot waste time in talking. I have to tell them! I must tell them!"

The Marquis realised as she finished speaking that she had disappeared and hurried after her.

When he reached the top Trina was still ahead of him and he followed her seeing that as she reached the end of the corridor, she intended to leave the Castle not by the front door but by the back.

He caught up with her as she was moving across the lawn, having slowed her pace a little because she was breathless.

"I suppose it is useless to ask you what all this is about?" he enquired.

"I cannot talk now . . . I have to get . . . back to the . . . Château!" Trina gasped.

As if he accepted the inevitable the Marquis was silent until the Château was just ahead of them.

"I told the *Comte* when he called for you," he said, "that you had already gone home and he should look for you in the garden."

She was still running although the Marquis managed to keep up with her by walking quickly, and Trina flashed him a smile.

"I guessed . . . that was . . . what you would . . . say."

Her fair hair was blowing in the warm wind, and with a dirty hand which left a smear of grey on her forehead, she swept it back.

The Marquis smiled but he said nothing, and a moment later Trina had reached the French windows leading into the Salon.

She rushed into the room to find as she had half-expected her mother and the *Comte* sitting on the sofa talking to each other.

At the sight of her they stared for a moment and the *Comte* jumped to his feet.

"Trina—what has—happened . . . ?" Susi began.

"I have found it!" Trina cried. "I have found it . . . it is there in the dungeon . . . *Comte* Bernhard's treasure . . . where he must have hidden it all those years ago!"

She was so breathless from her long run that her words fell over each other and sounded almost incoherent.

She saw the expression of astonishment on the *Comte*'s face and said again:

"It is all there . . . the gold plate . . . a huge

casket filled with . . . jewels . . . and bags . . . or
what were once bags . . . of golden . . . coins!"

"The treasure?" the *Comte* questioned, but Susi
moving towards Trina said:

"Dearest, what have you done to yourself? You are
so dirty, but you are not hurt? Tell me you are not
hurt?"

"No . . . Mama . . . I am not hurt . . . only excited because I have . . . found it for you . . . now
you can get married . . . and live at the Castle . . .
and stop . . . worrying!"

As she spoke she remembered for the first time
since she had come into the Salon that the Marquis
was standing behind her.

She turned round to see that he was just inside the
window with a look in his eyes that it was impossible to
interpret.

"His Lordship wants to know the . . . truth of
what we have been doing," she said a little sarcasti-
cally. "I think we can now give him a very adequate
. . . explanation . . . and there need be no further
pretence."

"Yes, we must," Susi agreed. "I hated it anyway.
But, dearest, you must wash and change. I cannot
bear you to look like that."

"What does it matter?" Trina asked. "We have to go
and get the treasure out so I shall only get dirty all
over again."

She looked at the *Comte* but he was too dazed by
what she had said to be able to express his feelings.

"What are we waiting for?" she asked. "You must
come and see it!"

"Yes, what are we waiting for?" the *Comte* agreed as
if he forced himself to speak calmly. "And as it happens the carriage is still at the door waiting instructions."

"Then quickly! Quickly!" Trina cried impatiently. "I
want you to come and see what I have found . . .
immediately, in case I have . . . imagined it."

She seized Susi by the hand as she spoke and pulled her across the room.

"Of course we want to come," Susi said, "but . . ."

As if the *Comte* suddenly entered into the spirit of the excitement, he cried:

"We are all going! How can we wait? If it is true, then it is the most fantastic thing that has ever happened!"

"It *is* true!" Trina declared.

She had reached the Hall and was drawing her mother towards the front door, when Susi said:

"My bonnet—I cannot go like this!"

"What does it matter, Mama?" Trina replied. "And if you touch the treasure . . . you will soon be as dirty as I am."

"We will all touch it," the *Comte* said firmly.

Trina had pulled Susi into the carriage and the *Comte* got in after them and was followed by the Marquis.

It was as if he was quite content to allow Trina to have her way, but Susi noticed as the carriage drove off, that his eyes were on Trina's face and she was aware of how disreputable her daughter looked.

She drew a small lace-edged handkerchief from her belt and bent forward to start wiping the dirt from Trina's face as she had done when she was a child.

Trina would have put up her hands to do it for herself, but Susi said quickly:

"No! Do not touch anything! You might at least have stopped to wash your hands!"

Trina laughed.

"Oh, Mama, after all these centuries, does it really matter if my hands are clean or not? Think what this means to you. I can wash my hands for the next hundred years!"

Susi, however, continued to take the worst of the dirt from Trina's face, then she put the handkerchief into her hands.

"Perhaps this will be more effective," the Marquis suggested.

As he spoke he drew a large clean linen square from his pocket.

Trina smiled at him.

"I was trying to find a secret passage by which I could escape from you!"

"I wondered if there was one, when we heard how many the Castle contained," he replied. "But I thought it unlikely, as the dungeons are below ground."

"Who told you about the secret passages?" the *Comte* enquired.

"The servants have talked of nothing else ever since we arrived," the Marquis answered, "and actually I had read about your eccentric ancestor after I agreed to rent the Castle."

The *Comte* laughed.

"I had forgotten that you were likely to be a student of history."

The Marquis looked at Susi.

"Now I am beginning to understand why my mother was not told there was a second beautiful woman staying at the Château!"

The *Comte* laughed again.

"I see that among other talents you can add that of being a detective."

"I shall be interested to hear the whole story," the Marquis said, "but of course, after we have seen the treasure."

"That naturally comes first," the *Comte* replied.

Trina thought there was a slight acrimony between the two men. It did not surprise her when she remembered the scathing things the Marquis had said about the *Comte*.

She told herself that none of it mattered now.

She was sure that the treasure, because of its age, would be exceptionally valuable, and perhaps neither

Jean, nor any future *Comtes* of Girone would have to marry a wife with a large dowry.

At the same time when they reached the Castle and Trina led the way back along the passages that led to the dungeons, she was just a trifle apprehensive.

Supposing, after all, she had been mistaken and the treasure that was black with age was, in fact, worthless except for a few pieces which would be appreciated by a Museum?

She and the Marquis had left the door of the dungeons open and she ran down the steps and across the stone floor to the opening she had made in the wall.

"We can only go in one at a time," she said.

She looked at the *Comte* as she spoke.

"I claim my right of being the first," he replied with a smile.

"Of course!"

He took off his coat and put it on the floor and going down on his knees crawled through the opening, as Trina had done.

Susi picked up his coat and held it in her arms.

"It is cold and damp down here," she said. "Why did you come here in the first place?"

Trina's eyes twinkled and she looked at the Marquis.

"Are you prepared to explain to Mama," she asked, "why I was in the dungeon?"

"Certainly," he replied. "I locked your daughter in here, Lady Sherington, because she refused to tell me the truth."

"You—locked Trina in the—dungeon?" Susi repeated in horrified tones. "How could you do—such a terrible thing?"

"I think perhaps you rather spoiled her when she was a child," the Marquis replied, "but now I see you together I am persuaded that she cannot be more than thirteen or fourteen!"

It took Susi a moment or two to realise he was paying her a compliment. Then she said:

"Trina is eighteen—but I do not like to think that you have been—unkind to her."

The Marquis smiled.

"You will understand, Lady Sherington," he said, "that as she was pretending to be you, I expected her to tell me the truth."

"I am sorry—very sorry," Susi said. "I knew we should never have done—such a thing—but I wanted to help—Jean—and also—although you may not believe it—to save your mother from that wicked and horrid man in Italy."

"What man in Italy?" the Marquis enquired.

Susi looked at Trina.

"Should I not have said that?"

"Yes, of course you can say it, Mama," Trina said. "I intended to tell His Lordship myself when the opportunity arose."

She saw the Marquis was waiting for an explanation and went on:

"Your mother told the *Comte* that if we did not find her the Elixir of Youth, she was going to leave here immediately to go to Rome and put herself in the hands of a man called Antonio di Casapellio who would have hypnotised and drugged her."

"I have heard of Casapellio," the Marquis said sharply. "But are you sure of what you are saying?"

"You can ask the *Comte*," Trina said. "Although what we have done may be reprehensible, we at least will not have harmed your mother physically, which is what I understand this Italian would do."

The Marquis was frowning.

Then before he could speak, there was a shout from the *Comte* and he appeared through the opening in the wall pushing in front of him a large casket.

It was the one Trina had seen amongst the other things and had opened to see the jewels it contained.

The *Comte*'s white shirt was as dirty as Trina's gown, but he had managed to keep his face clean and as he got to his feet, he walked straight to Susi, put his arms around her and said:

"Tell me how soon you will marry me, my darling? For thanks to your daughter, I am now a very rich man!"

CHAPTER SEVEN

The *Comte* raised his glass.

"To Trina!" he said, "and to our future happiness!"

He looked at Susi as he spoke, saw the expression in her eyes and thought he was the most fortunate man in the world.

He could still hardly believe it was true, that after all these centuries, *Comte* Bernhard's treasures should have been discovered at exactly the right moment.

While he had been prepared, because he loved Susi, to give up his Castle and a great many luxuries which he had thought were necessary to his comfort, he was aware that she, because she was so sensitive, would have always felt guilty.

Now everything would be perfect because he was well aware that what was lying at the moment on the dungeon floor had a value which was almost impossible to assess.

He had found it hard to believe when Trina had said that she had found the treasure, that it could, in fact, be anything like as impressive as he hoped.

When he and the Marquis had taken turns to drag

or push the pile through the narrow passage into the
dungeon, every journey had made the *Comte* realise
more fully the wonder of what Trina had discovered.

The de Girones might have guessed, he thought,
that *Comte* Bernhard with his passion for concealed
passages, staircases and secret chambers of one sort or
another would have also contrived a secret place in
which he could keep safely everything that was valuable in a time of war.

Although the history books had fulsome accounts of
his magic, strangely enough there was little about his
death.

In fact, the Girone family did not even know where
he had died or how.

It might have been in battle, on one of his travels, or
in the Castle itself.

Now the fact that there was so much treasure left in
the Castle made the *Comte* think that perhaps his ancestor had been away from home when his life had
come to an end.

But what was important at the moment, was what
he had concealed.

As the *Comte* and the Marquis passed the treasure
through the hidden entrance, Susi and Trina took
them and laid them out on the stone floor of the dungeon, and the piles of what they collected grew and
grew.

Where Trina had seen one gold plate there were
dozens. There were also goblets and flagons, bowls of
every size, all of gold and ornamented with precious
stones.

There were also other caskets like the large one
which the *Comte* had brought out first, and they were
not only masterpieces of fine craftsmanship, but contained jewellery mounted in gold and silver which he
knew would be the delight and envy of every Museum
in the country.

A large part of the value of what they had found was
in the coins.

The bags in which *Comte* Bernhard had stowed them had crumbled into dust in the passing centuries and the *Comte* and the Marquis first of all tried to carry handfuls of them through the passage until Trina ran to collect something to contain them, from upstairs.

It was important, the *Comte* said, that nobody, for the moment, should know of their discovery.

She had therefore contented herself with snatching everything that seemed available in the nearest room, including two waste-paper baskets.

Then she had the bright idea that pillow-cases would be even more convenient as there was no chance of obtaining sacks.

She therefore went up to the nearest bedroom and pulled the cases from the pillows to carry four of them down to the dungeon in triumph.

Even then there were still quite a lot of coins which the *Comte* and the Marquis decided must wait until another day.

When they finally emerged, Susi gave an exclamation of horror at the *Comte*'s appearance while Trina laughed both at him and the Marquis.

"You look like a pair of blackamoors!" she said. "I cannot imagine what your valets will think you have been doing!"

"We shall have to think up some reasonable explanation," the *Comte* said. "But remember—not a word about the treasure in front of the servants."

"Are you afraid they might steal them?" Susi asked.

"My servants would never do such a thing," the *Comte* answered quickly, "but we could not prevent them talking. At first the village would be agog with excitement, next, reports in the newspapers would bring sightseers from all over France."

He smiled before he added:

"*Comte* Bernhard still remains a celebrity, at least in this part of the world."

"We will be very careful," Susi promised.

He smiled at her and she added:

"For Heaven's sake, let us go back and have baths. My hands are so dirty I am afraid to touch anything."

"Your gown is dirty too, Mama," Trina said, "but it has been in a good cause."

"A very good cause," the *Comte* agreed positively, "and I cannot remember ever being so happy in the whole of my life."

He was looking at Susi as he spoke and because she knew what his happiness meant her eyes met his. For a moment everything else was forgotten.

They walked from the dungeon and as the *Comte* locked the door carefully and put the key in his pocket, Trina felt that the Marquis was being left out of the excitement.

"I suppose," she began hesitatingly, "you . . . would not wish to . . . dine with . . . us tonight?"

As she spoke, she felt she was rather presuming on the *Comte*'s hospitality.

At the same time, if she was honest, she wanted the Marquis to be with them and she knew she was curious as to what he felt about her, now that he knew the truth of her deception.

"Of course you must dine with us!" the *Comte* agreed before the Marquis could speak. "I was . . . in fact . . . just about to invite Your Lordship. We have a lot of things to discuss."

"I shall be delighted to accept your invitation," the Marquis replied.

"We had better make dinner a little later than usual," the *Comte* went on, "it will take us some time to get clean."

When they drove away in the carriage which had been waiting for them, the *Comte* put out his hand, dirty though it was, to take Susi's.

"It does not seem possible that all these wonderful things have been hidden there for so long," she said. "Are they really as valuable as you hoped they would be, when Trina said she had found the treasure?"

"I cannot begin to estimate their worth," the *Comte*

replied, "but that is unimportant beside the fact that we can be married immediately—tomorrow, if it can be arranged."

Susi gave a little cry.

"Tomorrow? But that is too soon!"

"Very well—the day after!" he conceded. "But I will wait no longer than that!"

Susi did not speak and Trina interposed to say:

"The *Comte* is right, Mama. There is no point in waiting. It will be lovely to know you need no longer worry about anything—except of course, your husband!"

She gave a mischievous little glance at the *Comte* who said quickly:

"If you are going to frighten Susi about my being a roué, I shall put you back in the dungeon and lock you in, as the Marquis did!"

"It was an unforgivable thing for him to do!" Susi cried indignantly. "How could you let him treat you in such a way?"

"I had very little choice," Trina answered.

She did not however wish to talk about what had happened between the Marquis and herself.

She was glad when the carriage arrived at the Château and she could run upstairs to her bedroom.

The maid who looked after her was horrified at the condition of her gown.

"What have you been doing, *M'mselle?*" she cried.

"We have been exploring the older parts of the Castle," Trina answered.

She did not say any more and the maid went away muttering that her expensive gown would never be the same.

Soaking in a warm bath scented with jasmine flowers, Trina thought with satisfaction, that she had solved the problem she had set herself as to how to help her mother.

The only worry was a personal one—what she would do herself.

She obviously could not force herself, for the moment, on her mother and the *Comte.*

The one thing they would want on their honeymoon was to be alone, and she had no wish to return to England.

There her aunts would not only make her life miserable, but would be scandalised by the thought of her mother marrying so quickly after her father's death—and to a Frenchman!

She decided that at least for a little while she could stay with the *Duchesse.* After that, she would have to think again.

She could not help knowing that she would like more than anything else, to get to know the Marquis better, but she had the uncomfortable feeling that he might think very differently.

No man liked being made a fool of, and he had been deceived by her pretence that she was an older and more sophisticated woman.

This, if nothing else, might make him decide that he was no longer interested in her, even as a sparring companion.

The idea was very dispiriting, and yet Trina could not help a little lift in her spirits because he was coming to dinner.

She chose what she was to wear with the greatest of care, changing her mind a dozen times, before she finally decided on a gown of white lace, so fine that it gave her an ethereal appearance, almost as if she was dressed by fairy hands.

The maid arranged her hair in a different manner from the style she had worn previously and instead of wearing jewels, she took a white camellia from a vase of them in her bedroom, and set it amongst the curls on top of her head.

"C'est charmant, M'mselle!" the maid exclaimed, and Trina could only hope that the Marquis would think so too.

When he arrived for dinner, she thought that no

man could look more magnificent or more imposing in his evening-clothes.

But when he kissed Susi's hand in a conventional fashion and only bowed to her, she wondered apprehensively if he was still angry.

The dinner was a meal at which they all laughed and it was impossible to be gloomy about anything.

The *Comte* was in such high spirits and he and Susi were so happy that their excitement was infectious and Trina saw a different side to the Marquis than she had ever seen before.

He was witty and amusing and all through the meal he and the *Comte* tried to cap each other's stories.

Only when the servants had left the room did they talk of the subject which lay at the back of all their minds.

"What are you going to do about what lies on the dungeon floor?" the Marquis asked.

He was being discreet in not directly mentioning what was actually there and the *Comte* answered:

"I have already sent a telegram to the Curator of the Louvre, whom I know, asking him to come here with all possible speed. It will obviously take him a day or so."

He paused to look at Susi and say:

"You will not mind, my precious, if we start our honeymoon here?"

"I would not wish to be anywhere else," she said in a low voice and blushed as she spoke.

"I have been thinking," the Marquis said, "about your position now you are to be married, and I have a suggestion to make."

They all looked at him and he went on:

"I know more than anything else you will want to take your wife to your own Castle. I would therefore like, if it is at all possible, for my mother to move here to stay with your grandmother."

The *Comte* was obviously surprised and the Marquis went on:

"I have heard a great deal about *Madame la Comtesse* from the French Ambassador in London. His father, the *Marquis* de Vallon, was, I understand, in love with her for many years."

"Of course!" the *Comte* interposed. "I remember my grandmother speaking of him and I think I also met him."

"His son speaks of your grandmother as one of the most interesting as well as the most beautiful women, he has ever seen."

The Marquis paused before he went on:

"I have not met the *Comtesse,* but I cannot help thinking, from all I have heard, that she is just the sort of person who might help and influence my mother at this particular moment in her life."

"That is a marvellous idea!" Susi exclaimed.

"Perhaps," the Marquis continued, "if she could see how another woman, as beautiful as she was, has not only accepted old age gracefully, but has also been exceedingly brave about her disability, I think there would be no further need for her to seek the assistance of quacks and crooks."

"Which we tried to be," the *Comte* said frankly. "And that reminds me—I forgot this in all the excitement."

As he spoke, he drew from the inside pocket of his evening-coat a cheque which he passed across the table to the Marquis.

"If it is made out in your name," the Marquis said, "I would like you to endorse it."

The *Comte* looked surprised and he explained:

"I intend to cash it and keep the money for the moment, so that my mother will not have so much to spend. I am also determined that whatever happens, I will not allow her to get into the clutches of someone like Casapellio or anyone else who will extract large sums from her."

"I am afraid it might be a somewhat difficult task," the *Comte* remarked.

"I realise that I have been at fault in the past," the Marquis said, "because I left her alone and did not provide her, as I should have done, with the right sort of companions."

"I think loneliness might have had something to do with it," the *Comte* said.

"That is what I must prevent in the future," the Marquis answered, "therefore I would like, if you will permit me, and if the *Comtesse* will agree, her to stay here."

"I am sure that can be arranged," the *Comte* replied. "When I told *Grand'mère* this evening what had happened she was so excited that she is determined to-morrow to inspect the treasure for herself."

"I thought she would be pleased," Susi said.

"She is even reconciled to my marrying an English-woman without a large dowry," the *Comte* said with a smile.

"You are—sure?"

Susi's question made him put out his hand towards her as he said:

"Quite, quite sure. *Grand'mère* loves me, and I told her with considerable eloquence that I could never be happy without you."

"Oh—Jean . . . !"

Susi could hardly breathe the words, but they were very moving.

"Will you speak to your grandmother tonight?" the Marquis asked, as if he wished to get everything set-tled.

"But of course. I promised her anyway that Susi and I will say good-night to her after dinner."

"Did you invite her to join us?" Susi questioned.

"Of course I did," he replied, "but she was so ex-cited by what had happened that I think the effort of getting up and dressed would have been too much. But she insisted on a glass of champagne with which to drink our health!"

"I am sure your grandmother is often lonely too,"

Trina remarked. "It must be very hard when one has been the centre of admiring friends, to be alone, even in a place as beautiful as this."

"I am quite certain," the *Comte* smiled, "that *Grand'mère* and the Marchioness will find a great many interests in common, and as His Lordship has said, in future we must see that they have the right sort of friends to keep them amused and happy."

It flashed through Susi's mind that what every elderly lady really wanted was grandchildren who would occupy both their thoughts and hours of their time.

As she met the *Comte*'s eyes she knew he was thinking the same thing and it made her feel shy.

She looked so adorable that his fingers tightened on her hand which he still held.

There was no need for words. They were so closely attuned to each other that they vibrated to each other's thoughts as if to music.

"As we have finished dinner, I think we should go to your Grandmother now," Susi said. "It is growing late."

She rose as she spoke and as she and Trina left the Dining-Room, the gentlemen followed them.

Susi walked up the stairs beside the *Comte,* his arm round her waist, and Trina went into the Salon tinglingly aware that the Marquis had followed her and they were now alone.

She walked to the window to look out onto the dusk of the night.

It was very warm, the faint wind there had been earlier in the day had gone and now there was a stillness, as if even the earth had stopped breathing.

Unexpectedly, the Marquis took Trina's hand in his and drew her through the window and onto the lawn.

She did not speak, but his clasp was firm and she thought there was something determined about him which made her quiver.

The stars were glittering overhead and the moon

turned the Castle to silver so that it looked as if it had stepped out of a fairy-story and into their dream.

The Marquis drew Trina towards the cypress trees and she knew he was going to the place above the river where they had listened to the nightingales.

Only when they reached it did he release her hand and she stood where she had stood that first night when he had joined her and she had thought he was the *Comte*.

She did not look at him but at the river below shimmering in the light of the moon, the country beyond it undulating away into the darkness of the horizon.

It was then she heard very faintly in the distance, the trilling note of a nightingale.

She held out her hand, just as she had done that first evening, to warn the Marquis not to speak. Then as the birds seemed to come nearer she felt as if she had stepped back into the past.

What had happened then was happening again, and yet in the days between so much had occurred that she felt almost as if she had lived a lifetime of emotions.

One nightingale was singing; and now as if it was inevitable it was joined by another, and they sang in unison.

The sound was so exquisite, so moving, that without even meaning to, Trina turned her head to look at the Marquis and see what he was feeling.

He was nearer to her than she expected, his eyes were on her face, and as she looked up at him he said very quietly, almost beneath his breath:

"A song of love, my lovely one, and that was what I was waiting to hear."

At the term of endearment Trina's eyes widened for a moment, then without realising what she was doing, she was in his arms.

She felt his lips take possession of hers and she knew this was what she had been waiting for, what she had been longing for and what she had been afraid of losing.

His kiss swept her up into the sky as it had done before, only now it seemed more insistent, more wonderful and more ecstatic than it had been.

She felt her heart beating against the Marquis' and she knew as he drew closer and still closer that as their bodies merged into each other's, so did their hearts and minds.

She was his, and she surrendered herself completely to the power and dominance of him because she had no resistance left.

Now there was not only the song of the nightingales, but Trina felt as if there was the music of the angels singing not in her ears, but in her heart, and the rapture the Marquis gave her, was part of the stars, the moon and God Himself.

The Marquis raised his head.

"I love you!"

Because it was impossible to speak Trina turned her face against his shoulder.

"I fell in love with you," he went on, "when I first came through the cypress trees and saw you looking up at the sky and thought you were too beautiful to be human."

"You . . . really do . . . love me?"

"I love you until you fill my world and there is nothing else but you, but I am in fact, at the same time —angry!"

"Angry?" she whispered, "because I deceived you?"

"Not with your magic tricks," he replied, "they are immaterial, but because you led me to believe that you were your mother, and I believed that she belonged to the *Comte.*"

"And that . . . upset you?"

"So much so," the Marquis replied, "that after I kissed you, I decided I would never see you again!"

"Oh . . . no!"

It was a cry of horror as Trina remembered how much she had wanted to see him.

"When I left the day before yesterday for Monte Carlo, I decided I would not return to the Castle as I had intended."

Trina drew in her breath.

"How could you have thought of anything so . . . cruel when I was . . . longing to see you again?"

"How was I to know that?" the Marquis asked. "I thought you were just a very lovely, flirtatious woman, wishing to have every man she met at her feet, and I had no wish to add to their number."

"There is . . . no-one."

"Then I was right—nobody has kissed you except me?"

"N . . . no!"

"Oh, my darling, you do not know how I fought against believing what my instinct told me. Are you surprised that I am angry?"

"Please . . . forgive me."

He looked down at her eyes pleading with his, thinking in the moonlight, she was so beautiful, that he would impress this moment on his mind for ever.

Then as if he realised that her beauty was not only ethereal but very human, his lips sought hers again and he kissed her until the world seemed to swing dizzily round them and they were both breathless.

The Marquis drew Trina towards the stone seat on which they had sat before.

She sat down with his arms around her and with a little sigh of sheer happiness, her head fell back against his shoulder.

"Now we will make plans," he said. "If your mother and de Girone are to be married the day after tomorrow, I suggest we are married tomorrow evening."

"T.tomorrow?" Trina exclaimed in sheer astonishment.

"Why not?" the Marquis asked. "But because we are in France it will have to be a Civil ceremony first, in front of the Mayor, then I imagine there is an English Church of some sort in Arles."

"That is very . . . soon!"

"What else are you suggesting we should do without your mother to chaperone you? I can hardly believe you intend to spend her honeymoon with her?"

"No . . . of course not," Trina replied. "I was actually planning I would go to Paris and stay with the *Duchesse* d'Aubergue. She did in fact, ask me to."

The Marquis's arms tightened.

"And you imagine I would allow you to do that?"

Trina gave him a questioning little smile and he laughed.

"All right—I am jealous—madly jealous! That is why I intend to marry you now and at once, before I lose you."

"You need not be . . . afraid of . . . doing that."

"How can I be sure?" he asked. "I am not sure of anything where you are concerned. You have taunted me, teased me, and fought me in a manner I found extremely irritating, and at the same time, quite enchanting!"

His lips were near to hers as he added:

"I want you! I want you as I have never wanted anything in my whole life, and I love you as I never thought it possible to love any woman. You are mine, Trina, and I do not intend to wait!"

There was a determination in his voice which made Trina thrill to the mastery of him.

She knew that however much she prevaricated she would, in the end, do exactly as he wanted not only now, but for the rest of her life.

He was the conqueror, the victor, the type of man she had always admired. Someone she might coax to get her own way, but who otherwise would always be her master.

At the same time, Trina knew it would be fun to be with him, fun to make him fight for what he wanted, and even more marvellous and exciting when she finally surrendered.

"Supposing," she asked in a small voice, "I prefer to have a . . . grand wedding? After all, you are of great . . . importance in England. Your friends would expect that we should be married in St. George's, Hanover Square, with at least two pages and ten bridesmaids, besides a Reception for five hundred guests."

"Then they will be disappointed," the Marquis said firmly, "and so will you! I am not taking you back to England until I am sure that you love me as much as I love you, and I need no longer be afraid of letting you out of my sight."

"And . . . where are you . . . suggesting we should go for our . . . honeymoon?"

She knew even as she asked the question, that he had already planned it.

"My yacht arrived at Marseilles today, on its way to Monte Carlo," he answered. "I have telegraphed the Captain to have everything ready for our arrival!"

"You were quite . . . confident I would . . . agree to . . . marry you?"

"If you refuse I can always lock you in the dungeon again until you agree!"

Trina gave a little laugh, then she said:

"I was trying so hard to escape so that when you unlocked the door, you would find nobody there and would be puzzled as to what had happened to me."

"I would still have caught you again," the Marquis said. "You can never escape me! I knew that even while I tried to leave."

"Would you . . . really have . . . stayed away and . . . forgotten me?" Trina asked in a low voice.

"If I tell the truth—no!" the Marquis replied. "I knew when I spent a sleepless night in an Hotel at Nice before I caught the earliest train possible back to Arles, that I had to see you again. Had you belonged to a thousand *Comtes*, I would still have made you mine."

As if the fear that she might have belonged to some other man still frightened him, he put his fingers under her chin and turned her face up to his.

Then he kissed her fiercely, possessively, demandingly, in a different way from the kisses he had given her before.

Only when his passion became so tempestuous that Trina gave a little murmur of protest and put up her hands as if to protect herself did he set her free.

The fire in his eyes was unmistakable and when he looked at her, he said, his voice very deep and a little unsteady:

"Forgive me, my darling. I love you so wildly, so overwhelmingly that I forget how young you are, and how, although you pretend to be otherwise—inexperienced."

"Will . . . will that . . . bore you?"

"I will find it very exciting, so exciting in fact that you must not allow me to frighten you."

He pulled her close to him, but more gently.

"Oh, my darling, you are everything I looked for in a wife, but thought I would never find."

"Are you . . . sure about . . . that?"

"I thought young girls were gauche, stupid and with no brains. I was wrong."

He moved his lips gently against her skin as he went on:

"I thought I wanted sophistication and a woman who had a knowledge of the world, and again I was wrong. What I want is you, every precious scrap of you, to be mine now and for all eternity."

Trina put her arm around his neck and drew his head down to hers.

"That is what . . . I want too," she whispered. "I want to . . . belong to you. I want to make you . . . happy. Please . . . please teach me about love . . . so that you will . . . not be . . . disappointed."

"I will never be that," the Marquis answered, "and teaching you about love, my precious one, will be the most thrilling and wonderful thing I have ever done in my life."

He was kissing her again, not so fiercely, but at the same time demandingly, as if he wooed her with his kisses, and Trina thought that not only her whole body responded to what he wanted of her, but her heart, her mind and her soul.

Vaguely, somewhere far away, she heard the nightingales singing and she thought as they sang they were soaring high into the sky.

Only now she and the Marquis were flying with them towards the stars, and the light and the glory of it made them, too, part of a song of love.

Revenge of
the Heart

Author's Note

The reign of Tsar Alexander III of Russia opened
with a persecution of the Jews which was unequalled
until fifty years later, when Adolf Hitler assumed
power in Germany. He ordered that one third of the
Jews in the country must die, one third emigrate and
one third assimilate.

This appalling programme resulted in thousands of
Jews being murdered and their property confiscated,
while 225,000 desolate Jewish families left Russia for
Western Europe.

In 1892 the Emperor's brother the Grand Duke
Serge, a sadist, evicted thousands of Jewish artisans
and small traders from Moscow. Their quarters were
surrounded by Cossacks in the middle of the night
while police ransacked every home, driving the unhappy people out of their beds. Classed as criminals,
they were forced along the roads to nowhere.

In the summer of 1894 the doctor announced that
Alexander III was suffering from dropsy, which was
the result of the kidney damage he had suffered in a
train disaster. Desperately ill and shrunken to half his
size, he lingered however until 11 November.

His son Nicholas II, whom the Prince of Wales described as "weak as water", reigned until 1917. The
following year he and his family were assassinated by
the Bolsheviks.

Chapter One

❧

1894

*W*arren Wood walked into the *Hôtel* Meurice and made himself known to the Receptionist.

He had not been in Europe for nearly a year and only after the Receptionist had sent for the Manager was he recognised.

"It is delightful to see you again, *Monsieur* Wood!" he said in excellent English. "I hope you enjoyed your trip abroad."

'Trip' was hardly how Warren would have described his journey through North Africa in which there had been moments of delight but a great deal of acute discomfort, besides times when his life had been in danger.

He was however too glad to be back in Paris to be argumentative, so he merely asked if he could have a room, if possible the one he usually occupied and if his luggage, which he had left at the *Hôtel* nearly a year ago, could be sent up to him.

All this was promised with a politeness which was characteristic of the French.

Then as he would have turned away from the desk the Manager said:

"I have some correspondence for you, *Monsieur*. Would you like it now, or shall I send it up to your room?"

"I will take it now, if you have it handy."

The Manager disappeared into an inner sanctum and returned with a large packet of letters fastened together with string.

Warren Wood took it, put it under his arm, then waited for the page who was carrying a piece of his small baggage to go ahead and show him the way.

The room, if not the same one in which he had stayed before, was identical and on the Fourth Floor, from which he had a delightful view of the roofs and trees of Paris.

As he stood at the window while the porters brought in his luggage, he thought there was nothing so attractive and beautiful as Paris in the sunshine.

High above the houses with their grey shutters, which he thought when driving from the station he would recognise anywhere in the world, rose the Eiffel Tower, nine-hundred and eighty four feet high, which had been completed for the Exhibition which had taken place five years before.

Its metal structure, as one Frenchman Warren had met at the time had boasted, was symbolic of the creativity, vigour and brilliance of France.

But at that moment, Warren had not been interested in anything else except his own feelings of frustration and despair.

Almost as if the Tower silhouetted against the sky made him remember what he had determined to forget, he turned from the window, tipped the porters who were waiting expectantly and sat down in an armchair to look at his letters.

He was surprised there were so many and he wondered who, except his mother, could have bothered to write to him after he had left England.

Then as he undid the string and removed the neat band of paper that held the letters together, he looked at the one on top of the pile and stiffened.

For a moment he could hardly credit what he was seeing.

Yet there was no mistaking the flamboyant lettering, the pale blue envelope which was so familiar and the subtle, seductive scent of magnolias which personified the writer.

He stared at the envelope as if it fascinated him, and yet at the same time he was afraid to open it.

Why, he asked himself, should Magnolia, of all people, be writing to him here in Paris?

That she had done so meant that she must have obtained his address from his mother, who was the only person who knew where he would be staying on his journey home.

He told himself that if there was one person he did not wish to hear from at this moment, it was Magnolia.

Then with a frown between his eyes and a tightening of his lips he carefully opened the envelope.

Warren Wood was an extremely good-looking young man, but his appearance had altered in the last year from the personification of an elegant 'Man-About-Town' to become more intensely masculine and at the same time harder and more ruthless.

It would have been impossible to live through the experiences he had shared with Edward Duncan without learning that life was not just a round of amusements and pleasure as it had been in the past and that it could never be the same again.

At times on their journey in Africa Warren had thought he could not stand it any longer and must admit he was defeated by the elements, the incredibly unpalatable food and most of all the camels.

If there was one thing Warren had grown to hate, it was the camels. They were lazy, tiresome, unpleasant beasts, difficult to handle, smelt abominably, and at first made him feel sea-sick.

After nearly a year's endurance he had learnt to master them, but he knew that while he loved horses and could not imagine his life without dogs, the camel was undoubtedly his *bête noire*.

He even thought they reminded him of some of his

friends and acquaintances and once had said to Edward:

"I shall certainly avoid these people in the future!"

Edward had laughed almost derisively. When they left each other the morning before at Marseilles he had said:

"Goodbye, Warren! I cannot tell you how much I have enjoyed your company and what a delight it has been to have you with me."

He spoke so sincerely that Warren felt almost embarrassed thinking of the times when he had cursed himself for accepting Edward's invitation.

However, he knew when he looked back on these last months that they had enriched his character and broadened his horizons in many ways that he had never anticipated.

And yet now, the first thing he had found on his return was a letter from Magnolia.

And it was because of Magnolia that he had gone to Africa to forget.

He had been sitting in his Club in St. James's with a large glass of brandy beside him when Edward had sat down in an adjacent chair.

"Hello, Warren!" he had said. "I have not seen you for some time, but then I have been in the country."

"Hello!"

The tone of Warren's voice made Edward look at him sharply.

"What is the matter?" he asked. "I have not seen you look so down in the dumps since you were beaten in the Long Jump at Eton!"

Warren did not reply, he only looked down at the glass beside him and Edward asked in a different tone:

"What has upset you? Can I help?"

"Not unless you can tell me the best way of putting a bullet through my brain!" Warren answered.

His friend looked at him searchingly before he enquired:

"Are you serious?"

"Very! But I suppose if I did shoot myself it would distress my mother, who is the only person I can trust in this damned crooked, filthy world in which everybody lies, and lies, and lies!"

He spoke so violently that Edward glanced around the room hoping he was not being overheard.

Fortunately there were only two other members, elderly and half-asleep, in the big leather chairs at the other end of the room, oblivious to everything except themselves.

"It is not like you to talk like that," Edward remarked. "What has happened?"

Warren had given a bitter laugh and Edward, who had kwown him since they had been at School and Oxford together, realised he had had a lot to drink, which was for him very unusual, and was at the talkative stage.

"Tell me what is wrong," he said coaxingly.

As if he was glad to have somebody with whom to share his feelings, Warren replied:

"It is not a very original story, but I have just learnt that the only thing that counts is a man's possessions—not himself!"

"You cannot be speaking of Magnolia?" Edward asked tentatively.

"Who else?" Warren replied. "When I took her down to stay at Buckwood it never crossed my mind that she was not, as she had assured me, as much in love with me as I was with her."

He paused and his fingers tightened on his glass as he said fiercely:

"I loved her, Edward, loved her with my whole heart! She was everything I wanted in a woman and as my wife."

"I know that," Edward replied quietly, "but what happened then?"

Again there was that bitter and unpleasant laugh before Warren replied:

"You may well ask! She met Raymond!"

Edward stared at him.

"Do you mean your cousin? But, good Heavens, he
has only just come of age!"

"What did that matter, beside the fact that he is an
Earl?"

In a mocking, sarcastic voice Warren went on:

"My dear Edward, you must realise, as I was stupid
enough not to do, that all a woman needs to make her
happy is a title and money. What the man himself is
like is utterly and completely immaterial!"

Edward would have spoken, but Warren continued:

"He may have bow legs, crossed eyes, warts on his
nose, but if he is likely to become a Marquis, then the
idea of being his wife supersedes every other feeling in
what she quite erroneously describes as her—heart!"

He choked over the last word and drained what was
left in his glass, then put up his hand to attract a
waiter.

Fortunately there was not one in the room at that
moment and Edward said:

"Before you get too drunk, Warren, tell me the
whole story. I am not only interested, but very sympathetic."

"Thank you, old boy!" Warren replied. "I suppose I
can trust you not to let me down, although I swear to
God I will never trust a woman again—never!"

"But surely," Edward protested, "Magnolia does
not intend to marry Raymond?"

"Oh, yes, she does!" Warren replied. "And now I
look back, I realise she made a dead set for him the
very moment we walked into Buckwood! I suppose,
now I think about it, Raymond had not got a chance
as soon as she looked at him with her large dewy
eyes!"

Edward knew this was very likely true.

Magnolia Keane was not only beautiful, but she had
practised the art of fascinating men until, as Edward
was well aware, she could exert an almost hypnotic
influence on anyone she desired.

He had known quite a lot about Magnolia before she met his friend Warren Wood, and the first time he saw them together he had thought it a mistake for him to become embroiled with her.

Coming from a good county family, Magnolia had come to London determined to find herself a rich and important husband.

It should have been easy, Edward thought, considering how extremely beautiful she was, while her father, who was Master of a well-known pack of fox-hounds, was popular and had a number of friends in sporting circles.

But Magnolia's father was not a rich man, and while by a great deal of scrimping and saving Colonel Keane could afford to take a house in London for the Season, it was not in the most fashionable area, and he did not contemplate giving a Ball for his daughter.

This meant that the invitations she received were not as numerous as they would have been if she had been able to reciprocate in the usual manner.

The whole process of bringing out a débutante was very much a 'cutlet for a cutlet' and Colonel and Mrs. Keane and their daughter Magnolia had not been invited to any Balls given by the leaders of London Society!

This therefore resulted in Magnolia meeting considerably fewer eligible bachelors than she had hoped.

She did not, in fact, receive a single proposal of marriage during her first Season, and although a great many men admired her, unfortunately most of them were already married.

In consequence the Dowagers gossiped about her and her name was crossed off a number of the lists which every hostess kept punctiliously.

The following year, after having shone like a star at a number of Hunt Balls and attended Race-Meetings and Points-to-Points at which she was inevitably encircled by a group of admiring men, both old and young, Magnolia came to London again.

She was determined that this time she would end the Season with an engagement ring on her finger.

There was no engagement ring, but she did meet a distinguished Baronet eighteen years her senior, who became her constant companion and in private pursued her as relentlessly as any hound pursued a fox.

Magnolia played him skilfully as a fisherman would play what appeared to be a hooked fish, but at the last moment, when she had actually started to plan her trousseau, he got away.

She could hardly believe it was true when he told her that he had made some extremely unfortunate investments and found it would be impossible for him to keep up his house and estates unless, to put it bluntly, he 'married money.'

Magnolia decided to put a good face on what was a disastrous set-back and a humiliation she was determined not to acknowledge.

The moment she realised she had lost her Baronet, she told her friends most convincingly that she had found it impossible to marry a man who was so much older than herself and 'set in his ways.'

"It may be very stupid of me," she had said, "but I want somebody I can not only love, but also laugh with, and enjoy life as poor James found it impossible to do."

If a few people guessed the truth, the majority merely assumed that as Magnolia was so beautiful she had plenty of time to find somebody who really suited her.

Only Magnolia herself was aware that time was passing, and if she was not careful she would find herself 'on the shelf.'

She was well aware that most men married a girl because she was young and innocent, and what they considered to be an ideal wife.

If they wanted anything else, there were always the sophisticated Beauties who were to be found in the 'Marlborough House Set,' and who were acclaimed wherever they went by the public and in the news-papers.

At nearly twenty-one Magnolia was desperate when she met Warren Wood.

He was everything that she thought a man should be, handsome, exceedingly well-bred and welcome in the most distinguished Social Circles.

His father, Lord John Wood, was the younger brother of the Marquis of Buckwood and, as Magnolia was well aware, there was no family in the whole of the British Isles more respected and admired than that headed by the Marquis.

The house from which the 1st Marquis had taken his name stood on an estate which had been given by Queen Elizabeth to Sir Walter Wood after he had sunk three Spanish galleons.

He had brought her not only the spoils of victory, but also some exceedingly fine pearls which he had taken from his prisoners.

As soon as Magnolia met Warren she told herself he was her fate.

Although as far as she could ascertain he did not have much money, she knew that every Social door would be open to her as his wife and she would un-doubtedly embellish the 'Marlborough House Set.'

Warren, who at twenty-eight had enjoyed a great number of love-affairs with the Beauties who found him both handsome and charming, was surprisingly bowled over by Magnolia.

There was something irresistible, he thought, about her large, dark liquid eyes, and her soft white skin which really did have the texture of a magnolia.

It was only later that he learnt that she had not in fact been christened 'Magnolia' but the more com-monplace 'Mary,' but had changed to a more glamor-ous name when she was old enough to appreciate her own charms.

She was in fact very beautiful and attractive, and

had, when she wanted to use it, a charm that few people especially men could resist.

Unfortunately for Magnolia, at the time when he proposed her mother had died most inconveniently two months earlier.

This meant that it would be considered extremely improper and heartless for her even to think of an engagement until at least four more months had elapsed.

Then they would still have to wait another three months before they could be married.

Magnolia had no intention of starting off her marriage on the wrong foot from a social point of view.

She had therefore accepted Warren's proposal with alacrity, but told him that for the time being it must be a precious secret between the two of them.

"I understand, my darling," he said, "and of course I will do anything you want, except that I cannot wait one moment longer than is absolutely necessary to make you my wife."

"I love you! I love you!" Magnolia had said. "If it is difficult for you to wait, it is equally hard for me!"

He thought nobody could be more adorable as he kissed her passionately and she had appeared a little shy.

Then she had extricated herself from his arms while still holding closely to his hand.

"We must be very careful that we are not talked about," she said. "At the same time, darling, wonderful Warren, I would love to meet your family."

He smiled.

"I expect really you want to see Buckwood!" he said. "It is the most beautiful house in the world, and I only wish for your sake that I owned it!"

He laughed before he continued:

"It would become you, and I could not pay you a higher compliment!"

He had then explained to her that his uncle was extremely kind to him, and although his parents lived in a charming old Manor House on the estate, he was allowed to use Buckwood as if it was his own home, to ride his uncle's horses and to shoot in his woods.

"We are a very close family," he said, "and I know that Uncle Arthur will love you, as he loved my father."

Lord John had died about fifteen months ago, and Warren missed his father so desperately that he had instinctively put his uncle in his father's place.

He was quite certain his uncle would find Magnolia as lovely and as charming as he did himself. At the same time, he wanted his approval and he therefore took her down to Buckwood at the first opportunity.

They stayed of course in the Manor House with his mother.

While he thought she was a little cooler than he would have liked towards Magnolia, he put this down to the fact that, although she wanted him to marry, she was understandably over-anxious as to whether any woman would make him as happy as she wanted him to be.

The Marquis however had found Magnolia just as charming as Warren had anticipated.

Because Magnolia had told him to keep secret the fact that they were engaged, Warren had merely hinted to his uncle that he might be considering 'popping the question' and asked his advice.

"A very pretty girl, my dear boy!" the Marquis had said. "Very pretty! I hope she likes the idea of living in the country. She is no use to you otherwise."

"She was brought up in the country," Warren had replied, "and her father is Master of the Ferriers."

"So you told me, so you told me," the Marquis said, "and I think I have met him. Nice chap. Well, his daughter should certainly be able to ride to hounds."

"She can certainly do that!" Warren enthused.

At the same time, although he hated to admit it, when he saw Magnolia on a horse he was not as impressed as he had thought he would be.

He had the idea she was nervous and, although it had never crossed his mind before, that she was afraid of falling and damaging her lovely face.

This however was a very minor flaw in somebody who otherwise appeared to be absolutely perfect.

As usual, there were a number of guests staying at Buckwood who were the Marquis's friends, and almost as soon as they arrived Raymond appeared with three of his.

They had just come down from Oxford and were in tremendously high spirits, noisy and ready for any sort of 'fun,' from tobogganing downstairs on teatrays to playing practical jokes on each other and of course on Magnolia.

She responded to them in a way that made Warren admire her even more than he had done before.

It seemed to him excellent that instead of moving with a certain dignity and grace as she had in London, and competing on their own ground with women much older than herself, she could enter wholeheartedly into the laughter and fun of the young men who teased her as if she was a pretty kitten.

It was freezing weather and the next day when the ice on the lake was bearing, skates were produced for everybody as if by magic and it did not surprise Warren that Magnolia was an excellent skater.

She certainly looked exquisite on the ice, her slim figure showing to its best advantage when she was on skates, and her dark hair and large eyes framed by a fur hat of white fox.

The young men fought with each other as to who should skate with her next, and usually there was one on each side of her as they sped over the ice at what seemed remarkable speed.

Warren had watched them benignly.

He enjoyed skating but had no wish to indulge in acrobatics, and later in the day left them to enjoy themselves while he went riding with his uncle.

The Marquis had grown very stout in his old age and liked to take things easy.

As they rode over the Park they talked of the estate and the steps he had taken to have everything working in perfect order for the time when Raymond should inherit it.

"I wish he would take a little more interest in what I am doing," the Marquis said. "When you have a chance, Warren, have a talk with him and make him see that an estate of this size depends entirely on its owner taking a personal interest in everything that is done and in every person who is employed to do it."

"I am sure Raymond appreciates that, Uncle Arthur," Warren replied. "But he is still very young, and I thought this morning he and his friends were more like a lot of puppies playing with each other. I am sure in time he will settle down and learn to be as good a landowner as you are."

"I hope so, I sincerely hope so," the Marquis muttered.

Then as if he wished to change the subject he went on:

"I want to talk to you about this new tenant of ours. I am not sure if I have put the right man in charge of . . ."

It was quite late as they returned to Buckwood.

It was almost dark, and the skaters had gone in and were now playing some mad game around the billiard-table which resulted in a lot of joking, and what Warren privately thought of as 'horse-play.'

Magnolia seemed happy, and he thought how lovely she looked with her cheeks flushed, her hair a little dishevelled.

He wanted to take her in his arms and kiss her, but when he tried to draw her away from the others she told him in a whisper that she thought it would be a mistake for them to disappear together.

"I love you, darling," she said softly, "but we must be very, very careful!"

He understood, and instead went to the Study to read the newspapers which had arrived from London.

He thought as he did so how lucky he was to have found somebody so adaptable that she would undoubtedly make him a perfect wife.

It was four days later, when he was taking Magnolia back to London that the bomb-shell fell.

When he thought back he realised he must have been both stupid and blind not to realise what was happening.

There had been dancing in the evenings with young people coming in from neighbouring houses at Raymond's invitation, some staying, the others arriving after dinner.

He had organised it all very skilfully.

Besides the more formal dancing when Magnolia waltzed with Warren, there were also noisy Lancers, Quadrilles and Scottish Reels which usually resulted in girls being swung off their feet amid screams of delight.

It all seemed very young and amusing, but it had passed through Warren's mind that he was getting rather old for so much ragging.

Nevertheless the Prince of Wales had started the fashion for practical jokes and a great deal of 'horse-play' in the parties he had enjoyed a few years earlier.

Now Warren had begun to prefer the Bridge table.

It was only when he saw Raymond whispering to Magnolia the night before they returned to London that he wondered what they had to say to each other, but was glad they could be such good friends.

Then, as they travelled back alone in a reserved carriage with Magnolia's maid in the next-door compartment, she said a little tentatively:

"I have something to tell you, Warren."

"What is it, my precious?" he asked. "And have I told you how beautiful you look today? Every time I see you, you are lovelier than yesterday!"

"Thank you," she replied, "but I want you to

understand that while I still love you, I cannot marry you!"

"What do you mean?" Warren asked.

He spoke sharply because he was so astonished, and then thought he could not have heard her aright.

She raised her eyes pleadingly to him as she said:

"I do not want you to be angry with me."

"Of course I will not be angry with you!" he replied. "How could I be? But I do not understand what you are saying!"

"I am saying, dear Warren, that while I love you, I am going to marry Raymond!"

Warren just stared at her, feeling as though his head was suddenly filled with cotton-wool and he could not take in what she was saying.

At length, in a voice that did not sound like his own he ejaculated:

"Marry Raymond? How can you? He only came of age last November!"

"He wants to marry me, but of course we shall have to wait until I am out of mourning."

"And you really think you can do this to me?" Warren managed to ask, the words coming jerkily from between his lips.

"I am sorry, dear Warren, but you have to understand."

"What have I to understand?"

She hesitated. Then he knew the answer.

"You mean that Raymond will one day become the Marquis of Buckwood!"

"You did say yourself that the house would become me!"

"So that is how it is!"

He felt as if the train was spinning dizzily round him.

Then as he realised they were drawing into Paddington Station he knew that Magnolia had timed her revelation very cleverly to coincide with their arrival.

A minute later the carriage-door was opened by a

porter, Magnolia's lady's-maid appeared, and there was no more time for intimate discussion.

Her closed carriage was waiting outside, and as they reached it Warren raised his hat to Magnolia, then walked away.

He had not spoken one single word since they left the train.

Only as he climbed into a hired hansom and directed it to drive to his Club was he aware that he was shaking with anger.

At the same time a desperate sense of loss pervaded him, making him feel as if the very sky had caved in on his head.

He had loved Magnolia, he had loved her in a way he had never loved anybody before, and he had believed in her protestations of love.

Now scraps of conversation were coming back to him.

"I am afraid we shall not be at all rich, my precious," he had said. "Although my father had an unusually generous allowance from my uncle, I still have to provide for my mother."

"I love you because you are you!" Magnolia had said in her soft, sweet voice. "If you had not a penny in the world, I would love you just the same!"

"Darling, could anybody be more wonderful?"

On another occasion he said:

"As soon as you allow me to tell my uncle we are engaged, I know he will offer us a house somewhere on the estate. There are quite a number of small, attractive Manors, and I know you would be able to make any one of them look very lovely."

"What I want to do is to make a home for you."

"I know you will do that," Warren answered, "and of course we will try to afford to have a small house in London as well."

"I hope it will be big enough for me to entertain your friends," she said. "Just because we are married, I must not deprive you of all the people who love you because you are so wonderful. But I know the women will be very envious of me for having such a clever, handsome and attractive husband."

"We will buy a house with a large Dining-Room and a large Drawing-Room," Warren promised.

At the same time, he wondered if he would be able to afford it.

Because he loved Magnolia he had already begun to economise, so that he could save money to buy her all the things she would want once she was his wife.

Fortunately, because he did have so many rich and what she called 'important' friends, he knew they would stay away a lot in house-parties, where he had always been welcomed in the past.

That would mean she would require a number of glamorous gowns, and he told himself he would have to curtail some of the small extravagances with which he had indulged himself as a bachelor.

However, because he loved Magnolia he felt that nothing could be too great a sacrifice, and he felt as if he wanted to lay himself and everything that belonged to him as a tribute at her feet.

Now he could hardly believe that, loving him as she had said she did, she could marry a boy who was hardly any older than herself and also, as Warren knew, very immature.

Raymond was not at all intelligent and had very few positive attributes except for a straight-forward character and a youthful desire to enjoy himself without worrying about anything else.

The Marquis was, although he had never admitted it, slightly disappointed in his son. Raymond's reports at School had not been good, and twice he had nearly been sent down from Oxford for making no effort to study.

Then when his father tried to teach him about the estate, Raymond showed no real interest in it, except for the amusement it could afford him.

Warren had never really thought of Raymond as

being grown up and certainly not as anybody's husband, let alone Magnolia's.

To think that she was marrying him just because he would one day be the Marquis of Buckwood made him feel appalled, disgusted, and at the same time humiliated that he still loved her, still desired her and felt that life was insupportable without her.

By the time he had reached his Club and drunk an inordinate amount of brandy he told himself that it was not a question of wondering how he could live without her, but more that he did not intend to do so.

It was then that Edward had found him.

"Now listen, Warren," he said, "I have a suggestion to make, and I want you to consider it seriously."

"The most sensible thing I can do is to jump into the Thames!" Warren replied somewhat thickly. "I am not likely to drown because I am a strong swimmer, but I may die of the cold!"

"I have a better suggestion."

"What is it?"

The question was surly and Edward replied:

"You can come with me to Africa!"

"To Africa?"

There was just a note of surprise in the question which made Edward think he was at least curious.

"I am going there to find material for a new book," he said. "I am also going to explore parts of the desert and Morocco where few people, and I imagine no Englishman, has ever been before. We might have some game-hunting too. We could also lose ourselves in a sandstorm or be killed by some hostile tribe!"

"That would solve my problem, at any rate!" Warren remarked.

"I agree it would save a lot of trouble and be an interesting and unusual way to die."

There was silence. Then Edward said:

"Come with me! I do not think you will regret it, and at least you will not have to sit here crying over

Magnolia and wondering what she is doing with Raymond."

He paused before he added:

"You are much more likely to be fending off reptiles or other dangerous animals and thinking of how draughty and uncomfortable it is in a tent which is likely to blow away at any moment!"

"You certainly make it sound very unattractive!"

"I cannot promise you a feather-bed or the exotic pleasures of the East!" Edward replied. "But it will give you something to fight, and I think that is what you really need at this particular moment."

There was silence.

Then, as if Warren was seeing Magnolia and hating her with a violence which could only come from a man who had been 'crossed in love,' he said:

"All right, if you want me, I will come with you. But you must make all the arrangements, while I become disgustingly and I hope obliviously, drunk!"

Thinking back, Warren could hear himself saying it, and while he spoke despising himself for being so weak, so stupid as to love a woman who had rejected him for a title.

And yet now, a year later, the letter he was holding in his hand seemed to disturb something within him that he thought he had forgotten.

As he looked down at the letter he could smell Magnolia's perfume coming from it, and he could remember as he looked at the curves of the letters she had written, the curves of her breasts and the smallness of her waist.

He thought he could feel the warmth of her lips beneath his, which had made not only his heart but also hers beat faster.

He had known that if he desired her as a woman, she also desired him as a man.

"Magnolia! Magnolia!"

His whole body cried out for her.

But why the hell had she written to him now?

335

CHAPTER TWO

*F*or a moment the words on the blue writing-paper seemed to dance in front of Warren's eyes.

Then he read:

Dearest, Most Beloved Warren,

How could you have gone away so cruelly without telling me where you were going? I could not believe it when I learnt you had left England.

I knew then how foolish I was and that I had been swept away by a sort of madness which I cannot explain, but which I think made me temporarily insane!

Now I have had time to think it over I know there is only one man in my life and that is You!

I love you, and I can only beg you on my knees if necessary, to forgive me.

I cannot believe that I have really lost something so precious, so marvellous, as your love. My only excuse for not appreciating it was that I had never known anybody like you before.

Your uncle tells me you are somewhere in Africa and he has no address, so I can therefore only send this letter to Paris where I have learnt you will stay first when you return.

When you read it, darling, forget my stupidity and think only of how happy we were before we went to Buckwood, and let me once again creep into your heart.

336

*Forgive me and let us know the bliss we both felt when
you first kissed me.*

I love you! I love you!

Your very penitent and humble
Magnolia.

Having read the letter Warren stared at it as if he
could not believe his eyes.

He looked at the date and saw that it had been written nine months ago, in fact only a month after he had
left England.

It really did not seem possible that Magnolia should
have changed her mind so completely and so quickly,
and because it seemed so incredible he read her letter
over again.

He felt he must find some explanation, although
what it could be he had no idea.

He looked through the pile of letters and under
several bills and half-a-dozen envelopes containing
what he guessed were invitations, all of which had
been sent to White's Club in London and forwarded
on, he found a letter addressed directly to the *Hôtel*
from his mother.

He thought as he looked at her neat, aristocratic
writing that it was very different from Magnolia's
somewhat flamboyant style.

But having no wish to criticise, he opened his
mother's letter and read:

My darling son,

*I was so delighted to receive a letter from you yester-
day from Casablanca to tell me you were on your way
home.*

*I have been desperately anxious to get in touch with
you, and it seemed almost an answer to my prayers that
you should have written to tell me that it would not be
long before you are in England again.*

*What is important is that as soon as you receive this
letter you should come home immediately.*

I know that you will be extremely upset and sad to learn that Raymond had a fall out riding three days ago and I have just learnt that he died this morning from his injuries.

It was apparently in some wild midnight Steeple-Chase in which he was taking part when staying with a friend and I think all the competitors had enjoyed a very good dinner and perhaps too much to drink.

Now poor Raymond is dead, and Dr. Gregory, who came to tell me what he had just learnt, also brought the grave news that your Uncle Arthur has had a heart-attack.

He has not been well for the last few months owing to the fact that he is so over-weight. On top of this, the news of Raymond's accident had been too much for him.

He is in a coma, although still alive, but Dr. Gregory says frankly there is little chance of his recovering.

You will therefore understand, Dearest Warren, that you are needed here urgently, and I can only pray that you will get this letter quickly. Please telegraph me when you receive it.

I am so sorry that your home-coming should be spoilt by such unhappy news, and the sense of loss which we will both feel.

At the same time, I know that you will take over your responsibilities and perform them conscientiously with the same dignity and compassion that was so characteristic of your father.

Bless you, my darling son, I am waiting anxiously to hear from you.

Your devoted and affectionate mother,
Elizabeth Wood.

If Warren had been shocked and surprised by Magnolia's letter, his mother's left him gasping.

He could not believe it possible that his Cousin Raymond, so young and full of life, should be dead, or that his Uncle Arthur should not be expected to live.

He realised that in consequence his whole life had

changed, while at the same time he could hardly credit that what his mother told him was true.

He had never in his wildest dreams ever thought of himself as being the Marquis of Buckwood. Just as he knew it had never crossed his father's mind that he might have inherited instead of his brother.

Lord John had no ambitions of that sort, nor had he an ounce of envy in his whole body.

"No one could be a better head of the family than Arthur," he would say frequently.

When he was ill and aware that he might not recover from what had been a very serious operation, he had said to Warren:

"Look after your mother, and help Arthur in every way you can. I know that he relies on you."

"Yes, of course, Papa," Warren replied.

His father had given him a faint smile.

"You are a good son, Warren," he said faintly. "I have always been very proud of you!"

As he remembered his father's words, Warren could not help wishing that he could have taken his brother's place.

Then he found himself wondering who would help him to carry on as head of the family.

He was well aware how many Woods there were who would look to him for help and guidance and to do honour to the family name.

Just for a moment the immensity of the task which had suddenly been thrust upon him seemed almost overwhelming.

There were not only huge estates in many parts of England for which he would be responsible, but also Orphanages, Alms Houses, Schools and so many Charities that the list of them, as he knew, filled three pages of foolscap.

There were also the hereditary duties of the Marquis of Buckwood at Court, and he was well aware that Queen Victoria had a soft place in her heart for his uncle and frequently had demanded his presence at Windsor Castle so that she could ask his advice.

When Warren thought of the Queen it was almost as if he drew himself to attention.

He not only respected but also fervently admired Her Majesty and he recognised how much the expansion, prosperity and prestige of the British Empire owed to her presence and the manner in which she inspired those who served her.

Then he remembered how urgent was his mother's need of him and he looked at her letter again and found that she had written it three days previously.

"I must leave for England first thing in the morning," he told himself, and thought he would ask the Concierge for the times of the boat-trains from the *Gare du Nord*.

He would at the same time ask for a Telegraph Form with which he could relieve his mother's anxiety by saying he was on his way.

Then as he pushed aside the rest of his correspondence he saw that the *Hôtel* had written a date on his mother's envelope which told him it had arrived yesterday, two days after she had written it.

Written quite clearly was: *"June 27th"* with the seven crossed in the foreign fashion.

It was then an idea came to him and he picked up Magnolia's blue envelope which lay on the floor at his feet.

Written on that, also by the *Hôtel*, was: *"June 27th."*

For a moment he stared at it as if he could hardly believe his eyes.

Then he referred to Magnolia's letter on which there was engraved the date quite clearly: *"October 20th 1893."*

Then he understood, and for a moment the cynical lines around his mouth made him look older and almost unpleasant.

He told himself it was what he might have expected; that Magnolia, the moment Raymond was dead, had tried to make sure of him.

Because the idea of such perfidy made him feel murderous he threw her letter down on the floor, and walking to the window stood looking out with unseeing eyes.

The sun was sinking and the last dying glow over the roofs of Paris was breathtakingly beautiful.

But Warren was only seeing Magnolia's lovely face as she concocted her plot to make herself the Marchioness of Buckwood, by hook or by crook.

He wanted to kill her.

How could any woman he had once loved behave in such an appalling manner or imagine that he would be deceived by such lies?

He knew as he stood there that the last vestige of feeling he had for Magnolia had finally been driven out of him as if by the thrust of a knife.

Now he knew that even if she was kneeling at his feet and looking up at him imploringly with her large, dark, liquid eyes, his only impulse would be to strike her.

He felt he could almost see her crafty brain at work when she realised that having lost Raymond she must now win back Warren at all costs.

She had, therefore, concocted what had seemed a very clever plan of sending him a letter which purported to have been written almost as soon as he had gone abroad.

If the *Hôtel* had not been so punctilious about marking the post as it arrived, he might never have guessed that what she had written was not a genuine change of heart when she had learnt that he had left England.

In order to make sure that he was not making a mistake, he looked at the other letters he had received and saw on each one of them the date of their arrival scrawled by the Concierge.

He had not himself actually given instructions regarding his mail to the secretary of White's Club, but he knew that Edward had ordered his own letters to be sent to Paris and he supposed he had made the same arrangement for him.

The only person to whom he himself had given this address was his mother, and he wondered how Magnolia had extracted the information from her without her being suspicious of what she was about to do.

Then he had another idea, and looking amongst the pile of letters now scattered on the floor he found one he suspected might be there.

It was dated, as his mother's had been, three days earlier and was from his uncle's Solicitors in the neighbouring County Town. He guessed it was from them that Magnolia had obtained his address in Paris, and that they had got it from his mother.

The Solicitors' letter was signed by a Partner he knew well, who had been a friend also of his father's.

He conveyed his deepest sympathy and his regret at having to inform him of his Cousin Raymond's death.

He asked him to return as soon as he received the letter, as it was important he should attend to all the things appertaining to the estate which at the moment his uncle was unable to do.

It was quite obvious from what Warren read that the Solicitor, like his mother, thought there was no hope for the Marquis, and he felt as if they were placing the burden of authority on his shoulders almost before his uncle was buried.

Then as he laid the Solicitors' letter tidily on a table, he deliberately put his foot down hard on Magnolia's sheet of blue writing-paper, pressing it brutally into the carpet.

The moon was high in the sky and the stars were shining like diamonds as Warren walked along the bank of the River Seine.

When he was in Africa with Edward they had sometimes talked of what they would do when they got back to civilisation.

"We will stay a few days in Paris, old boy," Edward had said. "I have always found it is the right place to 'bridge the gap' between the primitive and the sophisticated."

Warren had looked at the desert stretching away to a lazy horizon so that it was difficult to know where the sand ended and the sky began.

"I suppose," he said mockingly, "you are thinking of the *Moulin Rouge* and *Maxim's!*"

"When I am on a journey like this," Edward replied, "I find myself almost forgetting what an attractive woman looks like! I would certainly welcome one of the Sirens from *Maxim's* at the moment and enjoy seeing the girls kicking their legs in the 'Can-Can' at the *Moulin Rouge*."

Warren had laughed. Then he said:

"What I would like is a glass of cold champagne! If I have to drink water out of a goat's-skin very much longer, I think I shall go mad!"

"You would certainly go mad without it!" Edward retorted, glancing up at the blazing sun overhead.

They had been trekking for nearly four days and, as Warren had said, the water they drank from the goat's-skin grew daily more and more unpleasant.

"Tomorrow we will be able to replenish our stores," Edward said. "Although I am afraid it will not be like the food we could enjoy at one of those expensive Restaurants in the *Palais Royal*. And after all the privations you are suffering at the moment, your clothes will need inches taken in before you can wear them again."

Warren had laughed, but he knew when he changed for dinner tonight that Edward had been right.

His clothes, if they were to fit as perfectly as they had before he had left for Africa, would certainly need the attention of an experienced Tailor.

At the same time, his muscles were harder and he had a feeling, although of course it was absurd, that his shoulders were broader.

But he knew the endless hours of riding on either one of the desert horses or on a camel had resulted in his body becoming athletically stronger, despite the fact that the food he had eaten had been rather to keep him alive than for enjoyment.

In spite of all he had to ponder over, he could not help appreciating the excellent dinner he had eaten at a small Restaurant not far from the *Hôtel*.

He remembered thinking vaguely that if he had not been so worried about what was waiting for him at home, he might have looked up a very attractive lady with whom he had spent several delightful evenings when he had stayed in Paris previously.

When he had passed through the city with Edward on his way to Africa, he had merely deposited his clothes at the *Hôtel* and because he was feeling so knocked out by Magnolia he had let Edward choose what they should do that evening.

They had started at the *Folies Bergères* but he had left Edward at *Maxim's* without even dancing with one of the extremely alluring hostesses.

Although in Africa he had had very different ideas about what he would do on this first night in Paris, now he only wanted to think, and he had therefore eaten alone and as it was warm he decided to take a walk before he retired to bed.

The *Hôtel* had found him an Express train which connected with a steamer leaving Calais at midday, and he calculated that if he was fortunate he could arrive at his mother's late the following evening.

He therefore telegraphed her to say that he would be with her at about ten o'clock, but not to worry if it was later.

It was all a question of timing, but in the summer there was less chance of being delayed on the Cross-

Channel Steamer than there was at other times of the year when the sea might be rough.

Tonight there was not even a breath of wind or the rustle of leaves in the trees that bordered the river.

Warren, walking slowly beneath them, thought the moonlight shining on the great buildings and turning their roofs to silver was very different from the moonlight that had percolated through the palm trees of an oasis where they had slept when they could find one.

At other times, when they erected their tent amongst stones and rough shrubs they had had to be wary of snakes, scorpions and the innumerable unpleasant insects which all seemed to have an irresistible desire to creep into his sleeping-bag or down the back of his neck.

He thought now with a twisted smile that the clip-clop of the horses' hoofs moving down the tarmac-surfaced roads was very different from the grunts of the camels, and the coarse manner in which their Arab servants would clear their throats before they spat.

'This is civilisation,' he thought.

He felt as if it was like silk in which he could wrap himself after wearing sack-cloth for a long time.

He crossed over a bridge so that he could look at *Notre-Dame* with the moon shining on the Seine beneath it.

He was remembering how when he had first come to Paris as a very young man, he had stayed on the Left Bank because everything there was so much cheaper.

He recalled how on leaving his *Hôtel* and walking towards the Seine, the first thing he had seen was *Notre-Dame* and he had found the ancient Cathedral irresistibly romantic.

Now he leaned his arms on the cool stones of a wall which bordered the great river and watched a barge with its red and green lights reflected in the water, passing slowly downstream.

It was then he became aware that there was somebody below him on the towpath which had been built for the horses which pulled every barge that passed through Paris towards its destination.

Without really paying attention, he noticed the slim figure of what appeared to be a very young girl moving along the edge of the water and looking down into it.

Strangely she was not wearing a hat or even a shawl over her head, and the moonlight seemed to touch her hair with silver.

Warren watched her while he was still thinking about himself, noticing that she had a grace that made her move almost as if she was walking on the water rather than on the ground, and that her waist was very small.

Then as she reached the shadows of the bridge she stood looking down with a curious intentness.

Almost unconsciously, but with the perception of a man who has lived with danger and becomes aware of it almost before it happens, Warren knew what she was about to do.

It was not that she moved or even bent forward; she just stood looking into the water, and he was aware almost as if someone had told him that she was choosing her moment.

Without really thinking, without considering that he did not wish to be involved, Warren walked quickly to the opening in the wall just beside the bridge from which steps led down to the towpath.

They ended only a few feet from where the girl was standing.

Moving silently because he was wearing soft-soled evening pumps, Warren reached her side.

Deep in her thoughts she was unaware of him and he said quietly, so as not to startle her:

"*Faites attention, Mademoiselle! Ici la Seine est dangereuse.*"

He watched her as he spoke, and the girl stiffened.

Then, in a voice as if the words were jerked from between her lips, she said:

"Go . . . away! Leave me . . . alone!"

To Warren's surprise she spoke in English and he answered in the same language:

"How can you think of doing anything so foolish?"

"Why should you . . . care?"

"Some *Gendarme* is bound to see you, and then you will be in trouble."

He still spoke very quietly, and now the girl turned to look at him.

In the shadows he was aware of a small, white pointed face with two huge eyes that seemed to fill it.

She looked at him and he thought, although he was not sure, that she was surprised that he was in evening-dress.

Then she said, still speaking in English:

"Go away! It is no . . . business of . . . yours!"

"As we are of the same nationality, I find that hard to believe."

"Please . . . please . . . leave me alone!"

Now her voice held a hopeless, pleading note in it and he said:

"You say it is none of my business, but because I am English I should feel obliged, if I saw a dog or a cat struggling in the river, to try to save it, and I have no wish to get wet!"

"Then let me die in my . . . own way . . . without . . . interference!"

Her words were very low and, Warren thought, there was a lost note in them that had not been there before.

"So you want to die," he said reflectively. "That is what I wanted to do nine months ago, but a friend prevented me from doing so, and now I am glad to be alive."

"It is different for you . . . you are a man!"

"I am still a human being, and where I have just

347

come from human beings have to fight to live. It has made me appreciate life in a way I never did before."

She turned her face away from him and he could see her profile silhouetted against the water and thought, although he was not certain, that she was attractive.

At the same time there was something about the sharpness of her chin that made him think she was unnaturally slender.

"Because I was saved by a friend from doing what you are contemplating doing," he said, "I suggest we sit down somewhere, preferably with a glass of wine, and you tell me why you are taking such a desperate step."

As he spoke he saw her whole body stiffen and she said quickly:

"I have told you to go away . . . if you want a woman . . . there are . . . plenty of them in the . . . streets."

It was the obvious interpretation she could put on what he had just said, and Warren said quickly:

"I swear to you, I was not thinking about you like that! If I wanted what you suggest Paris caters for it without my having to come to a towpath on the Seine!"

He spoke as he might have done to a rather foolish child, and as if she understood she said:

"I apologise . . . that was rude . . . when you are trying to be . . . kind."

"You must be aware it is the sort of thing you must expect if you walk about Paris late at night alone."

"I am not walking about Paris," she said fiercely. "I came here to . . . drown myself . . . and you are preventing me from doing what I . . . want to do."

"As I have already pointed out, it is unlikely you will be successful. Suppose you consider my suggestion and talk it over with someone who has once been in exactly the same position as you are?"

"I doubt that very much."

"It is true, and I really feel it is fate that I should have seen you and known what you were about to do."

"How . . . did you know?"

The question was curious and Warren answered it truthfully:

"I was aware you were in danger just as a month or two ago I was aware that I and the man with whom I was travelling were in danger before it actually occurred. My instinct, or whatever you like to call it, saved our lives in the same way that I hope I have been able to save yours."

The girl to whom he was speaking gave a little sigh. Then she turned from the river and took a step away from it as if she realised that what she had intended was for the moment at any rate impossible.

They walked side by side up the steps to the road, and now in the moonlight Warren looked at her and realised she was very young—in fact so young that despite the fact that her hair was heaped on top of her head, he thought she was only a child.

Then he realised that she was too tall to be so immature and that the illusion of childishness was caused by the fact that she was so pitifully thin.

She was a replica of some pitiful sights he had seen amongst some of the tribes of Africa, and was obviously suffering from malnutrition.

It was an explanation anyway for her wishing to die, but he merely said:

"There is a small Restaurant near here where I used to eat when I was young. If it is still open I suggest we go there while you tell me about yourself."

"I have no intention of telling you anything, so perhaps I should not accept your . . . invitation under . . . false pretences."

"Then I will talk," Warren said, "and you can listen!"

The girl stood for a moment undecided, as if she thought it might be wiser to run away from him.

Once again he knew what she was thinking and he said:

"As it happens, I would like to talk to you, because I have a tremendous problem on my mind. It is one that would not have been helped by the music and the laughter that I could have found across the river, and that is why I was walking here. You may in fact, be the 'guiding light' for which I was seeking."

"You do not look as if you had any problems," the girl remarked.

He knew as they walked under the light from the streetlamps that she was impressed by the smartness of his white shirt-front and long-tailed evening-coat.

"You would be surprised at those with which I have suddenly been confronted!" he said. "So please do as I ask, and I promise that when you want me to escort you back to wherever you are staying I will do so—immediately."

He felt a little shudder go through her as if his words evoked something unpleasant.

Then he crossed the road and walked a little way further before there was a turning where he remembered the Restaurant had been.

He found it was open, but the tables outside on the pavement under a red and white striped awning were empty.

Inside half-a-dozen customers were seated at tables in the centre of the room, while those at the side where there were sofas against the wall were unoccupied.

At the sight of Warren in evening-dress the Proprietor hurried forward and led him to a sofa-table in a corner.

As he sat down, Warren was aware as the girl seated herself beside him that surprisingly she was not embarrassed by her surroundings, nor by the fact that she was without a wrap or gloves.

Then he noticed that the gown she was wearing was threadbare. She had a long, swan-like neck, and he thought if she was not so thin she would be very attractive.

She made no attempt to look at the menu which the Proprietor put in front of her at the same time as he handed one to Warren.

"Shall I order?" Warren asked.

"Thank you."

Glancing at her without appearing to be too curious, he realised he had been right in thinking she was suffering from lack of food and was in fact, near to starvation.

He could see the prominent bones at her wrists, the thinness of her fingers and, as he had noticed before, the sharp line of her chin.

Her eyes were unnaturally large and he knew she was remarkably pretty, in fact the right word was 'lovely.'

Knowing it would be ready, he ordered first some Vichyssoise, a cold soup which was nourishing because it was made of potatoes and cream.

Then he ordered a chicken dish which the Proprietor informed him was the *Spécialité de la Maison.*

"I think I remember it when I came here many years ago," Warren remarked.

"Then I am delighted to welcome you back, *Monsieur,*" the Proprietor replied.

Warren then ordered a bottle of champagne and made it clear that he required it to be served without delay.

As the Proprietor took the wine-list from him, Warren turned to look at the girl beside him and said with a smile:

"Now suppose we introduce ourselves? My name is Warren Wood."

There was a little pause before she replied:

"Mine is Nadia."

"Is that all?"

"Charrington."

"So you *are* English!"

Even as he spoke he was sure, again with a perception which was instinctive in him, that although her English seemed perfect, her appearance denied it.

There was nothing he could put his finger on, but he was certain there was some other nationality to which her blood owed allegiance.

Yet Warren thought it was a mistake to sound as if he was questioning anything she told him, and he said:

"Now we know each other, suppose you tell me what you are doing in Paris and why you are so anxious to leave it?"

As if she found the way he was expressing it almost amusing, he thought there was a slight smile on her lips before she replied:

"You promised we would talk . . . about you!"

"Very well, I will keep my word," Warren replied, "which incidentally, I always do."

He knew she would understand he was reassuring her that he would let her leave the moment she wished to go, and he had no other designs on her.

"I arrived," he continued, "in Paris tonight from Africa, and I am leaving first thing tomorrow morning for England."

"You have been in Africa? What have you been doing there?"

"I was travelling with a friend who is writing a book on the tribes of North Africa, particularly the Berbers. We have been to places where they had never seen a white man before, and very nearly left our bones behind."

"It sounds very dangerous!"

"It was! At the same time, as I just told you, it cured me of wishing to kill myself."

She looked at him and he knew she was taking in the smartness of his evening-clothes and was aware of how expensive they were.

After a second she said:

"You do not look as though there was . . . any reason for you to want to . . . die."

"There are other reasons why people commit suicide besides lack of money!"

"Yes, I suppose there are," she agreed, "but being absolutely penniless and . . . alone is very . . . frightening!"

The way she said 'alone' made Warren lower his voice as he asked:

"Who have you lost?"

"M.my . . . mother."

"And you have no father?"

"My father is . . . dead."

There was a tremor on the last word which made Warren feel there was something particularly painful about the way she had lost her father.

"And you have no other relations who could look after you?"

"N.no . . . not in Paris."

It was quite obvious she had not the money to go anywhere else and he said:

"It seems impossible that anyone in this overcrowded city should be completely without friends, relatives or acquaintances."

She looked away from him as if she did not wish to reply, and he noticed her eye-lashes were very long and dark.

After a moment he said lightly:

"Then perhaps I have been sent as your 'Guardian Angel' to save you from yourself."

"Which is something you . . . should not have done."

"Why not?"

She sighed.

"Because it is only . . . prolonging the agony."

There was no time for him to reply because the Proprietor brought the Vichyssoise soup and set down the bowls in front of them.

They were accompanied by a basket containing

crisp rolls warm from the oven, and there was a large pot of butter.

It was then that Warren knew how desperately hungry Nadia was, not because she rushed at the food, but because she deliberately waited, almost as if she was counting the seconds before her hand went out to touch the roll.

Slowly, so slowly that he knew she was forcing her will to behave with propriety she broke it, helped herself to the butter and spread a very small piece of the crust with it.

Then again she waited before she lifted it to her lips.

Warren pretended not to notice.

Instead he tasted the champagne, asked that there should be just a little poured into the glasses and the bottle then returned to the ice-cooler.

He also asked for a bottle of mineral water.

By the time all this was done Nadia was delicately and slowly drinking a spoonful of the soup.

As she did so, Warren thought, although it might have been his imagination, there was already just a touch more colour in the deathly whiteness of her skin.

She made no sound until the soup was finished.

Then, as she took a sip of the Evian water, Warren said:

"Try to drink a little champagne. It will give you an appetite."

"Do you think I need a stimulus to . . . acquire that?"

"I have learnt from experience," he replied, "that when you have been without food for a long time and you think you are very hungry, it is surprising that when the food is actually there you suddenly have no desire to eat it."

"Did you learn that in Africa?"

"Yes," he answered, "amongst a great many other things."

"I would like to hear about them."

"Are you really interested, or just pretending to be?"

For the first time she gave a little laugh.

"Actually I am interested, but I admit I have not thought about anything except my own troubles for what seems a long time."

"When did your mother die?"

He thought for a moment she would not reply. Then she said:

"Two days ago. She was . . . buried this morning."

Then, as if without his asking her she knew what he wanted to know, she added:

"I sold Mama's wedding-ring, her clothes, and everything I possessed to pay for the Funeral. Even so, the Priest had to help me from the Charity Funds."

She said the word 'charity' as if it was an insult, and Warren said:

"I understand. So you have nothing except for what you stand up in."

"M.must we . . . talk about it?"

"That is why we are here."

"Very well . . . you may as well know the truth. I have nothing, and nowhere to stay tonight. In the circumstances the river seems very inviting."

"As long as you end there, and not in some extremely uncomfortable prison."

She looked at him sharply before she replied:

"You seem very certain that I should be prevented from doing what I want to do. But every day dead bodies are discovered in the river, and no one has prevented them from drowning."

"You are one of the lucky—or unlucky—ones, whichever way you like to think about it."

"Unlucky? Of course I am unlucky!"

He was thinking of what he should say to her when the chicken arrived.

It was deliciously cooked with cream, and there were vegetables and sautéed potatoes to go with it.

As he had anticipated, Nadia could eat only a very little, despite the fact that he noticed she took several little sips of the champagne.

Then she put down her knife and fork, looked at him pleadingly and said:

"Forgive me . . . when you have been so kind . . . but you are quite right . . . and it is impossible for me to . . . eat any more."

A waiter took away their plates and Warren ordered coffee and said:

"Now, suppose you tell me how you are in such a plight when it is obvious that you are educated, and are also what is called a 'Lady'?"

To his surprise Nadia stiffened and again looked away from him.

"I . . . I am not being rude," she said, "but . . . I cannot answer that question."

"Why not? I wish to understand."

She clasped her hands together and he knew that she felt she was being very obstructive before she said:

"It is a story I can tell . . . nobody . . . but Mama and I came to Paris because . . . if you like . . . we were in hiding . . . and our money gradually grew less and less. Then . . . Mama became ill."

"So you spent what you had on doctors' fees!"

Nadia nodded.

"But they were hopeless. They could do nothing for Mama and as she was in pain and I could not afford the right food . . . or the proper attention for her . . . it was perhaps a . . . good thing that she . . . died. I . . . I mean . . . good for her."

"I know what you are saying," Warren said sympathetically. "There is nothing worse than watching somebody you love suffer, and not being able to help."

He was thinking as he spoke of his father, and he could understand how frightening it had been for somebody like the girl beside him who was obviously well-born.

"I wish you would tell me the whole story," he said.

She shook her head.

"I . . . I cannot do that. All I can say is: Thank you very much for giving me such a . . . delicious meal!"

She looked at him as if she expected him to get up and leave, and he replied:

"You are not so foolish as to think that I would walk away and leave you here. Even if I gave you some money, which I could quite easily do, I would not be able to sleep at night wondering what had happened to you."

He smiled before he added:

"I am sure you would feel the same. We all want to know the end of the story!"

"Perhaps there will not be one!"

"Nonsense! You are well aware that is not true! One chapter is finished, but life at your age and mine, I hope, will perhaps be more enjoyable in the next chapter than in the one which we have just completed."

Nadia's eyes seemed to fill her whole face as she said:

"What . . . can I do?"

It was the cry of a child who was afraid of the dark, and Warren answered:

"I have an idea which has suddenly come to me almost as if I heard it spoken by somebody outside myself, and yet I am almost afraid to tell you about it."

"There is no need for you to be that."

"Very well, I will risk your saying it is quite preposterous, and yet it is in my mind and I can see it falling into place like a jig-saw puzzle."

"You are making me . . . curious."

At the same time as she spoke Warren saw there was a wary look in her eyes, and he knew that she was afraid that his suggestion, proposition, or whatever it might be, was what she had feared in the first place.

Almost as if he could read her thoughts, he was aware that she was measuring the distance between her seat and the door.

If he said what she anticipated he might say, she could get up and run from the Restaurant and be down the road and out of sight before he could follow her.

"It is nothing like that," he said very quietly.

Now the wary look in her eyes changed to one of startled surprise because he had read her thoughts, and as he saw the colour come into her cheeks, it made her look surprisingly lovely.

CHAPTER THREE

*C*hoosing his words carefully, Warren said again:

"I arrived back in Paris tonight having been in Africa for nearly ten months, during which time I have had no letters and seen no English newspapers."

He realised that Nadia was listening intently to what he said and continued:

"The reason I went to Africa was that a woman to whom I was secretly engaged changed her mind because she found a man in a more advantageous social position than myself, and decided that a title was more important than love."

He was trying to speak in the same calm voice he had used all the evening, but now he remembered what he had felt when Magnolia had told him she preferred Raymond.

He was also furious at the deceitfulness with which she was trying to get back into his life, and this changed his voice and, although he was not aware of it, the expression on his face.

"I was wondering when I went for a walk by the Seine," Warren went on, "how, when I return to England tomorrow I can avoid the scenes which I will undoubtedly have to endure from a woman who is incapable of speaking the truth."

Again the condemnation seemed almost to vibrate from his lips and he finished by saying:

"Now I have no wish to die, but instead I would find it very easy to commit murder!"

If he had intended to startle Nadia he certainly succeeded.

He saw her large eyes widen, and her fingers were clasped together as if she was personally disturbed at the violence of his words.

Then as if he remembered how young and frail she was, he said in a different tone:

"Forgive me, I should not speak like that, but I wanted you to understand and help me."

There was a little pause before she said:

"I would like to help you, but I cannot see how it is . . . possible for me to . . . do so."

"When I walked by the Seine tonight," Warren answered, "my thoughts were of vengeance; how I could hurt somebody who had made me suffer so acutely that, like you, I wished to end my life."

There was silence as if he was feeling for words before he added:

"A dozen different ideas rushed through my mind, one of them being that I might hire an actress to return to England with me."

Nadia looked puzzled.

"Why should you wish to do that?"

"Because I thought the one certain way to show the woman of whom I am speaking that I am no longer interested in her," Warren explained, "would be to come home with either a wife or a *fiancée*."

Now Nadia was very still as if she understood what he was saying to her.

Then as if she thought it was impossible for him to entertain such an idea she said:

"And you . . . intended to find this . . . actress?"

"It was just a wild idea, which is impracticable because I am leaving tomorrow and have already telegraphed to my mother to expect me."

"Then . . . what are you . . . saying?"

Her words were very low, but he heard them.

"I am saying," he replied, "that it seems to be fate that you should come into my life at this particular moment, or should I say that once again our Guardian Angels have taken a hand in making things easier for both of us?"

"I . . . I still do not . . . understand."

"What I am suggesting is that you should come back to England with me as my *fiancée*. You will not come under your own name, so there will be no embarrassment for you as a person. We will give you a name and, to make my revenge really effective, a title!"

He almost spat the last words, then seeing Nadia draw in her breath he controlled himself to say without any expression in his voice;

"I will ask you to play your part for only as long as it is necessary. Then we can announce to the few people who will be interested that we find we are incompatible, and I will pay you enough money to keep you in comfort for a long time. I will also try to find your Charrington relations who can look after you."

He paused and realised that Nadia was staring at him as if she could not believe what she had heard.

Then as if she was convinced it was a fantasy she said:

"I . . . I suppose you are joking?"

"I have never been more serious."

"But it is . . . impossible! How could I do . . . such a thing?"

"Why not?"

"You have only just met me . . . you know . . . nothing about me."

"That is immaterial. What is important is that nobody in England knows anything about you. They will therefore accept exactly what we tell them."

"I would . . . make mistakes . . . I would let you . . . down!"

"I see no reason why you should do that. I think it would be a mistake for you to be English, and foreigners are not supposed to be *au fait* with all the protocol of English social life."

Nadia looked away from him, then quite unexpectedly she laughed.

"I do not believe . . . this is true!" she said. "I must be dreaming, or perhaps by mistake I am . . . acting in a very . . . strange Comedy."

"As far as I am concerned, it is a drama which might easily have become a tragedy."

Warren was frowning as he remembered how desperate he had been when Edward had joined him at the Club, and how agonising the wounds Magnolia had inflicted on him had been, for months after he left England.

It was only when the difficulties, problems and discomforts of everyday life in the desert had occupied him almost exclusively that she had ceased to haunt him.

He knew however that what she had made him suffer had left scars that would remain on his mind and what he thought of as his heart for the rest of his life.

As if, while he was thinking, Nadia was also turning over in her mind what he had told her, she said:

"Suppose when you see . . . this lady again you . . . realise that you . . . love her so much that you will . . . forgive her as she . . . wants you to do?"

"Never!"

As he spoke a surge of rage seemed to sweep over

him and he brought his clenched fist down on the table, making the glasses jump.

"Never! Never!" he declared. "Let me make this quite clear, Nadia: I have finished with love, and if I do marry eventually because I want an heir, it will be a marriage of convenience such as the French have and which proves in most cases exceedingly successful."

The cynical lines on his face seemed to accentuate as he added:

" 'Once bitten, twice shy!' I will never allow myself to be humiliated again."

"I can understand your feelings," Nadia said. "At the same time perhaps, although you did not realise it, it is better to have learned what the lady was like . . . before she became your . . . wife rather than . . . afterwards."

This was something which had never occurred to Warren before, and he thought that Nadia certainly had a point.

He visualised, because he had a very fertile imagination, what he would have felt if after they had been married he had had to watch Magnolia yearning to be with Raymond instead of with him.

What was more, she could have been deeply envious that she could not live at Buckwood, or eventually become a Marchioness.

He would have tried to please her, tried to ensure that she was not discontented in the small manor house they would have lived in on the estate.

Yet he knew now as Nadia had suggested, it would have been a slow and painful agony to acknowledge the truth, and better to endure the short, sharp blow Magnolia had given him which had nearly knocked him out.

As if he could not bear to think of what might have been, he said abruptly:

"Let us concern ourselves with the situation as it is. Will you help me?"

"Do you really think I can?"

He looked at her and said:

"Shall I be very frank? You are a Lady. I know without your telling me that you are well-educated, and if you were properly fed and well-dressed you would be strikingly beautiful."

He spoke quite impersonally as if he were cataloguing Nadia's finer points, and yet the colour swept into her face, making her seem not only very young, but also very human.

Because she was so pale, so thin and so unhappy, she had seemed somewhat divorced from reality, but now she was only a young girl who had received a compliment.

Then she gave a little cry:

"You said: 'Well-dressed!' I have already . . . told you that I possess . . . nothing! I have sold . . . everything . . . even my shoes."

"In which case we have to work very swiftly."

He drew his gold watch from his waistcoat pocket and looked at the time.

It was almost eleven-thirty.

He raised his hand to catch the Proprietor's attention, who understood that he wanted his bill.

It was ready and as he put it down on the table Warren placed a large number of francs on the plate and rose to his feet.

"Come along!" he said, "we will find a *voiture,* then I will tell you where we are going."

He knew as Nadia rose that she was still contemplating whether she would do as he suggested, or run off and find her way to the river without his interference.

Then as if something young and irrepressible within her told her that she would rather live than die, she gave him a faint smile.

They walked into the street and when they reached the main road that ran alongside the Seine they saw a *voiture* for hire coming towards them.

"Take us to the *Rue de Rivoli,* to the late market!" Warren ordered.

The cab-driver touched his hat with his whip and obviously impressed by Warren's appearance replied:

"*Bien, Monsieur!*"

Warren got in beside Nadia who asked:

"Why are we going there?"

"Because it is the only place open at this time of the night," Warren explained, "and I have to buy you a cape and perhaps a hat before I can take you into my *Hôtel*."

She looked at him quickly, and he said:

"I am going to ask the Manager's wife, who I remember is a very able woman, to find you enough clothes in which you can travel to England. After that my mother will provide you with those that you lost while you were travelling to Paris."

"Will your mother believe that?"

"You must make certain she does. At the same time we first have to have a convincing story to tell *Madame* Blanc who, I am quite certain, will be very inquisitive."

He was silent as the *voiture* drove over a bridge across the Seine and a few minutes later they were in the *Rue de Rivoli*.

At the smart end where it joined the *Place de la Concorde* the shops at this late hour were of course all closed.

But Warren had remembered that beyond the Louvre, where there were the big, cheap Emporiums, there were also some small shops which stayed open late.

There was also an open market where one could buy food as well as all sorts of strange objects which the French considered bargains.

When the *voiture* came to a standstill Warren got out and told the man to wait.

He took Nadia by the arm and then they mingled with the throng of ordinary people who had just come out from the Restaurants or the Theatres and a number of rag-pickers who were doubtless also pick-pockets.

Warren steered Nadia through the crowd which was very good-humoured, joking and laughing amongst themselves, until he found a shop that was illuminated and had its door still open.

There were a number of flashy gowns and some very seductive under-garments in the window, but inside there was a clothes'-horse with a long rail on which there hung some long cloaks which the Parisian women wore at night over their evening-gowns.

He picked out one which was on a hanger but thought it too gaudy, then found another in a dark blue material that he placed over Nadia's shoulders.

It reached almost to the ground, concealing her threadbare gown, and he thought it suited her.

"You will have to choose the hat," he said.

He pointed to where there was a miscellaneous collection of hats: straws, velvets, some decorated with feathers or flowers, some gaudy, all heaped together on the side of a counter.

Nadia hesitated.

Then with what he thought was unerring good taste she picked out one that was plain and yet unmistakably had a touch of Paris *chic* about it.

It was a light felt, obviously left over from the winter collection, but it was small and trimmed only with one large black quill stuck into the band around the crown.

She put it on her head and looked at him for approval.

"Excellent!" he exclaimed.

He paid an indifferent saleswoman who looked tired and was obviously watching the clock for closing-time.

They walked back to the *voiture*, Warren gave the address of his *Hôtel* to the cab-driver, and as they set off up the *Rue de Rivoli* he said:

"Now you have another part to play, and I shall be interested to see how good an actress you are."

"You are . . . frightening me!"

"You certainly need not be frightened of *Madame* Blanc, although I admit I have found her somewhat intimidating in the past!"

Nadia realised he was laughing at her and she said:

"Please tell me quickly what I have to do."

"This part of the story is rather complicated," Warren said. "I left the *Hôtel* telling the Manager I had to leave first thing in the morning for England. He was to make all the arrangements for me. I return with a very beautiful young woman, for which the French have only one possible explanation!"

He did not wait for Nadia to reply to this but went on:

"I should have asked you this before, but what other languages do you speak besides English and French?"

He knew from Nadia's momentary hesitation that she was considering what reply to make.

It was strange how he could read her thoughts and was aware when he intruded on something she wished to keep a secret.

He did not even think it was extraordinary that he was so perceptive about her. He only knew that his instinct told him so much more than she would put into words.

Hesitatingly she said:

"I . . . I can speak . . . Hungarian."

"Good! That is exactly what I hoped, or rather, that it would be the language of one of the Balkan countries of which most people are lamentably ignorant."

He smiled at her in the darkness of the *voiture* as he said:

"This will fit in with the tale we will tell when we reach England, so at least you need not change your identity."

"It sounds like something in a novel!" Nadia exclaimed.

"We have to make it credible!"

"Very well then . . . I am Hungarian."

"Tell me an Hungarian name."

"Ferrais, or Kaunitz!"

"Ferrais will do," he said, "and your father is an extremely wealthy nobleman."

Nadia did not speak and he continued:

"Because he is so wealthy, you were kidnapped when you were travelling to Paris and held to ransom."

Warren spoke every word as if he was seeing it happening as he described it.

"The men who captured you were utterly and completely ruthless. They starved you, told your father you would die unless he paid them an enormous sum of money, confiscated your clothes, your jewellery, in fact, everything you possess."

"It sounds . . . terrifying!" Nadia exclaimed, but there was a hint of laughter in her voice.

"Then today, by some great good fortune," Warren went on, "I discovered among my letters an anonymous communication telling me where I would find you. Because your captors were not expecting you to be rescued, I was able to steal you away without their preventing me."

Nadia clapped her hands.

"It is exactly like one of the novelettes Mama would never let me read."

"Well, now you can not only read it but live it," Warren replied, "and make it convincing."

"To *Madame* Blanc?"

"Exactly! We are relying on her not only to believe you, but to provide you with the clothes in which you will travel to England, and in which you will look very attractive, despite all the privations you have suffered at the hands of your kidnappers."

367

"And you really think she will . . . believe us?"

"It depends on how well we tell the story!"

When several hours later Warren went to bed, he stood for a moment at the window looking out over the moonlit view beneath him.

There was a smile of satisfaction on his lips which had not been there when he had looked at it before.

He had known, when he told his dramatic tale to *Monsieur* and *Madame* Blanc in the Manager's Office and saw their absorbed attention to what he was saying, that Nadia would not fail him either here in France, or when they reached England.

She played admirably the part of a shocked and frightened young girl who had suddenly been subjected to the horrors she had endured after being kidnapped.

Wisely, she said very little except to exclaim piteously over her sufferings.

Her thin face and huge eyes were so pathetic that he knew *Madame* Blanc's heart had been wrung with sympathy.

"Because I could not bring my cousin here to the *Hôtel* in the state to which she had been reduced," Warren explained, "I bought her a few clothes at the market in the *Rue de Rivoli*. But you understand, *Madame*, she must have something very different in which to travel to England."

"I can of course buy clothes very easily, *Monsieur*," *Madame* Blanc assured him, "but not until the shops are open, and *Mademoiselle la Comtesse* must have the best!"

"Yes, of course, the very best!" Warren agreed. "And money is no object."

He thought as he spoke of the huge fortune he would inherit when he became the head of the family in his uncle's place, and knew that for the first time in his life there was no need for him to count the cost of anything.

He made it clear to *Madame* Blanc that Nadia's father would reimburse him for anything he spent, so that it would be foolish to buy cheap things which they would throw away when they reached England.

"My cousin is used to having clothes that are the envy of all her friends," he said with a smile, "so I must look to you, *Madame,* to replace those which have been stolen from her."

"But of course, *Monsieur!*" *Madame* Blanc said eagerly.

Then she looked at her husband.

"How long do I have, Etienne, before *Monsieur* wishes to depart?"

It took quite a lot of argument and pleading from *Madame* before Warren finally agreed to leave Paris on a later train which would connect not with the morning Cross-Channel Steamer from Calais but the afternoon boat.

This would mean their arriving much later, but he knew it was impossible for him to take Nadia to England without the right clothes.

He had no wish to tell the kidnapping story to his mother, or to anybody else on the other side of the Channel.

That story was for French consumption only, and in England he intended to say that he had met Nadia in Paris *en route* to Africa, that he had fallen in love with her and she had waited for his return to Paris before they announced their engagement formally.

He felt this was a safe story considering that nobody except Edward knew how long they had stayed in Paris before they went to Africa and there was no reason why Nadia should not have met him at Marseilles on his homeward journey.

This would mean that he would not have read his mother's letter, or for that matter, Magnolia's, until he arrived in Paris.

It all seemed to fit in very well, and he knew, if he was honest with himself, that he had rather enjoyed the intrigue and working out the plot he had invented himself, although Nadia was very important in it.

After they had talked for a long time in the Manager's Office, he realised she was looking tired and suggested to *Madame* Blanc that Nadia should go to bed.

"I am sure, *Madame,*" he said in his most charming manner which was difficult for any woman to resist, "you will look after my cousin tonight and chaperone her very effectively. Tomorrow, I intend to take her to my mother, who will be horrified at what has occurred."

"I am sure that is true, *Monsieur,*" *Madame* Blanc replied, "and *Mademoiselle* can sleep in the room next to mine because my daughter who usually occupies it is staying with friends."

"I am very grateful, *Madame.*"

Madame Blanc bustled Nadia upstairs, gave her a hot drink to help her sleep and helped her to undress.

She exclaimed in horror at the condition of the gown which was all her captors had given her to wear!

She promised that tomorrow she should have the most beautiful gowns that Paris could provide, besides mantles, hats, gloves and everything else that could be bought at a moment's notice.

"What I intend to do, *Mademoiselle la Comtesse,*" *Madame* Blanc said in her firm, practical voice, "is to set off at dawn without you to find what is available in your size. You are very slim, so it should not be difficult. Then later, when you have had *petit déjeuner,* one of my staff will bring you to join me and see if you approve of my taste."

"I am sure, *Madame,* that anything you select for me will be delightful and very *chic!*" Nadia replied.

She knew by the smile on Madame's face that no Frenchwoman could resist the chance of spending unlimited money, even if it was for another woman!

Nadia was in fact exhausted, and almost as soon as her head touched the pillow she fell asleep.

Madame Blanc then returned to her husband's Office where he and Warren were still talking.

"La pauvre petite est très fatiguée!" she commented.

"I only hope the journey tomorrow will not be too much for her," Warren said, "but I have to go home."

"I thought perhaps the urgency concerned your family," *Madame* Blanc said, "but I did not like to mention it before."

"What do you mean?"

In answer the Manager handed him from his desk a copy of *Le Temps* and pointed to a paragraph low on the front page.

It was almost what Warren had expected as he translated:

DEATH OF A DISTINGUISHED ENGLISH NOBLEMAN

It is with deep regret that we learn today of the death of the Marquis of Buckwood at his home in Oxfordshire . . .

The newspaper went on to describe the Marquis's importance at Court, his vast possessions, his visit to France at the opening of the Exhibition and finished:

The Marquis's only son died very recently after a riding accident. The heir to the title is his nephew Mr. Warren Wood, who has been abroad for some months and is not aware of his new position.

Every effort is being made by the Solicitors to the estate to get in touch with Mr. Wood.

Warren finished reading the account and as he put down the newspaper the Manager said:

"My condolences, *Monsieur*, and also my congratulations!"

"Thank you," Warren replied. "Now you understand why I must go home as quickly as possible."

"Of course, *Monsieur,* but as *Madame* has said, clothes cannot be purchased until the shops are open."

"No, of course not" Warren replied, "and clothes even in these circumstances are very important."

Then *Madame* exclaimed:

"You do not intend, *Monsieur,* that I should buy everything in black for *Mademoiselle la Comtesse?*"

Warren thought quickly, remembering that Nadia was in mourning for her mother.

At the same time it would spoil his return with her if she was, as Magnolia had been, restricted by the strict protocol of mourning.

He shook his head.

"No, there is no need for *Mademoiselle* to be in mourning," he replied. "Our relationship is through my mother's family, and there is therefore no reason why she should be affected in that way by my uncle's death."

"I am glad!" *Madame* Blanc exclaimed. "Mourning makes us all, as I have said before to my husband, look like a lot of black crows!"

Warren smiled.

He knew if any country in the world could make mourning look attractive and even seductive, it was France.

The little touches of white on a black gown, the transparency of chiffon or lace over the skin, were very different from the heavy crêpe, the profusion of jet, and the gloom of British black.

He merely said aloud:

"I suggest, *Madame,* that you make my relative look as young and as beautiful as she was before she suffered so acutely at the hands of those villains."

"I hope, *Monsieur,* they will receive their just deserts!"

"Her father the Count will certainly see to that,"

Warren replied. "But it is best for us to get out of the country before anything untoward happens. Such men if thwarted in their desire for money, can be very dangerous!"

"That is true, *Monsieur*," *Madame* Blanc agreed. "So you must certainly catch the second Express as my husband has suggested."

"Everything will be arranged, *Monsieur*," the Manager said. "A private compartment in the train, the best cabin on the Steamer, and a Courier to travel with you who will see to everything."

"Thank you!" Warren replied.

He thought now as he stood at the window that it was almost amusing.

Suddenly as if by a magic wand, his whole life had changed.

From now on there would be Couriers, valets, footmen to run at his bidding, and waiting for him in England would be Secretaries, Managers and Agents who had helped his uncle run the estates.

They saw to it that each one of his houses functioned like a well-oiled machine with no breakdowns and no problems to cause him sleepless nights.

'I am lucky, unbelievably lucky!' he thought.

He drew the curtains to shut out the moonlight and got into bed.

Sitting beside Nadia in the reserved carriage on the Boat Train carrying them from Dover to London, Warren thought she looked if a little tired, exceedingly lovely.

He knew she had slept in the comfortable cabin that had been engaged for them for the Channel crossing.

He on the other hand, had walked the decks feeling he needed the fresh air, and finding the smooth sea and the last rays of the afternoon sun delightful.

He appreciated, although he did not say so, every

luxury they had enjoyed so far, not only because it was
so very different from the discomforts of Africa, but
also because he knew it was prophetic of his whole
future.

He had waited until now to tell Nadia his new name
and title, although he had noticed she was astute
enough to look puzzled when the Manager addressed
him as: *'Milord'* rather than *'Monsieur.'*

"When you had gone to bed last night," Warren
said to her, "the Manager showed me a copy of *Le
Temps* in which there was a report of my uncle's
death."

"I am sorry if it has upset you."

"It was what I expected," Warren said, "because my
mother had warned me. After his son was killed he
had a heart-attack and was in a coma. This means that
I am now the 6th Marquis of Buckwood!"

Nadia did not speak for a moment. Then she asked:

"Does that make you feel very important?"

"Yes, very!" he replied. "Especially as I never anticipated for one moment that I would ever inherit such a
position!"

"Then I am glad for you, but it will make the lady
who wishes to marry you very angry!"

"Very angry indeed!" Warren said with satisfaction.

Then as if he had no wish to talk about himself he
added:

"We must go over our story to be quite certain before we arrive that you are word-perfect."

"I am so afraid of making mistakes . . . then you
will be . . . angry."

"I promise you I shall not be that," he said. "And
after the splendid way in which you carried off our
fantastic tale last night, I am sure there is a fortune
waiting for you on the stage at Drury Lane!"

She laughed as if that was such an impossibility that
it was but a figment of his imagination.

Then Warren said:

"Judging from the amount of luggage which you

now possess, I imagine there is no hurry for us to visit any English shops, and you can cope at any rate for a few weeks in the country."

"I am afraid *Madame* Blanc has spent a great amount of money," Nadia said.

"That is immaterial beside the fact that you have to look right for the part."

"I should certainly do that," Nadia said in a low voice. "I have never seen such wonderful gowns, nor did I imagine it was possible to buy so much so very quickly!"

She gave a little laugh before she said:

"I really believe *Madame* was up all night hammering on the doors of the dressmakers. In fact she told me that at one shop the seamstresses had been paid extra to go to work at four o'clock in the morning because they had a special wedding-gown to finish."

Warren laughed.

"They cannot have been very pleased to see another customer!"

"According to *Madame* they were delighted, and actually that particular bride will have three of her gowns delivered late!"

Warren laughed again.

"If there is one thing the French are really adept at, it is the turning of any emergency to their own advantage! I am certain the gowns that were switched cost double in the process, but were well worth the expense!"

"I only hope you will think so," Nadia said, "and I am very embarrassed at costing you so much."

"I would pay a hundred times more to be sure of creating the effect I want."

The hard, bitter note was back in his voice and Nadia looked at him apprehensively.

Quickly, because she thought the violence of his emotions spoilt him, she talked of other things, asking him further about the history of Buckwood and to describe the members of the family whom she would meet.

Because she seemed to have grasped so quickly the different relationships and even the different titles she would encounter in the family tree Warren, as he talked, was quite certain that it was not new ground to her, but something she was familiar with in her own life.

The more he was with her, the more he looked at her, the more he was certain she was blue-blooded to her finger-tips.

Although she would tell him nothing more about herself, he was aware of a mystery which intrigued and fascinated him and he knew he would never rest until he had learnt her whole secret.

At the same time, he knew it would be a great mistake to upset her in any way, or for her to resent his prying into things which did not concern him.

All that mattered at the moment was that everybody should be convinced that he was intending to marry somebody with whom he was not only deeply in love, but who was also eminently suited to become the Marchioness of Buckwood.

"I was wondering," he said aloud, "whether I should make you a Princess, but I think that might be dangerous because there must be Hungarians in England who would at least know those in their country who were of Royal blood."

"That is true," Nadia said seriously, "and as almost everybody one meets in Hungary is a Count, that would be very much safer."

Warren was aware that if a Count had even a dozen children they all inherited his title, each one of them becoming a Count or a Countess, unlike in England where the title went only to the eldest son.

As if she wished to please him, Nadia said:

"There is however no reason why my mother should not have a little Royal blood in her, if you wish to improve the story."

"That sounds a good idea," Warren said.

"There are on the Russian border," Nadia said hesitatingly, "quite a number of families who consider themselves . . . Royal . . . although they play no part . . . in the governing of the country."

"I am aware of that," Warren smiled, "and it is clever of you, Nadia, to suggest that your mother should be Royal. I imagine you can give me the name of some large family to which she could quite easily belong."

"Of course," Nadia replied. "There are so many Rákócitz that I doubt if anybody but a Hungarian could count them all!"

"Very well, your mother was a Princess of the family, and you had better give me her Christian name."

"Shall we say Olga?"

"Excellent!" Warren said. "Princess Olga! And as the daughter of a great landowner, Count Viktor Ferrais, you are of course, by no means overawed by or in any way subservient to the Marquis of Buckwood!"

"Of course not," Nadia agreed her eyes twinkling. "In fact, I am only afraid that my family will not think him good enough for me!"

They both laughed and Warren told himself that he had been certainly in luck when he had seen a slim figure looking down into the dark waters of the Seine and realised what she was about to do.

It was however, a little after midnight when finally they reached his mother's house, and Nadia was very tired.

On Warren's instructions telegrams had been sent before he went to bed the night before to his mother and to his uncle's secretary at Buckwood House in London and, as he expected, there were carriages to meet them at Victoria Station.

They were carried swiftly across London to where it seemed almost as if at his command the train was waiting to convey them to the nearest station to Buckwood.

More carriages, more servants, and at last they walked into his mother's house to find her waiting for him, her arms outstretched.

"You should be in bed, Mama!" Warren said as he kissed her. "You should not have waited up for me."

"I could not rest until you were safely home," his mother replied. "Oh, dearest boy, I am so delighted to see you!"

She kissed him again before she looked curiously at Nadia.

"Mama," Warren said slowly and impressively, "may I introduce the Countess Nadia Ferrais, who has come with me and who I am very proud to tell you has promised to become my wife!"

He knew what he had said was a shock to his mother, but as he expected, she took it with her usual gracious dignity, saying:

"My dearest, I hope you will be very happy!"

Taking Nadia's hand in hers she said:

"I am very glad I shall have a daughter-in-law who will look after my son, and whom I know I shall love."

She spoke so gently and movingly that Warren saw the tears come into Nadia's eyes and knew she was thinking of her own mother.

Quickly, in case she should become emotional, he started to talk to his mother of how they had met when he was on his way to Africa, and how they had known they were meant for each other.

He told her how she had been waiting for him when he arrived with Edward at Marseilles.

"Of course she had one of her elderly relatives with her," he said, having just thought of it, "and although I begged her to come with us to England, she unfortunately had to return home to Hungary."

"I thought from your name you must be Hungarian," his mother said to Nadia, "and of course like all your countrywomen you are very beautiful, my dear!"

"Thank you," Nadia replied.

"She is also very tired," Warren interposed, "and I suggest, Mama, that she goes to bed immediately, and we can tell you everything about ourselves tomorrow."

"Yes, of course, dear boy."

His mother took Nadia upstairs to hand her over to an elderly maid who helped her into bed, and only after she herself also had retired did Warren go into her room to sit down beside her.

"I am so glad you are back in time for the Funeral," his mother said. "That you are engaged to be married will be cheerful news for the family, after they have been stricken first by Raymond's death, and now by poor Arthur's."

"I could hardly believe it was true when I read your letter," Warren said.

"It seems unbelievable," his mother agreed, "but dearest, first thing in the morning you must take charge of everything as they are expecting you to do."

"Of course, Mama!"

He rose to his feet as he spoke and added:

"Now I am going to bed, for I too am tired. I seem to have been travelling for a very long time."

"You look very well, and I rather like the new colour of your skin."

"You mean my sun-tan? At times in the last few months I have been as dark as any Arab could be!"

"You look very handsome, as I am sure that charming young lady you have brought with you has told you already."

"She has been very ill, and is rather shy, Mama."

"She looks very young, and very sweet!" his mother replied.

She spoke with a note in her voice which made Warren know she was entirely sincere.

After a little pause she went on:

"You may be surprised to learn that Magnolia Keane is staying at Buckwood!"

Warren started.

"Staying at Buckwood? Why should she do that?"

"She moved in with an elderly cousin whom she calls her chaperon after Raymond's accident. She appeared then—to be overcome with sorrow. But your uncle's secretary, Mr. Grayshott, tells me she asked him searching questions about you and made it very clear that she wanted to get in touch with you."

"She has not come here, Mama?"

"Not since I refused to see her after you had left England."

"She tried to see you then?"

"I think after she learned you had gone away she was curious enough to want to know what had happened. Anyway, she called here and asked to see me, and I sent a message to say I was not well enough to receive strangers!"

Warren thought that his mother, when it suited her, could put down very cleverly somebody who was pretentious or pushing, but aloud he said:

"You will understand, Mama, that I have no wish to see Magnolia again. Although I had no chance of talking to you about it, the reason why I left England was that she told me she intended to marry Raymond."

"I knew that," his mother replied.

"How did you know it?" Warren asked curiously.

"Oh, my dear, I am not so stupid as not to be able to put two and two together! Moreover, although it is very regrettable, servants talk and nothing one can do will stop them!"

Warren drew in his breath.

"Do you mean to say that the servants at Buckwood realised that Magnolia was trying to capture Raymond while she was secretly engaged to me?"

"That is so, dear," his mother said, "and I can understand it makes you feel bitter about her. Personally, if you want the truth, I never liked Magnolia, nor did I trust her!"

"Then you were far more astute than I was!"

"Of course!" his mother agreed. "Women always find it very hard to deceive other women, and although, darling boy, so many women have loved you for yourself, I was always suspicious that where Magnolia was concerned, she put your background first and you second!"

Warren sighed.

"You make me feel very foolish, Mama, and in a way ashamed of myself."

"There is no need for you to be that," his mother said. "But I am thanking God that you have found somebody whom you can love and who will be marrying you, rather than your Family Tree!"

Warren laughed and it was quite a natural sound.

"Nadia assures me," he said, "that ours is quite a young sapling compared with her father's."

"I would not be at all surprised," his mother replied, "for the Hungarians are a very proud people. Anyway, my dearest, I wish you every happiness which I have the unmistakable feeling is what you have found this time."

Only when he was in bed did Warren wonder if it was very reprehensible of him to start his new life by acting out a lie and deceiving somebody who trusted him as his mother did.

Then he told himself that at least Nadia provided him with an excuse for immediately turning Magnolia out of Buckwood and it would give him great pleasure to do so.

"Damn her!" he muttered. "How does she dare to come here, forcing herself upon the family as if she was Raymond's wife, and at the same time writing to me as she did?"

He knew as he asked himself the question that it would be a mistake to under-rate Magnolia. She would fight desperately and in the most underhand and devious manner possible to get her own way.

"There is no reason why I should be afraid to take her on," Warren told himself.

At the same time he was not sure.

CHAPTER FOUR

❧

*W*arren was having breakfast at seven-thirty the next morning when Mr. Greyshott came into the room.

He had been his uncle's chief Secretary ever since Warren could remember and was a grey-haired man of over fifty.

He was exceedingly efficient and had the character to exercise an authority which nobody disputed.

He had been at the station last night to meet Warren, who now looked up with a smile to say:

"Good-morning, Greyshott! Despite the late hour at which I got to bed I am ready for all the burdens with which you no doubt propose to confront me!"

Mr. Greyshott laughed and replied:

"I hope they will not be too overwhelming, My Lord."

"Sit down and tell me about the arrangements for tomorrow," Warren said in a different tone.

Mr. Greyshott sat down at the table and waved away the suggestion of coffee which the Butler offered him.

Then as the servants left the room Warren said:

"First I would like to know who is staying in the house and how many more you are expecting to-night."

"I thought Your Lordship would ask that," Mr. Greyshott answered, "and I am afraid it is a very long list. I had no idea until your cousin's funeral that so many Woods existed!"

"I have always known ours was a very large family," Warren replied, "but a great number of them did not concern me until now."

Mr. Greyshott handed him the list on which he saw the names of great-uncles, great-aunts, uncles, aunts, and innumerable cousins, besides close friends who had already arrived to be present at the Marquis's Funeral.

"I should think if they all stay with us the house will burst at the seams!" Warren remarked.

"We can manage," Mr. Greyshott replied reassuringly, "and I think, if you will permit me to say so, they will expect Your Lordship to move into the Master Suite tonight."

Warren accepted this because it was traditional and merely said:

"That is what I will do."

He was still reading the list as he spoke. Then at the bottom of it he found the names he was looking for.

Miss Magnolia Keane
Mrs. Douglas Keane

He looked up and chose his words with care as he said:

"I see no reason for Miss Keane to be staying in the house, and I suggest that if she wishes to attend the Funeral, which we cannot prevent her from doing, she should move to an *Hôtel* or to friends in the neighbourhood!"

His voice sharpened as he spoke, and as Mr. Greyshott did not reply he went on:

"As I expect you are aware, I have brought my fiancée with me, intending to announce my engagement formally. As things are, we shall have to wait a little while, but I would like you, Greyshott, to make it clear to the family why she is here."

He thought Mr. Greyshott looked at him in surprise and he added:

"It will be a little difficult for me in the circumstances, and it would be better if it came from you."

"Very well, if that is what you wish," Mr. Greyshott agreed, "but I think, if you will forgive my saying so, My Lord, that it would be a mistake to turn out Miss Keane."

"Why?"

"Because she would certainly resent it, and she is getting a great deal of sympathy because, although it was supposed to be a secret, everybody knew at your cousin's Funeral that they were engaged."

Warren's lips tightened. Then he asked curiously:

"I cannot understand why their engagement had not been announced! After all, it would have been quite correct to have done so in March or April."

"That was what she wanted," Mr. Greyshott replied, "but your uncle insisted that there should be no formal announcement until Christmas."

Now Warren was surprised and raising his eyebrows asked:

"Why did he insist on that?"

Mr. Greyshott hesitated, and Warren said sharply:

"Tell me the truth, Greyshott. I want to know!"

"I think His Lordship did not like Miss Keane and was aware that when you brought her to stay with your mother you intended to marry her."

Warren was astonished.

"How could Uncle Arthur know that?"

"No one can stop servants talking," Mr. Greyshott said quietly, "and your uncle was very fond of you. In fact I think it would be true to say that he often wished you were his son rather than his nephew."

"In consequence he disliked Magnolia!" Warren said beneath his breath.

"I know that she pleaded with him and so did Raymond over the announcement of their engagement, but your uncle was adamant. He told them that if they

were both of the same mind at Christmas or perhaps
at the time of the Hunt Ball at the beginning of De-
cember, their engagement could be announced then."

Warren knew that his uncle could be very dictato-
rial when it suited him, and he could understand
Magnolia's frustration.

Then when Raymond was killed she had realised all
too clearly that she had lost the substance for the
shadow.

There was a hard look in his eyes and a cynical twist
to his lips as he said:

"All the same she has no part in Buckwood now,
and the sooner you get rid of her the better!"

He knew by the expression on Mr. Greyshott's face
that it was not going to be easy, and he asked sharply:

"Raymond did not make a will in her favour, or
anything like that?"

"I understand she asked him to do so," Mr.
Greyshott answered, "but your uncle heard about it
from the family Solicitors, and forbade Raymond to
do anything of the sort."

Because he disliked everything he had heard, Warren rose from the desk and said:

"I have no wish to see her, Greyshott. Tell her that I
am here with my fiancée and will need the rooms she
and Mrs. Keane are occupying."

"I will do that," Mr. Greyshott agreed.

At the same time, Warren knew he felt anxious.

There was a horse waiting for him at the door, and
Warren rode across the fields to the big house.

As he saw it looking magnificent in the distance,
with the Marquis's standard flying at half-mast, he
thought it must be a dream that it now belonged to
him.

The sunshine turned the hundreds of windows to
gold and glittered on the lake and it seemed to Warren as if it had stepped out of a fairy-story.

He loved Buckwood as it had always been so much
a part of his childhood and the memories of his father.

He knew that now he had come home he must devote himself to serving the house and the family traditions as his ancestors had done before him.

As he reached the front door he found there were several carriages outside.

He knew that the moment he entered the huge marble Hall with its statues of gods and goddesses and the flags commemorating battles in which members of the family had fought valiantly, there would be the chatter of voices.

Whatever happened either in joy or sorrow, the Woods always made Buckwood a meeting place, where they could get together and talk about themselves.

He was not mistaken.

He could hear their voices in the Drawing-Room as he entered the hall and saw the row of top-hats laid out on the table beneath the staircase.

Then with a faint smile because it was all so familiar, he opened the door and joined them.

It was nearly an hour later when he extricated himself from the clinging arms of his female relations who had always been eager to kiss him because he was so handsome, and the hearty hand-shakes of the male representatives of the family.

It warmed his heart to realise that they were all genuinely glad that he should take his uncle's place as head of the family.

They had loved his father, for nobody ever managed to quarrel with Lord John, and in consequence they had adored and spoiled Warren ever since his birth.

It was only as he moved towards the Study where his uncle had always dealt with any business which affected the estate that he realised they had not yet learnt of his engagement and wondered what they would think of Nadia.

He had made it clear to the servants at his mother's

house that she was to be allowed to sleep until she woke.

He decided that she should not attend the Funeral, although she would be expected to have luncheon and to dine with the family today when she would be introduced to them as his future wife.

He thought it would undoubtedly surprise them, but not so much as it would surprise Magnolia.

Mr. Greyshott was waiting for him in the Study.

He put down in front of Warren the arrangements for the Funeral, a copy of the Service which had already been printed with a wide black band on the outside cover, and a list of the guests at luncheon.

"The rest of the family will be arriving this afternoon," Mr. Greyshott explained, "and I will let you have the seating for dinner later on."

"Have you spoken to Miss Keane?"

"Yes, I have," he replied, "but she refuses to leave until she has seen you."

"I have no wish . . ." Warren began.

At that moment the door opened and Magnolia came into the Study.

A quick glance told Warren that she was even more beautiful than when he had last seen her.

He knew however, as she moved towards him with a sensuous grace that somehow made the plain black gown she was wearing seem almost immorally seductive, that his only feeling for her was one of hatred.

With a murmured apology Mr. Greyshott moved quickly from the room.

As the door closed behind him Magnolia said in the soft, caressing voice that Warren remembered so well:

"You are back! Oh darling, it seems an eternity since I last saw you!"

He had risen to his feet when she appeared, but he had remained behind his desk and he replied coldly:

"I am surprised to find you here!"

"If I had left immediately after Raymond's funeral,

I might have missed you. Did you not receive my letter in Paris?"

"I received your letter which arrived three days before I did!"

He knew as he spoke this was something she had not expected he would know and her long eye-lashes flickered.

At the same time she was quick-witted enough to say after just a faint pause:

"I wrote it soon after you left, but there was no point in sending it until I knew you were on your way home."

"Which, most conveniently, was after Raymond had his accident!"

Magnolia made a little gesture with her hands which was very expressive. Then she asked:

"Why are you talking to me like this? I told you I loved you, Warren, and I have always loved you. Surely you can forgive me a moment's madness?"

She gave a deep sigh.

"When I saw this house I thought it was so beautiful that I could think of nothing except living in it and feeling as if I belonged . . ."

She spoke very softly and as if, Warren thought, she was trying to weave a spell around him from which he would find it hard to extricate himself.

Then in a hard voice he interrupted her to say:

"It is no use, Magnolia! I am not prepared to stand here and listen to your lies! I told Mr. Greyshott to ask you to leave and that is what you have to do."

"He also told me you had brought your fiancée with you," Magnolia said. "Is that true?"

"Greyshott invariably tells the truth, as I do!"

"And you really intend to marry somebody other than—me?"

She asked the question mockingly and there was a laughing note in her voice.

Then deliberately, so that she took him by surprise,

she moved round the desk and was standing close beside him.

She threw back her head to look up at him in a way he had always found irresistible and her lips were near to his as she whispered:

"Warren! Warren! I love you, as you love me. How could either of us forget the wonder and the glory we found when you kissed me?"

Then before Warren could move she pulled his head down to hers and her lips were on his.

He could feel the passion on them, could feel too the softness of her body against him and smell the seductive fragrance of her perfume that had something exotic about it.

But as she kissed him, her lips moving sensuously against his, he knew that her power over him had disappeared.

This contact with her dismissed the last lingering doubt in his mind as to whether she still had some hold over him.

His fingers closed over her wrists and he removed her arms from his neck.

"It is no use, Magnolia."

As she realised he was completely unmoved by her, he saw an expression first of incredulity in her dark eyes, then it was replaced by one of frustration and anger.

For a moment there was only silence, as if she found it hard to believe what he had said. Then she asked:

"Are you really sending me away?"

"I insist upon your leaving my house! While you are here it is only an embarrassment, and as your engagement to Raymond was not announced you have no official standing."

He released her wrists as he spoke and she rubbed one of them with her other hand as if he had hurt her.

"I believed that you—loved me."

"I did love you," Warren answered. "I loved you

completely and whole-heartedly until I learnt that you were merely using me to serve your social ambitions and were not interested in me as a man!"

"That is not true!" Magnolia cried. "And I love you now as I have never loved you before!"

"Only because you have lost me!" Warren replied cynically. "And you do not like being a loser."

"Have I really lost you?"

Now her voice was very soft and beguiling and he knew she was making one last desperate effort.

"As you already know, I am engaged to be married to somebody I love, a woman I can trust!"

Again his voice was sharp. Then he added:

"Goodbye, Magnolia. As you will understand, I have a great deal of work to do, so I hope you will excuse me if I do not come to see you off."

He spoke with a formal politeness that was more shattering than if he had raged at her.

Magnolia walked slowly to the door and only as she reached it did she turn back to say:

"You will be sorry, Warren, that you treated me like this! And do not think that you can forget me so easily or find another woman who will excite you as I was always able to do!"

She paused before she went on in a voice that seemed to vibrate towards him:

"When you are kissing your *fiancée* you will remember my kisses. When you touch her skin it will not feel like mine. You will miss the beating of my heart and the sound of my voice telling you of my love!"

Now the tone of her voice was hypnotic, mesmeric, but as Warren listened he knew it was a very skilful performance and that the audience to whom it was addressed was not himself as a person, but the Marquis of Buckwood.

"Goodbye, Magnolia!" he said sharply and sat down at his desk.

She lingered for a moment longer, then she was gone.

Only when he was certain she would not return did he rise to walk across the room to the open window.

He felt he needed fresh air.

He felt too as if he had been fighting against something which threatened to envelop him against his will and if he was not careful would destroy him.

Then he told himself he was being as threatrical as Magnolia had been, and the sooner he got back to sanity the better.

At the same time, he felt almost as if his collar was strangling him and it was hard to breathe.

Nadia came downstairs a little after eleven o'clock, feeling ashamed that she had slept so late.

The Butler met her in the hall to say:

"Her Ladyship has asked me to apologise, M'Lady, and to inform you that as she was very fatigued through being up so late last night she will not be down until luncheon-time."

"I quite understand," Nadia replied, "and I am late too."

"That was to be expected, M'Lady," the Butler said. "It's a very tiring journey from Paris, I understand."

"Yes, very," Nadia agreed.

He opened the door of the Drawing-Room which had long French windows opening out into the garden.

Outside Nadia could see there was a formal rose-garden and because it was summer the roses were all in bloom; crimson, white, yellow, pink and gold, they made a lovely picture.

Everything was very quiet, except for the humming of the bees buzzing over the blossoms, and the birds singing in the bushes.

It was like stepping into a fairy-land after being condemned to the squalid bedroom which she and her mother had occupied on the Left Bank of the Seine.

Even to think of it after her mother had grown so ill made Nadia shudder.

A breakfast-tray had been brought to her bedside after she woke and as she had looked at the beautiful china, the silver cover which kept the eggs hot and the fine linen napkin embroidered with Lord John's monogram she wanted to cry.

How could her mother have endured the cheap, badly cooked food, served on cracked plates in their dirty, dilapidated attic?

It was not surprising, Nadia thought, that she had died not only of her illness, but also of starvation because it was impossible to provide her with the right nourishment.

"Oh, Mama, if only you were here now!" she cried out in her heart.

Then she knew it was no use grieving over the past and instead she had to think of the future.

"I am so lucky, so very, very lucky," she told herself, just as Warren had done.

She was thinking that if he had not saved her she would by now be buried in a pauper's grave and because she had committed suicide, without the prayers or the blessing of the Church.

At least her mother had had that.

Because she was aware how desperately tired she had felt last night and almost on the point of collapse, she forced herself to eat everything on the breakfast-tray even though it was a great effort.

"If I am to help him as he wishes me to do," she reasoned, "I have to be strong and, what is more, I must have my wits about me!"

Last night when the maid had been helping her undress, the woman's voice had kept fading away and she had felt as if she was moving in a fog.

Now everything was clear, but it was inevitable that the weeks—or was it months?—of misery and privation overshadowed with fear had taken their toll.

Now she was in England, her fear had receded into

the background, and with her new identity, even though it was just play-acting, she need think of nothing except getting herself well and trying to do what kind Mr. Wood asked of her.

Then she remembered he was now a Marquis and wanted to laugh because it all seemed so incredible.

How could she have imagined for one moment when she went down to the Seine to drown herself that so soon she would find herself living in the luxury of an English mansion, waited on by attentive servants, such as she remembered in the past?

And knowing that hanging in the wardrobe were expensive, elegant gowns such as she had never expected to see again, let alone own?

"It is not true! I am dreaming!" Nadia exclaimed.

But because it was so exciting, she wanted to get up and see everything and do everything in case she woke up . . .

The sunshine in the garden, the roses, the red-brick wall enclosing them which she knew was very old and mellowed with age all seemed again part of her dreams.

Her mother had often described to her what an English garden was like.

Although she had never seen one, she knew now this was exactly what she had expected.

It was all so beautiful and there was no need to look over her shoulder or fear that somebody was approaching her, or lower her voice in case what she was saying should be overheard.

"I am in England and I am safe!" she said aloud.

Because the sun was very hot she turned and walked back through the French windows into the Drawing-Room.

This again was exactly as her mother had described to her; the comfortable sofas and armchairs, the tables on which there were innumerable and fascinating *objets d'art*, snuff-boxes, pieces of Dresden china, silver photograph frames with photographs of beautiful women which they had signed boldly and proudly.

There were portraits on the walls too, which were, Nadia thought, what she might have expected.

There was a beautiful painting by Sir Joshua Reynolds over the marble mantelpiece and a very attractive Greuze on one wall.

There was a 'Conversation Piece' of a family wearing the clothes of the previous century with a magnificent house in the background that she was sure was Buckwood.

It had been too dark last night to see the big house, and she hoped that Warren would show it to her today.

She already knew how much it meant to him. His voice had softened when he spoke of it and she had the feeling that it was as dear as the woman he had loved.

When she thought about him, seeing how handsome and attractive he was and, as she had found, kind and understanding, it seemed impossible that any woman should have thrown him over so cruelly that he now wished to have his revenge.

Nadia was far too perceptive not to be aware that the woman who had jilted Warren had made him suffer in a manner which he would never forget.

At the same time, she thought to herself, his bitterness was a flaw and seemed unworthy of him.

It was as if, she thought, looking across the room, somebody had deliberately damaged the beautiful 'Conversation Piece' that she realised now had been painted by Gainsborough.

Then as she was looking at it, thinking that one day Warren should be painted in the same way together with his family and the house he loved behind him, the door of the Drawing-Room opened.

Nadia turned her head, hoping it was Warren.

Instead she saw a woman who was so beautiful and

so different from anybody she had seen before that she could only stare at her.

She was dressed in black which seemed to reveal every curve of her breasts and hips, and somehow made her seem theatrical as if she was on a stage.

There were two long strings of pearls round her neck and her hat was trimmed with black ostrich feathers.

Beneath it her skin was dazzlingly white and had the same translucence as her pearls.

Her eyes were dark, liquid and fringed with long lashes.

She came gracefully across the room as Nadia watched, spellbound by her appearance.

Then as she reached her the woman exclaimed:

"I understand you are trying to marry Warren!"

The rude way she spoke and her form of words was so surprising that for a moment Nadia could not find her voice to reply.

Then because she thought to hesitate might seem weak she answered:

"We are . . . engaged."

"Then let me tell you," Magnolia said, "that you are not going to marry him! And if you try to do so, you will be sorry!"

She spoke in a low voice which was venomous. Nadia could now see the fury in her eyes and it made her afraid.

"I . . . I do not understand," she answered and heard her voice stammering.

"In case you do not know, my name is Magnolia Keane, and Warren is mine, as he has always been. If he thinks he can escape me, he is very much mistaken. As for you . . ."

Magnolia looked her up and down in a way that was insulting before she finished:

". . . go back to where you came from and find another man. You shall not have mine!"

"I do not . . . know what you are . . . saying!"
Nadia cried.

But Magnolia, having almost spat the words at her,
turned away.

She walked back towards the door, moving slowly,
sensuously, almost, Nadia thought, as if her body
writhed like that of a snake.

Then the door was closed behind her and Nadia
was alone.

For a moment she could not believe that what had
happened was real.

Then she thought she could understand why Warren had been so much in love with Magnolia that
when they parted he had wished to kill himself.

She could understand that with somebody like the
woman she had just seen, love would not be a soft and
contented happiness, but a burning, fiery rapture
which would consume those who felt it.

Then when it was gone it left them sucked dry of
everything but a sense of despair.

"Now I can understand," Nadia said beneath her
breath. "But why, if she still wants him, does he need
me?"

It all seemed incomprehensible. She knew when
Warren had told her in Paris how he had been disillu-
sioned, she had thought he had lost the woman he
loved for ever and had not expected to find her here,
claiming him as obviously Magnolia Keane was doing.

She sat down on a chair because her legs felt as if
they could not carry her, and tried to work it out in
her own mind.

Then, because she was very intelligent, she began to
understand what had happened.

Magnolia, as Warren had said, had refused to
marry him because she had the chance of marrying a
man with a title.

That must have been his cousin who had died
through an accident.

Now the cousin was dead she wanted Warren back again, but he no longer wanted her.

It all seemed somewhat complicated.

At the same time, Nadia could understand his pride would not allow him to be thrown down and picked up again by any woman, even one as beautiful as Magnolia Keane.

"She is lovely, but dangerous!" Nadia murmured.

Then as she recalled the expression in Magnolia's eyes, she felt the fear she thought she had left behind in Paris creeping over her again, the fear she had lived with for so long that it seemed cruel that it should be with her again, just when she believed she had escaped from it, and she felt herself shiver.

The door opened and Warren came in.

He looked so handsome, so elegant, in his riding-clothes with polished boots and wearing a whip-cord jacket and there was also something strong, comforting and safe about him.

Without meaning to, Nadia gave a little cry of delight.

"I was thinking of you."

Warren shut the door behind him and walked towards her.

"What was that woman doing here?" he asked. "Has she upset you?"

"How . . . how did you know she was . . . here?"

"I saw her carriage driving away," he said, "and I knew she must have called either to upset my mother, or you."

"Your mother is not yet down."

"Then you, Nadia, what did she say to you?"

Because he was still speaking sharply and his voice was hard, Nadia felt herself tremble and her face as she looked at him was very pale.

As if Warren understood, in a very different tone he said:

"You are upset, and that is the last thing I wanted. I

am very sorry, Nadia. I might have expected this to happen."

"But . . . how could you?"

"I told her to leave my house, and she was very angry. Then because she had been told we were engaged, she came here to vent her anger on you."

"She is . . . very beautiful!"

"I once thought so."

"And now?"

Nadia glanced at him and saw to her surprise that he was smiling.

"She no longer has the power to upset me."

"I . . . I am so very glad!"

"But she has upset you, and that is unforgivable!"

"No, I am all right now. It was . . . just that she was . . . rather frightening . . . and she said you belonged to her."

"That is where she is mistaken."

He gave a sigh as he added:

"I suppose I really should not talk to you like this, but as you are helping me you may as well know the truth. I was secretly afraid, although I would not have admitted it even to myself, that when I saw her again she would somehow get me back into her clutches."

"And you . . . did not feel like that?"

Warren recalled how Magnolia's lips had meant nothing to him and he said:

"I am free, completely and absolutely free!"

He walked across to the window as he spoke and looked out into the sunlit garden, thinking that the beauty of it was his, just as the house, the lake, the great oaks under which the deer were lying were his.

Now he felt he could enjoy them without any shadow on his happiness.

Then behind him a soft voice said:

"P.perhaps you . . . no longer . . . need me . . . and I should . . . go away."

He turned and saw Nadia's eyes looking at him beseechingly, and knew she was afraid he might wish her to leave at once.

"Of course I want you," he said reassuringly. "Nothing could be more disastrous than for Magnolia to guess for one moment that I had brought you here just to confront her, and that as soon as she had left you had left too."

"You . . . want me to stay?"

"I insist upon your staying! That was our agreement. If you remember, I said you would stay as long as I considered it necessary."

"And it is . . . really necessary? You are not just . . . saying that to help me?"

"You are necessary to me," he said, "and I am being entirely selfish when I say I want you."

He thought the expression of relief which swept over her face was very touching and he added:

"I learnt when I was in the Army that one should never underrate the enemy, and I have the feeling, though I hope I am wrong, that Magnolia will not give up easily."

"That is what I thought . . . too," Nadia said, "but . . . surely she cannot . . . hurt you now?"

"No, of course not!" Warren replied. "The only way she could hurt me would have been through my heart, as she did before."

"And now?"

"I shall enjoy myself without giving her another thought."

"At the same time," Nadia said a little hesitatingly, "while I do not see quite what she can do, I think she might still be dangerous for you."

"Nonsense!" Warren exclaimed. "We are just frightening ourselves with 'bogey-bogeys,' as I used to do when I was a child."

Nadia laughed.

"I used to be frightened of them too."

He saw a shadow pass over her face and knew the

fear had not only been when she was a child, but also when she was older.

He wanted to ask her about it because he was curious, but knew it would be a mistake.

Perhaps one day she would confide in him, but for the moment he would respect her desire for secrecy.

Instead he said:

"I am going to ask you to come to luncheon to meet my relatives. Quite a number are here already and you will meet the rest at dinner. Now, as we have plenty of time to spare, I thought perhaps you might like to drive a little way round the estate, and of course admire my house."

Nadia clasped her hands together.

"May I . . . really do that?"

"I am inviting you to come with me."

She gave a little cry of joy. Then she said:

"I will not keep you a minute while I fetch my hat."

"I am prepared to wait," he replied, "but do not be any longer than you can help."

She did not answer him, but ran from the room and he heard her footsteps crossing the hall.

He smiled and thought that although their conversation had been serious, she was still at times spontaneous and impulsive, almost child-like.

"It was clever of me to bring her here!" he murmured. "It has made it far easier to be rid of Magnolia than it would have been otherwise."

Then he wondered what his relatives would think of Nadia and was certain they would consider her far more suitable to be the Marchioness of Buckwood than Magnolia.

He was well aware that women always eyed Magnolia with suspicion, if not an active dislike.

She was far too sensational and beautiful in a way they would think somewhat immodest and theatrical.

The Marchioness of Buckwood should by tradition be beautiful, but with an indefinable dignity that came from being exceedingly well-bred, and what the servants would call 'a proper Lady.'

Strangely enough, that was exactly how Nadia looked, and Warren found himself wondering who the Charringtons were, and how she and her mother could have been left to starve.

'Charrington' was not an uncommon name, and yet he could not remember whether he had ever met one.

"I will ask amongst my friends," he decided, "and when I go to London I will have a word with the secretary of White's."

He knew that the man, who had been there for years, had every member's antecedents at his fingertips.

Then as he realised that Nadia was running down the stairs he told himself he must be careful to remember that she was the *Comtesse* Nadia Ferrais, and she came from an old and very respected Hungarian family.

For the first time it crossed his mind that if she was Hungarian she would be expected to ride well, and for her not to do so might arouse suspicions.

He helped her into his Phaeton which, drawn by two superlative horses, was waiting for them outside.

As they drove off he said:

"I have never had time to ask you before, but do you like riding?"

She looked at him and he saw her eyes were twinkling as she replied:

"I know what you are really asking me is whether I ride well enough to convince anybody who sees me that I am really an Hungarian!"

"You are reading my thoughts!"

"But of course! As you sometimes read mine!"

"Then answer my question."

"I can do that quite easily. I ride very well, but I have not ridden for a long time. Although one never forgets, I shall doubtless be red and stiff after riding one of your spirited horses."

"It is something you must certainly do, once the Funeral is over."

There was a little pause. Then Nadia said:

"Perhaps you will think it was wrong of me to be so . . . extravagant, but I did insist upon *Madame* Blanc buying me a habit, just in case you asked me to ride with you."

Warren laughed, and it was a genuine sound of amusement.

"The trouble with you, Nadia, is that you are not only unpredictable, but usually one step ahead of me. It has only just occurred to me that people would expect you to ride well, while you tell me you have already anticipated that is what they would do!"

"It seemed somehow rather presumptuous when we were in Paris, but perhaps one day I shall be able to pay back the money you have spent on me."

She made a little helpless gesture with her hands before she added:

"But for the moment . . . I cannot think how."

"You forget, it is I who am in your debt, not you in mine," Warren replied. "And I am so grateful that I want to thank you over and over again, and think of some way in which I can tell you how much your being here means to me."

He looked down at her as he spoke, and as she was looking up at him their eyes met.

It flashed through his mind that the obvious way to prove how pleased he was would be to kiss her.

For a moment it was hard to look away.

Then as if he remembered the horses needed his attention, Warren looked ahead and said:

"Now you will have your first view of Buckwood, and I know you will not be disappointed."

CHAPTER FIVE

*W*hen the Funeral was over and the family began to leave, everybody was congratulating Warren on his engagement, and especially on Nadia.

Although he had expected them to be effusive he realised they spoke with a sincerity which had nothing to do with ordinary politeness.

He had noticed himself that after luncheon the first day and again after dinner, Nadia made a point of talking to those of his relatives who were rather dull and uninteresting and would otherwise have been ignored.

He felt it was very tactful of her and could not help comparing her with Magnolia, who invariably made herself the centre of attention to the male members of any party at which she appeared.

He noticed that Nadia seemed particularly kind to older women, especially those whom the other members of the family had for years classified as bores.

When everyone had left he drove across the Park to his mother's house and found her having tea alone with Nadia in the Drawing-Room.

"We are rather late, dearest," his mother said when he came into the room, "but I felt a good cup of tea was what I needed to sustain me."

"You were marvellous, Mama!" Warren said,

bending down to kiss her. "I only hope it has not been too much for you."

"It was certainly rather upsetting," his mother said quietly, "because I was very fond of Arthur. At the same time, he did not linger on for months like your poor grandfather did."

Warren had always thought he would hate to die slowly with everybody thinking in the words of Charles II that he took 'an unconscionable time' in doing so.

In fact, if he had his choice he would rather die in battle or by accident, than be nothing but a body which breathed but could not think.

Because the Funeral had left him feeling sombre, he tried to smile as he said:

"Now, tell me what you have planned for this evening, although it seems incredible we should be alone. But now the family has left, it is quite eerie to have the house so quiet."

He was thinking also that it was almost unnerving to realise that it was now his, and that everybody was looking to him to bring in changes and perhaps new restrictions.

He had already made up his mind he would move slowly and try not to upset anybody.

He was well aware the old servants were set in their ways and, as Mr. Greyshott had everything running so smoothly he had no wish to ruffle the surface of what appeared to be a very calm sea.

"What I think would be best," his mother answered, "is if either you dine with Nadia, or she comes to you. I, personally, want to retire to bed."

"You are not over-tired, Mama?" Warren asked hastily.

"No dearest, but I hate Funerals, and also I found a great number of relatives all at the same time extremely indigestible!"

Nadia laughed, and it was a very pretty sound.

"Perhaps they would all look better if they were not

draped in black," she said. "My father always hated black. He said it was a dismal colour which only suited dismal people."

As she spoke her eyes met Warren's and they knew they were both thinking as he had told her, that *Madame* Blanc had said that women in mourning looked like black crows.

"I think as the cooks have had a lot of hard work in preparing luncheon for so many people," Warren said, "I will dine here, Mama."

"Very well, dearest, and being upstairs I shall feel that Nadia is adequately chaperoned even from the most ill-natured gossip."

"She has certainly given them enough to talk about at the moment," Warren said.

Then his eyes darkened as he remembered the same was true of Magnolia.

Unbelievably she had come to the Funeral, even though after he had turned her out of the house he was sure that she would return to London.

Instead of which, after almost everybody was seated and the Service about to begin she had appeared at the West Door.

One of the ushers had hurried forward and, because Warren had not given any orders to the contrary, she was led up the aisle and squeezed into the family pew just behind where he was sitting.

She obviously intended to cause a sensation, and she was dressed in a manner which made every woman as well as every man in the congregation find it difficult to take their eyes from her.

Her gown was as elegant as the one she had been wearing the day before, but far more elaborate.

Nevertheless it revealed her figure in the same seductive manner and the long veil which fell from the small bonnet on her head and covered her face was more suitable for a widow than for an ordinary mourner.

Warren, who just glanced at her, was sure it was

what she had worn for Raymond's Funeral and it had seemed equally sensational then.

As she knelt behind him he could smell the fragrance of her perfume, and he suspected that she was willing him to be aware of her.

All through the Service he felt as if her eyes were boring between his shoulder-blades, and although he tried to ignore her, it was impossible.

The coffin was carried down the aisle by soldiers of the County Yeomanry of which the Marquis had once been Colonel-in-Chief.

Warren walked behind it and was aware as he did so that Magnolia had pushed her way to the forefront of the other mourners.

It was then he realised that she carried in her hand a small bouquet of white orchids.

When the coffin was lowered into the grave she dramatically threw the flowers on top of it.

Then she put her hands to her eyes, staggered, and appeared about to collapse.

Because she was standing close to him, instinctively Warren put his arms around her to prevent her from falling into the grave.

Then as he half-carried her away he was aware that while her eyes were closed there was a faint smile on her lips and she was play-acting.

He handed her over to another member of the family as quickly as he could.

At the same time he was furiously angry that she had indulged in a sensational scene which would lose nothing in the telling.

There would also, he was quite sure, be reports in the local newspapers.

After such outrageous behaviour, he was not surprised when the whole party arrived back at the house to find Magnolia ensconced in a comfortable chair in the Drawing-Room with one of the maids ministering to her with smelling-salts.

He made no effort to speak to her, but other

members of the family went to her side, and Warren
could hear her lamenting in a low but clear voice how
much she would miss the Marquis.

"He was always so kind to me," he heard her say,
"and I shall not only miss him but this house. I feel as
if it is my home, and I cannot bear to lose it!"

There was a most convincing little sob in her voice
as she said the last words.

Warren thought, although it might have been his
imagination, that one or two of the relatives glanced at
him as if they thought he had the answer to her problem.

It was not until she left almost immediately after
luncheon, so as to receive the maximum amount of
attention, with half of the men present going to the
front door to see her off, that Warren was able to
heave a sigh of relief.

"Now there is no excuse for her to come back
again," he told himself, although he had the uncomfortable feeling that she might try.

He wished then that he had asked Nadia to attend
the Funeral luncheon and there made it clear that the
date of their marriage would be announced as soon as
possible.

Yet since she had met all the family the previous
day, he had thought it unnecessary for her to appear
to be mourning the Marquis whom she had never
met.

As soon as Magnolia had gone he therefore made a
point of saying to all his relatives as he bade them
goodbye:

"I hope when you come here again it will be in
much happier circumstances."

It was impossible for them not to realise what he
meant, and the majority of them replied automatically:

"You mean your wedding, Warren dear!"

"I think perhaps we should have an engagement
party before that," he said with a smile. "It could not

of course be a Ball, but perhaps a garden-party or a Reception at the beginning of August."

"We will look forward to it!" everybody exclaimed.

He knew that for the family any party at Buckwood was always hailed as something particularly enjoyable.

Now, looking at Nadia across the tea-table, he thought how attractive she looked in a gown that appeared simple, but had all the elegance that only France could create for a woman.

Even though she was still very thin, there was colour in her cheeks that had not been there before, and while her eyes were still too large for her face there was a light in them that seemed as if she had captured the sunlight.

"Tomorrow," he said, "I suggest as I have the farms to visit and it would be far quicker to ride than to drive, that you accompany me on horse-back."

There was no need for Nadia to speak in order to express her excitement, since the look on her face did it for her.

Then Warren's mother said:

"I know how thrilled and delighted everybody will be to meet Nadia, but if you go to one farm you must visit them all, otherwise there will be a great deal of jealousy."

"I have already thought of that," Warren replied. "I remember how in the old days when I called at the farms they always said:

" 'We've not seen ye're mother lately! Tell her I've a pot of home-made jam waiting for her.' "

His mother laughed.

"Or else it was a jar of pickles or honey, or a cut of the newly-cured ham. The people here have always been so generous!"

She put out her hand to touch Nadia on the arm.

"I know they will love you, my dear," she said. "I noticed today how kind you were to the older members of the family."

Nadia laughed.

"Mama always said if at a party there was somebody left out or alone, it showed that one was a bad hostess."

"That is true! At the same time, most young people are too busy thinking about themselves to have time for those who are no longer young."

The way his mother spoke told Warren very clearly how much she approved of Nadia, and he congratulated himself for being so lucky as to have found somebody who would play the part so well.

He had never realised until his mother told him so that she had not liked Magnolia nor had she thought her good enough for him. So it was slightly surprising that she had taken so quickly to Nadia.

He was just holding out his cup for his mother to refill when a footman came into the room with a package on a silver salver.

"What is it, James?" Lady John asked.

"This 'as been left for th' Countess, M'Lady."

As he spoke he held out the salver towards Nadia, who looked at it in surprise.

"For me?" she asked.

"I cannot believe it is a wedding-present already," Warren joked.

Nadia took the parcel from the salver, which seemed to be a small box.

She looked at it, thinking there must be some mistake, then saw it was addressed in capital letters very clearly: *"THE COUNTESS NADIA FERRAIS."*

"Open it!" Warren said. "It must be a present, although it seems surprising that any of my relatives should be so generous so quickly."

"Now, darling, that is rather unkind!" his mother reproached him. "Ever since you were small the family always spoilt you with gifts at Christmas and on your birthday, and you used to complain bitterly when I made you write and thank them."

"That is true," Warren said, "and you taught me never to 'look a gift-horse in the mouth'!"

His mother laughed, and by this time Nadia had undone the outer covering of the parcel to find a box of chocolates.

They came from Gunter's in Berkeley Square, who were famous for their special sweet-meats which Warren had often bought for his mother.

She had now however a touch of diabetes and had been forbidden to eat anything containing sugar.

Nadia looked first at the box, then at the paper in which it had been wrapped before she said:

"It does not say who sent it."

"I expect the servant who took it at the door will know," Warren replied.

Nadia undid the ribbon that tied the box, opened it and said:

"They certainly look very delicious! Will you have one?"

"Not now," Warren replied. "Perhaps after dinner."

"I am not allowed chocolates," Lady John said, "so you will have to eat them all yourself, my dear."

"Not after such a big tea!" Nadia protested.

She looked at Warren as she spoke, and he knew she was telling him she was making a tremendous effort to eat, but was still finding it difficult.

She was just about to put the lid back on the box when Lady John said:

"Look at greedy Bertha!"

Ever since Warren had come home the two dogs which had always been at his uncle's side had attached themselves to him.

One was a fairly young spaniel who he knew was an exceptionally good gun-dog, the other a bitch who had been a field-trial winner in her day, but was now very old, crippled with rheumatism and finding it hard to see.

But ever since his arrival she had been at his heels and now had followed him into the house where she had laid down quietly beside his chair.

Now however Bertha was sitting up on her hind legs, begging.

Nadia looked at her in surprise and Lady John explained:

"Poor Arthur developed a very sweet tooth in his old age and one of the reasons why he grew so fat, which undoubtedly contributed to his heart-attack, was that he was always eating chocolates."

She looked at Bertha and smiled as she added:

"Bertha is as greedy about them as he was. As you can see, her mouth is watering as she can sense what you have in your hands."

"Then she must certainly be the first to enjoy my present," Nadia said.

She picked out what she thought was a soft-centred chocolate and held it out to Bertha who quickly gobbled it up, then was sitting up begging for more.

"That is enough," Warren said. "She will get so fat that she will be slower than she is already."

"Just one more," Nadia pleaded.

She smiled at him as she spoke, and held out another chocolate to Bertha.

The dog snatched it from her, then suddenly as she did so, she seemed to shake all over.

So quickly that the three people watching could hardly believe it was happening, she turned and rolled over on her back.

For a few seconds every muscle in her body seemed to be twitching.

Then suddenly she was completely still.

Nadia gave a little cry and asked:

"What has happened? Has she had a fit?"

Warren went down on his knees beside Bertha.

He was feeling for her heart. Then he said:

"She is dead!"

"It cannot be true!" Lady John exclaimed. "How could it happen so suddenly?"

"Because she was poisoned!" Warren replied.

He reached out and took the box of chocolates from

Nadia's lap, then he put his arms around his mother and lifted her to her feet.

"I want you to come upstairs and rest, Mama," he said. "I am going to send for the Veterinary Surgeon to examine both Bertha and the chocolates. Something unpleasant is happening, and I do not want it to upset you."

"But it does upset me!" his mother protested. "How could anybody be so wicked, so evil, as to give poisoned chocolates to Nadia?"

Warren knew the answer, but he did not reply.

Instead he led his mother across the room and Nadia followed them.

She was very pale and her heart was beating frantically with a fear which had been her constant companion for nearly three years.

Now she told herself that there was no escape from it, not even in England.

She did not see Warren until dinner-time.

When Lady John had gone to rest, Nadia had gone to her own room, having been urged to rest also.

Instead she could only lie on the comfortable bed, watching through the open window the sun sinking behind the trees, and hearing the rooks making their usual noise as they went to roost.

"How can this have happened?" she kept asking herself.

She knew if Bertha's death had not warned them, she undoubtedly would have died, and perhaps Warren as well if, as he had intended, he had eaten one of the chocolates after dinner.

The whole idea was so terrifying that even though it was very hot outside she felt herself shivering beneath the sheet that covered her.

It was so unexpected after she had begun to feel relaxed and happy for the first time, with somebody as kind and sweet as Lady John, who reminded her of her mother.

Warren had also given her a wonderful feeling of security every moment she was with him.

Poisoned chocolates! How could it be possible? How could anybody think of doing anything so diabolical, except those who had haunted her thoughts and dreams for so long?

Because she was so frightened, Nadia prayed:

"Please, God, do not let me die like that! Please let me live a little longer."

Then as she felt her prayer winging up into the sky, she thought it strange how only a few days ago she had longed to die, and now she wanted to live.

She knew it was because Warren had saved her and brought her away from a world in which everything was ugly, sordid and painful to a place where everything was beautiful and until this moment she had thought peaceful and normal.

Now she was aware that it was very different and she felt an irrepressible fear.

She might so easily have put one of the chocolates in her own mouth, just because she thought it would please Warren that she was eating.

The colour had left her face and her eyes were dark and troubled when after her maid had helped her dress she had gone downstairs to dinner.

She had wanted to say goodnight to Lady John, but her lady's-maid had told her she was already half-asleep, and it would be a mistake to disturb her.

"Supposing she had died?" Nadia asked herself. "It would have been my fault, and I would have felt I was a murderess!"

She was early, so she had not expected the Marquis had yet arrived, but when she went into the Drawing-Room, he was standing at one of the open windows, a glass of champagne in his hand.

He turned towards her and watched her walk into the room, aware without her having to say one word what she was feeling.

He gave her the glass he was holding, then

returned to the side-table to pour another from the bottle that was standing in an ice-cooler.

When he came back to her side, she asked in a voice he could hardly hear:

"What . . . did you . . . find out?"

"What I suspected," he answered, "that the chocolates had had a poison injected into them very skilfully! It would have been impossible for you to realise they had been tampered with until it was too late!"

He saw the shudder that shook Nadia's body. Then she said:

"I must go away! I . . . cannot stay here because . . . they must have . . . found me, and if they . . . strike again, it might . . . harm you!"

She was speaking without thinking. Then she saw the expression of astonishment in Warren's eyes before he asked:

"What are you talking about?"

She looked at him blindly for a moment, then away again, and he said quietly:

"I think we should be honest about this, and face facts. The poisoned chocolates came from Magnolia Keane!"

He realised as he spoke that this was not what Nadia had been thinking.

She stared at him for a long moment before she asked a little incoherently:

"Are you . . . sure of that? Are you . . . quite sure?"

"Absolutely sure, and the only question the Surgeon kept asking me was how anybody who was not experienced could have inserted poison so skilfully without there being any outward sign of it."

Nadia drew in her breath.

Then in a voice Warren was aware she was trying to make normal she asked:

"But . . . why should Miss . . . Keane wish to . . . poison me?"

Warren's voice was hard as he replied:

"I should have thought that was obvious."

"Yes . . . of course . . . how stupid of me!" Nadia said. "She did say that . . . you belonged to her . . . and she would never let me . . . have you."

"Tell me exactly what she said."

It was an order and although Nadia hesitated she knew she must obey him.

"She said first: 'I understand you are trying to marry Warren!'"

"And what did you reply?"

"I said we were engaged."

"Then what happened?"

Again Warren's voice was very authoritative and Nadia replied:

"Miss Keane said: 'You are not going to marry him, and if you try to do so, you will be sorry!'"

As she spoke Nadia thought it was very stupid of her not to have thought in the first place that it might be Magnolia Keane who had sent her the chocolates.

She had never imagined any English Lady would behave in such a manner, or that it was possible for her to be in that sort of danger in an English country house where there were servants to protect them and Warren never very far away.

"I can only say how sorry I am, and it is my fault that she has upset you," Warren said in a quiet voice. "I thought she might try to hurt me, in some way I could not even imagine, but it never struck me that she would attempt to murder you!"

"Perhaps it would be . . . better if you m.married her as she . . . wants you to do," Nadia said almost in a whisper. "After all . . . you . . . loved her once."

Even as she spoke, as she had done spontaneously on a sudden impulse, she knew that she could not bear Warren to marry such a woman.

He was too fine, too noble, far too magnificent to waste himself on anyone who would stoop to murder to get her own way.

Then she saw the scowl between Warren's eyes and realised how angry he was as he said:

"I would not even try to save Magnolia from the gallows, which is where she would have ended had it not been for poor Bertha."

"The Veterinary Surgeon could not . . . save her?"

"She died instantly, as you would have done if you had eaten the chocolates as Magnolia intended you should."

His lips tightened before he said:

"She had not foreseen that I would be here, but anticipated I would still be looking after some of the relatives who might be expected to linger until it was quite late."

His voice was deep with anger as he continued:

"She knew that Mama was not allowed chocolates, and that left only you, who she expected would be here alone when you received her present."

As he finished, he gave an exclamation which seemed almost like an oath as he added:

"That is what happened, and there is nothing I can do about it, no charge I can bring against her, although only by a miracle are you alive!"

Without thinking Nadia moved and held onto him with both her hands.

"It is frightening . . . very frightening," she said, "but at least you did not eat one . . . as you might have done after dinner."

"Bertha saved us, and we should be grateful for that," Warren said. "I have left orders for her to be buried in the Dogs' Cemetery where all our dogs lie, and where I like to believe they are happy and undisturbed."

For the first time since she had come into the room, Nadia smiled.

"We, too, had a Cemetery for our dogs," she said. "When I was a little girl I used to put a bone on their graves thinking they could eat it when nobody was there, and it had always disappeared in the morning!"

"Where was your Cemetery?" Warren asked.

As if Nadia realised she had been indiscreet she took her hands from his and said quickly:

"We were talking about poor Bertha, and tomorrow I would like to see where she is buried."

"You were also telling me about your dogs," Warren said. "What sort were they?"

"I do not . . . want to . . . talk about it," Nadia replied. "You must tell me how I can be . . . safe from Miss Keane . . . and perhaps for your sake . . . I should . . . go away."

She knew as she spoke she had no wish to leave him. In fact, it would be very frightening to have to do so.

As if he knew what she was feeling, Warren reached out and took her hand in both of his.

"Now listen to me, Nadia," he said, "I promise I will look after and protect you, and that I shall prevent anything like this ever happening again."

He felt her fingers quiver in his and after a moment he asked:

"You still trust me?"

"You know I do," Nadia said.

Then as she looked up into his eyes it was impossible for either of them to look away.

After dinner at which Nadia had tried to eat a little of each course, they went back into the Drawing-Room.

The last dying rays of the sun were crimson on the horizon, and as they instinctively walked towards the open window the peace and fragrance of the garden made it impossible to believe there was danger and hatred in the world beyond it.

They walked towards the sun-dial and stood looking down at the ancient figures carved in the worn stone.

"I want you to be happy here," Warren said, as if he was pursuing his own thoughts.

"I am happy," Nadia answered, "and now I am no longer afraid of Miss Keane . . . or anything . . . else."

He knew from the way she spoke the last few words that she was in some other kind of danger which she kept a secret and which was very different from what had just occurred.

Warren longed to ask her once again to tell him the truth about herself, but he knew it would only upset her, and he was certain that she would refuse, as she had already, to satisfy his curiosity.

She looked so lovely, and at the same time so fragile and insubstantial in the fading light, that he thought it seemed almost absurd that she should be involved in such dramatic and dangerous circumstances.

"I have not had a chance to tell you," he said, "how magnificently you played your part yesterday. All my relatives were captivated by you, and think I am very lucky to have found such a suitable wife to reign at Buckwood."

"They were all very kind to me," Nadia said in a low voice, "and your mother has been . . . wonderful!"

"My mother says you are everything she hoped for in a daughter-in-law."

"I am sure she is very upset by what has just occurred."

"After I saw the Veterinary Surgeon I explained to her who was responsible, and she merely said it did not surprise her."

"But she feels afraid . . . as I am . . . that Miss Keane might try to . . . hurt you."

"I do not think she wants to kill *me*," Warren remarked.

Nadia gave a little cry and once again put her hands towards him.

"If she cannot get her way . . . if you do not marry her after all . . . even after she had . . . disposed of

me . . . then she will . . . hate you for not doing
what she wishes . . . and might try to avenge herself
. . . as you are doing."

The last words were very faint, but Warren heard
them.

Then as if he thought it was a mistake to be too
serious, he said lightly:

"I am quite certain that whatever happens you will
save me, as you have done already, very effectively."

"Have I . . . really been able to help you?"

"You know you have," he answered. "If you had not
been here, Magnolia somehow in some crafty way of
her own might have persuaded my relatives that I was
under an obligation to make her my wife. That was
what I foresaw and feared when I asked for your
help."

There was silence. Then Nadia said hesitatingly:

"I . . . I thought perhaps now you would . . .
want me to . . . go away . . . but I can see that
might be a mistake."

"A very great mistake," Warren agreed. "I want you
to stay here, I want you to go on playing the part of
my *fiancée* until we are both absolutely convinced that
Magnolia will try no more tricks."

After a moment he added:

"Perhaps I am asking too much of you? You have
been through so much already in your own life, although you will not tell me about it, and I should not
ask you to risk being murdered by a jealous woman
who is obviously mentally unhinged."

Nadia smiled at him, and he thought it was a very
brave and rather touching little smile.

"You promised to protect me."

"And that is what I will do," he answered, "but,
please, Nadia, stay. I want to have you help me getting
to know the people who are now my responsibility,
and when it comes to planning alterations or improvements, two brains are obviously better than one."

"I think you are flattering me," Nadia replied, "and

really you are quite capable of doing all those things without any help at all! At the same time, you know I want to stay here."

He knew there was a fear behind the words that she would not express or explain, and he said with the smile that many women had found irresistible:

"I am pleading with you to stay! In fact, I should be very hurt and upset if you run away and leave me."

"Then I will not do so."

"Now I am going to send you to bed," Warren said. "When I said good-night to Mama she said that if she needed her beauty-sleep, so did you, and as you are aware, I want you to look very much fatter than you are at the moment."

Nadia laughed and the sound seemed to ring out like music in the quietness of the garden.

"I keep forgetting now that I have such lovely gowns that you are shocked by my appearance," she said. "I really am trying very, very hard to eat, but you will have to give me time."

"I can think of quite a lot of things I should give you as well as time," Warren answered, "but you will have to wait until I get to London."

He had forgotten as he spoke that Nadia was unlike all the other women he had ever met, wanting everything he was ready to give them and pleading for a great deal more besides.

Nadia took her hand from his and said in a serious little voice which he knew so well:

"Please . . . I have accepted these beautiful gowns from you because I could hardly appear as your *fiancée* in the threadbare dress which was all I possessed. But I do not expect . . . anything else, and I should be very . . . upset if you tried to give it to me."

Warren thought for a moment. Then he said:

"Surely you must be aware that everybody will expect me to give you, as my *fiancée*, all the things that would express my love rather more eloquently than words."

"No!" Nadia said.

She spoke so firmly that Warren was surprised.

Then as if she felt she must explain herself she said:

"When you asked me to help you, you said you thought of me as a lady. So as a lady, I will not and cannot accept anything from you except what is absolutely essential for the part I have to play."

She spoke with a dignity that was very impressive.

Then she added in a child-like and very pleading voice:

"I know Mama would not have approved . . . so please . . . do not embarrass me."

Warren knew there was nothing he could do but capitulate and he said:

"Very well, Nadia, but I can only say that you are a very unusual and very surprising young woman, and apart from that, somebody I respect and admire for the courage you have shown."

Because of the way he spoke he saw the colour flood into Nadia's cheeks.

Then as her eye-lids flickered and he knew that she was too shy to look at him, he thought it was very attractive, very endearing, and in every way very different from Magnolia.

CHAPTER SIX

*N*adia walked round the sitting room looking at the pictures and ornaments.

Every time she did so she thought how beautiful

they were and how each one had a history of its own which she wanted to remember.

She had asked Warren about the pictures and he told her how they had come into the family, one of them being a present to his father and mother on their marriage.

"Everything in this house Mama treasures because it is part of her life with my father, and of course mine," he said with a smile.

"I knew it was all chosen with love," Nadia said softly.

He smiled, thinking it was the sort of remark that only she would make, and which he found himself remembering when he thought about her during the night.

For her, he felt sure, every day was an enchantment which she could not express in words.

He knew that her sufferings, which must remain a secret, were something she did not wish to talk about because they had been so painful and had resulted in her mother's death.

But he could not be unaware that for Nadia to have come to Buckwood was like being lifted from the horrors and terrors of hell into a special Heaven which was filled with sunshine.

"How could I have wanted to die, when I can live here?" Nadia asked herself.

Then as always, when she reflected how marvellous everything was, there was a little stab of pain in case it should suddenly all come to an end.

She would wake in the night, thinking how wonderful the previous day had been and how much she was looking forward to the next.

Then she would ask herself how many days there could be before Warren told her that her usefulness was at an end.

It was such an agony to think of it that she tried to force herself to live for the day, the hour, the second, and miss nothing.

Now as she looked at the Sir Joshua Reynolds portrait over the mantelpiece she knew she was thinking it was something she would never forget, and wherever she might be she would see it in her mind's eye.

The same applied to the 'Conversation Piece' which was particularly important because it portrayed Warren's ancestor and his family with Buckwood House in the background.

'He has everything,' she thought.

Then she was ashamed of feeling a touch of envy, being homeless herself.

"I wish I could be in a picture and live there like the people the artist has portrayed, then I would be immortal!"

It was a fantasy which she found intriguing, and she imagined herself, if not in that particular picture, then being painted by some famous artist who would portray her body while she would give it her heart and soul.

She played with the idea because it delighted her and tried to think what would be a suitable background.

"As I do not own a house," she told herself, "it would be more appropriate if I was out in a garden."

Thinking of it made her walk through the window towards the sun-dial, and standing by it as she had done with Warren she touched the figures engraved on top of it.

Then she heard a strange sound which came from a door in the red brick wall.

Nadia knew it led out into an orchard where the apples on the trees were just beginning to change colour.

She wondered what the sound could be, and going down the flagstoned path which bordered each side of a well-trimmed box hedge, she pulled open the ancient door which had been there as long as the walls themselves.

When she could not hear anything she moved a few

steps into the orchard, still wondering what the sound had been.

The next moment she gave a cry of sheer terror for something heavy and dark was thrown over her head.

Before she could even struggle she was picked up and carried swiftly away, in what direction she had no idea.

Warren was in his Study dealing with a pile of correspondence which Mr. Greyshott had left for him to sign.

There were several new leases for tenants who had taken over farms that had remained empty during his uncle's illness, and there was also a report from the Manager of his estate in Devonshire which had to be read carefully.

He thought as he did so that he would soon have to visit his other properties, and especially the one at Newmarket where his uncle had kept most of his race-horses.

In the meantime however there was still a great deal to do here.

He had already had a number of calls from prominent people in the County inviting him to take up various positions of importance which it would have been impossible for him to refuse.

He was just reading a letter from the Deputy Lord Lieutenant who had taken over his uncle's duties while he was ill, when Mr. Greyshott came into the room.

He looked up and Mr. Greyshott said:

"I thought you would like to know, My Lord, that I have just seen the Veterinary Surgeon who confirms that the poison which was inserted into the chocolates was, as I suspected, taken from here!"

Warren frowned.

He had been very angry when Mr. Greyshott had

told him that he guessed that the poison which might
have killed Nadia had actually come from the house.

Apparently his uncle had an aversion to shooting
any of his horses or dogs which had become too old or
too ill to go on living, and had trusted nobody but
himself to 'put them to sleep.'

He had therefore persuaded the Veterinary Surgeon to find him a poison that was so strong and acted
so quickly that the animal died almost immediately it
was swallowed.

What had first puzzled Warren was to know where
Magnolia could have so quickly obtained the deadly
poison which had killed Bertha.

It was then that Mr. Greyshott, who was the only
person to be let into the secret of the poisoned chocolates, said that he recognised the box from Gunter's
which had been ordered by the Marquis before he was
taken ill.

Secondly, he suspected the poison itself came from
a locked cupboard in the Gun-Room where the Marquis had kept it, thinking it would be impossible for
anybody to get hold of it without his permission.

"Why should Miss Keane have known of it?" Warren enquired.

"I imagine your cousin told her," Mr. Greyshott replied, "or perhaps His Lordship did so. They both
spoke often of how distressing it was to dispose of any
of the animals they loved."

He thought for a moment before he added:

"I remember now that while Miss Keane was staying here the Marquis put one of his dogs, who was
suffering severely from a growth in the throat, out of
its misery."

"So I suppose," Warren said, "Miss Keane took the
poison with her when I turned her out of the house."

Mr. Greyshott paused for a moment before he answered:

"Actually, the cupboard had been broken into and
the lock smashed!"

There was nothing more to say. At the same time Warren had insisted on an autopsy the report of which Mr. Greyshott now handed to him.

Because it only confirmed what he already knew, he set it to one side and started to talk of matters concerning the estate until Mr. Greyshott left him so that he could finish signing his letters.

"I will come back for them in half-an-hour, My Lord."

Some of the letters were quite long, and Warren had only completed half-a-dozen when the door opened again and without raising his head he remarked:

"You are too quick for me, Greyshott. I have not yet finished!"

There was no answer and he looked up, then stiffened.

It was Magnolia who had come into the Study looking exceedingly alluring, and no longer in mourning.

She was wearing a very elaborate gown of rose pink chiffon inset with lace that made her look more exotic than usual, and her wide-brimmed hat was trimmed with flowers and ribbons of the same colour.

For a moment Warren just stared at her. Then he rose slowly to his feet, as if he was resentful at having to do so.

Magnolia walked slowly, as if deliberately displaying herself before him, towards the desk.

Only as she reached it did Warren ask:

"What are you doing here, Magnolia? You know I have no wish to see you."

"But I have every wish to see you, dearest Warren," Magnolia replied, "and I think when you hear what I have to say, you will realise it would be wise to listen to me."

"I do not want to listen, and we have nothing to say to each other," Warren said firmly. "Go away, Magnolia, and leave me alone!"

He sat down again as he spoke and looked at her

across the desk, wondering whether he should accuse her of trying to murder Nadia or whether it would be better to say nothing.

She was looking at him seductively, and he thought her eyes which seemed half-veiled by her long lashes had a glint of triumph in them he did not understand.

She was holding a paper in her hand, which she put down on the edge of the desk and there was something seductive about the way she slowly drew off her long kid-gloves.

Then she put out her left hand and asked:

"Do you see what I am wearing?"

Because he was puzzled by her behaviour Warren looked down and saw that on the third finger of her left hand she was wearing a ring he had given her.

He could so well remember purchasing it in Bond Street, then giving it to her and kissing first the ring, then her finger before he said:

"Because it is impossible at the moment, my darling, for us to become engaged or married, I am binding you to me with a ring that symbolises that you are mine for eternity."

"Oh, dearest, that is what I want," Magnolia had exclaimed.

"And you will never escape me!" Warren replied. "Although you cannot wear this ring in the daytime until we can announce our engagement, I want you to promise me you will wear it at night when you dream of me."

"You know I will do that."

She had looked down at the ring which was a very pretty one with small diamonds set with gold all round it.

She had then lifted her lips and Warren had kissed her passionately, possessively, until they were both breathless.

Now the memory of what he had felt at that moment made Warren feel disgusted and he said harshly:

"I told you to go away! If you do not do so, I shall ring for the servants to show you out."

"I doubt if you will do that after you have heard what I have to say," Magnolia replied.

Now she picked up the paper she had put on the edge of the desk and said with a note in her voice he did not understand:

"I have here a Marriage Licence made out in your name and mine!"

"What the devil are you talking about?" Warren exclaimed.

"It will be easy for us to be married immediately," Magnolia said. "I have made enquiries and the Vicar is at this moment at home in his Vicarage."

"I can only imagine you are insane!" he replied. "I would no more marry you than I would marry the Devil himself!"

He spoke violently because his temper was rising, but Magnolia remained quite unmoved.

She merely set down the Special Licence in front of him before she said:

"If you do not marry me, then that woman you call your *fiancée* will die!"

Warren seemed for the moment to be turned to stone before he enquired in a voice which with a deliberate effort he made quiet and calm:

"I should be interested to know exactly what you mean by that!"

"I mean," Magnolia replied, "that she has been taken to a place where you will never find her and where, if you do not marry me as I have asked you to do, she will die of starvation!"

For a moment there was silence.

"I do not believe you!" Warren exclaimed.

Magnolia looked at him under her eyelashes and smiled, making the whole conversation seem more horrifying than ever.

He knew she was deliberately being seductive,

feeling quite confident that it would be impossible for him not to respond.

Then she lifted her face to his in a manner that was contrived because she knew it displayed the curves of her long, swan-like neck.

"The young woman has been carried away from the garden at your mother's house and hidden so that clever though you are, my dearest Warren, you will never be able to find her."

She shrugged her shoulders so as to display the sinuous lissomness of her figure before she added:

"Even if you search and eventually find her, it will be too late, for she will, as I have said, die of starvation."

Warren drew in his breath as if he still could not credit what he was hearing.

He looked down then at the Special Licence lying in front of him and saw on it was written his own name and that of Magnolia.

He knew her well enough to realise that she was wildly elated by the feeling that she had him cornered, and that there was, she believed, nothing he could do but accept her terms or else allow Nadia to die.

After a moment he said quietly:

"Surely we can come to some better solution than that I should accept what, as you well know, Magnolia, is criminal blackmail?"

Magnolia gave a little laugh.

"Fine words! And they mean there is nothing you can do, my adored one, but make me your wife!"

Warren wanted to shout at her that nothing and nobody would make him do that.

Then in his mind's eye he saw again Nadia's face as he had seen it when he saved her from drowning herself in the Seine, and had realised she was suffering from starvation.

He had been well aware how in the last five days since they had been at Buckwood the marks of privation were gradually disappearing day by day and almost hour by hour.

It had given her a new beauty.

He had seen that as her chin became less sharp, the bones in her wrists less prominent, and the lines at the sides of her mouth and under her eyes disappeared, she looked as young as her years.

And when she was animated and laughing she was so beautiful that he thought it was difficult to recognise the unhappy, frightened girl who had wanted to die.

He was sensible enough, however, to know that if she was subjected again to such privation it might be difficult to save her a second time.

Almost as if she was following his thoughts, Magnolia said with what was now an undoubted note of triumph in her voice:

"It is no use, Warren! Clever and brilliant though you may be, I have won this time!"

She paused and when he did not speak she added:

"And, darling, when we are married I will make it up to you. I shall be everything you want in a wife and very much more as a woman that you love."

She gave a little laugh before she added:

"I know that nobody could be a more ardent and more passionate lover than you, and however much my brain wanted to marry a coronet, my body has always responded to yours, and now we will be very happy."

As she finished speaking she realised that Warren was not listening. He merely asked, and his voice was sharp:

"Tell me where you have put Nadia!"

"Of course I will do that, just as soon as we are married. We can go now to the Church and you can tell your carriage to follow us. As soon as you replace this ring on my finger, we will send him to find that woman, but keep her out of my sight!"

Magnolia spoke sharply and it told Warren how

much she hated Nadia because she thought she had taken her place. He was certain there would be no chance of saving her unless he did as she demanded.

Once again he stared down at the Special Licence on his desk, trying frantically to think what he could do.

It flashed through his mind that he could ring the bell and call for the servants.

A search could be made, organised by Mr. Greyshott, all over the estate.

It would cause a great deal of gossip and scandal and might eventually reach the newspapers.

He knew nothing could be more damaging from his own point of view, or that of his family.

He also had the uncomfortable knowledge that it would be appallingly difficult to find Nadia without having the slightest clue as to where Magnolia had hidden her.

He owned five thousand acres of land around Buckwood, and all the time he had been away in Africa, Magnolia had been staying here with Raymond except when they were together in London.

She would by now know hundreds of places where somebody small and weak like Nadia could lie for weeks, even months before she could be found.

In addition to his blotter, on which the Buckwood coat-of-arms was embossed in gold, were all the items that were considered essential to a gentleman's desk.

There was a large gold ink-pot, a pen-tray, a pot containing game-shot in which pens could be cleaned, a tiny candle in a very elegant candlestick which was used to heat the sealing-wax with which he sealed his letters.

There was also a gold ruler, a pair of gold scissors, and a gold letter-opener, all bearing the Buckwood crest.

As if another part of his brain had taken over, Warren noticed that the letter-opener was long and very sharp, and suddenly he knew what he must do.

"Give me your hand," he said aloud and held out his own towards Magnolia.

She did not seem surprised, but put her hand in his; on it was the ring he had given her and as his fingers closed over it she smiled into his eyes seductively.

It was then that Warren slashed her sharply across the back of the hand with the letter-opener.

Magnolia started, then gave a shrill scream.

As she did so she looked incredulously at the long wound from which the blood was already oozing.

She would have snatched her hand away but Warren held tightly onto it as he rose to his feet.

Still holding onto her he walked around the desk until they were facing each other.

"How dare you cut me!" Magnolia screamed at him. "You have hurt me, Warren, you have hurt me terribly!"

"I am going to hurt you a great deal more," he said, in a quiet voice, "unless you tell me where you have hidden Nadia."

"My hand is bleeding!"

Warren glanced down and saw the blood was actually running over the side of her hand onto his own.

Still in the same quiet manner in which he had spoken before he said:

"It will undoubtedly leave a nasty scar and if you do not tell me immediately what I wish to know, I will scar your face in the same way, first on one side, then on the other."

"You would not dare!"

The words were defiant but he could see as she recoiled away from him the fear in her eyes.

"You have driven me far enough," Warren said, "and I shall not hesitate to disfigure you. Now which shall it be?"

He raised the letter-opener as he spoke and now Magnolia could see its long, sharp end almost like a stiletto pointing towards her.

For a moment it seemed as if she would go on fighting him.

Then as if she knew she was defeated she surrendered.

"Very well," she said sullenly, "she is in the State Mine."

"You are not lying to me?"

"No!"

"If you have deceived me," Warren warned, "I swear I will find you and carry out my threat!"

He paused before he added:

"Make no mistake, Magnolia! I shall mark you and make certain that in the future your beauty shall not blind another fool to the vileness of your character!"

As he spoke Warren took his hand from Magnolia's so suddenly that because she was straining away from him she almost fell to the ground.

Then as she staggered to keep her balance he flung the letter-opener down on the floor, and walking out of the room slammed the door behind him.

The men who had carried Nadia away from the garden had put her in a carriage which set off quickly the moment they closed the door.

They had thrown her down roughly on the seat and she was aware they had got into the carriage after her and were sitting opposite with their backs to the horses.

She was so frightened that for a moment she could not think and was finding it hard to breathe because of the thickness of the cloth which covered her.

She could feel her whole body trembling and her lips were dry.

Although she wanted to scream it was impossible to do so, and anyway she was quite certain nobody would hear her crying for help.

She was also frightened that the men might strike her to keep her quiet.

Then, because she thought they were the same men who had pursued her and her mother across Europe, she prayed she might die.

She knew it would be impossible to face what might lie in store for her and remain sane.

"Let me die, please God, let me die!" she whispered in her heart, and at the same time she prayed for Warren.

"Save me! Save me!" she cried out to him.

Then she knew he could not help her and somehow she must find a way to kill herself before the men sitting on the other side of the carriage killed her in an agonising way.

She was so frightened that she could feel her teeth chattering and the tears running down her cheeks.

Then she heard one of the men speak to the other.

"Be it far?" he asked.

"Nay," the other man replied. "We be nearly there."

It was then Nadia felt a relief that was so overwhelming that she felt almost as if she was free instead of a captive!

No one could mistake the voices of the men in the carriage for anything but English, and she had feared something very different.

Her captors, she then knew, had been ordered to abduct her by Magnolia Keane.

It was frightening, but not as terrifying as she had thought it a few moments ago when she had known she must die.

Then, because she was sure it was Magnolia Keane who had sent these men to kidnap her, somehow, although she could not think how, she knew that Warren would save her.

She was certain, so certain that once again she was praying to him to come to her rescue, feeling as if she sent her thoughts towards him on wings.

"Save me! Save me!"

She could almost see him listening to her plea for help, his grey eyes reassuring her.

It was then, at that moment, almost as if it was a blinding light in the suffocating darkness, that she knew she loved him.

She loved him and she had done so for a long time, but had not realised it was love.

She had known it was a joy beyond words to ride with him, to talk with him, and that every time he came into the room she felt as if her heart leapt towards him because he looked so strong and so handsome.

"I love him!" she told herself. "I love him, but I am nothing to him, except as somebody he has hired to help him get rid of that wicked, murderous woman!"

Almost without thinking, her prayer to Warren became one of gratitude to God because he had not married Magnolia Keane, nor did he want her any more as his wife.

How could he, when she had attempted murder, and had only failed in what she had set out to do because a dog was greedy?

Nadia had lain all that night feeling the horror of what had occurred was like something cold and hard pressing into her breast.

It was only after she had been alone with Warren the next day, visiting the farms as he had asked her to do, that the pain had gone away, and when she was with him she could forget about it.

Now she knew that Magnolia was trying once again to murder her, and the only person who could save her from death was Warren.

"Save me! Save me!" she cried out in her breast.

Yet she was afraid the men would shoot or stab her before Warren could reach her.

Then because she was very intelligent, Nadia worked out in her mind that if they meant to kill her

they might have done so without taking her away
from the garden.

If they had intended to drown her, the lake was
quite handy, but now they were driving away from it,
although in which direction Nadia was not sure.

Their only alternative, she thought, was to throw
her into a deep pit, or imprison her somewhere so
that she could not escape and would therefore eventually die slowly and miserably of starvation.

It was all very frightening, except for a faint ray of
hope still lingering that Warren would defeat Magnolia's nefarious plan, even at the last moment.

It was almost, Nadia thought, as if it was a battle
between the two of them, a battle of love which had
turned to one of hatred.

They were therefore all the more vindictive, more
violent, because they had once felt so differently towards each other.

She reasoned it all out and somehow, although she
was still terrified, she felt as if God was on her side and
good must triumph over evil.

The carriage came to a halt and she heard one of
the men opposite her say:

" 'Ere we be! Now, don't be in 'urry. We've ter get
t'door opened first.''

They got out of the carriage, and Nadia knew she
had been left alone.

There was silence for what seemed a long time before she heard a horse shake its head, making the har-
ness jingle and then the coachman cleared his throat.

She wondered if it would be possible to free herself
from the confines of the thick blanket that covered her
from her head to below her knees.

But she was afraid that if she moved, long before
she could escape from the carriage the man on the
box would give the alarm and the two men would
come hurrying back.

They might then beat her until she was unconscious!

"I am . . . frightened! Oh, God . . . I am . . . frightened!" Nadia whispered.

Once again she cried out to Warren:

"Save me! I love you! Oh . . . save me!"

She repeated the words under her breath over and over again.

Then she thought wildly that if she were out of the way Magnolia might by some means trick him into marriage, or perhaps if he would not agree to marry her, she might hurt him in some way.

'She is ruthless and mad!' Nadia thought.

Suddenly with a constriction of her heart, she heard the two men talking together in the distance, their voices coming nearer as they approached her.

One of them pulled her out of the carriage and they both picked her up to carry her down a steep incline.

At moments, because the ground beneath their feet was rough, Nadia thought they would drop her.

Then the descent had ended and as they walked a little way on the level, one of them said:

"Moind yer 'ead!"

Nadia was sure they were stooping as if there was a low doorway above their heads, or else they were in a tunnel.

It took her by surprise when they suddenly put her down on the ground so roughly that it hurt.

And before she could get her breath she heard them walking away, their footsteps crunching on what sounded like hard, rocky ground.

In the distance a door was slammed noisily into place, a key turned in a lock, and a few minutes later Nadia could hear the sound of wheels as the carriage drove away.

It was then for the first time she moved from the place where they had thrown her down.

With an effort she eased the heavy blanket up to her shoulders, to throw it back from her head.

For one terrifying moment she thought she must

have died, or gone blind, for the darkness was just the same as it had been under the blanket.

Then she was aware of a dank, damp smell and a long way from her she saw a glimmer of light.

After looking at it for some time she decided it must come from the door which the men had closed and locked.

Afraid to move, and yet realising she must find out where she was, she rose tentatively to her feet, and remembering how the men had to crouch as they carried her to where she now was, she put her hands above her head.

She touched something cold and with sharp edges.

She could just stand upright. At the same time she knew that if she moved she would be wise to bend her head.

She looked again towards the light and picking up the blanket from where it lay on the floor at her feet she walked very slowly, bending her head and feeling her way before she took each step.

The light grew stronger as she drew nearer to it, and she realised that it was coming from the sides of the door.

It was then she realised she was in a Mine. Strangely it did not smell like coal but she could not recognise what it was.

She put out her hands to touch the door and found it was very strongly made.

She pushed at it, then hammered on it with her clenched fists.

"Help! Help!"

Her voice seemed to echo back at her along the tunnel, but she was sure there could be nobody outside to hear her, otherwise the men would not have brought her here.

She could feel the fear of being alone and the horror of how she would die sweep over her, and knew that unless Warren could somehow find her, Magnolia would have won.

She would die slowly of starvation, and it might be months or even years before anybody came to what she guessed now was a disused Mine.

Nadia threw the blanket with which she had been covered down onto the ground.

She sat down on it, leaning back against the door, and covering her face with her hands she began to pray.

It was not a prayer to God, but to Warren.

"Save me!" she called to him again and again. "Save me . . . save me! I love you . . . and I do not want to . . . die before I have seen . . . you again!"

CHAPTER SEVEN

Outside the front door Warren found waiting the cabriolet which he used to drive round the estate and carry him to his mother's house.

Without speaking to anybody he got into the driving seat, the groom holding the horses' heads jumped in beside him and he drove off at a tremendous pace.

He knew where the Slate Mine was, although he had not visited it for years and thought it strange that Magnolia should know of it.

He imagined she might have seen it during the hunting season when the woods and the thick stubble around the old Mine, which had not been worked for years, nearly always produced a fox.

But all that really concerned him was Nadia, for he

knew what had happened would shock, frighten, and distress her, so that she would quickly be in the same state of desperation that she had been in when he had first found her.

Even to think of her suffering made him feel murderous towards Magnolia once again.

At the same time, he was so deeply concerned for Nadia that it was in itself a strange feeling almost like a physical pain that he had never known before.

Then as he drove on, deciding how he would comfort her and try to make her understand this would never happen again, he knew that what he had been feeling for her for a long time was love.

It seemed impossible when he had sworn to himself that never again would he humiliate himself in loving another woman after the way Magnolia had treated him.

Yet if he was honest, he had to admit that almost the moment he had met Nadia, because she was so pathetic and at the same time brave, and there seemed to be some close affinity between them which he could not put into words, he had fallen in love.

When they played their charade first to deceive *Monsieur* and *Madame* Blanc, then his mother and his relations, he had realised how exceptional she was, and how perfectly she fitted into the part he had designed for her.

Yet for Nadia it had obviously been quite natural to behave like a great lady and to be charming to his relatives.

She had moved with an indescribable grace around the great rooms at Buckwood as if she was part of them, and as he watched her something he had thought was dead within himself came to life.

At first he had not recognised it because it was so different from his initial feelings for Magnolia.

What Magnolia had awoken in him was a fiery desire, and the flame that lit within them both was a seething, uncontrollable passion that was entirely physical.

What he felt for Nadia was spiritual and while she attracted him because of her beauty, he knew it was her mind which kept him amused, interested and intrigued.

Overriding everything else was his longing to look after her, to keep her from coming to any harm, and most of all to sweep away the fear from her eyes.

He drew in his breath sharply as he thought of how frightened she must be now.

Although she knew nothing of the Buckwood Estate, she would guess that in a place as obviously unused as the old Slate Mine, she could remain undiscovered for ages.

It hardly seemed possible that Magnolia should have brought into the quiet English countryside such horrors as poison and kidnapping!

Yet Warren rebuked himself for being so obtuse as not to have realised before that she was determined to have her own way almost to the point of insanity.

She had longed so desperately to become the Marchioness of Buckwood, then she had lost her chance after, if only she had married him, it had been within her grasp.

The disappointment had brought out all that was fiendish and vile in her character.

"How could I have guessed, when she was so beautiful, that beneath the surface lay the heart of a devil?" he asked.

It suddenly struck him that possibly because she was so determined to be rid of Nadia she had even instructed the men who had kidnapped her to kill her before they left her in the Mine.

He knew as the thought came to him that the horror of it was like a sword piercing through him.

If he lost Nadia now he would have lost everything that was precious, so incomparable that never, however long he lived, would he find it again.

He pressed his horses to go faster in a way that surprised the groom sitting beside him.

Jim was however one of the younger lads in the stable, and Warren was glad that he would be too shy, and perhaps too stupid, to ask questions or even to think that what was occurring was extraordinary.

He knew as he settled down to drive the horses that he had to travel along a rough track that led through a wood, then cross a stubble field before there was another clump of trees, and beyond that the land dipped down to where the Mine had originally been excavated.

He remembered how when he was a boy his uncle had said that the slate was not worth the trouble of excavating or the cost of paying the men who worked in it.

He had therefore found them jobs elsewhere on his land, and working on the Mine had ceased.

Because it had been left neglected, the tunnels became dangerous, and before long his uncle had ordered doors to be put up at the entrance in order to prevent children from playing games inside it.

It was extremely uncomfortable driving across the rough field, but Warren hardly slowed the pace of his horses.

When they passed through the clump of trees and he knew it would be easy for him to reach the Slate Mine on foot, he brought the cabriolet to a standstill and gave the reins to the groom.

"Wait here for me, Jim," he said, and jumped down to the ground.

Then he was running, driven by a feeling of urgency which told him that if Nadia was not dead, she would be terrified at being imprisoned in the dank darkness of the Mine.

He had reached the top of the dip in the ground and saw as he expected that on the heavy doors which had been erected at the entrance there was a padlock.

For the first time he wondered if Magnolia had the key and wished he had demanded it from her.

Then he thought it more likely that the men who had imprisoned Nadia had either thrown the key away or else had taken it with them.

He hurried down the incline.

Then as he reached the doors he stood for a moment to wonder if after all Magnolia had tricked him and Nadia was somewhere else.

In a voice that did not sound like his own he called her name:

"Nadia! Nadia!"

He thought afterwards that the few seconds he waited for her reply was a century of apprehension.

Then he heard her give a little cry before she asked:

"Warren . . . is that . . . you?"

"I am here!"

"I knew you would come . . . I have been . . . praying that . . . you would . . . save me!"

"I will," he answered, "but first, I have to discover how I can open the door."

He looked at the padlock and realised it was a heavy one, and it would be difficult without the right instruments to break it away from the wood.

He saw that the doors were somewhat primitively made by the estate carpenters, and merely hanging at the sides on iron hinges.

It was then that Warren knew that fate had had a purpose in building up his exceptional physical strength in his long journeyings in the desert.

With a strength he knew he would not have had a year ago, he put out his arms and lifted one of the doors upwards and off the hinges.

For a few seconds the strain of it seemed almost insupportable, then the door fell to the ground with a resounding crash and Nadia was standing inside.

As soon as she could see Warren's face she scrambled over the fallen door towards him, reaching out

her arms so that he could lift her from the darkness of
the Mine into the sunlight.

With his arms around her she knew that she was
safe and that her prayers had been answered, and she
burst into tears.

She hid her face against his shoulder and as he held
her very close against him she sobbed:

"I . . . I was so . . . f.frightened that you would
not . . . know where I was . . . and that you would
not . . . hear me calling for . . . you."

"I have found you," Warren said in a deep voice,
"and I promise you, my darling, this will never happen again."

Because she was so surprised at the endearment she
turned to look up at him, the tears running down her
cheeks, her lips trembling.

Warren looked down at her and thought that despite her tears she had never looked more beautiful.

Then his lips very gently touched hers.

To Nadia it was as if the heavens opened and everything she had longed for and dreamt of and thought
was impossible suddenly came true.

Warren was kissing her, and it was the most perfect,
the most marvellous thing that could possibly happen.

Her lips were very soft and she trembled against
him, not with fear, but with a rapture which he also
felt within himself.

Because it was so perfect and so very different from
any kiss he had known, his lips became more insistent,
more possessive, but still he was very gentle.

He knew that he must comfort her for what she had
been through, even while at the same time she entranced him.

Only when it seemed that as he kissed her time
stood still did he raise his head to ask:

"My precious, my darling, you are all right? They
have not hurt you?"

"Oh, Warren . . . you are here! I was so . . .
afraid you would never . . . f.find me!"

"I have found you," he said as if he must reassure himself, "and this will never happen again!"

Then he was kissing her with long, slow, possessive kisses, as if he made her his and he would never lose her.

It was a long time later when he looked down at her again and thought that no woman could look so radiant, so ecstatically, gloriously happy, and still be on earth.

"I love you!" he said again and again, as if he could not say it too often.

"I . . . love you!" Nadia replied. "But I . . . never imagined . . . never even dreamt that you might . . . love me!"

"I love you as I have never loved anybody before! And so that I can keep you safe from all these horrors which should never have happened and must never happen again, we will be married very quickly!"

It was then, to his surprise, that Nadia stiffened, and turned her face to hide it once again in his shoulder.

"What is the matter?" he asked. "I cannot believe that you do not love me enough to marry me."

"I love you with my whole heart. I love you until you fill the sky . . . the world and there is nothing else but you . . . but I cannot . . . marry you."

Warren's arms tightened around her as he asked:

"Why not?"

She did not answer, and after a moment he said:

"You must tell me your secret, my precious one, and I swear that whatever it is, nothing and nobody will prevent me from making you my wife."

"No . . . no!" she murmured. "It is . . . impossible . . . and might . . . hurt you!"

"The only thing that could really hurt me," Warren said, "is that you should not love me enough to trust me."

He felt her quiver and knew she was deeply perturbed.

"You have been through enough," he said quickly. "We will talk about it when we get home. Besides, this is not a very romantic place to be talking of our love."

Nadia raised her head and he saw she was smiling through her tears.

"Wherever we are . . . it is romantic when you tell me that you . . . love me," she said, "but . . . do you really . . . mean it?"

"I love you in a way I did not know existed until this moment," Warren said. "But come along, I refuse to stay here any longer."

He took her by the hand and helped her up the stony incline and across the rough ground of the wood to where the horses were waiting.

He lifted her into the cabriolet, picked up the reins and Jim climbed up behind.

As they drove off, Nadia lay back against the cushioned seat feeling as if nothing mattered except that her heart was singing because she was with Warren and he had said he loved her.

Then she told herself she had to be firm, and that however much she loved him she could not let him become involved in the terror that had stalked her these last years, culminating in her mother's death.

"I have to go away and leave him," she told herself, and felt her whole body cry out at the agony of it.

Because the groom could hear what was said they did not talk, but Warren drove as quickly as he could back through the wood, into the Park and down the drive.

He did not take Nadia to his mother's house, but to Buckwood.

He did so deliberately because he felt that already she belonged there, and that was where they should decide their future.

He determined to make quite certain they would be together, and she would be his wife.

He drew up alongside the stone steps, then sprang

to the ground to go round to the other side of the
cabriolet and lift Nadia down.

Then he put his arm protectively round her shoulders and led her into the house across the hall and
into the Drawing-Room.

For a moment the Study was too closely associated
with Magnolia for him to wish to take Nadia there.

The Drawing-Room was filled with flowers and the
last rays of the evening sun coming through the windows glittered on the huge crystal chandelier.

Warren shut the door behind them and drew Nadia
to one of the elegant gold-edged sofas by the fireplace.

She sat down and he said:

"My precious, you have been through so much!
Shall I get you a drink?"

"I want nothing," she answered, "except to be certain that you are here and I shall not die of cold and
starvation in that . . . horrible damp Mine."

She realised as she spoke that Warren was looking
at her as if he had never seen her before.

"I must look terrible after having a blanket thrown
over my head, and I am sure the Mine has made me
very dirty."

"You look perfectly lovely!" he replied, and his
voice seemed to vibrate on the word. "Lovelier than
any woman I have ever seen! Oh, my darling, how
lucky I was to find you!"

She knew he was referring not to saving her from
the Slate Mine, but to finding her by the Seine.

"I . . . I seem to have brought . . . you a lot of
. . . trouble," she said in a low voice.

"It is all over now," he said, "but I want you to
understand that the only way that you can be safe and
be sure that Magnolia will never trouble us again is by
becoming my wife!"

He was holding Nadia's hand, and he felt her fingers tighten on his as she said in a very low voice:

"I cannot imagine anything more . . . perfect than
to be . . . married to you and to be with you . . . all

the time. But because I . . . love you I cannot put you in . . . danger."

"Why should I be in any danger?"

As Warren asked the question Nadia looked away from him, and he knew she was wondering whether she should tell him the truth, or go on hiding her secret.

As he waited the door of the Drawing-Room opened and Mr. Greyshott came in.

"I heard you were back, My Lord," he said, "and thought you might like to have the newspapers which have just arrived."

He walked across the room with them in his hand and putting them down on an embroidered stool in front of the fireplace said conversationally:

"There is news that Tsar Alexander III is dangerously ill with Dropsy, and is not expected to live. You will remember your uncle visited St. Petersburg in 1882 to represent the Queen at his Coronation."

When he had put the newspapers down Mr. Greyshott looked towards Warren as if he expected an answer, and with an effort, because he found it difficult to think of anything but Nadia, he replied:

"Yes, of course, I remember!"

Then in a very odd voice that seemed as if it came from a stranger Nadia said:

"D.did you . . . say . . . the . . . Tsar is not expected to . . . live?"

"That is what it says in the newspapers," Mr. Greyshott replied. "In fact, according to the *Morning Post* the doctors say his life is despaired of."

As he spoke he stared at Nadia in astonishment because she had put her hands up over her eyes, and Warren who was sitting close to her knew she was fighting for self-control.

He looked at Mr. Greyshott meaningfully, making a slight gesture as he did so, and with his usual tact his secretary understood he should leave them alone.

He walked quickly from the room, and as the door

closed behind him Warren put his arms around Nadia and drew her close to him.

"I think what we have just heard means something important to you, my Precious," he said quietly.

"It . . . it means . . . that if the . . . Tsar dies . . . I am s.safe!" she said in a voice that trembled. "Oh, if only . . . Mama were still alive!"

Warren drew her closer still. Then he said:

"Tell me about it, darling. I hoped you were going to tell me anyway, before Greyshott interrupted us."

"I want you . . . to know," Nadia said. "I . . . hate having any . . . secrets from you."

"Then let us be rid of them."

She looked up at him and despite the tears in her eyes he felt in some strange way that she was suddenly transformed.

It was not only her love for him that made her face radiant, but also it seemed as if the misery he did not yet understand had slipped away from her and she was free to be herself again with all the joy and happiness of youth.

She drew a deep breath before she said:

"My real name is Princess Nadia Korzoki and my father was Prince Ivan Korzoki."

"You are Russian!" Warren exclaimed.

"Well yes, half Russian," she confirmed. "You thought I was not . . . wholly English."

"I was sure of it," he said, "but tell me your story."

"Mama was the daughter of the British Ambassador to St. Petersburg, and Papa fell in love with her and she with him the moment they met."

She glanced up at Warren as she spoke and he knew how much she loved him before she went on:

"They had to have the permission of the Tsar Alexander II to marry, which he gave them only reluctantly, because Papa had Royal blood in his veins. In the end he agreed on condition that they went to live in the country on Papa's large estate which bordered on Hungary."

449

Nadia then paused, as if she was looking back before she went on:

"They were very, very happy, and never regretted missing the gaieties, or indeed, the intrigues and problems of St. Petersburg."

"So it was in Russia that you learned to ride so well!"

"I rode in Hungary also," Nadia answered, "but I have not got as far as that yet."

"Go on, my lovely darling."

"I shall always remember how happy everything was at home, but Papa was deeply shocked when Tsar Alexander II was assassinated thirteen years ago, and his son when he came to the throne revised all the reforms that were being made in the country."

Warren was listening intently as Nadia continued:

"The first thing the new Emperor did was to tear up an unsigned Manifesto which had provided for a limited form of representative Government in Russia. It was something that was very dear to Papa's heart, and it soon became clear that Alexander III was determined to bring back into Russia all the cruelties which his father had begun to eliminate."

Nadia's voice was very moving as she said almost in a whisper:

"Worst of all he was . . . determined to destroy . . . the Jews."

Warren had heard this and knew how everybody in England had disapproved of the Tsar's action.

But he did not say so, and let Nadia continue:

"The new Tsar decreed that one third of the Jews were to be exterminated, one third assimilated and one third driven out of the country."

She gave a deep sigh before she went on:

"You will understand that as Papa's estate was on the border many of those who were rounded up by the Cossacks were driven over our land, chained, starving and whipped into Western Europe!"

She fought against her tears before she went on:

"Mama used to cry at night because she had seen their suffering, and Papa helped where he could, telling our own people to give them food and sometimes, when the Cossacks were not looking, a little money."

"Then what happened?" Warren asked.

"Papa had a Jewish friend who was a very famous and brilliant surgeon, and had operated on him and on many of Papa's friends. One night he arrived at our Castle saying that he had learnt he was to be arrested the next morning and taken to St. Petersburg for investigation."

Nadia's voice was very low as she said:

"We knew this meant torture and a slow and lingering agony before he died."

"And your father saved him?"

"Papa smuggled him and his wife into Hungary and gave him enough money so that he could start life again in Europe."

Nadia made a helpless little gesture with her hands before she said:

"But of course somebody reported to the Tsar what Papa had done and he was furiously angry with him for helping such a well-known Jew to escape."

Warren began to understand what had happened.

"In fact, the Tsarevich Nicholas, who had always been very fond of Papa and was a quiet, gentle, rather weak young man, was courageous enough to send one of his trusted servants to warn Papa of the danger he was in."

"That was brave of him!" Warren exclaimed.

"Very brave, because he was frightened of his father. Anyway, as soon as Papa received the warning he hurried Mama and me to the border, knowing it was only a question of days, perhaps only hours, before he was taken to St. Petersburg."

"He did not leave with you?"

"Both Mama and I begged him to do so, but he was adamant."

" 'I will not be a Refugee from my own country!' he

said. 'I do not believe the Tsar would dare to execute me for a kindness to an old friend!' "

"But he did die?"

"He was . . . murdered but we did not hear about it until we were told the Tsar had commanded that Mama and I were to be brought back and stand trial also for helping the enemies of Russia, who were the Jews!"

"So that is why you were hiding!"

"We had to hide unless we wanted to . . . die like Papa."

There was a break in Nadia's voice which made Warren hold her closer to him.

"Tell me another time, if it upsets you," he said softly.

"No, no!" Nadia replied. "I want to tell you . . . I have wanted to tell you before . . . but I have been too afraid to do so."

He kissed her forehead before she went on with a determination he admired:

"Everything after that became a nightmare. We had been staying with friends in Hungary, but of course we could not involve them in our troubles. Then we thought it wise to go to France, and from there to England to Mama's relatives."

"That sounds very sensible."

"That is what we thought when we started off," Nadia answered, "but we soon realised that the Secret Police when they are intent on revenge, never give up. They tracked us all through Hungary and were not far behind us when we passed through various small Principalities until eventually we reached France."

She gave a little sob before she said:

"It is . . . difficult to remember the details . . . but it was all terrifying. All we knew was that the Russians were looking for us, determined not to let us get away, and we realised that we must involve as few people as possible."

She paused for a moment before she went on:

"Nevertheless everybody was very kind, and we passed from friend to friend but as our money grew less and less we had to sell the jewels Mama had brought with her. That was dangerous because the Russians following us recognised them and knew they were only a few days behind us."

"So when you finally reached Paris you had nothing left," Warren said.

"Only the clothes we stood up in and so few francs that we could only afford to stay in an attic in a dirty, squalid lodging-house which made Mama more ill than she was already."

Nadia made a little helpless gesture as she said:

"You know the rest of the story. Mama died, and because I had nothing, really nothing . . . I wanted to . . . die too."

"Thank God I prevented you from doing that," Warren exclaimed. "But now, my precious, it is all over. The Tsarevitch is your friend, and I am sure the programme of cruelty against the Jews will cease as soon as he comes to the throne."

"Do you really . . . think I am . . . safe?"

"You will be safe as my wife," Warren said, "and we are not even going to wait until the present Tsar dies. We will be married immediately, but everyone except my mother will still know you by the name we invented."

He pressed his lips against her cheek before he went on:

"Later, when it is safe to do so, we will tell the truth, and I know everybody will think it a story of great bravery, as I do."

"I.it was not very . . . brave of me to . . . want to . . . die."

"It was very brave of you to let me save you and to come here and do everything I asked of you."

She turned her face up to his and he said:

"I adore you, my beautiful little Russian Princess, and all the horrors and miseries are over. You will live a very quiet, uneventful life here in England, which perhaps after all the dramas you have been through you will find dull."

He was teasing her, but Nadia gave a little sob and put her arms round his neck to say:

"May I really do that? It sounds so wonderful, so like being in Heaven, that I feel I must be dreaming."

"It is a dream come true," Warren said, "and I assure you that when you are my wife and the Marchioness of Buckwood, there will be no Secret Police lurking in the shadows, and I will make sure there are no jealous women either."

"How can you be . . . certain of . . . that?"

Warren smiled.

He knew he had threatened Magnolia in a way which had frightened her more than he could have effected by any other means, and would ensure they were free of her in the future.

Her beautiful face was the only thing that really mattered to her and to risk damaging it would be unthinkable for her.

"She will never worry either of us again," he said reassuringly.

Then he had an idea.

He remembered the Special Licence with which Magnolia had tried to blackmail him.

His uncle had been a close friend of the Archbishop of Canterbury, and Warren had met him on several occasions.

He happened to know that he was in London at the moment because it had been reported that His Grace was officiating at a Memorial Service for a famous Politician who had recently died.

He was sure that if he wrote to the Archbishop asking for a Special Licence for his marriage to Nadia, and explaining that because he had just returned from abroad he was unable to come in person, the Archbishop would understand.

He could then marry Nadia immediately in the

Chapel attached to the house without anybody except his mother being aware of it.

Later their marriage could be announced and their secrecy could be explained as being necessitated by his being in mourning.

Then they could entertain his relatives as he had promised them he would.

All that mattered at the moment was that Nadia should not be left alone and frightened either by day or by night.

He felt his heart give a leap of joy at the prospect as he said:

"Leave everything to me, my lovely one. There are no more problems to be solved, no more difficulties to seem insurmountable. All you have to do is to love me."

"I do love you," she said. "I love you so much . . . but are you . . . certain you are . . . wise to marry me? After all . . . there may be some way in which it might harm you to be married to a Russian who is . . . wanted by the . . . Secret Police."

"Nothing can harm me, except that I might lose you," he replied. "What I want you to do, my adorable one, is to forget all the horrors that have pursued you from Russia, and remember that your mother was English."

He laid his cheek against hers and said:

"We will find your mother's relatives, and I know they will make you feel very much at home and a part of England. You have not been able to enjoy this country until now, but it is my country, and as we are now one person we will make it a home for ourselves and for our children."

"That is what I want to do," Nadia cried, "but I still cannot believe it is true that after so much misery and so much fear I really have come . . . home."

"I will make you sure of it," Warren said. "Oh, darling, I love you, and I swear that you will never be frightened or unhappy again."

He kissed her until the room seemed to whirl round them.

Only when Warren raised his head were they aware that the sun was sinking outside in a blaze of glory and the rooks were going to roost.

"I love you!" he said, and his voice was very deep.

"I thought you told me that you intended, if you really had to marry, to make a *mariage de convenance* as the French do!" Nadia whispered.

"I am marrying because I love you and I want you. The feelings I have for you are very different from anything I have ever known or imagined."

"What do you . . . feel?"

"Very excited—very much in love—and something more."

"What is . . . it?"

"I feel as if I have found the most precious treasure in the world which is so perfect, so unique that I will keep it and protect it for ever."

"And . . . that is . . . me?"

"You, my beautiful darling."

Warren rose from the sofa and pulled her to her feet beside him.

"I am going to take you back to my mother," he said, "and I want to tell her the truth, but nobody else. Then I am going to send my letter to the Archbishop and we will be married the day after tomorrow."

He smiled before he went on:

"Then we will leave here ostensibly to visit the other properties which I have inherited but really to spend our honeymoon together—alone."

Nadia drew in her breath and whispered:

"That will be . . . wonderful."

"We will go first to Devonshire where my house is very comfortable and very quiet and then we will go to Leicestershire to look at . . ."

Nadia gave a cry which interrupted him.

"You are doing . . . everything so quickly that I am . . . afraid."

REVENGE OF THE HEART

"Of me?"

"No, I could never be afraid of you," she said, "only that you have not . . . thought it . . . over."

"I have nothing to think over," Warren replied firmly. "I am so lucky, the luckiest man in the whole world, and all that really matters, my precious, is that we are alive, we are together, and I am certainly not taking any more risks of losing you!"

He put his arms around her.

He did not say anything, but she knew he was thinking of the poison that Magnolia had tried to give her and of the men who had kidnapped her and hidden her in the Slate Mine.

And most of all, how he had saved her as she looked down into the Seine, meaning to take one fatal step into the darkness of oblivion.

"Three times I have been . . . saved," she whispered, "and now . . . I belong to . . . you."

"I will make sure of that," Warren smiled. "Fate, or God, has given you to me, and I never dreamt it was possible to own anyone so completely adorable."

There was a passionate note in his voice which made Nadia move a little closer to him and lift her lips to his.

He looked at her before he said very softly:

"I will love you, adore you and worship you for the rest of our lives. Will that be enough?"

"It is the only thing I ever want," Nadia whispered, "and I will love you until the world comes to an end, and the stars fall from the sky!"

Then Warren was kissing her, kissing her demandingly, passionately, at the same time tenderly, and she knew he was right.

She had "come home."

About the Author

DAME BARBARA CARTLAND, the world's best known and bestselling author of romantic fiction, is also an historian, playwright, lecturer, political speaker, and television personality. She has now written over six hundred and twenty-two books and has the distinction of holding *The Guinness Book of Records* title of the world's bestselling author, having sold over six hundred and fifty million copies of her books all over the world.

Barbara Cartland was invested by Her Majesty The Queen as a Dame of the Order of the British Empire in 1991, is a Dame of Grace of St. John of Jerusalem, and was one of the first women in one thousand years ever to be admitted to the Chapter General. She is President of the Hertfordshire Branch of The Royal College of Midwives, and is President and Founder in 1964 of the National Association for Health.

Miss Cartland lives in England at Camfield Place, Hatfield, Hertfordshire.